THE EPIC OF ARYA

ABIR TAHA

THE EPIC OF ARYA

IN SEARCH OF THE SACRED LIGHT

SECOND EDITION

ARKTOS
LONDON 2016

Copyright © 2016 by Abir Taha.

All rights reserved. No part of this book may be reproduced or utilised in any form or by any means (whether electronic or mechanical), including photocopying, recording or by any information storage and retrieval system, without permission in writing from the publisher.

Second edition.

First published by AuthorHouse, USA, in 2009.

Printed in the United Kingdom.

ISBN 978-1-910524-54-1

EDITOR

John B Morgan

COVER DESIGN AND LAYOUT

Tor Westman

ARKTOS MEDIA LTD.

www.arktos.com

*To the Light bearer,
Zarathustra the eternal*

CONTENTS

PREFACE ix

PROLOGUE xi

PART ONE: The Veil of *Maya* 1
   In the land of eternal night 1
   Among the sleepless dreamers of the desert 7
   Arya's sermon 32

PART TWO: *Heimkehr* 53
   The woman from the North 53
   On the suffering that bestows 61
   The prophet 68
   The Sons of Light 75
   On the meaning of Life 83
   On the plight of gods on earth 99
   The mission 114
   Arya's journey 121
   The divine odyssey 131
   The rise and fall of the Master Race 153
   The Inner Fatherland 177
   Time 188

PART THREE: Kali Yuga 193
   In the land of gloom 193
   Among the dreamless sleepers of the city 196
   The inverted pyramid 227
   The worm in man 230
   The darkest man 233
   Arya's lament 236
   The vision 240

    The plea 244
    Kshatriya 249
    The dream of love 256
    Of higher love 259
    The great temptation 260
    Arya's rebirth 262
    The message 270

PART FOUR: Shambhala, Sanctuary of Light 277
    Beyond the Gate 277
    The realm of the gods 278
    Moksha 279
    The King of the World 281
    The Spirit of Shambhala 288
    The new religion 297
    The coming god 303
    The Armies of Shambhala 305
    A call to arms 307
    Hymns to Life 311

EPILOGUE 317
    The departure 317

NOTES 320

ABOUT THE AUTHOR 321

PREFACE

By writing the legend of Arya, I am embarking upon the secret journey that leads to the Inner Self, treading the sacred path that unravels Man's eternal destiny. With my blood and my tears, I am writing this story, an epic of Truth and Love, of duty and passion, where Light falls and loses itself in darkness, and darkness finds and redeems itself in Light. This is our past, our path, our destiny.

Abir Taha
Avignon,
April 8th, 2007

PROLOGUE

1

When Arya, the human goddess of Light, woke up from her long dream, following an endless night in the arms of Eternity, she found herself in a strange land where darkness reigned supreme, a gloomy world she had hitherto never seen. "Am I still dreaming?" she asked her perplexed mind, overwhelmed by the boundless obscurity surrounding her, "or have I just awoken? Is not Night the time for the soul's awakening? Does not the soul blossom in the depth of the night, and dance with the stars and gods above, even as reason rules the earth and men below during the day? Am I awake, or is my awakening itself a dream?"

"My eyes, wide-open, tell me that I'm conscious, but what do my eyes know of consciousness! They belong to the earth and see only the crude things of the earth, the hollow shell and the outer form; they remain blind to the subtle essence of divine truth and higher consciousness. The spirit alone, this spark of infinity, this glimpse of eternity, is blessed with divine sight, while the body totters aimlessly in the eternal darkness of blind matter. My eyes tell me that I am awake, yet my spirit looks beyond and contends that reality lies elsewhere, that what men call 'the world' is but a deceptive dream, a cruel illusion of the senses, a shadow of reality."

As Arya thus questioned Truth, wondering about Life's manifold forms, Her hidden meaning and purpose, she again asked herself: "are we awake when our eyes are open and our reason is sovereign, or does the soul truly see when the eyes are shut and the spirit roams the ether? Does not Night unfold its deepest mysteries and reveal our inner infinity, the god within, as it unravels the secrets of the universe? But who, save a god, could answer such questions?"

"Alas! I am only a *human* goddess, that is, a goddess with a mission on earth. The law of Nature commands that, lest they become mere idols, *all* gods must go down to men, must become men, so that men can become gods. It is their divine vocation, for only by going down do they uplift life; only by living among men, and through them, do they fulfil their own divinity. Nature's will thus has it: gods must descend to men, and men must ascend to gods; only thus is the purpose of life accomplished, for the world is a sacred circle of absolute Unity."

"It is God's will that gods, His messengers, angels, and warriors — the noblest manifestations of the Unmanifested, the multiple forms of the One, the highest expressions of divine Force — must first fall into the depths and the abyss of existence, before they can rise to the higher spheres and soar to the heights of Supremacy. For only thus does life fulfil its first and last commandment, which is to eternally overcome itself and create beyond itself. Only thus does God turn into life, and Life becomes divine; only thus does He embrace Life and impregnate Her with the hallowed gift of creation."

"I am a human goddess, that is my joy and my misery. It is a joy, for all gods yearn for incarnation, it is their ultimate destiny, as perfection lies in creativity, which can only be conceived, and achieved, whenever a lofty thought assumes a noble form. It is a misery, for in vain do all humans long for divinity; in vain do they seek out eternity and dream of immortality. Perfection, to them, remains an impossible dream and an unfulfilled hope, and they die unsatisfied with a bitter taste of unquenchable thirst upon their lips."

"I am a human goddess, and though my divine spirit floats on its own river of perpetual bliss, there in the realm of the Absolute, its form below remains bound to the shackles of earthly life's limitations and frustrations, hampered by the fallible senses of its own humanity. That is the price for incarnation: the form allows the spirit to unfold and reveal itself, yet it binds it to the human chains of time and space. Alas! The tragedy of life is that perfection is always achieved at the price of freedom, and freedom at the price of perfection. Thus God remains unattainable save for those who earnestly seek Him and pay the ultimate price of elevation, by sacrificing their finite souls for the eternal glory of divinity."

Having touched the heart of her existential plight — indeed, the plight of all human gods —, Arya, despondent and lost, cried out to the wind: "alas! Could it be that the gods themselves have forbidden men from fathoming the riddles of the universe, jealously keeping the sacred flame of Truth as the blessing and the privilege of the sole immortals? Prometheus thus remains the symbol of man's endless quest to equal the gods, for death that overcomes itself is a hymn to life which leads man away from himself and closer to God."

"All martyrs are immortals. Immortality, however, as all greatness, comes at the highest price — for how else would it justify Life? — and that is: to sacrifice one's humanity and shed all finite thought and earthly desire. My unknown brothers, who strive to become immortals and dwell in the boundless abode of the gods, I entreat you to sacrifice the evanescent glories of the earth for the eternal glory of God; to abandon all earthly pleasures for the divine bliss of the higher world. Forsake all lower life, fellow Warriors of Light, and you shall gain everlasting Life; offer your perishable egos on the altar of divinity, and your immortal selves shall bathe in the fountain of Eternity. All sacrifice is an offering and a blessing, for life gives back to the earth what it took from the earth; it bestows its most precious gems and its sweetest fruit to him alone who, seeking to find himself, loses all and everything; and it takes away everything from him who gains everything, but loses himself."

"Is not Life itself a dream of the gods, a fanciful play of joy and sorrow, elation and despair, wrought on humans by the powers that be, as a blessing to the eternal and a curse on the transient? Should not man welcome death — instead of dreading it as a daily tragedy cast upon men, as the end of all existence -, should he not welcome it as liberation, as a pathway to a higher life, a threshold to a higher awakening?"

"Could it be that in our waking state, we dream Life and suckle the breasts of Her sweet illusion, and only in our sleep do we truly exist? Is sleep merely a time of rest for the body and the mind, or is it the time for the awakening of our souls to a higher reality, to Truth and Beauty? Is not death a deep and constant sleep lifting man's indestructible Self into the realm of infinity, where only gods dwell?"

After a short moment of inner silence, pondering the meaning of the human cycle of life and death, of night and day, of slumber and awakening, Arya thus questioned her Higher Self: "is not sleep man's only link with the divine, the only trace left of the reign of gods on earth, before Time itself began? And yet, we become humans once more when Night passes and the world of senses again holds full sway, when magic and mystery fade, washed away by the first light of day."

"We remain ignorant and limited in our aspiration and elevation, so long as we remain humans, that is, thinking beings who use cold logic and plain reasoning, calling their ignorance 'enlightenment', instead of contemplative beings endowed with intuition — that last trace of divinity in men -, who dream in the brightest daylight and awaken in the darkest night, humans who live and fulfil the dream of the gods."

"A veil of ignorance covers humanity, a veil of silent shame that can only be lifted by man's sincere longing for the eternal, for that longing is the last sigh of God on this earth. That is the plight of man: he remains poor in spirit though the earth is full of riches; he remains human though the gods walk among men and talk through them. Alas!

The god in man remains a child waiting to mature. Shall man grow into a god, or is he doomed in his humanity?"

2

It was dark, and all Arya could see was the pale gleam of the moon and the faint sparkle of distant stars, countless drops of a forlorn light, remnants of another age, silent witnesses to the dawn of the gods. The moonlight unveiled the ebb and flow of the nearby sea. A mild breeze caressed the glowing waves, in a symphony of beauty and harmony. Arya, lying on the sandy beach, gazing at the sea, home and refuge to all the streams of Life and Love, was all alone, having as sole companion the invisible presence of Pan. Yet she thought it was fine, and spoke thus to the sea:

"Is it not the fate of gods to live and die alone, having as sole companions, as you, boundless ocean, the shadow and the whisper of Infinity, and the sacred breath of Eternity? In solitude lurks divinity… Gods remain alone, it is their fate and misfortune, though they may stand in the middle of their worshipping crowds, these damned souls aimlessly seeking the way to salvation, these wretched creatures who will know neither God nor Truth, for they tread not their own sacred path, which is engraved in the immortal Self of the highest and the lowest of men."

"Men have hitherto blindly followed the crooked ways of fake prophets and false gods, kneeling before a lifeless idol that is but the human shadow of a god, more a fool than a god. The blind and the deaf, blind to the spirit of the earth, and deaf to the heartbeats of creative life, seek in vain a god who shall forever remain distant and unknown, an invisible idol for the world's countless fools and cowards, a faceless tyrant who enslaves souls and slays the spirit of men."

"Alas! The god of men is no beacon of life pushing them forwards and upwards into their destiny and their heights; he is but a reflection of men's imperfections and frustrations. The god of men is no fountain of love that pours the blessed wine of creation upon their thirsty souls and gaping mouths longing to taste the sweetness of Wisdom — that forbidden fruit of mortals -, and yearning to feel the ecstasy of Supremacy."

"Alas! The god of men is unworthy of divinity! And humans remain little lambs seeking in vain to redeem their lost, damned souls, lost in the vain search of an imaginary world that negates all life, and damned for having severed man's magic link with Nature, the only abode of God… for they look upon the boundless horizon as an unattainable goal that one dreams of, but never pursues, hopelessly awaiting a sign of salvation from above and beyond, while their agonising souls and their weary bodies cry out to them and bid them to find themselves and forsake all gods. For gods dwell within and through us, and our Inner Self — which remains unknown to most men — is the supreme deity."

"O you wretched mortal souls, seek the god within, for he alone shall redeem you and lift you up to the heavens above, whose roots lie in the bowels of the earth. Although God's spirit pervades all life, His body, His temple, is none other than His supreme manifestation in Mother Nature and her noblest creatures."

3

Arya was naked, and the cool breeze of the night gently caressed her rosy skin and stroked her golden hair. She was naked, but it was fine, for, she asked the mild, warm southern wind, "is not innocence itself naked, do not the angels, these faithful messengers of the gods, stand and remain naked in the Sun and the wind, naked as pure innocence itself, before you, great breath of God, as a blank page tells its tale to posterity and unfolds its destiny, there where the Spirit dwells and grows eternally, where the dead letter fades away, slowly, gradually, victim of Time, the slayer of love, glory, and memory?"

4

It was night, yet Arya thought that this, too, was fine, for even she, the eternal bringer of Light, knew that it is from the depths of darkness and in the cosmic mysteries of the night that divine Light is conceived, to be born at dawn and to blossom at the sacred noontide. Thus, creation is conceived at night, the cradle of birth, and fulfilled in the day, the temple of Awakening.

"Does not dusk carry the seeds of dawn? Is not night pregnant with the light of day?" murmured Arya to her inner ear, relishing the magic of the sacred silence around her, shuddering with awe at the sight of the starry heavens above her. It was night, and Arya's soul was serene and pristine, for she knew that, as the soul longs for overcoming the body and the physical plane, so too does night long for the day to honour its promise of creation and achieve its dream of elevation. For night is to day what the soul is to the body: a glimmer of divinity, a stairway to infinity, and a foretaste of eternity. Night is to day what spring is to winter: a new beginning and a promise of rebirth, Life everlasting that perpetually renews and perfects itself, death that forever overcomes itself by flowing out into the stream of everlasting Life."

5

Hours passed, then days, yet the liberating rays of the god of all life, *Surya* (1), came not to relieve Arya's soul from the overwhelming darkness that stifled it; for she, the human goddess of Light, who found her inspiration in the stillest hours of the night, yet fulfilled her cosmic dreams in the blessed light of dawn, could not live and thrive without the sacred flame of Truth that ever lit the temple of the gods since the dawn of time. And so, Arya's sublime soul grew weary and hopeless, for night followed night, and darkness gave way to darkness in an endless cycle of despair, in this strange land that seems to have been forsaken by all gods.

In vain did she wait for the new dawn that her soul longed for with the eagerness of desperation and the hope of salvation. Night became eternal and darkness prevailed, covering the skies and earth with its sombre mantle of mystery and expectation, in this uncanny, unreal world where hope seemed like an impossible dream. Thus Arya's dejected soul asked the night, "is this, too, a fleeting dream, a shadow of reality that will soon fade away with the first light of day? Will this illusion wither away with the break of dawn — cradle of awakening — washed away by the ocean of the divine, golden rays of Light and Life? Or is this dream... reality itself?" she wondered.

"But *what* is real, what is unreal? Who can tell the true from the illusory? Is not life in the eye of the beholder, in the ear of the listener, in the faith of the worshipper, in the soul of the saint, and in the revelation of the prophet? Does not each man behold life as a mirror to his own inner self? Does not each man behold God, his own god, as the reflection of his Higher Self in the sky? Is not the whole world my own will and my own representation? Does not reality consist of man's own inner world? Is not 'the world' our inner universe? Ah! Life is but a bitter chalice of questions left unanswered, broken dreams, and unfulfilled hopes."

After a short moment of silent meditation, Arya continued her introspection and asked her inner self: "is this darkness a dream of an illusory reality? Is reality a mere continuation of the cosmic dream of God? Is the real but a cloak of the unreal? Is the veil of *Maya* (2) the only true and lasting reality? Is truth doomed to remain an illusion, a faded hope, an unattainable fantasy?" Thus Arya's perplexed soul asked the wind, only witness to her solitary predicament and her silent pain. She then went on questioning Life's deepest mysteries and strangest riddles:

"Am I the dreamer or the dream? Does not Eternity express itself in our dreams — only repositories of supreme Truth — and manifest itself through them? Does not Infinity borrow space and time, our bodies and minds, as vehicles to realise its cosmic scheme of creation and elevation? Does not the dream of Night finally flow into the ocean of Day, fulfilling its destiny? Thus should the vision of the night achieve its purpose with the first rays of dawn."

With a last sigh of despondency, Arya again asked herself: "is not darkness the veil worn by Light in its sacred hour of prayer, a veil that it removes when comes the time for work and fulfilment? For the moon is a goddess as the Sun is a god, and every day, dusk and dawn celebrate this holy union of the gods, when the darkest hour turns into translucent brightness. Night is a prelude, never a closure; night is the beginning, never the end. And if it were to become an end, it would reap nothing but ignorance and death."

PART ONE

THE VEIL OF *MAYA*

In the land of eternal night

1

As time passed, irreversible in its thrust towards eternity, Night perpetuated itself endlessly, and so Arya's soul, stifled by the gloomy darkness that dimmed its sacred inner flame, grew weary, and it spoke thus to the starry heavens above, for they were the only drops of light and hope in that sea of darkness and despair: "all darkness that does not turn into Light is but a doom cast upon life. All night that does not turn into day is but death perpetuating itself, the demise of all longing and all faith. For what is it to live without longing, and to love without faith? It is but wretchedness and gloom. Faith and longing are the pillars of the temple of perfection, where the eternal flame of all creativity and elevation burns, radiating its redeeming rays of light that usher in the dawn of the divine Life. For the light of day redeems all that is dark, base, awry, and fake in man and in the world."

"If not a prelude and a forerunner to day, a promise of Light and Life, darkness begets nothing but death and oblivion; night is but sickness, ignorance, and illusion, if it does not flow into the sea of light, even as the stream that does not flow into the ocean turns into mud and dirt. And how many human swamps have been formed each time darkness shunned the Light, and men chose the bliss of ignorance over the thorns of Truth! For Truth hallows lofty souls and harms base and ignorant ones, even as the sunlight comes as a blessing and a crowning to those who seek it even in the darkest abyss, while it blinds those whose dark souls — unfit for, and unworthy of divine sight — prevent them from beholding God's reflection on earth."

"O you heavenly stars above, show me where is the light that would lift this obscure veil of gloom, this endless night, twilight of all gods and graveyard of all hope! Where is the light that shall rekindle my inner flame, so that it venerates, once more, its source and its end, the star of stars, *Surya*?" Thus Arya lamented her cosmic pain and her secret hope to the Great Silence about her, mystery of all mysteries, for she felt that it alone understood her, she whose emerald eyes were repositories of the world's mysteries, as are all divine eyes; yet they could still not behold before them the light that they bore within, the light that they reflected.

In vain did Arya's eyes seek the light of life and love in the overwhelming black void that made her soul feel gloomy and grow dark and weary. In vain did her exalted soul search for the sound of magic murmurs of the sacred forest that bore her, since the dawn of time, there in the abode of the gods where the North wind blew, there in the island of abundant and overflowing life, at that sacred time before Time itself began, when gods walked the earth and men roamed the heavens, and Nature separated them not.

In vain did she seek the cool, refreshing breeze that once caressed her skin and played with her hair, to soothe her tired face, worn out by the sweltering summer heat of this strange land of desolation, where the infinite ocean seemed to be the only promise of freedom and hope for lost souls and desolate hearts. But in the land of darkness, light holds no sway, and so the long-awaited day never came, to Arya's utter despair. "What am *I*," she thought, "I, the earth goddess of eternal

Light who, throughout the ages, spread the Word of Truth, Wisdom, and Beauty, what am I doing in the midst of all that darkness? Is it a curse or a sign that I should live among death's ghastly forerunners and gruesome symptoms, ignorance and ugliness? Should I embrace death, or redeem it? Should I rest in eternal peace, or thrive in eternal life? All this darkness overwhelms me!"

"Why am *I*, the favourite daughter of *Surya*, that mother of all life, trapped here in this land of perpetual night?" she asked herself again, as though hoping to force an answer out of Life. "Is this my reality? Has the dream become real, or has reality itself become a dream, a mere illusion to the mind and the senses? Am I henceforth doomed to belong to this waking dream, this land of illusion that I could never call home? Will I remain engulfed by this sea of darkness, like a lost shipwreck that finds no shore, and sails forever, aimlessly, on the high seas? Like a wingless bird hopelessly struggling to fly and soar in the sky where it belongs?"

"O *Surya*, Mother of All, wherefore art Thou? What befell the world? Has it been cursed by the powers of darkness and the messengers of doom? Alas! A ray of light once touched the face of darkness, but darkness chose to look away; it shunned the Light when it did not understand it, and banished it forever when it did. And so today in vain do I seek you, brightest star of all, like a newborn seeks his mother's warm breast in a dark and cold night, as a refuge and an abode."

"Have the gods cursed you, cursed the world, O mother of all gods? Have Thy beloved sons gone blind and forsaken Thee? Have all gods gone mad, turning truth and wisdom into illusion and folly? Have the children damned their own mother, so that her healing rays no longer shine upon the world? Or have you, star of stars, in your infinite wisdom and divine justice, cloaked yourself in this veil of darkness, to punish the sons of the earth, whose conceit and ignorance turned them away from you, the only god and supreme truth, worshipping instead false gods, idols of clay, dust, and sand? O, that I may again behold your golden beauty, life-giver and life-sustainer, propagator of Truth and Love!"

"Shall this night last an eternity? Are we hereafter meant to live in perpetual darkness? Is not ours the darkest of ages? The worst curse wrought upon men? O *Surya*, may that this be a bad dream that will soon fade away with the first light of the new dawn." Thus spoke Arya to her dejected heart, and she resolved to discover this strange new world, for she had to find out why the gods had chosen this uncanny fate for her; she had to unravel her own mystery and solve the riddle of Providence.

2

And so began Arya's long and solitary journey across the desert, under the moonlight, in search of the living, in search of men, far from the oasis of Light which bore her, there where the Sun never sets and the spirit finds no boundaries, there where the stream of awakening finds its source and its ocean, where light flows into light, and life blossoms ever anew. Deep in her heart, Arya felt that, though she was in the middle of this deserted landscape where all life ends and all hope fades, her spirit still belonged — as it ever will — to the land of white nights and endless elevation, the cradle of divinity and the fountain of enlightenment.

As she walked across the desert desperately seeking a sign of life, Arya wondered why she, who has always longed for the night as the sacred time for the awakening of the soul, and the blessed moment for the ripening of the spirit, why did she now dread the night and flee it as one flees death itself, though he knows it shall meet him, evermore, at the threshold of his path to Eternity, as the crowning of a fruitful life, or liberation from an unworthy existence? Why did she, Light made flesh, the light that longs for its shadow as the day longs for the night, why did she now pray for night to end and lift its dark veil of doom off the radiant face of day?

"Is it not because night and darkness should turn into day and light, in the divine order of things, in the eternal cycle of Life?" thought Arya, "for whenever the ring of supreme unity is not complete, nature's sacred laws are violated, truth is slandered, beauty mutilated, and the whole world turns upside down; it is in that darkest of hours, when all hope seems lost, and all faith forsaken, that gods issue their ultimate sentence on a fallen mankind, unleashing their wrath upon those guilty of the worst crime of all, the crime against Mother Nature, while redeeming those worthy of redemption. Yet that time has not come yet, it is in the making, it is near, it cometh soon, it lurks in all corners, and only the Awakened Ones see it and await it as a secret hope and a hidden promise."

After a short moment of meditation, wondering about life's occult meaning and veiled purpose, Arya continued questioning the Silence about her and spoke thus: "does not Night draw its inspiration and its magic from its secret longing for day, a longing that heralds the dawn, that sacred time when souls blossom and gods awaken? Alas! Night was my muse, the sacred fountain where my soul bathed and shed the worries of the day; now night is but a source of gloom, for it heralds not a new day and a new birth, but is a curse upon itself and rots in its own dirt. It is a void that seeks the void, darkness that sows and reaps itself, for wisdom without consciousness is blind and remains unfulfilled, and the wisdom that grew ripe at night needs the daylight to deliver its sweetest fruit."

"It is the blessing and command of Nature that day should follow night and night follow day, even as death turns into life and life into death, in the sacred ring of Eternity; even as spring follows winter and returns, evermore, to reinvent and redeem Life. It is the will of the gods that body and spirit, reason and passion, logic and intuition should be united in the holy harmony of divine Infinity. Spirit should be to

Nature what the soul is to the body: a force of life, a creative will that elevates the body and sanctifies the form. Thus this endless darkness is but death perpetuating itself, becoming itself, instead of overcoming itself; it is an endless cycle of gloom and misery."

3

Walking for hours on end under the faint reflection of the moon and the countless stars in the dark skies above, Arya could still not see anything other than the boundless desert of sand and dust. Hope seemed to fade away like dust in the wind, with every new step that she took towards the unknown, in a hopeless search for a sign of life amid this sea of melancholy; there seemed to be no way out of this dark circle of nothingness, and a deep feeling of dejection gnawed at Arya's heart. Yet she realised that, whether she was living a realistic dream or an illusory reality, *this* was now her new reality, the fate that Life had woven for her, and so she had to accept the will of providence, for divine Wisdom has Her own reasons and Her own purpose, and gods and men are but Her agents and warriors. "Even the worst tragedies have a veiled meaning and serve a hidden purpose, in God's great scheme in the universe," muttered Arya to herself, hoping to find consolation in this justification of her woes.

Thus she bowed to her fate and to the will of divinity, out of respect for the spiritual hierarchy, resolving henceforth to accept all that would befall her with courage and grace.

Among the sleepless dreamers of the desert

1

Finally, after a long journey across the desert, in the middle of that ocean of sand where the wind perpetually moves the dunes like blond waves of a restless sea, Arya reached a region blessed with life, a rich landscape of pine forests, thick woods and green hills. In the midst of this luxuriant vegetation, there was a small lamplit village, and her heart rejoiced at this scene, for she could at last behold the living again and drink the sacred wine of Life, following her eerie encounter with the soul of death.

As she entered the village, Arya saw men at work, actively going about their daily tasks, apparently unencumbered by the absence of the Sun, this gravest breach of Nature's laws. When she reached the main square of the hamlet, she thought: "finally *some* company... for gods, hermits, and prophets, even bad company is welcome." Then she sought to find out the name of that strange land where the Sun was banished, that twilight zone where nature's golden reign had come to an end, and men's dark rule had begun.

Drawing the men's admiration and the women's envy, she soon became the centre of attention, for her tall stature, her fair and well-defined features indicated that she was from the North, there where the cold air and the harsh weather mould the fairest maidens and the mightiest warriors. Like a sun unto herself, she seemed to shine on these natives, as her inner flame radiated its golden rays unto her surroundings, piercing the dark soul of the night with the divine spear of awakening.

Unperturbed by all the commotion around her, Arya noticed a tall, distinguished-looking elderly man standing apart from the crowd, on the threshold of his home, who was carefully watching her from a distance. She approached the man who looked at her with a mix of affection and admiration. There was a certain gleam in his eyes when she finally came face to face with him, as though he felt that somehow, she was no stranger to him, that there was something in her that belonged to his inner world and his inmost thoughts. She saluted the old man and she too had the same feeling of familiarity, the feeling that somewhere in time, in this world or another, she had known that man with noble features whose eyes reflected a timeless wisdom from a forlorn divine age.

There was a strange mixture of sadness and contentment in the wise man's mysterious eyes, and Arya felt a strong affection for that person whom she had just met, but whom she already knew, though she could not tell how or when their paths had previously crossed in the labyrinth of time. But that made no difference, for time and space never were boundaries to those whose souls are akin, and destiny always unites those who share the same ideas and pursue the same ideals.

The old man invited her inside his modest home so that they could talk with discretion, away from the crowd. "Don't let the mob annoy you," he said as they went in, "they are not used to seeing a strange face here in the middle of nowhere. You see, it is not often that foreigners come to such a remote place, save those who are lost or *want* to be lost, those who want to escape from men and the ignorance of men, who seek to lose mankind in order to find themselves… only to find out that there are no limits to men's stupidity; it follows you to the confines of the earth, and wherever man sets foot, Nature decays and gods depart."

"Man is the only imperfect creature on the face of the earth — though he is the highest —, for he alone has not *become* who he is — a god in the making —, he has silenced the voice of the god within, choosing the inertia of survival over the creative selection of evolution; and all that does not go upwards and forwards, goes downwards and backwards. Hence, the ape in man has killed the god in man, and so he remains locked in his infinite conceit, trapped in the realm of possibility, and, save for a few godlike men — who are more gods than men —, man has yet to cross the threshold of Impossibility and walk the path of divinity, which is engraved in his body and his immortal soul and still waits to be trodden." Thus spoke the old man, while he looked through the window into the boundless sky. "My child," he added, "you should know that no man comes here save he who is desperate, he who has decided to quit life and retire away from its absurdity and injustice… for there is nothing to give or take from life here in the land of sterile thought and hollow faith."

He then bid her sit down and drink a cup of mint tea with him. They sat for a moment in silence, drinking their tea, each absorbed in his thoughts. She then told him: "never have I seen such a strange world that defies the order of Nature and the law of Life; is it a dream, a mirage? Where is the Sun, source of all life and all truth? Where has it disappeared? *Why* has it vanished, drowned by all this overwhelming obscurity? Can there be Life without Light? Those who choose to live in the dark are but dead men walking in the labyrinth of Nothingness, hollow beings whose souls have long been buried in the abyss of eternal darkness; for those born blind can never behold Life's beauty and glory, and they live forever in the shadow of existence. What, pray tell, is the name of this cursed land that has been forsaken by the gods? For all gods, as life itself, are the sons of the One God, *Surya*; pray tell, my friend, what befell our Great God?"

Looking at Arya with tender eyes filled with a certain nostalgia, the wise man replied: "this, my child, is the land of Eternal Night, the home of darkness, graveyard of all hope and freedom; this is the land of idle dreamers, who dream while they're awake — who dream *that* they're awake — those whose life is but a long dream, though they call their dream 'awakening', their ignorance 'truth', and the road to Nowhere that they tread, 'the right path'; those whose god is but an illusion, though they call him 'the supreme'. This is the land of all possibilities and no reality, the land where the 'if' and the 'ought' have buried the 'is' and the 'shall', where the Unattainable has buried the soul of life. This is the land where dreams are conceived and take shape, but do not conceive and shape the real, where the eternal and the transient, the real and the illusory mix together, unite, and clash; the land where the Word was crucified when It became flesh, where God was shunned when He became Man, where hope was slaughtered when it became truth, where the Idea was slain when it took form."

"This is the land where the word 'God' sounds hollow in the ears of Truth, where divinity is robbed of its meaning, where religion kills the Spirit in the name of the letter, and slays the soul of Life in the name of heaven and hell." As the old man thus revealed his secret thoughts and his occult truth, a bittersweet feeling of melancholy shook his serenity and detachment, yet he went on speaking his word: "once, the radiant star reigned over humanity, its sacred light kindling the inner flame of men and illuminating their minds. Once, Supreme Truth pervaded the world with Her holy rays of Wisdom and Elevation."

"But that was the dawn of mankind, when gods trod the earth and men followed the golden path to divinity, at that sacred time when the real was imbued with magic and the divine walked on human limbs, when nature was God's supreme manifestation, and God was nature's ultimate destination, and God and man were united in the bosom of life. Today, however, is the twilight of man. Today a god of darkness casts his shadow over the land of the rising Sun, a mighty idol numbs men's minds and stifles their spirit. An invisible tyrant, who has divorced life, suffers no company among gods and men, and sits lonely upon his pitiful throne, a sad and lonely ruler ruling the sad and the unfree; and what kind of a god rules over slaves? He remains the god of slaves, and to rule over slaves is to rule over nothing, to be a slave oneself."

The old man fell silent for a moment, as a feeling of resentment and powerlessness in the face of life's strange ways and invisible and crooked purpose overcame him. He then said: "today an unknown god rules the world of men, in the name of a kingdom that shall never come, for it is not, never was, and never will be, of *this* world. And is there anything more pitiable than a king without a kingdom? A ruler whose reign never comes? But what kind of a god is a stranger to life and to divinity itself? What kind of a creator shuns his own creation? Such a god shall remain a strange god, a lonely god whose soul was lost when it no longer served existence and ceased to elevate the depths to its heights, severing the bridge of Life which binds the potential and the actual, the possible and the real, the ideal and the true. For the kingdom of God lies in our hearts, not in some distant heaven; thus taught the Son of Man, but men did not understand him. But was a prophet ever understood? Will the human ever fathom the divine?"

"Alas! The god of men shall remain a mystery unto himself and the world, an unsolved riddle that eternally tortures the mind and haunts the soul, a lifeless idol that is a blessing to the ignorant, and a mystery that is a source of shame to the enlightened."

"Life, in the eye of God, is a perpetual ascent, an eternal thrust upwards, a shining path that those in search of the Absolute tread on their way to the realm of immortality. But now that the reign of men is upon the earth, life is but perpetual decay, a continuous fall in the bottomless chasm of darkness; nature's timeless beauty has been distorted by the baseness of men which wants to conquer, and by conquering slays the soul of the world. Nature's divine innocence has been tainted by greed, that indelible sin of mortals. Man: that most divine and vilest, that highest hope and lowest creature… he stands guilty of the greatest crime, the crime against Life; for he has turned Nature from the abode of divinity into a battlefield for men, these eternal children, dwarfs of the Spirit. Man has turned God against Himself, when God ceased to be the Way and became the end."

"Today men no longer believe in the god of Life, the Father, the All, the Great God Pan, whose kingdom is nowhere and everywhere, whose reign is not imposed from above, but comes from within, whose free spirit blows like a liberating wind over men, lifting their minds and sanctifying their souls… and so, Life's supreme symbol, its essence and purpose, has vanished from the face of this wretched world, its very name has become sacrilegious, and doom is knocking on mankind's door… My dear child, Syria and *Surya* no longer rhyme today, and the land of the rising Sun no longer deserves its ancestral name, for it now follows an alien god. And so the desert has invaded Our Sea (3), and Night has fallen on our dawning Sun."

"The truth is that he *deserved* to die, this failed artist (is not man his masterpiece?), for true divinity thus commands: *all* failures shall perish… and God is the biggest failure today. He deserved to die, this imperfect god, when he rose above Life and thus killed Her soul, the sacred breath that imbues the world with meaning and purpose, the sublime Light that fills all darkness with hope and expectation. These people do not know it yet — for they live outside life, here in the desert of existence —, yet the god they worship is but a ghost, a shadow, a relic of divinity… he is indeed dead, this idol who haunted the souls of men, though the stench of his decomposing spirit has not yet reached deserts, mountains, and forests — wherever Nature is still at home -, for it is in the cities that God's death is most felt. It is the fumes of the cities — the fumes of lust and greed — that killed the soul of God, for Nature remains divine, and evil has a human face."

"God died when Truth was slain in his name, when Life ceased to justify itself, and death became a goal and a promise. Darkness fell upon mankind when God's heaven became man's hell; when, instead of hallowing Life, God's name became the worst curse cast upon existence."

"God is dead, and everywhere man lives in darkness. Man, seeking God in the beyond, killed the god within, and so in vain he roams the earth, desperately seeking the Light that once kindled the flame of his divine soul. But the earth has become a desert, and deserts harbour no gods, for there the Great Breath is stifled, there Life declines, Spirit decays, and all that lives on in this valley of death is an unquenchable thirst upon men's dry lips, and an unfulfilled hope in their empty hearts."

"God is dead, and we are all orphans lost in the abyss of existence, in that dark void where no hope ever sparkles, where deserts grow and Life withdraws. The world has lost its divine innocence, for only the divine is innocent, and innocence alone is divine. That is why doom stands at the gates of mankind, for the age of men is the darkest of ages."

"Yes, my child, man is a dark cloud in Life's clear sky… for in his conceited ignorance, he has 'humanised' Nature — that is, he made everything flat and small and devoid of mystery — so he could call it home. But to nature belongs divinity, for nature is innocent. And man is Nature's enemy, that is why he will never be divine; he is a mere passing wave in the sea of Impermanence."

"Man killed the soul of Nature in the name of reason, and he killed the spirit of God in the name of faith. Whatever he touches, he distorts and slanders, this arch-enemy of Life, this anti-God… But how could these twin daughters of Truth — Faith and Reason — become enemies, how could they become the very enemies of Life, save in man's twisted mind? For to separate them is to kill them both, and so today the spectre of death casts its dark shadow on our wretched earth."

"Today everything lies and cheats, everything is fake and crooked… everything is *human* today. Woe to all gods, in this dark age of men! Pity all men, in this twilight of the gods! For gods and men are bound by the same destiny, and whenever their paths do not meet, life goes astray and the world loses all meaning. Gods should become men, and men should become gods… that is Destiny's ultimate commandment. Only thus will the human and the divine finally be reconciled, and the

God-man, conceived out of this blessed union, shall inherit the earth. But ours remains the age of men, the darkest of ages."

"God died, though his ghost lives on in deserts and forests, wherever man has not sullied the soul of Life. I tell thee, dear child of Light, God's disgrace came at the hands of man: when man himself ceased to see God in his own shadow, when he ceased to be a god in the making, he condemned *all* gods, for the fate of man is linked to the divine in a holy union made in the heavens… when man ceased to be that bridge which leads beyond and above itself, he sank in the stagnant waters of death and decay. Thus today he worships the shadow of the god that once was, as it is better to believe in the void than not to believe at all, for life has no meaning but the meaning it gives itself."

"Man forgot whence he came, thus he became blind to whither he was going, for the past casts its light onto the path of the future, to reveal the will of destiny. And so the Light of God went down when man's soul ceased reflecting it; for the source of light dies out when it no longer bestows its healing rays upon the world. Light always springs from within, so when the inner flame dies, the world turns into a cold desert. When man fell, God failed… for God is man's dream, and the dream is shattered when the dreamer awakes."

"Man killed God when he ceased to seek Him within, for it is in man's depth that divinity takes root and grows into the Boundless Being that governs all existence. It is from the depths of Being that the heights of Becoming are conceived and that the Tree of Life blossoms forever anew, elevating men into gods… for gods are but higher men who have overcome themselves; and the abyss that gazes at the peaks grows wings that rise to meet them."

"God died when life lost its meaning. But when God died, life lost its purpose, and so it became unbearable. So where is *our* god, the God of Life, *Surya*, source of all Light and all creation? Alas! Today the star of stars is forbidden in the world of men; today the tyrant-god, the ruthless ruler and lawmaker above the clouds, has replaced the all-encompassing, all-pervading god, father to gods and men, the god of lovers, poets, saints, and all Warriors of Light. Today the lost reign of gods on earth is but a faint memory kept alive in the souls of those Sons of Truth; now, man rules the earth, and he has made it in his own image, a petty, empty planet for petty, empty creatures. Nobody today believes in gods or human gods, noblest sons of Mother Nature; men now either believe in *one* god or in *no* god, and both are blasphemy, for what is God without gods? A father with no children, — as Nature without Life is a childless mother — ; and Life itself is but the home and soul of God."

The old man paused for a moment, reflecting on the lost divinity in heaven and on earth, then he said: "today the land of the rising Sun lies in the shadow of perpetual gloom, and its people, turning their backs on the past and shutting their eyes to the future, bow down before the pale reflection and the unfaithful imitation of the star of stars; for the moon is but a distorted and faded mirror of Supreme Truth, and its gleam is but a shy recollection of the Eternal Light. Yet Truth never dies, it always prevails — for Truth is divine, and nothing is above divinity —, though it sometimes bends its proud head under the heavy weight of deceit (and the deceit of millennia weighs heavily), only to lift it higher when comes the time of renewal and rebirth. Thus, the mysteries of the Natural Religion still linger, in this dark day and age, in the heart of every Son of God, in the mind of every seeker of Truth, and in the soul of every lover of Wisdom, for they alone are the true faithful, they alone serve Life itself and for its own sake."

"The Eternal Religion belongs neither to time, nor to space, but to the boundless ocean of Being; it claims no holy land or chosen people, but speaks the universal language of God. Banished ages ago from this land by the sons of the desert, — when the desert grew and life withdrew —, the religion of Divine Wisdom, whose father is the Sun and whose mother is Life, still lingers in the spirit of those select few who have neither forsaken their selves nor lost their way, those who bear the sacred flame of Truth within, upholding the faith that inspires them in times of unbelief, and guides them in times of enlightenment. However, the greatest majority of humans have chosen — as herds always do — to live in darkness, and so the Light has gone down, for whatever you cease to believe in fades away. Thoughts are the only reality, the world is but the thought and dream of God."

2

Thus spoke the wise old man, and his words filled Arya's soul with sorrow mixed with hope, joy mixed with nostalgia, for she felt and knew that she was not alone, that there was a secret community of believers, unknown brothers in faith and spirit, living in silence, waiting to be reunited again when the Occult rises to the surface and Truth reclaims Her right. "I know what land this is," she said, "I had heard about it from travellers who went East in search of new lands to discover or conquer. They call it 'the land of the sleepless dreamers,' the place where reality itself is an illusion, a dream where reason slumbers and superstition rules, where obscurity overwhelms the mind and spirit and covers truth with an impenetrable veil, in the name of 'faith' and 'virtue.'" Having said that, Arya stood up, approached the window, and gazed through it at the night-revellers and worshippers of the village; they were kneeling before the moon, saying prayers and singing songs of praise to their god. She reflected a moment, and then spoke thus:

"Just look at them, my friend, how they know but one reality: darkness, eternal night, and how they worship the shadows of Truth and Light… for he who has ever lived in the dark sees a dawn in every twilight and a sun in every star; and he whose soul has never touched the divine venerates a ghost as a god… but a stream is not the spring, and a drop is not the ocean."

"Woe to those who have not beheld the Light, for they shall never know the glory of a higher life and the bliss of a higher love; instead, they vegetate, throughout their empty existence, in the swamp of human ignorance and deceit, in this world of the living dead and decaying life. For he who has not seen the light of Truth with his inner eyes, and he who has not heard the voice of God in the depths of his being, and he who has not felt the soul of Life in his inner infinity, will never tread the divine path. And though the shadow follows the light wherever it goes, it can never become Light; and so man can never become divine unless he ceases to be a shadow and turns himself into Light, the source and beginning of All."

"Pity those dwarfs of the spirit who rest in the comforting peace of idol veneration, for they bow down before an unknown god whose soul forever eludes them. Divine incarnation is heresy in their blind eyes, and there is nothing worse, in the eyes of God, than the blindness that comes from within, the blindness of the soul. Thus they kill the idea by denying its form, for an idea that is not expressed fades into oblivion."

"Pity those who only find peace by kneeling before the void, for theirs is the peace of the faint-hearted and weak-minded, a peace borne out of defeat, not the peace that crowns the greatest victory — and what greater victory than victory over oneself? — and that is: to look Truth in the face and whisper in the ear of God the word: Supremacy. For Supremacy is man's only destiny."

"These people remain blind to the shining truth that says: 'God is in All and All is in God'. For the One takes on motley forms so that He may express Himself in life, as the Father embraces life through the Son. And are not all men gods in the making? Are we not all sons of the Light? Are not all gods shining drops in the radiant ocean of God? For, as you said, what is God without gods? A Message without messengers, Spirit devoid of form, a holy ghost that only haunts but never transforms."

"God is one, God is whole, yet the Whole manifests itself in its parts, and so God manifests Himself in the gods, His messengers and forms. But one needs the profoundest depth, one should be able to see beyond sight, to hear beyond sound, and to feel beyond the senses, in order to comprehend such truths; one needs to be one with the purpose of the universe in order to fathom the Unfathomable, to seize the Unattainable, to perceive the Unmanifested, and to grasp the essence of Truth that lies in parable, metaphor and symbol." Thus spoke Arya, and her heart was swollen with a feeling of deep gratitude to Life for granting her the gift of higher consciousness, for to live without consciousness is to be blind in the kingdom of light. Still gazing at the night worshippers who were now performing the basic rituals of their religion, under the watchful eye of their clergymen, Arya remained silent for a moment, reflecting on how faith ceased to be in the service of truth, as Truth ceased to be man's highest goal and purpose. She then spoke thus:

"The age of darkness fell on *this* mankind," she said, "when the mind ceased to guide the heart into performing miracles undreamt of, when reason became the slave of passion and thus became blind; for the blind can never guide the blind on the path of Light, and so they all totter aimlessly in this void that life has become, here in the land of Nowhere and Nothing."

"These people worship a strange god above the clouds and beyond understanding, for their narrow hearts and blind minds reckon that only by putting their god above life do they truly do him justice and glorify him; but do they not see that God's soul is to be found in Nature, and His glory rests in His Sons, the gods? That the One and the multiple drink from the same divine source? That the Whole lives through its parts, as they draw their essence from it? That all opposites are none, and all Being is one? These people do not know God nor will they ever, for their eyes do not see beyond their minds, thus they can never *truly* see, — as true sight comes from the soul — ; they can never see that gods are Nature's forces at work in the service of Providence and Destiny, for only the natural is true, and only the true is natural."

"The only thing that is *real* is the one thing that is hidden from the noise of the world; it is the meaning behind the absurd, the sublime behind the uncanny, the divine behind the human. It is the idea behind the form, the alpha behind the omega, the eternal behind the transient. The only thing that is *true* is the one thing that is unknown to men's limited minds and narrow souls, for man is *not*—as he claims—Nature's masterpiece; he is only a bridge, a stepping-stone, a prelude to the higher act of creation. Man is an experiment of the gods…"

"They put their god above Life and beyond Truth, these obscure men of the East… but is not God the soul of Life and the heart of Truth? Their god is but a figment of a child's imagination; but true faith requires maturity, hence men remain eternal children of the spirit."

"They put their god above Life, these 'believers', but what good is a god who is a curse upon life? Is God not the supreme life-giver? And they boast of their 'faith', which they claim puts them high above common mortals; but is not faith without reason bondage of the spirit and tyranny of the senses over mind and soul?"

"I would rather perish by lightning—and thus overcome myself—than kneel before an idol that enslaves my soul and numbs my mind… I would rather die free and proud, with hope as my last sigh, than live in the eternal bondage of human ignorance, wrought by this blind faith which blights man's reason and creates fake gods, and thus neither elevates the mind nor the spirit, but sinks man ever deeper in the whirlwind of unbridled passion. Better to die while aspiring after divinity, than to live in the comforting mediocrity of humanity… better to perish in the shadow of the Light than to live in eternal darkness, for darkness only begets darkness, and faith devoid of reason only breeds barbarity, fanaticism, and superstition."

"Yes, faith in the 'only god' only begets ignorance and decay, for this god… does not exist! And when God himself becomes an escape from life,—instead of being a glorification of life—, Life loses all meaning.

The god of men is a disgrace to divinity... hence all *this* god breeds is ignorance, whether it is called faith or godlessness... and so everywhere you look today, you see either pious fools or godless morons."

"Therefore, let this god from the desert stay away from me, away from us *truly* chosen ones, — we who have chosen Pan over Yahweh -, for *his* lost tribes are doomed to aimlessly wander the earth in search of a promise that never was, and a time that will never be. *That* is the curse of the gods: those who stray from the Inner Path shall nowhere feel at home and never find peace, though they may wander the earth in search of their lost soul; the desert remains their only home, a burden they carry like a camel's hump wherever they go."

3

Upon hearing Arya's fiery rejection of the god of men, the god that man's poor imagination has fashioned in his own image, the old man was bewildered by these bold words, arrows of wisdom that struck at the very heart of truth; words that, though full of godlessness, were also full of faith, an outcry of the Inner God who wants to break out and conquer life anew, in this dark world which lost its soul when it slew the soul of Truth. "These are the words of an alchemist," he said, "words which transform the poison that man spreads — whenever his sick mind wanders, and wherever his clumsy foot ventures — into Life's divine elixir of Beauty and Eternity... words that turn all that is base, fake, awry and rotten — everything human — into divine Truth, perpetual creation, and endless elevation."

Thus spoke the old man, as his heart was filled with the sacred hope and silent aspiration of those exuberant yet unfulfilled souls who have long searched, but never found. Then he told her: "Arya, my dear child! Never have I heard such saintly words, though saintliness is often cloaked in unbelief, in this world of contrasts and shadows... never have my ears listened to this holy melody of God, though holiness often wears the veil of godlessness, when God himself loses His soul to men's folly. For those with subtle ears and pure hearts, these most godless words are filled with piety, as they strike right at the heart of divinity... they are filled with the faith that emanates from within, the faith that destroys idols of clay and builds in their place temples of the Spirit."

Having said that, the wise man was still dissatisfied, for he felt that there was something incomplete in Arya's discourse on the failed god; there was still a note missing from Arya's Symphony of Life, he thought, something that remained unsaid; for destroying an idol means little if it does not lead to creating a god, as godlessness is no worthier than superstition, and both are alien to divinity and dwell in the eternal darkness of illusion and folly. Therefore, he asked her: "you condemn the god of men as a fake god, a hollow shell of divinity; yet this is what you *do not* believe in, this is the god you deny... I need to know what you *do* believe in, the god that you embrace. I need to discover the creator in you, not just the destroyer; for to be truly divine, one has to create, as destruction is always a prelude to creation, the opening act of the Masterpiece — and where it is otherwise, it is but evil and baseness, the void seeking the void."

"You despise mankind and its all-too-human god, Arya, yet mocking the human means little if it does not entail glorifying the divine, and destroying the temple of deceit remains an act that is void of significance, if it is not guided by the will to erect the temple of Truth. Thus, preaching man's demise remains an empty speech that cries out in the desert of existence, if this preaching does not turn into a vision, a promise, and an act of divine creation. My dear child, your wisdom flatters my truth, yet it still needs to mature in the deep well of the Spirit before it can shine on the peaks of Supremacy. Your wisdom needs to overcome the 'ought' and preach the 'shall', your wishing needs to turn into commanding. I need to hear about *your* god, Arya, the god that *you* venerate, for only gods can talk about God, and I see the spark of divinity in your mysterious eyes."

Having heard the old man's exhortation with great attention, Arya looked at him with gratitude and a sense of satisfaction, for he had asked her to give out her most precious gift, to bestow her most priceless jewel — and what good is a treasure that remains buried? What good is a jewel that is not offered? — and that is: the secret of divinity, the truth behind the mystery. "You ask me to unveil the divine beneath the human, the eternal beneath the transient, the infinite beneath the limited. For is not God the Absolute in all things? Life at its highest, Love at its profoundest, Force at its supreme height, Beauty in its most sublime form, Wisdom in its infinity, and Innocence at its purest? But where, pray tell, have you ever seen such heights in the world of men? Nowhere and never have I seen God's shadow reflected on this wretched earth, except during the Golden Age, when men still believed in gods and accepted them as their teachers and guides, before the germ of equality infested men's brains and darkened their souls."

"You ask me to talk about my god, O wise one; yet surely your wisdom must ask: what sublime words could express the Unutterable, what great metaphor could reveal the Unmanifested? You ask me to talk about my god; yet how can I speak of something I have yet to discover? For what am I roaming the earth for, if not in search of my god? And though I hear His voice in every beat of my heart, and His presence fills my every breath, and though I touch His soul with every thought, I do not know Him yet, for I am still not ready: I am wise enough to know it, and humble enough to admit it. And one should not speak of that which one does not know, that is what wisdom dictates, and Wisdom is the greatest teacher, the teacher of Life. For those who are not ready, silence is the greatest teacher, as thoughts need the silence of the gods to mature, and the words of men kill the soul of ideas — the soul of God. Hence, the wise do not talk, and the talkative are seldom wise; for the void that is in man — the void that *is* man — seeks to fill itself with the noise of the world, whilst Wisdom is a world unto itself."

"No, my friend, I cannot yet speak of my god, though I am a goddess; for there is still too much *woman* in me... the inner goddess has yet to unfold and conquer the woman, before *I* can speak to God and about God, for, as you said, only gods can talk about God. I say *my* god, for even gods have their own god and seek him out, as perfection is an endless path that leads to the Boundless. Even gods must experience their own hell before they can be baptised in the divine Spring of Life. And our hell — that purgatory of men — is called earth... Yes, earth is our hell, for down here the infinite is bound by the limited, and the eternal by the transitory. And there is nothing more stifling for a god than the chains of time and space. But earth is also the mirror of heaven, and the fleeting image that passes below reflects the timeless essence that dwells above."

"I have yet to *find* my god... I have yet to discover my Self and tread my path. And my path is engraved in my memory, which is the cosmic memory of God. However, even though I travel the earth in search of the lost truth and the coming god, still my soul knows that my search is but the path that leads to a deeper, inner quest, for the whole universe speaks through our depths. And so, everywhere I look for *signs*... milestones of the Spirit that would lead me back to my inner Self, to my inner God; for the outer is only the gate to the inner, and the whole universe is but the reflection of the infinite in us. Hence my *true* search is ultimately inwards — as is all search for the divine, as is all soul-searching —, and the world is only the form that the Idea takes to express its inner essence... as the Word is but the breath of God cloaked in human language."

"Yes, wise one, I have yet to *know* my god; my quest has just begun... I seek Him as a lost child seeks his mother, in this strange world where no one is at home. I seek the *coming* god, for the old god is dead — and who could still believe in a dead god? —; and to live without faith is not to live at all, for faith is the breath of life. Hence, they look the same to me, these believers and these sceptics of today; they all hold on to an illusion, whether they call it 'God' or '*Nihil*'... they either worship an idol of clay and sand that kills their reason, or kneel before their own unbelief as an idol that slays their spirit."

"God's absence has become unbearable today, for life is unworthy if it does not serve a higher purpose; and what higher and nobler path than that which leads to the divine? And so men desperately seek to fill the void left by God's demise; but nothing on this earth, not power, not riches, not glory, not even love — that most divine gift bestowed upon men — nothing can fill that gulf left in Life's womb, a gulf that is most felt in those whose unbelief has killed their soul and rendered the world a lifeless desert. When God died, something died in man... and today my soul, too, is an empty shell, though I am a goddess; for nowhere else can you most feel the death of God than in the mourning hearts of His children, the gods."

"I need to believe again so that I can live again, for how can one live without hope? And faith is the highest hope... I seek *my* god, I await *my* dawn, I need to breathe the fresh air of the heights, there where all hopes are born, where everything becomes possible and all ideals become real. I seek a *new* meaning; for how could one live if Life lacked all meaning? One would have to set a new goal and create a new god in order to live, for the divine remains the highest goal."

"Alas, my friend, I cannot speak about my god, for I have yet to know Him; and one cannot talk of the glory of Light when all one sees is the wretchedness of darkness... thus I seek a drop of light in the midst of this ocean of night. But I know the *way* and I see the gate of His temple, though the sacred flame that hallows His sanctuary has yet to kindle the hidden fire that lies buried underneath my human sheath. I only see the Gate, though I have yet to tread beyond it into the realm of the immortals; that is all I see now, for the way to God is long and steep, as are all paths that lead there where the air grows rare for humans, up yonder where gods dwell."

Having unveiled her misgivings and her highest hopes, Arya remained quiet, and the old man stared at her with eyes full of satisfaction and admiration, for her humility in the face of Life's mysteries unveiled a deep wisdom and a noble soul, as only those who have seen the light of Truth can bestow its redeeming rays unto the world. After a moment's meditation, he told her: "very well, then, talk to me about the Gate… speak, dear child of Light, of what your inner eyes see, and what your soul feels… enter the realm of your vision of divinity, and tell me what you see. Tell me what god you *seek*."

Arya stood still for a while, then she went into a trance, looking within, delving into her depths, contemplating her inner infinity, the boundless that dwells in her soul; after a lapse of time that resembled eternity, she said to the wise man: "the god I seek is unattainable, and yet He is reality itself; He dwells in the here and now, He lives in every lofty thought and through every noble feeling, and yet remains beyond time and space, always a distant hope and a fleeting dream that overcomes itself each time it fulfils itself. God, seen through *my* eyes, is perpetual will to creation and elevation that drives life ever beyond and above itself; He is the highest idea expressed in the simplest form; He is Nature at Her best and in Her purest innocence; He is nowhere and everywhere, below and above, unseen and ever unreachable, yet again evidently expressed in the magnificence of Being."

"God — as Life — is Justice, Goodness, Wisdom, Reason, yet in the shadow of His Light grow the germs of injustice, evil, and folly. God pervades our world and touches our lives, yet His remains the realm of Infinity; He expresses Himself through the Word, yet His language remains ineffable; He takes on different forms, yet His essence remains elusive, beyond the reach of all that does not endure; He manifests Himself through opposites, yet His Truth belongs to the realm of the

Absolute. Thus God is Order veiled in chaos, Love expressed through Force, Being ever unfolding through the whirlwind of Becoming."

"God is like Nature, He *is* Nature: pure innocence that knows no limits either in good or evil, pure energy that pervades all that is and shapes all that becomes. God is nameless, for the Whole cannot be named nor can it be judged, the Whole cannot be conceived outside itself. God is eternal, for Eternity knows no limits and lives in its own realm of Ideas; He is perpetual elevation, an endless ascent towards the endless peaks of Being, a sacred thrust that lifts man's soul into the divine heights and draws it ever closer to its beginning and end, the source of the stream and ocean of Life."

"*My* god does not oppress, nor does He judge — only man, the limited, does that —, for how could the Whole oppress and judge itself? *My* god neither rewards nor punishes, for man alone, through his actions, issues his own sentence upon himself, rising above or sinking below himself: and *that* is divine justice: the deeds of man weighed on the scale of life — for accident and chance do not exist. Life itself is God's kingdom, and His soul dwells in the depth of my being. I need not seek Him outwards or above, for He is within me and speaks through me: is not man's longing for immortality the last sigh of divinity on earth? That is how we, the Sons of *Surya*, view and live divinity: always as the Light that pervades the All, always as inwards and throughout, flowing eternally and shining on All and Everything, bestowing everlasting truth, divine wisdom and energy; Light that turns all shadows and darkness into radiant pathways to Infinity."

"*My* god embraces His world, He does not shun it; for He is infinite Love that lives and grows through all-encompassing Energy, and we are all the sons of Life bathing in the vast ocean of His Being. God is Light, and Light knows neither boundaries nor limitations; in its presence, all darkness vanishes and all shadows retreat. Thus only those select few — the elect among the elect — whose eyes reflect the divine spark, and whose forehead bears the sacred flame, count among God's lineage. Men, however, are not worthy of treading the path to divinity. They remain closer to the apes than to the gods. *Their* god is the dark shadow of Supreme Light. Theirs is a strange deity, indeed. So let them keep their judge, their punisher and tyrant-god above the skies, that eternal father to eternal children… let the god of men stay away from us Sons of Life."

As she spoke of her own burgeoning vision of divinity, Arya felt that there was something eternal in her that was speaking *through* her. By talking about God, she was unveiling the goddess within. That, she felt, was how she would discover the god she was seeking. "Could it be," she asked the old man, "that man travels the earth in search of something higher than himself, something that eludes his mind but captures his soul, only to discover that all he is seeking ultimately dwells in his inmost being? When will man realise that the Quest should start where it usually ends: in the Self? For the whole universe is contained in our inner depths, the whole world is a drop in our ocean of Being, as we are the drop and we are the ocean. Yet hopelessly we still search, hopelessly we still yearn, we seek to find ourselves by losing ourselves, embracing the world while shunning its soul… man has grown accustomed to search for, to ask, and never to find. Man has grown accustomed to being limited, to being human; he has forgotten what it feels like to be divine. We have forgotten our own memory of heaven; we have become deaf to the divine melody of Life."

Thus spoke Arya, and there was an expression of contentment on her face, for she had said aloud, for the first time, what she had always kept within her heart and soul: the doubts, the questions, the answers that had always haunted her. "Certain truths are better left untold," she said, "and certain questions unasked, when those they are destined for are lacking. But then comes the time for pruning and reaping, and only those chosen for rebirth and renewal are then allowed to taste the fruit of Truth that has long ripened in the millenarian wells of the Occult."

The wise man, who was carefully listening to each word of Arya's solitary sermon, rose and embraced her tenderly, as a father embraces his long lost daughter on her return home. "My child," he told her with a great sigh of relief, "my spiritual godchild! You flatter my wisdom with your truth! Your humility betrays the greatness of your soul, for only the great are humble, and only the wise admit their ignorance."

"Finally we meet again! For it *is* you, it is *you* that I have been waiting for, during all these long years of inner struggle and longing… a kindred soul to share my sacred beliefs, a higher soul *worthy* of such beliefs… And though my will has often faltered, I never lost faith, knowing that the day will come when the Chosen Souls meet again and together build the Holy Temple of the New Age; for Destiny always finds a way, and Fate always has its say: noble blood draws noble blood, and so the Holy Brotherhood of Masters lives on, beyond time and space, universal and eternal, indestructible, invincible, supreme. And even the darkest night carries the golden dawn within its womb. Arya, you are the first Chosen One whom I encounter; you are the first ray of light in this overwhelming ocean of darkness … could you be the ray that announces the Sun? Could you be the dawn that ushers in the noontide? The breeze that precedes the storm? The hope that heralds the winds of liberation?"

"Ah, the joy of *real* company, the bliss of *true* comradeship! All my life, I have lived as a hermit in my own land and among my own people. All my life my exalted soul has known nothing but the cosmic solitude of gods among men, lonely stars shining in the midst of a dark universe of blind matter. I have chosen to lead a solitary life, for I always thought it better to live the silent solitude of gods than to suffer the noisy company of men; and nowhere more than in a crowd have I felt the loneliest, an eternal stranger among strangers… yes, dear Arya, *this* is *my* secret: the people you see before you are *not* my people, for they no longer share *my* truth… the finest among them have long departed, leaving behind a land of desolation."

"This land you tread on is *not* my land, for the soul of Truth no longer dwells here, and all that's left from its former splendour is a lifeless desert of sand and dust, with the ruins of gods' monuments standing as sole witnesses to the glory that once was; for even the sacred fades away if it does not fulfil itself and realise its dream of perfection, turning its promise into an achievement. The sacred becomes a curse when it does not create beyond itself. And so, the cradle of civilisation has become the silent museum of mankind, where memories and relics of another age and another race are stored as symbols of the greatness of this once glorious nation."

"No, Arya, I no longer recognise this land, though I was born and raised on its soil, and though I have shared my bread with its sons. But birth has no value on its own; it means little if it does not occur in the right place, at the right time, and for the right reasons. Birth means little if it is not willed by fate, for all else is accident and chance; and alas, how many men are the illegitimate sons of that capricious woman, Chance! How many births unnecessary, how many lives unworthy… Birth means little if it does not serve a higher purpose and follow a sacred path. One is born to fulfil oneself, to look ahead, not behind, for birth is a beginning, a means to an end, but not the end itself; and when it becomes an end, it only breeds sterile thought and declining values."

"And that is what is wrong with nobility today: it no longer justifies itself. That is what is wrong with the *world* today: all values have lost their meaning — and is not God the highest value and the deepest meaning? — but even *he* is dead. Yes, all values, all identities have lost their soul, even the highest among them, those that made life worth living: class, nation, race, culture, religion … today these are but empty names, idle labels and futile tags the cleverest and the most foolish of men acquire upon one's birth, without merit, without a purpose. But values should justify themselves, they should be earned with the sweat of struggle and the blood of honour, on that battlefield of ideas and values that is Life. Birth should serve beyond itself, otherwise it becomes death — and how many dead men walk among the living today! — but in the era of decline, all values have become common, even the noblest ones, even the highest ones, and so we wander aimlessly on this empty planet, lonely atoms desperately searching for our forsaken souls."

"Today, the highest man — as the lowest — has little value, for he has lost his soul, his purpose, his meaning, which is to rise above himself and equal the gods; for that is man's ultimate destiny: to sit at the table of the gods, an equal among equals. But today men follow the short and smooth road of mediocrity that leads nowhere, shunning the long and steep path that leads to glory, a road not travelled save by the boldest and wisest of men, those with a divine mission and a sacred cause."

"Man means nothing today; he is neither a bridge nor a goal, least of all here in the land of illusion and frustrated hopes. No, dear child, I *could* never, I *will* never belong to this land — or to any land, for the whole world has become a desert of the Spirit —; I could never embrace its beliefs, for it now follows crooked paths and false gods. My only home is called the Temple of Truth. It is a temple that could be found anywhere and anytime, a temple that only he who serves the eternal could enter, for it is a tribute to that which endures, unaltered by time's ruthless cycle of birth and death. Where Truth is, *there* is my homeland. And where you see lovers of Wisdom, know that *these* are my people. No religion, no nation or culture, no god is above Truth, for Truth is the soul of God, and God is supreme."

"Truth is the highest religion, it is the *only* religion, for it is the Religion of Life. Hence Truth is my nation, the only place I call home — the only place *God* calls home — and Her sons and warriors are my only companions in arms and brothers in race; for a true warrior — a Warrior of Light — is he who wages a spiritual war on the world and on himself, he who believes in the sanctity of a holy war;

and nothing is holier than Truth... for war is only righteous if it serves a noble cause — and what nobler cause than Truth? — but war waged for its own sake is nothing but death and destruction."

"And a true race, a race worthy of that name, is not defined by the language that it speaks, the land that it inhabits, or the history that it shares, however great these may be; *that* is only called a *people*... but Race — Ah! Glory and misery of race! — race is a divine word that has been tainted and belittled by men's stupidity... race lies not in language but in the blood, and the blood never lies; but blood is tied not only to flesh, but to spirit. Noble blood runs not just in the veins, but also in the soul, as the body inherits the body, and the soul inherits the soul, in the endless cycle of birth and rebirth that governs human life. A race is a spiritual brotherhood of blood and honour; it is defined by the dream that it shares, the truth that it reveres and fights for, the god that it venerates... and only he or she who shares *my* truth and believes in *my* god do I call a brother or a sister, a son or a daughter, for blood means little if it does not serve the soul, and the beauty of form remains an empty shell if it does not transpire in the greatness of the spirit."

"Arya, favourite child of the gods, your words are drops of wisdom that have filled my thirsty heart with hope and joy. You have spoken aloud what my soul has secretly revered all my life. For I, too, am a Sun worshipper, a seeker of Truth, a Son of the Sacred Light. And one never really forsakes his beliefs, as one's beliefs are his essence, his only true and lasting possession... and only that which is not material, only that which cannot be grasped and counted and weighed and exchanged, is that which lasts. Truth speaks thus: only that which cannot be grasped is that which endures and prevails."

"No, Arya, I have not forsaken my beliefs, though I have buried them in the secret garden of my immortal soul, away from men's wicked ignorance and boundless stupidity. But one never really loses himself, one always finds his inner path. In the end, one always re-conquers himself, for salvation awaits him who earnestly seeks, and in seeking errs. Therefore, know that nothing can take away one's faith, — not oppression, not tyranny, not delusion or deceit —, for faith is indestructible and eternal, it survives beyond death, and soars high above all of Life's contingencies and miseries. Hence, my soul belongs to no land, it is as infinite as the universe; it creates its own world, its own heaven and hell, its own god and its own devil. And so it is with every man, whether he knows it or not, whether he accepts it or not. For those to whom Truth is the supreme value and the ultimate goal, no religion can replace Wisdom, as there is no religion and no god above Truth, for God is Truth."

"The moon can never become a sun, and so I could never worship the shadow of Truth. The moon steals away what it can of the Sun's light, yet all it ever gathers is a faded gleam that can never compare to the source of All. The lunar god is therefore but an unfaithful imitation, a pale reflection of the all-embracing divinity. And as the moon is a faint reflection of the Sun, source and fountain of Life and Light, so is the faded god that men worship today a pale imitation of the true and eternal god, a clumsy cloning of the all-encompassing cosmic principle."

"Blessed be the hour that has united us, my child… now I know that we are not alone, that our brothers lie in wait for our Great Reunion, to raise again the sacred banner of Truth — our *Sol Invictus* — on the world's temples and monuments, at the Great Noontide, at the hour of the Great Awakening."

Arya's sermon

1

Arya was deeply touched by the wise man's words, as she noticed that the years had done little to dampen his spirit's fervour and his inner flame, and she felt compelled, by an irresistible inner urge, to address the venerating crowds outside, to tell them *her* truth, as she took pity on these people who knew not what they were doing; hence, she went out, walked towards the main square of the village, stood among the worshippers in their hour of prayer and interrupted their ritual, speaking thus:

"You idle dreamers of the desert, can you not smell the stench of God's rotting corpse and decaying spirit? Do your eyes not see that you are kneeling before the Void, though you call this void 'God'? And this in itself is blasphemy, that God has ceased to be an incarnation of Mother Nature and a manifestation of the Spirit of the Earth! You blind seekers of the Light, you have hitherto only known darkness, for faith has blinded your eyes instead of enlightening your souls. You live in eternal night, though you call your night 'awakening', and your ignorance 'supreme truth'! You call your god the greatest and the unique, though you know him not save in the dead letter of the scriptures — and God knows that the Spirit is above all letters! — , not as the supreme life-giver, but as a lifeless idol that remains a sombre mystery... not as a liberating, elevating inner Spirit, but as an enslaving, debasing inner tyrant."

"God, as humanity has hitherto worshipped, is but a dream of man, for this is what man essentially is: a dreamer and a creator of dreams and gods and heaven and hell. Or could it be that man himself is a dream that dreams itself evermore and endlessly, until death tolls the hour of awakening, lifting the impenetrable veil of *Maya* that covers all life below?"

"*My* god is innocent of you, you strange worshippers of a strange god; the god I *see* is not the god you imagine; the god I *feel* is not the god you conceive; the god I *know* is not the god you suppose. When *you* say 'God', you escape from your selves and look beyond for salvation and perfection, severing yourselves from Nature — that divine source of all life — , separating the Creator from His creation, and the macrocosm from the microcosm. When *I* say God, I look within and I delve into my depths to find my abode of Infinity; I see Him *as* everything and *in* everything, for the Whole cannot be conceived away from its parts, as the world is a whirlwind of creation that continually reinvents itself."

"When *you* say 'God', you picture a higher being and a higher force that remains beyond the reach of mind and soul. When *I* say God, I live the divine experience within and embrace this higher force as my origin and my end, for we are all shining seeds of Light in the sacred fields of Absolute Unity. God and Nature are one, even as the soul and the body cannot live separately, as they imbue one another with the divine breath of life. The particular longs for the universal, in reminiscence of a lost unity, and the universal manifests itself in the particular, to fulfil its dream in deed, and turn the word into an act of creation; and so the divine cycle of life is complete, for creation is a sacred circle which merges Self and Ego to elevate and express Life."

"You say 'God' and you await divine justice, seeking heaven as a reward for your good deeds, and dreading hell as punishment for your bad ones. Well *I* say unto you, justice is not a commodity that you buy and sell on the market of life — for Life is not a market! — though the shopkeepers of faith have ever taught you that everything can be bought and sold in this world where quantity crushes quality and possessions possess the soul. Justice cannot be bought or sold: it is *earned*. And divine justice does not occur 'above' or 'below', in a distant and indefinable tomorrow. Justice unfolds here on earth, heaven and hell unfold here on earth, God Himself lives among you, and His justice is a blessing that you bestow upon yourselves or a curse that you bring unto yourselves."

"Your rise and fall are of your own doing, not willed by 'fate' or 'God' or any outside force or circumstance; you rise or fall through *your* actions, for karma reigns supreme, and all else is illusion and deception. Karma reigns supreme, and no escape to another world or another time is possible — save in the deluded minds of the fainthearted —, for all accountability died with the old god. Know that freedom is not mere absence of restraint, though as eternal slaves, that is how you will ever perceive it. Freedom, *true* freedom, *higher* freedom, is being able to say to the face of Fate: 'come and do your thing, come with your blessings and misfortunes, your glory and your misery, for *I* willed it thus, and thus shall *I* will it evermore and forever until the wheel of existence stops turning'. *That* alone is Freedom, that alone is accountability, which is responsibility for one's own actions, and control of one's own life. But only the masters know that kind of freedom, and most men remain willing slaves of deceit."

"You petty worshippers of a god without a face, firm believers in a shaky faith built on the sands of illusion, when shall you cease blaming God and cursing the devil for your misfortunes? When shall you stop regretting the past and dreaming of a new life, and instead start taking control of the present, which is the steering wheel of your own ship, Destiny? For man is the sole commander of his ship, and the wind that moves its sails hither and thither, sometimes taking it into unknown seas that only his soul knows — for it drove him to them — is but the breath of man's immortal spirit ever longing to go deeper into new seas, to discover new lands and experience new beginnings."

"Man alone determines whether his ship remains in safe haven or wanders deep into the high seas where the winds of change and renewal blow, where Life ever unfolds before the eyes of God. So when shall you act, idle believers, and cease being acted upon? When shall you be achievers, and cease being spectators? You alone determine your destiny and write your own life on the pages of your inner legend, whether you are conscious of it or not, whether you admit it or not. For God dwells within, justice is your own doing, your fate is engraved in your will, and you reap what you sow throughout your lives, throughout the ages."

"But still, as all herds, you look away when the exhilarating wind of free will caresses your weary faces and fills your empty souls. Thus you choose to ignore God's *true* call, that cry of freedom — of a higher type of freedom hitherto unknown to man — which is carried on the wings of Supremacy and echoes for all eternity in the valley of Life: 'be perfect as thy Father is perfect; become Sons of God, become gods yourselves'. For that is God's *only* commandment, a call that is least heeded by man, that strangest of creatures. You shallow humans, you have not heeded God's call, though he has sent you all his saints and prophets bearing the same message cloaked in different forms. For thus speaks God: 'emulate me, do not idolise me, for each time you bow down before me, you kill something in me. Rise up to my peaks to meet me, do not debase me by debasing yourselves, for you are my Sons and remain my Sons, though you err and though you fall... only thus do *I* live eternally; only thus do *I* find meaning in the world that I have created.'"

Having spoken her word, which is the eternal word of God, Arya held a moment's silence, and there was a deep feeling of relief upon her face, as though a weight had been lifted from her conscience; for she had said aloud the only truth that men have never understood — yet when was Truth ever understood? —. But after a while, she went on sermonising the crowd, and spoke thus:

"Men's narrow souls are too small to drink from the divine, overflowing cup of Life; thus they remain alien to the truth which says: 'there is no heaven or hell, no good or evil, there is only wholeness, and being and becoming are merged in eternal creation, for creation is only possible when Spirit shapes matter, and the form expresses the word, as Life is perpetual evolution.'"

"For the spiritual person touched by the soul of God, happiness is within, it unfolds and realises itself through experiencing the boundless that dwells in every man. Yet temporal happiness, the evanescent joy of humans, always lies elsewhere, for it is the longing itself which is divine, not the object of the longing, as to yearn is to reminisce the divine origin of all that lives under the Sun. Wretched mortals, know that there is no end to pursue save eternal becoming, for the Path itself is the End. Life is whole, it is an endless hierarchy, from worm to man to God. The Tree of Life takes its roots in the seed man and bestows its fruit in God. But *your* god does not elevate, he levels and debases, for he is a human hymn to mediocrity, as his horizontal values betray the divine's ascending virtues."

"You dreamers of the desert, you have emptied Night from its mystery and magic, turning it from the sacred time of conception and hope, to a time of doom, impotence and decay. You dream of Truth, Beauty, and Harmony, yet your world remains wretched and empty, and your dream remains a dream that never blossoms into reality, night that never sees the day." By now everyone had stopped praying and was staring at Arya with astonishment, as though they were all spell-bound by what they were hearing. What an outrage, someone — and more so, a *woman!* — was questioning their undying beliefs, the word of God as they learned it in the 'Book of God'? That indeed was unprecedented in the land of faith and virtue. Yet, unperturbed by the menacing crowd that had gathered round her, Arya pursued her fiery speech:

"You falsely-called believers, what you call 'faith' is but crude religious dogma cloaked in the stolen wisdom of millennia; for wisdom in the hands of the unconscious turns into the worst ignorance, and faith without freedom becomes mere idolatry."

"You dark men living in the darkest of worlds, untouched by the sacred enlightening rays of *Surya*, that pure source of Truth and Wisdom, you are self-deluded servants of an illusory despot that you call God; you shall remain eternal sinners of a fallen world that cannot be redeemed, eternal dreamers of a better world that never comes, eternal worshippers of an illusion that insults the mind and betrays the soul, and thus slanders the divine, as true faith alone is divine, and only the divine is worthy of faith."

"You idle dreamers of light in the dark, in vain do you seek your unknown god in the beyond and remain blind to that spark of divinity, that sacred flame which kindles your inner universe, pouring its blessed drops of light into the sacred fountain of Life. You seek your god ever in the above and beyond, ever outside, remaining deaf to the voice of Truth that shouts in your ears: 'God dwells in the infinite, imperishable and universal Self of every living being... for God is Life, and Life is not, where God is not.' God is within you, so why do you refuse to be gods yourselves? Is it your human mind which betrays your divine Self and destiny, refusing to join anew the eternal Spring of Light whence it came? For the Divine is an internal state of mind and being engraved in the depths of your souls, not an unreachable dream in the distant stars above. But only the chosen among you know that truth and live it, for they have the seal of divinity on their shining foreheads."

"You sleepless dreamers whose dream will never end, lost lambs seeking a lost god, you shall forever remain seekers of ghosts and shadows, never contented, never fulfilled, never divine; you shall remain ever severed from your goal and your dream, ever strangers to the creative thrust of Life. For, by looking outwards, you drive the divine away from its inner abode in eternity, into the outer realm of the ephemeral and the illusory... by venerating the beyond, you deny Life; by dreaming the future, you deny the present; hence reality always evades you, and you live off the remnants of the past, eternal beggars of glory and eternal strangers to greatness."

"Sons of the South, *your* sun has set; therefore you know only the night of the soul and the twilight of the spirit."

"Sons of darkness, *your* light has dimmed, therefore you sow the poisonous seeds of death in the divine fields of Life, hoping in vain to reap the fruit of salvation from your unholy harvest. But how could the fruit of Life ripen in the dark caves of death, away from the redeeming rays of Light?"

"Sons of the Great Levant, has your memory betrayed its soul? Has your folly deceived your faith? Has your spirit forsaken its source? Have you forgotten *Surya*, Mother of All, O ungrateful sons, orphans of the spirit? Has your spirit gone blind, has your soul gone dark, so that they no longer see the sacred source whence they sprang? How *could* you forget that which made you great? For the soul of the past belongs in the heart of the present, and what once was augurs what shall be, as everything eternally recurs."

"But you are strangers to the *spirit* of this land — which is the spirit of the gods — and strangers you remain, for much of the desert runs in your veins, and deserts harbour no gods. Wherever you go, you carry the curse of the desert, turning all springs of Life into dry wells, and all fertile oases into desolate lands. Few of you are pure, and only the pure can transform and redeem, for they alone carry the soul of rebirth, they alone are the Lords of the Earth. Sons of the Levant, you follow a strange god, you follow a dark path that will lead you to your doom."

"You are strangers to *Surya*, as her true heirs, her only real sons, are nowhere to be found on the surface of this wretched planet, in this darkest of ages; for in the era of decline, the ones chosen for rebirth retreat from Life only to serve Her better; they retreat from mankind only to overcome it; they retreat from the world only to transcend it, and by transcending it, they transform it. Thus, dwelling in the bowels of the earth — for it is in the darkest depths that the radiant spirit of the heights is conceived –, they prepare the advent of the coming race, waiting for the new dawn to shine again on a world that has reinvented itself. Yet they toil away from the noise of the world, away from the fumes of mankind, unsullied by the stifling, reeking, impure air that men breathe and pollute; for today the purest air is *not* the open air; today the purest air is to be found only in the hidden temples of the Occult, in the holy sanctuaries of Eternal Truth, there where no man's foul breath has yet polluted the atmosphere, and where no man's profane foot has yet defiled the sacred."

"You debase God by worshipping His fleeting shadow, you debase the world by venerating its distorted reflection in a beyond that only 'comes' in a distant heaven; yet the Tree of Life cannot bear the fruit of tomorrow if it is not deeply rooted in the firm soil of the here and now, for the present bears the promise of the future. It is in the fields of the present that the seeds of the future take root and grow, to blossom when comes the time of the great harvest. But yours is the declining spirit of a dead past and the vain hope of a lost future."

"Sons of deceit, unholy servants of darkness, you claim to know all there is to know about God and Life, for all was written *for* you in that 'Great Book' that governs your lives and enslaves your will. Thus you reveal your arrogant ignorance that knows no shame, and only the wise know that it is through the portal of humility that wisdom is attained, and self-overcoming is achieved. But you petty mortals should know that no book is greater than life, and no god is higher than truth, for Truth expresses itself not in words and books and fables, but in Life itself, and Wisdom is none other than love of Truth and acceptance of Life. No book can contain the infinite ocean of truth, and Truth, when written, unfaithfully speaks of itself and turns against itself, for the spoken word is divine, and the letter dwarfs the spirit."

"Truth is out there in the fresh air of divine innocence; it breathes through that silent wind of a higher force which runs in the vast fields of Life and hallows all existence. Truth transpires in the wisdom that governs all, and in the divine harmony of Nature, which is none other than God's reflection on earth. But only an awakened spirit can truly feel and touch the heart of Truth, for Truth is a gift reserved for the gifted, the priceless wealth of those rich in spirit and pure of soul."

"Truth is out there in the pure sky of unbridled freedom and in the hidden justice that rules the world; it unveils itself in the beauty of this divine earth, and need not be buried in books — for only worms dwell in the dead letter of books, whereas Life is a soaring bird of Light — . Truth need not be taught and dictated or imposed, for Life is the greatest teacher, and Nature is the school of Life. And where there is Life, there Truth can be seen in both Her glory and Her simplicity."

"Truth need not be explained and dissected and analysed to death — for to analyse a thing too much is to kill its spirit -, Truth just *is*: it dwells in the divine hierarchy reflected on earth, and reveals its magnificence in the aristocratic law of Nature. But men cannot see it nor hear its enchanting melody, for their eyes only see the fleeting reality of the ephemeral, and their ears only hear the sound of greed and lust and lost opportunities knocking at the hollow doors of their wasted existence… Alas! Men's poor souls only know the despair of a finite life and the agony of separation."

"Truth is above all books and all solemn commandments, for it is an open book, the Book of Life that has no end and no beginning, as Life is eternal creation."

"You dark seekers of the Light, your only certainty is superstition, and your only reality is illusion, for you lack reason and cling to faith, not as love of truth, but as an escape *from* truth, as a last refuge against the emptiness and absurdity of existence; thus you reveal the emptiness and absurdity of *your* existence. You lack depth of spirit and, in a desperate bid to give meaning to your otherwise aimless life, you make up for this lack by clinging to base sensuality — and is not idol worship the worst sensuality? For idolatry glorifies the flesh and kills the spirit; and all that does not renew itself leads to torpor of the mind. And pleasure of the senses, that most treacherous delight, leads to death of the soul, for it is a curse disguised as a blessing, misery that borrows the garb of joy. It is the greatest illusion, the briefest joy which dies the moment it is born, a mere glimpse of the bliss of Eternity. Thus your existence remains chimera, and your ultimate hope, a mere promise scattered in the void of an inexistent beyond."

As Arya was speaking, all the villagers had gathered around her and were staring at her with shock and disbelief; for never before had anyone spoken to them and about them with such bold sincerity. Hitherto, only the elders of the village and the clergymen had the authority to deliver public speeches, and no one else — let alone a woman — ever dared infringe on that custom. For in the desert, women were not recognised as daughters and givers of Life. Hence the deafening silence of the crowds when Arya interrupted her sermon for a while, as her eyes seemed to look beyond, far into the distant stars where her spirit found its peace and fulfilment. But then she pursued her unrelenting speech, and spoke thus:

"I pity you, O sleepless dreamers of the desert who lack the light of reason to guide your lost souls on the way to self-overcoming; for evolution is the law of Life and the march of the Spirit towards Unity and Supremacy. And only those who overcome themselves truly live. Thus you have become slaves of the worst kind of tyranny — the tyranny of dogma — for its sweet poison, superstition, blights the mind and slays the soul of Truth. You remain trapped in that dark cage of idolatry which you call 'the world', zealously venerating an imaginary heaven, a lustful fantasy that is a mere self-delusion borne out of the perverted dreams of the lowest of men."

"You pious men of the South, your heaven reeks of lust and vileness; it is but a brothel for all of life's failures, who seek the baseness of pleasure as an escape from their inability to reach the heights of the Spirit. And even when you deny yourselves the joys of life in the name of virtue and chastity, yet like thieves you await the bounty of such fake abnegation in the unholy promise of hedonistic indulgence and wanton license of your lustful human, all-too-human heaven. Yes, you poorest seekers of Truth, your heaven is a human invention, and your god is a mere reflection of your frustrated hopes and forsaken dreams in the skies."

"If only you could despair… if only you *knew* the despair of living in the dark… for suffering and despair herald the dawn of a higher consciousness, and only the mindless live without a care. You serve your tyrant-god with the hopelessness and foolishness of those seeking liberation through bondage, sacrificing your freedom—that divine gift bestowed upon men—on the altar of a faith which enslaves you instead of setting you free. Hence in vain do you seek your lost freedom, and that is the nature of the slave: always to yearn for what is forbidden and denied, but never to dare and never to endeavour, for only the bold succeed, and only those who sacrifice achieve."

"Men of the East, you have faith and flaunt your 'faith' as the beacon that lights the dark world we live in today; yet your faith itself is but the veil that covers your cowardice and your fear of the unknown, and your god is the idol before which you lose yourselves when you despair of finding yourselves. Thus you shun the inner divine path upon which tread your inmost longing and your deepest aspirations."

"Your dream is but the dream of death and the graveyard of divinity… your god is a curse on Life, your life is a curse on God. You shall forever remain lost tribes as divided amongst yourselves over God and heaven and earth as you are fallen from the grace of the very god that you worship; for God is One, and in His soul beats the heart of Gaïa, the earth-goddess you so deny and debase."

"We Sons of *Surya* worship no ghosts; *we* look upon different horizons, we look inwards and venerate the god within, the inner god. *Our* god manifests Himself in man, for though man is but a distorted image of God, and though he is a failed god, he still remains a god in the making, a trial, a hope, and a promise. And for a thing to succeed, many trials are necessary, many attempts must be made, many failures must be overcome."

"*We* believe in the God-man, *not* the god in heaven, for the god who is in man, the god who *is* man, is higher than any unknown god. We are Free Spirits, and free spirits we remain; therefore, we kneel before no idol, and in our prayers our inner voice echoes the voice of God. Wretched humans of today, you shall never be free, for you are always escaping from yourselves—and freedom never was an escape, but an inner quest—, paying no heed to your own depths and your own possibilities — and how many possibilities lie in wait for man! — ; but you deluded minds will never attain wisdom, for the wise always admit their folly."

"Sons of the desert, your dark god casts a shadow of shame over the land of the rising Sun."

2

When Arya thus ended her sermon, there was a moment of heavy silence about her, as the people were still under the shock of that verbal tsunami that had just swept their slumbering minds and awakened their dormant souls; but suddenly, a voice cried out from the crowd: "blasphemy! Blasphemy! Death to the blasphemer!" Soon all the villagers followed suit, chanting this gravest of accusations in the land of faith, and some of them moved forward towards Arya, preparing to seize her. But the old man, anticipating what was about to happen, promptly stepped in to protect Arya, putting himself between her and the angry and menacing throng. With the boldness of those with an unshakable faith and an iron will, he shouted defiantly at the people:

"There are as many truths as there are people, but Truth itself belongs to God. This woman has spoken *her* truth. Let her be, for if her truth be higher than yours, then by condemning her, you would only be condemning yourselves. And if your truth be higher than hers, then you should pay no heed to her words, for they cannot reach you, as truth is untouchable, and only truth can slay deceit. But who amongst you dares claim what is right and what is wrong? Judge not what cannot be judged, for Truth alone can judge itself, and who are you to claim sole ownership of that which cannot be owned nor bestowed? For Truth is lived and felt; it lives in Wisdom and thrives in creation, and it drowns in the stagnant waters of uniformity and mediocrity."

As the old man realised that he had temporarily caught the mob's attention, diverting the villagers' anger away from Arya, he went on speaking, with a passion that had long remained unexpressed: "why do you become like wild beasts when anyone dares question your beliefs? Does your zeal betray a weak faith? Is your trust in your god so shaky that you need to defend him each time someone questions him? But true faith, as Truth, defends itself and speaks for itself. It needs no raised fists nor sharp swords, for only words can kill words, while the flesh only kills the flesh; and violence has always been a sign of weakness and defeat, as the spirit conquers the sword that slays it. Is not your staunch defence of your faith actually an onslaught on your own doubts? Is your faith, the temple of your spirit, so weak that it cannot withstand the winds of change that knock on the door of history? Is its roof so brittle that the slightest breeze can topple it? Are its foundations so frail that one cannot build higher levels on them, to get closer to the stars?"

"Leave this woman be. She speaks of other gods that you will never worship, and other truths that you will never embrace, for there is a god and a faith for each man and each race; thus speaks the voice of wisdom. The desert has claimed your souls, my poor friends, so seek not the cold, rejuvenating wind of the heights when all you know is the sultry heat of the lowlands. Worship your own god, and let the others worship theirs, as the wise live and let live, and only the narrow souls seek certainty for themselves and the world; for faith and change come from within and can never be imposed. Oppressors among rulers and peoples have never understood this simple fact: Truth can never be imposed nor bestowed, it imposes and bestows itself freely, as freedom guarantees authenticity, and only that which is real prevails in the end."

"If your god is truly the highest and the unique, as you claim, then nothing should shake your faith in him, and nothing should offend you; for those who live on the highest mountains, there in the realm of Light, look away from all shadows and all abysses. But I sense that your animosity betrays a weakness and a cowardice hidden deep beneath your pious souls and your bowed heads."

"You need a god before whom you can all be equal, yet know that we are only equal before death, and all that lives under the Sun is subject to the divine hierarchy of the pyramid of Life. You need a god before whom you can kneel and pray and hope, so that you rest in the comforting peace of the unfree, rather than face the war that your soul wages on itself in its endless quest for transcendence."

"You need a god before whom you can all be slaves — but *equal* slaves —, thus you sacrifice your freedom for the sake of that god of modernity: Equality. For you were born and chosen for slavery, and only by enslaving yourselves do you truly fulfil yourselves. You know not what it means to be free, as true freedom comes from within, and in your being dwells only bondage."

"You need a god before whom you can shun all accountability and escape from yourselves, forsaking what is rightfully yours — Life's gift of free will —, to serve a faceless idol who will never serve you. Thus you rest in blissful ignorance — for ignorance is always blissful, and only those who *know* carry the weight of the world on their shoulders —, praising the heavens for your joys and blaming hell for your woes."

"It is the sign of base and cowardly souls, and the beginning of the end, when a people cannot question their own beliefs and dare not stray away from the 'right path' set forth by the wrong prophets; it is a crime against human nature when a nation is forbidden to look into the mirror of its own soul, so it can praise Truth and Beauty, and condemn falsity and ugliness as *it* sees them, for each man sees the world through his own mirror. And when a people refuse to face their own fears and to overcome their own defects, they fall into apathy and degeneration, and they become the perpetual victims of slavery and ignorance; for freedom was meant for the free, and only the awakened ones are truly free."

"I pity you, my friends, for you will never rise above mediocrity, as poverty of mind and wretchedness of soul are beyond redemption…

therefore, go back to your praying and kneeling and grovelling before the Void that is *in* you, for tomorrow is yet another day in your grey sea of monotony that will wash away the memory of today." Thus spoke the old man, and there was now a deep silence among the crowd; but then the people, as though waking up from a deep slumber, again started moving hither and thither, and gradually dispersed, going back to their tasks.

3

After the villagers had resumed their normal activities and rituals — for nothing ever changes in the land of uniformity —, the wise man bid Arya to go back into his house, and they sat and talked all night long about the millenarian Wisdom that has survived all obscurantism throughout the ages, hidden beneath the cloak of secrecy, thus remaining pure and divine, unsullied by man's baseness and ignorance. "The Occult Truth," the wise man said, "is the only truth, for all that is hidden from men in this age of darkness is the fruit of yesteryear's wisdom and the seed of tomorrow's glory. Truth is the essence of God and the meaning of Life, and no force on earth can defeat divine will and destiny."

"Truth has been crushed to earth by the dark powers of deceit; but, as always, it shall rise again and shine evermore on the world, for it alone is supreme, and Supremacy is Life's only destiny, as it bears the soul of Eternity."

"Truth shall again bestow Her Sacred Light upon men, sanctifying their hearts and uplifting their spirit into new heights hitherto undreamt of. A new dawn cometh, a new hope is upon us, though our skies are now tainted by the dark clouds of doom and gloom. Have faith in Life, Arya, for there is wisdom even in its absurdity, and there is justice even in its misery, as Life has a hidden purpose and a deeper meaning, and only those who delve into Her Sacred Mysteries can touch Her divine essence. It is in the darkest hour that Light is conceived; it is from the heart of desperation that hope arises. In the end, Truth alone prevails, and the only real and lasting victory is Hers; all else is illusion."

"Yes, dear Arya, in the end, Truth always prevails. Yet, to survive untainted in the darkest of ages — and hence remain worthy of Her heirs —, Truth was kept in the deep wells of Wisdom by the bearers of the Sacred Light, so that She may one day shine again as the New Dawn of a New Age. Divine wisdom thus commands: Truth shall be known *by* the few, and reserved *for* the few, as man is not yet ripe for the fruit of the gods; he remains a lost hope and an unfulfilled dream."

"Therefore, dear child of Light, preach not the sacred to the profane, and speak not of the divine to humans, for men are still unworthy of God; that is why they remain imperfect men and failed gods. Others before you — prophets, saints, and Sons of God — have tried in vain to awaken men to a new reality and a higher consciousness; but their failure does not mean that *they* are failures, for God's messengers are rays of the divine Sun, and man remains Life's only failure."

"Preach not Truth to the many, the ignorant and weak of mind and spirit, as darkness is alien to light and can never understand it; day and night shall never meet, save in their brief encounter at dusk and dawn, when they greet each other only to part again evermore, eternal strangers to one another. And so men will always condemn Truth and shun it until they themselves turn into bright drops of Light in the boundless sea of Life. But *that* is the future of man. Today the mob rules and its values reign supreme; today the god of men has replaced the God of Life, as Nature has lost Her soul to the desert. Thus the genius — that god in the making — now yields under the heavy weight of dead numbers, and numbers never rise and never achieve. Alas! The slaves of the past have become the masters of the present, and the Higher Man, ever misunderstood, is condemned by men as a madman or a devil, a heretic among believers, and a hermit in a crowd."

"Today the Higher Man is rejected by a world that has unlearned belief in greatness and perfection, for men remain shadows in a world filled with light. To base souls, all that is lofty is unfathomable, and all that is unfathomable is either elevated to the rank of an unreachable god — if admired —, or debased to the level of absolute evil — if dreaded —; but Life is beyond opposites, as pure Light knows no contrasts."

"Therefore, God shall remain alien to man, so long as man remains alien to himself. How wretched are these mortals; they venerate all that is fake as holy, and extol all cowardice as virtue. Human perfection is forbidden among them, but permitted in heaven, away from Life, for men's imperfect souls bear not the existence of gods on earth — did they not crucify them? —; and so they give their distant god all the attributes that they lack, all their hopes and frustrations, and worship this idol instead of striving to become what they were born to be: gods themselves."

"They worship an idol that redeems all their imperfections and frustrations, these strange sons of the desert, but how *could* their idol redeem them when it is itself a product of their imperfections and frustrations? They need a god before whom all could be equal, to ensure that none would rise above mediocrity, for mediocrity is the rule today, and everything of a higher nature is feared and shunned… every exception is viewed with suspicion by the rule in this world gone awry."

"And if God did not exist, they would still invent *a* god and erect temples to venerate him, for by venerating an invisible tyrant, they guard themselves against the rule of gods on earth. And that is what the mob dreads the most: the God-man, the man who is a god, and the god who is a man; *he* is the mob's greatest enemy, for his sin is unforgivable among the wretched of the earth: he is perfect, he is divine, in a world of imperfection, in a world of men. Nowadays, perfection — that divine virtue — is forbidden in the human realm, as imperfection was forbidden in the realm of gods. Gods and men cannot share the power and the glory on earth; one either chooses to worship God and shun human perfection, or seeks divinity on earth and, as Prometheus, draws the wrath of the gods upon himself. Thus men prefer to kneel before an unknown and distant master rather than bow down before a human god, a real god in the here and now."

"Arya, beloved daughter of *Surya*, listen to the voice of Wisdom, and reserve Her sublime pearls to those who deserve and understand Her, those for whom She is meant and destined; and seek not to convert those who cannot be converted, nor to redeem those unworthy of redemption. Divine Wisdom has always been the blessing of the few and a blessing to the few, and thus it shall ever be. All great civilisations, all divine religions are the work of a few Initiates. Never have the masses achieved anything great nor come closer to God, for herds are born to serve, and never to create; to follow, and never to lead; and whoever heard of a lamb that roared like a lion? When has a dove ever soared like an eagle?"

"The masses could never know God, for, like dead matter, they live in the dark, whereas the Masters are the Light of the world, the soul of the earth. They are the last heartbeats of God in a lifeless, disenchanted world. And *that* is the vocation of the Higher Man: to redeem all that is dark, and sublimate all that is human. The masses remain in the dark, it is their element; thus they find their peace and fulfilment. Leave it be; you cannot change divine will, for it has its own reasons and its own goals, and we are only the instruments of the greater cosmic Will and Life's grand design."

"Go away, Arya, leave this land of darkness and seek your sacred light elsewhere, for it is vain to seek the Light in the bottomless pit of darkness. You cannot talk of the light to those who were born blind, for they could never see what *you* see, they could never understand that which cannot be taught, that which they have never known. Awakening belongs to those whose eyes are open; therefore, stay away from the blind, as they will only darken your soul and make your heart weary and dejected, for they are the hopeless and the unredeemable."

"Go, my child, and seek your path elsewhere, for — alas! — the sons of the East have forsaken the way to divinity. Go and seek *your* way, for each has his own way, and though there is one God and one Truth, many ways lead to them. Men have never understood that simple fact of life, and they keep on fighting each other for *The Way*, and thus the way has itself become the end, a dead end."

"Go and seek *your* way, for yours will never be theirs; the Golden Chain of divinity should never be broken, and so, divine daughter of Light, you should find your way and seek your god, for thus you would be joining anew man's lost bond with the gods. The flame of divinity should shine again on this dark world. That is your mission. That is your destiny. Seek the Light, Arya, where it is hidden, in the bosom of Life, not here in this desolate land. Follow the Light whence it came, look for it where it belongs, where it dwells. It is a strange thing indeed, that the Light does not dwell where 'God' is venerated; it is only to be found in the secret wells of the occult powers that pervade the world and rule its secret destiny. Search for the light inwards, for true divinity lies in the longing for perfection, in self-overcoming, in the creation of the God-man — the god on earth -, not in a transcendent world."

"What is divine is the will to divinity, not divinity itself. It is the journey, not the destination; the way, not the end, for there is no end to the eternal circle of existence, as perfection always surpasses itself. That has ever been the kernel of Wisdom; that is what these preachers of all-too-human religions will never understand, for they lead *away* from God, and not *to* Him. All that which leads you away from yourself leads you away from God, for God and Self are one, and Self is a ray of the divine Sun. Go, my child, and may the gods be with you on your journey to find yourself. For the Light you seek is the Self you long to unveil before your very eyes, as it stands naked before Truth itself."

Hence, following the wise man's advice, Arya decided to leave the land of darkness and, bidding farewell to the old man, she headed northwards on the way to find the Light. "The Levant is supposed to be the land of the rising Sun. But nowhere here have I found any trace of light. I have found only darkness, dark souls and dejected hearts. Very well! I, then, shall be this rising Sun, the Sun that rises in the East and sets in the West. That is my destiny: to be a sun unto myself and unto the world. To seek the Light and become the Light that redeems all darkness."

PART TWO

HEIMKEHR (4)

The woman from the North

As she walked away from the desert and headed northwards, in search of the Sacred Light that bore her, Arya came across a small, charming oasis, an island of abundant greenery in the middle of a boundless, colourless sea of sand. When she approached the oasis, hoping to quench her thirst, rest a while, and meditate under a palm tree, she was surprised to see an elderly woman sitting all by herself near a tent. A few sheep were grazing under the watchful eye of a German Shepherd.

Upon coming closer, Arya noticed that the woman had the ageless, piercing blue eyes and the radiant skin of the people from the North; she was intrigued by the presence of that solitary foreigner in such a remote place. The old woman greeted Arya, and, upon beholding her face, said: "what is a fair young woman like you doing here in the middle of nowhere? Why would someone like *you*, whose life has just begun to blossom, come to such a desolate land, where all life fades away and dies? Has Life ever sought death? My poor child, you are too young for the desert! Only hermits, saints, and madmen dwell in the desert… and I can see through your eyes that you do not belong here, that you belong nowhere."

"Your eyes speak of a sacred secret hidden deep inside your soul, a secret that can only be revealed to those it is destined for. But they tell *me* that: you do not belong to this world, for though your feet walk this earth, your soul soars in higher planes and your spirit serves the purpose of the universe. You seek a higher life and a new god. But what in heaven's name are you doing *here*? You are too young for the poverty of the desert; you have too many dreams unfulfilled, too many hopes unrealised... you have too many songs to sing, too many worlds to discover, too many gods to revere."

"You are too young for the desert. The desert belongs to those who have abandoned all hope and buried all dreams, those who have died before dying, those twice-dead, those who have witnessed the death of their spirit before the death of their body — and woe to him whose spirit departs while his heart still beats with life! — for the spirit, too, dies, and its death is of the worst kind, as the dying body nourishes the earth and is born again in new forms of life, while the waning spirit vanishes into the whirlwind of the void, never to come back. Young one, what do you seek in this desert where neither gods nor men dwell?"

"I could ask you the same question," answered Arya, — somewhat amused by the old woman's bold inquisitiveness —, "since it is obvious that you, too, do not belong here. But if you must know, I am lost; I did not choose the desert, the desert chose me... and I am running away from my destiny, I am trying to *change* my destiny, to challenge the fate chosen for me, by fleeing the desert and the people of the desert, seeking a more hospitable land where the Light has not yet been banished. But what are *you* doing here, in the midst of nothingness? Unlike me, *you* seem to have chosen this life... why is it so?"

The old woman gazed deep into Arya's eyes, as though she was trying to fathom the mystery that lay behind the portal of her soul, and she answered: "I came here all the way from the North, looking for warmth, away from the cold and grey sky of my homeland, which filled my heart with gloom and plagued my soul with despair... I came here looking for the Sun's redeeming rays, as I had grown weary of seeing grey everywhere and all the time; for when all you ever see is grey, your mind grows gloomy. And when all you ever *feel* is grey, your heart turns cold; but Life needs the warmth of Light to flourish and grow. Gloomy minds, cold hearts: *that* is what I was fleeing up there in the North, for I did not want to share the fate of my folk, and that is: to become a dark cloud which endlessly rains on itself with drops of sorrow and despair that slay the very soul of Life."

"There it is grey, but here there is only darkness! Can't you *see* that?" said Arya cynically, hoping to convince the old woman of her folly. "Yes," replied the old woman, "here I found only darkness and the sultry heat of a lifeless desert that blights the mind and crushes all will... here I found neither hope nor expectation, for there are no horizons to this endless sea of desperation, and death of body and soul awaits him who treads this land."

"But then, why did you come here," Arya promptly asked, as her curiosity gained momentum, "and why do you *stay* here?" The old woman stayed quiet for a while, as though she was recollecting some faded memories from the depths of her soul, then she said: "I came here looking for *magic*, for the magic of the East... *that* is what I came here for: to catch a last glimpse of the spectre of a departing god, to hear the last sigh of a dying god... for gods too, die, when they no longer serve beyond themselves and cease to create ever anew. And where I come from, up yonder in the land of disenchantment, magic lies buried beneath the ashes of the dead god. God died in the West, but his ghost still lives on in the East — for gods die hard where they were born — and his shadow still haunts men's imagination, giving hope to the hopeless and solace to the wretched of the earth."

"I came here to witness the twilight of the old god and the dawn of the new one, for dusk and dawn are forever intertwined, united by a common fate, joined in eternal becoming. The river of Becoming carries in its course the seeds of birth and death, as it flows into the boundless ocean of Being. Thus death is only a prelude to birth, even as birth itself leads to death. And this is the land where gods are born but also crucified, where prophets are most revered, but most misunderstood; this is the land where All begins and All ends, where the blood of Adonis flows into the veins of Christ, where the spirit of Mithras haunts the soul of Dionysus, where the flame of Agni kindles the heart of Orpheus... this is the land of the Alpha and the Omega, the land of Resurrection and Rebirth."

"But that magic I sought belongs to the distant past, at that sacred time when reality flirted with legend, before the dead letter of religions killed the immortal spirit of Truth, in the name of a god whose essence still eludes all and everyone... Ah! To behold again that vision of the everlasting glory of the godmen who walked the earth! What would I not give to experience once, just *once*, that divine feeling of human greatness which filled the hearts of all men, when philosophers were kings, and kings were philosophers, when religion brought men *closer* to God — not *away* from Him —, before the men of religion became men of power and thus slaughtered Religion, sacrificing Eternal Truth so that they could sit upon a shaky throne which itself sits upon lust, greed, and shame; a throne that all covet but none deserve... and none keep, save for a decade or a season."

Thus spoke the old woman, and her heart was swollen with a deep feeling of nostalgia, as memories from another age seemed to invade her frail but lucid mind, and, for a moment, she felt as though she was actually living these memories; for what are memories but the very soul of Life recollecting its own glory, the stream of Becoming that ever flows back into the endless river of Being? But Arya suddenly interrupted the old woman's reverie, saying with a pinch of impatience: "but what of *your* Great Levant today? Where is that Fertile Crescent, abode of the gods that Legend speaks of? Look around you! All there is to see is an arid land where no weed could grow, a graveyard of all human gods slain in the name of a tyrant-idol of clay and dust."

"Yes, young one, sadly you speak the truth… Alas! By coming here, I was merely pursuing an illusion, following the ghost of a glorious past, holding on to a divine dream that is forever lost in the memory of Eternity. But who *could* have known that the desert had grown *this* far? — no one realises that yet — and beware! It grows even farther with the decline of man… for all ascents are slow, but every fall is inexorable; the ascent is sublime, but the fall is terrible."

"Alas, the desert grows, my child, it invades our poor earth by the day, leaving behind nothing but death and misery. But there is nothing worse than the desert of the Spirit which wears the deceiving garb of civilisation, there in the grey land of mist where everything is half-and-half, wishy-washy, old and cold and faded; where no one clearly shouts 'Yes' or 'No', but all mutter 'maybe'… there where man aspires no more, where the reasonable has defeated the impossible, where cowards thrive and heroes perish, where the rich in possessions grow ever poorer in spirit… there where divine intoxication and love of the highest are forbidden dreams, crushed under the ruthless yoke of an illusion that calls itself reality."

"Nothing is more pathetic than the desert of the Spirit — which can be found nowhere save in man's mind, that gateway to all worlds —, where decay arrogantly calls itself 'progress', and the lowest instincts stifle the highest aspirations… there where no new dawn awaits man and no new horizons entice the bold traveller seeking new shores and higher seas. For, where Spirit lacks, where there is no aspiration, there is no elevation; thus apathy and decadence follow."

"Dear child, here there is only darkness, but black is better than grey, for death is better than agony. Thus I still prefer *this* desert of sand and dust to the wastelands of the spirit up yonder in the land of culture; for here you could still feel the last breath of God and caress his departing soul; but there God has long been buried under the rubble of man's forsaken dreams of greatness and his loftiest hopes of divinity, in the name of a cold reason that has never served beyond itself, and has thus betrayed its goal and killed man's soul. Forget not, my young friend, that Europa is the daughter of Phoenicia, and Arcadia is the lost child of Aghartha. But alas! When one speaks of the Levant today, one speaks in past tense…"

Clearly upset by what she had just heard, Arya interrupted the old woman's tirade, saying: "how *could* you compare the civilised world with *this* godforsaken land of doom and gloom? Stop ranting about the past, and speak to me of the present… Where *I* am going is surely a better place than *this* wretched desert you live in!"

The old woman, looking tenderly at Arya, as a mother looks at her crying child — with a mixture of affection and pity —, tapped her on the shoulder and said, smiling: "evidently, my poor, lost child, you have not yet *seen* this land of civilisation that you so earnestly seek… *there* you would discover what doom and gloom *truly* mean. For what was I fleeing, and what made me prefer this no-man's land to the company of men, save your 'civilised' world? Was I not running away from the empty noise of those dwarfs who deem themselves giants, those cavemen of the spirit who deem themselves 'developed' because they claim to have 'conquered' Nature, that is, they have slain Her in the name of a culture which is but ignorance disguised in fancy dress and pompous names?"

"Was I not running away from the men of culture who have strayed away from Nature's divine path and essence? But to stray away from Nature is to stray away from Life; thus culture, growing on the ashes of nature, awaits its own death, for the crime against Nature is a crime against Life, a crime punishable by the worst kind of death: the death of the Spirit. And though I found nothing here, still I am contented to live in solitude, to lead a simple life, living poorly but happily — for only poverty provides happiness, as wealth is the source of all woes —, and free from worry."

"For *I* see no civilisation where the Spirit is smothered by the dark smokes of lust, and the body stuffed with poisons that animals refuse to eat. I see no civilisation where the Higher Man, forerunner to the God-Man, lives under the yoke of a shapeless mob, in the name of a justice which only oppresses, and an equality which only breeds mediocrity. I see no civilisation where man has killed God in the name of freedom, only to replace the old tyrant-god with a new one, thrice worse, called money. I see no civilisation where men live in monsters of concrete, packed together like cattle, conditioned like slaves for both work and leisure, and boast of living the 'perfect life', in what only fools deem the ultimate stage in human evolution. For Nature alone is perfect and divine, and man fell from the grace of God when he broke his last bond with the Mother of All. *That* is man's original sin."

"Thus I chose this desert of sand to the desert of the spirit, for nothing is worse than the death of the spirit. I chose a poor and solitary life, away from the land of plenty, the land of the superfluous many, there where the life of abundance is emptier than all deserts… for there is nothing poorer than a wealth that does not flow from the heart and the spirit and thus bestows itself upon the world as a sacred hymn to Life and a silent blessing of Love. There is nothing emptier than a life of affluence, for true wealth comes from within and cannot be measured or counted. Wealth of possession is poverty of spirit; *that* is divine justice, for true superiority is innate, not accumulated."

"Woe to those who prefer to live rich in possessions but poor in spirit, for though they live abundantly, their hearts remain empty and their souls remain deserts… and the desert that is *in* man is worse than all deserts. You can *have* your 'land of culture', I have denied it forever. I have chosen to live a pure life in accordance with the divine law of Nature, untainted by the scars and fumes of what the soulless call the 'civilised world', and what *I* call the anti-natural world; and woe to those who transgress Nature's laws, for they are the enemies of Life."

When the old woman thus ended her passionate diatribe, Arya looked at her with bewilderment and said: "your bitterness betrays a disappointed love, your anger hides a frustrated hope. Your love has turned sour and your heart has turned bitter; thus you chastise what you love — and the greater the love, the deeper the disappointment. But rest assured, I am not heading towards the West, towards civilisation; I am heading *North*, I am going to the extreme North, back to my Spiritual Fatherland, the Hyperborea of my roots and my dreams, the land which bore my soul before Time itself began. I am heading towards the abode of Light, where the Sun never sets and where gods still walk among men."

"No, my friend, I am not heading West, but further North, towards the land where the divine odyssey on earth began, there where gods descended and taught men the god-like life; there where men worshipped the god within and thus became gods themselves; for involution begets evolution, and the God-man, the coming god, shall spring from man's inner longing for the divine, as all longing is a promise waiting to be fulfilled. I am heading there where all Higher Life on earth bloomed and flourished, where the Light shone on the whole world; the land where the Master Race was born, that golden race of Light, created by gods, bestowed upon men."

After hearing Arya's words, the old woman pushed a deep sigh of despondency, and, after a moment of silence, she said: "poor child, do you not realise that you are following the ghosts of a long-dead past? There is no light to pursue, there are no gods to revere, in this darkest of ages... for the *whole world* has become a desert, and darkness has descended upon our soulless, wretched planet. What are East and West, North and South? These words don't mean anything today, for geography is sacred no more, as it was in the days of yore. Today the earth has become one, not one in its glory, but one in its misery. Our poor earth is doomed... Gaïa writhes in the agony of the end."

"My poor child, the whole earth is now a desert... the end is near, and the shadow of death looms on our horizon. There is nowhere to go in that lost world of ours, for Life has issued Her deadly sentence on man. The light you seek is nowhere to be found save in your own soul, for everyone is a world unto his own, the whole universe is contained in every drop of your blood and every beat of your heart." Thus spoke the old woman, as tears filled her eyes and her heart was overwhelmed by the deep sorrow of those who have witnessed both the dawn and the twilight.

Arya was moved by the old woman's words, but they did not dampen her resolve, nor did they shake her trust in her destiny; therefore, she decided to continue her journey towards the North, in search of her lost soul. Thus she bade farewell to the old woman, saying: "you came here to lose yourself in a timeless world, to forget the petty worries of modernity, to live according to Nature; yet all you found is this desert. But I say to thee: even deserts harbour a promise of life; even darkness carries a future of light. So live your solitary life in peace, but *I* still have a world to discover, and I put my trust in Pan, god of Nature, to guide me on my way to my Higher Self, for He is the god of All."

The old woman embraced Arya tenderly and told her, just as she was preparing to leave: "mark my words, my child: you follow an illusion, you seek the void. All you will find is disappointment and despair." But Arya did not respond, as she was already hearing other voices; she was already in another world, her own world. She was already where she was heading.

On the suffering that bestows

On her journey back to her eternal home, there where the Spirit first took shape, where Light first gave life, as she was walking under the faded gleam of the stars, Arya was suddenly submerged by a deep apprehension, as the words of the old woman came back to haunt her, resonating in her head, shaking her faith. Consequently, in a moment of weakness which seizes even the strongest, she started to doubt the very freedom that she always upheld as God's gift to humans. Was she destined, she wondered, to wander the earth, searching in vain for her goal and purpose? Will she ever find the Light, or was she doomed to live in the dark? Was her fate sealed, or could she change it? "Is everything written," she asked her dejected soul, "or do we not ourselves write our personal legend on the pages of history? Are we born free, or do we blindly follow a path that was drawn by the powers that be? If man was born free, why is he everywhere in chains?"

As she was thus pondering the meaning of Life and the root of suffering, Arya continued her inner quest and faced her own doubts, again asking herself: "is man the master or the slave of his destiny? Does he deceive himself when he decides, or should he submit, as all is vain? Will man remain caught in the shackles of earthly limitations, until he realises that the freedom he so eagerly seeks lies in his inner indestructible Self, waiting for the salvation of the Spirit, that light which abolishes all shadows? Is not freedom an inner state of mind to be lived, not an outer quest to be pursued? But man's mind has ever been trained to think away from his spirit; that is why he remains human, and does not rise to meet his own heights."

"If man was born a slave who only dreams of a freedom that he will never truly and fully attain, then why does he cherish something he is not, and will never be? Is not longing a kind of remembrance, and a promise of revival? Is not Freedom the forbidden fruit of our lost paradise? The panacea denied us for a lost Unity? But what kind of a god creates slaves, promising them freedom as a goal never to be attained, a reward never to be earned? Is not God supposed to be merciful and just? How could Creation mix mercy with cruelty? Is Life naught but a play of the gods, and are men their playthings? But we were born to believe that *we* are the masters of our destiny, the shapers of our own world, the creators of our past, present, and future! What gave us this certainty, if not God Himself? We were born to believe that free will is the essence of justice, and justice is the meaning of the world, the law of divinity... thus we create our own justice, evermore and eternally on our journey towards Immortality."

"Is not man *both* free and determined? Free to make choices, and bound by these same choices? For Justice speaks thus: all that befalls man is the fruit of his own free will across the ages. Could Life, and even God, be our own creation? For the whole universe is reflected in our minds, and reality is only real, if *we* will it; the *world* is only real, if *we* will it. All that exists, exists in our mind; therefore, all that *is,* is the product of our consciousness, which is a speck of the absolute and infinite Mind of God. Thus *we* are our own creation, we are the source of All... God and man are One, there is no Creator, as Life is indivisible, and one cannot create that which is beyond creation."

"And so, whatever befalls man, man has already — silently or consciously — willed it. Fate is man's own creation; man is his own creation. Hence this suffering I incur has a meaning and serves a purpose... but what *are* they? How do I discover *my* meaning and *my* purpose? Am I treading the right path? Should I have stayed in the East? Does destiny await me there? Or do I belong up there, where I am heading? Oh! Cruelty of freedom! Freedom is a terrible thing, indeed, a very dangerous thing; for it removes all accountability, and weighs heavily on man's conscience, as *he* has willed whatever he has caused or incurred."

"Where will I find the Light? Where will I find *my* people? Who will guide me to it, and to them? My suffering will only end when I find my purpose, which serves the purpose of the universe, for the Whole needs its parts to fulfil its divine destiny. Does not all suffering hide an inner longing for unity with one's self and purpose? Is not all sorrow a lost Unity and a shattered Harmony? A broken link with the meaning of the universe?"

"Do I not suffer because I can neither find *my* peace nor *my* home in this flat world we live in? For sheer bliss, the bliss of Eternity, needs depth, the depth which bears new dimensions and higher worlds, so that it may behold itself in the mirror of divinity; *that* mirror never lies, as it speaks of itself. I am ever haunted by that strange feeling of belonging neither to time nor to space — for time and space only hide a deeper reality, a deeper truth that pure spirit alone can fathom —; my deeper Self belongs only to Eternity, and finds no abode in the transient world of forms, that heaven to the senses, that hell to the spirit."

"O that I may pass beyond human suffering, which is the worst kind of suffering, for it is suffering from lack. It is the suffering of the Spirit, the conscious suffering of the conscious man. Many times my soul has cried out to Life: 'all is vain... all is in vain... life is but the void perpetuating itself. God himself is but the void lost in itself. To live, to suffer, to die... *that* is what Life is all about, that is man's plight on earth. For man is an accident, and Life itself is a coincidence, a haphazard product of Chance, that favourite child of Chaos. All else is illusion and delusion'. But was that only illusion speaking through me? Was that only my ego revolting against its own bounds, against its own limited and finite nature? For fear and frustration thrive in the realm of the limited and the finite."

"But then my Self tells my ego: 'you condemn life, yet you condemn it as *you* perceive it, for you behold it through your own distorted mirror. Judge not Life, for Life is a blank page upon which you write your own story; and you are both the story and the storyteller. You are both human and divine, a destroyer and a creator; you are both wretched and sublime. Life is innocence; it cannot be judged nor can it be condemned, as it is but your will expressed or repressed, and your dreams fulfilled or undone. Did the old god, that ruthless judge, not die, so that no one would henceforth be made accountable? Was that not the great liberation? You should accept and trust your suffering, for it hides a deeper meaning and a higher purpose. Suffering impregnates man with the creative thrust. Everything great in this world is the product of great suffering. Thus all joy hides a secret pain, every beauty bears an inner scar, and the pleasure of today is but the tears of yesterday and the regrets of tomorrow'. Thus my Self teaches my ego to accept its limitations and to bless Life as a totality, for Life is One."

As Arya's inner struggle was unfolding on the battlefield of her soul, she kept on questioning her Self: "yet my suffering is not a mere human suffering. I suffer as an immortal spirit caught in a mortal body. I yearn to cross to the other shore, to that higher sphere where the Boundless basks in the beauty of eternal bliss; but there is something still pulling me downwards and backwards, and so I still endure life on *this* shore, down under where all dreams are permitted, but none are fulfilled. I have yet to cross the bridge, but how can I, when *I* still am a bridge? Will I become a goddess? Or will I remain human? But I am both, and neither! How do I choose what I already am, but have not yet become?"

"There is a raging war inside my world, I am torn between two loves: love of God and love of Man; the highest love and the deepest love... for the spirit is lofty, but the soul is deep. The mind aspires, but the heart desires; the mind resolves, but the heart falters... and happiness is only there, when these two meet. But alas! Happiness, true, long-lasting happiness, is forbidden here on earth; thus one cannot love both God and Man, one has to choose, for the heights and the depths never could meet. But to choose is to lose; to choose is to sacrifice, and all sacrifice is painful but divine."

"I long for greatness, for something more than this world has to offer... yet greatness is the fruit of great sacrifice; therefore, we surrender our right to *live* and to love, in order to serve divine creation. Did man not fall when he chose woman over God? Did Christ not rise when he chose Spirit over flesh, and thus defeated death? One cannot love both God and man. One must choose: he who loves God forsakes all that he *has,* and knows the sheer bliss of Wholeness, and he who chooses man loses all that he *is,* and suffers the pain of separation and finiteness."

"But that is the law of Life: every great victory involves several defeats, and one must climb on steps to reach the heights — will we be the steps or the heights? —. One must fall before one can ascend; one must suffer before one can transcend. Thus human love is forbidden to me — for I want to reach for the stars — but divine love is still beyond me, and so I suffer from both God and man, from both the Unattainable and the Unfinished… I suffer from the ultimate solitude, the solitude of him who has reached the Gate but has yet to tread the Temple of Eternity."

"The divine is struggling with the human in me. Thus I am torn between my being and my becoming, my beginning and my end. I yearn to dwell amid the stars and among the gods, but still I melt into the volcano of human passion which engulfs my soul with sweet but empty promises of bliss — for all that passion bestows are brief glimpses of eternal bliss. Love follows me like a shadow, and I run away from it — but can one run away from one's shadow? —; thus it always catches me, for love has long legs, and mine falter in its presence."

"I run *away* from love and I run *after* the Highest, but love ever catches me… my humanity ever catches me, and throws me back into the whirlwind of evanescent passion, tears, and regret. Yet can one resist the irresistible? And nothing is more irresistible than human love; but human love is like a sweet poison, its brief pleasure gives way to untold misery… Oh that I may rip my heart out to suffer no more! Oh that I may touch the soul of the divine, so that I can shed this human sheath which stifles my soul! I suffer the excruciating pain of an unfulfilled love, above and below. I run after an ever fleeting shadow of pure Light. But the more I resist, the more I yearn, and the more I yearn, the more I fall."

"Perfection is Unity, the idea manifests itself in the form, and the form lives through the idea… but the manifested is transient and evanescent; thus perfection carries the seeds of its own demise. Does not the form kill something in the spirit? Does it not take away from the spirit its boundlessness and eternity? Does not the spirit die when it takes shape and thus fulfils itself? Does not the goal kill itself when it achieves itself? Does not creation involve a certain death? For, as the form is born, something dies in the spirit. And so birth and death are joined together in the sacred dance of the Cosmos."

"Does not all achievement slay the very longing that strove for it? Is not all crowning also a crucifixion? For the wheel of existence turns all ends into beginnings, and all victories into defeats, and all contentment into thirst. We gods on earth pay the price of our divinity with the blood of our mortality. We achieve perfection and elevation at the expense of our immortality; hence we lift the world to the heights, while *we* decline and fall. The mirror of dawn reflects the shadow of dusk, and the sunrise owes its splendour to the sacrifice of the night. Every ascent was a fall, every fall will itself ascend. But then again, every fall was an ascent, and every ascent will itself fall… Is all vain because of the Circle? Or is the circle itself the purpose? Alas! Life begs too many questions and offers too few answers!"

"The divine shapes the human into fulfilling its hidden purpose and creating beyond itself, uplifting itself into the peaks of divine spheres. For all streams of Life which do not flow back into the ocean of Creation, lose themselves in the murky waters of decay. Gods need Nature and Life to experience their own immortality and their own infinity, for Spirit on its own cannot grow and create beyond itself and thus fulfil itself. The form needs the idea to be, and the idea needs the form to become. Thus the universe is the temple and sanctuary where the divine bestows its blessings upon itself. But creation entails suffering; that is the iron law of Nature."

"Such is the pain incurred by gods, a pain that is unknown to men — for men only suffer from lack of spirit, not from an overflowing spirit, that eternal fountain of Light which finds no river to pour its holy drops of Love and Life, and thus squanders its sacred rays into an arid soil where no seed can turn into a higher breed, and no higher life can grow. Such is *my* suffering, which flows not from lack of meaning, but from too much meaning, from divine meaning which wants to bestow its sacred fruit to redeem and lift a lost humanity beyond itself and into its divine destiny."

Thus spoke Arya's soul to itself, wondering about Life's true meaning and her own purpose in its Grand Design. Was she doomed to forever seek, and never find? To always long for, but never *be*? To always strive, but never to achieve? There was an inner strength that always pushed her to seek further, to look higher, to delve deeper, although she was yet unable to pierce the veil that blighted her eyes and numbed her inner senses; she had yet to discover what her soul already knew. She had yet to find what she already had. She had yet to become what she already was.

Despondent but resolute, Arya clung to her only hope: ever to seek, ever to strive, ever to hope. She had to tear the human veil that covered her divine essence, she had to shed her mortal shell to unveil the goddess within. For death of the transient is birth of the eternal, and only the twice-born are truly alive. Every death is a promise of life and renewal, and night bears the promise of a new dawn. The first birth is a trial, the second is divine.

The prophet

After a few days spent walking in the desert, in the same overwhelming darkness which greeted her upon her awakening, Arya finally came across a fertile land where the heat was less harsh and vegetation was abundant and enchanting. She realised that she had crossed the desert and was now in a land of mild climate and abundant life, getting ever closer to her beloved home. She ventured into a thick forest on a hill overlooking this charming landscape. As always, she was alone, yet she did not seem to mind, since she had accepted that it was her fate to be alone with the silent voices of the gods and the divine murmurs of Eternity.

She needed this solitude, she needed to be alone with herself, in order to explore the depths of her tormented soul. Perhaps she could thus find the answers to her many questions regarding her goal and purpose on this earth. For it is in the sacred silence of solitude that the divine reveals itself to the exalted soul. Silence is the language of the gods, and music is their prayer. Thus silence speaks its secret language to those who embrace their solitude as a secret hymn and a sacred song.

"Creators are often solitary," Arya said to herself, "and solitaries are often creators, for it is in the hallowed depths of solitude that the seeds of Creation are conceived, to blossom in all their splendour at the Great Noontide of Life." Thus she lamented her torment to the spirit of Hermes, messenger of the gods sent on earth to sow the seeds of the new breed, the Race of Light that shall inherit the earth when the Cycle renews itself. But by speaking to Hermes, Arya was also speaking to her Higher Self, to the goddess within, the goddess who knew not how to live among humans.

As she sat down under an old tree, contemplating the full moon and the starry heavens above, Arya fell into a meditative state of mind, plunging into the depths of her soul's timeless odyssey, reminiscing her cosmic origins and essence. She remained in a deep trance, communing with the Spirit of the Ages, feeling the gentle breeze that carried Life's hopes and longings for a better tomorrow. Suddenly, there appeared before her, as out of nowhere, as an angel, a man whose noble features revealed a higher soul, and whose divine eyes from another world reflected the mysteries of Being. He was observing her silently, from a distance, without uttering a word.

As she moved closer to him, she was struck by his uncanny resemblance to her. It was truly amazing how much they looked alike; their eyes, of the same essence, gateways to the secrets of the universe, spoke to each other, recognised and understood each other well before their minds could grasp the secret link and the sacred bond that united them. They were soul-mates, eternal companions on the endless journey of the Spirit towards Immortality.

Upon beholding the stranger's eyes, Arya felt that she was looking into the mirror of her own soul, reflected in the body of a man. It was as though their bodies were born from the same soul, carved out of the same original substance which created the universe. Her own inner world was unfolding before her very eyes when she looked deep into his. It was as though two worlds were meeting and merging into one reality, into the same divine essence. She had a strange feeling of *déjà vu* that she could neither explain nor comprehend. All she knew was that this stranger she had just met was no stranger. While their lips remained sealed, their eyes had already told each other their own story; for the soul speaks its own language and tells its own epic.

Arya felt a warm, secure feeling and a deep affection for this stranger who seemed like the closest being she had ever known; could it be that *he* was her long-lost soul-mate she had been searching for all her life? It was as though she had always known this man whose young face bore the wisdom of the ages, and whose countenance had both the innocence of a child and the roughness of a man. Thus she listened to her deeper, inner voice whispering to her: "this man is your soul-mate. You two were destined to be together, across time, beyond death, for all eternity."

After her initial surprise and bewilderment, Arya asked the familiar stranger: "who are you, and what are you doing on your own, here in the middle of nowhere? *I* am alone, but still I yearn for company, for *real* company… I am lost, but still I seek… I seek *my* race and *my* nation, my people and my home. Are *you* lost, too, or do you know your way and your purpose? For blessed is he who knows his way and his purpose in this age of chaos and emptiness."

The man looked at Arya with tender care, and he replied: "you ask me who I am and what I am doing on your path. I am your soul-mate, Arya, and I have come for you; Fate demands that our paths meet evermore on the endless Path of Time, for we share a common destiny and we serve a divine goal; and those who serve a divine goal share a common destiny."

"We Sons of *Surya* serve and embody the divine purpose on earth, we write the story of God on the pages of Eternity. And though we may be apart, solitaries longing for a Reunion that never comes, a Brotherhood that is felt but not seen, still our souls embrace each other and dance with each other and in their own sublime realms build the Temple of Absolute Truth, refuge to all those voluntary solitaries who have retreated from the world in order to redeem it — for only by transcending does one redeem —; and only when the Temple is built will its Sons come. Only then will the Warriors of Light — those brightest souls who patiently wait in the dark for their hour to come so that they can shine again and purify the earth from its bad seeds —, only then will they come and accomplish their destiny, which is the destiny of the Universe."

"But warriors need a leader, and Warriors of Light need a prophet. Therefore, *I* shall be your guide, Arya, for even *you*, dear Child and Warrior of Light, even *you* need guidance — and when I talk *to* you and *about* you, I am also talking *through* you, addressing *your* people, those who bear your name, for today they too are lost and confused… today your sons are neither warriors nor noble, they no longer lead and inspire, but follow and fall. For when Masters no longer lead, they fall… and when Masters fall, they fall deep, as they are the bold conquerors who know only the shining heights of Supremacy, and who thus falter and stumble when facing the dark abyss of defeat."

"You need guidance, Arya, you need someone to show you the Way, for you know not how to live today; but you need to be humble to accept that, and it is hard to be humble when one sits upon the mountaintops of the Spirit, as higher souls tend to think themselves worlds unto their own, and tend to dream themselves beyond and above this world of shadows and deceptions."

"I have come for you, Arya, to show you the way, the way to your inner legend. For though you think you know yourself, still you have not discovered the goddess in you; and I know you better than you know yourself — as the mirror faithfully reflects what it sees and sheds all illusions —, and I am the mirror through which you shall discover yourself." Thus spoke the stranger to Arya, as she carefully listened to each of his words, hoping to hear what her ears long yearned to hear, and to feel what her heart long yearned to feel. Seeing that he had caught all her attention, the man kept on talking to her:

"I know the real you, Arya, I know the eternal, indestructible Self which dwells in your innermost being, and which is beyond all suffering and transcends life's joys and miseries. I see the light in you, I see your great destiny unfolding before my eyes, and your destiny *is* great, Arya, but you do not know it yet — for you look not at the Whole, you only see the signs, but not the destination —; you seek and you yearn, but do you not know that your search and your longing ultimately flow into the ocean of your own Being? That your purpose finds its end in your inner Self?"

"All search is ultimately an inner quest, for the world is Spirit ever unfolding in manifold forms. You need not seek your god, for He dwells in you; you need only find yourself, and you will find God. Yet how can you find your god, when you seek Him among men? For where men live, gods die. How can you find the Light, when you seek it in the dark? You have yet to know yourself, Arya, only then will you become a goddess and serve your own god; for self-knowledge is the gate through which you enter the temple of divinity."

"But how can I find myself," answered Arya, "when I am lost? How can I find my path, when I know not where to look for it? For my world is still unknown to me, and I have yet to kindle the light of my inner flame."

The man looked at her with affection mixed with sternness, then he said: "you are not lost, Arya, for your soul belongs to the Eternal Spirit whence it came. How *could* you be lost, when the universe is your home? How could you be lost, when God is your guide? Time and space never could determine an immortal soul's identity and mission, for they are only vehicles for your eternal cause, the cause of divinity, the perpetual search for the Sacred Light of elevation and overcoming."

"How could *you* be lost, Arya, when you were born to lead? How could you waver, when you were born to affirm? How could you despair, when you were born to inspire?"

"How could you be lost, Arya, when *you* are the way? For we are our own path and our own destination… and your way ultimately leads to your Higher Self."

"How could you lose the way, when you were born to guide men *to* the way, the way that mankind has lost by seeking the crooked paths of greed, selfishness, and superstition?"

"You *know* the way, Arya, yet you turn your back on the future by clinging to a long-dead past; and has one ever moved forward, has one ever become who he is, by looking backwards, where only ghosts and shadows and dust dwell and dance with that killer of all dreams and all hope, death? You know the way, Arya, yet you are still trapped in the chains of human attachment — for attachment is human, and detachment is divine —, you are still trapped in the heavy chains of human identities that pull your spirit downwards into the dark void of ignorance and decay. For the more you transcend, the more you ascend, and the more you cling, the more you fall. Arya, there is still something human in you which you should sublimate, there is still too much woman in you which kills the goddess. Forsake your humanity and embrace your divinity, only thus will you fulfil your destiny."

Thus spoke the mysterious stranger to Arya, who remained silent for a moment, bewitched by such divine pearls of wisdom that came from higher spheres, pondering the meaning and the depth of her guide's counsel. But then, as though waking up from her brief meditation, she told him: "but how can I become who I am, a goddess, when I still cling to my last human chain, Love… love of Man, love of Race and Fatherland? And where there is attachment, there can be no transcendence and no elevation. And so I remain trapped in the throes of Nostalgia — that child of Illusion —, yearning for the ghost of a dead past, longing for the empty promise of a future that remains an elusive dream, and searching for a home that exists nowhere save in my inner world."

"And though I suffer, still I cling, and though I fall, still I yearn…" Arya suddenly fell silent, as a feeling of despondency gripped her soul, for she had touched the heart of her human drama. The stranger approached her, looked into her eyes, and said in a firm but gentle manner: "if you want to attain the divine, Arya, you must relinquish the human; that is the simple truth, but also the hardest to accept and to fulfil. And that in itself is divine justice, for to gain immortality, one has to sacrifice one's humanity; that is the price of divinity. Thus you should shed your mortal shell — your human desires, the highest and the lowest of them — to reach the gates of your own divinity."

"But is not Love *the* divine gift bestowed upon men?" asked Arya, "and is not the religion of Blood and Honour the highest kind of love? And so I still yearn for the land of the Goths, the land of the gods… for Goth and *Gott* (5) are one, that is what Legend tells us, and legends are the only reality, the golden core of Truth cloaked in metaphor and allegory. Thus my longing itself is divine, as it is that golden ray which leads me to my Abode of Light, there where my soul belongs, where my legend finds its beginning and its end, where my destiny unfolds and blossoms ever anew."

"I have many questions but one certainty, and that is: I must go back to my Home, I must find and redeem my lost people, for they alone are worthy of redemption; only then will I fulfil my destiny and seal my fate, for up yonder is the only refuge left on this human earth for gods and gods in the making, the last hope for the divine mission in this wretched age and this doomed world. I tell thee, dear friend, the salvation of the divine race — the only race worth saving — will come from the North, that eternal source of Light, birthplace of the Golden Race."

The Sons of Light

When Arya ceased talking, the stranger paused for a moment, and he had a peaceful expression on his face, as though he was relishing the reminiscence of the dawn of Time, that Golden Age of the Gods; but then his face grew sterner, as the power of the Eternal Present gripped his attention. "My dear Arya," he said, "know that Love is also a human desire, and, though it is noble and sublime, still it is human. Even the highest love is still human, for it comes from lack; it is a yearning, a yearning for a lost Unity. Love is a fallen idea of Perfection, a lost ideal of divinity. Thus you should overcome even your highest love if you wish to tread the path of Immortality."

"No one bathes in the same river twice, Arya. No nation is great twice; that is the cosmic economy, which runs in cycles... but the Circle grows in spirals, and so the past never repeats itself faithfully; thus our origin can never be our end, otherwise everything would be vain, since eternal creation is the law of Life, and renewal is its soul and its meaning."

"Today neither gods nor men dwell in your beloved North, but semblance of men and spectres of gods... have you *seen* your Fatherland lately? You would not recognise it; it is but the shadow of itself, a land of mist and gloom whose long departed soul nonetheless continues to live on in the blood of your sons, those noble Warriors of Light who, as true warriors, refuse defeat and fight until death takes their last breath away. For, to the noble, there is no defeat, there is only Supremacy or death."

"But today these warriors are nowhere to be found on the surface of this earth, for though they live among men, they live *above* them, having greater dreams and serving higher goals. And though they tread the earth, they serve the purpose of the universe; and, serving the divine, one becomes divine."

"Alas! Today the Sons of Light live in the shadow of Life, bright and lonely stars shining in the darkest of worlds, a world that has banished the Light from its heart and soul, a world that no longer dreams and no longer aspires and no longer inspires."

"Today the Sons of the Sun live in the darkness of death, defeat, and oblivion; but *they* alone are the Sun of the earth, they are the blessed rays of a New Sun that has yet to shine. They are the Black Sun which in its darkest bosom bears the brightest of stars and the highest of hopes for man's divine destiny — for man's destiny is divine, though today he is a fallen, wasted fruit —; still, new harvests will come, new dawns and new beginnings."

"Despair not, Arya, your Sons will come, your Sun will come, that Supreme Light of Truth which will purify and renew humanity. For that is what the Sun does: it purifies and renews, it gives and takes life, hallowing the living and redeeming the dead."

"Have faith, Arya, for though your sons live in the dark today, their wounded pride and their aching hearts find their solace in the sacred, invisible presence of the gods, and, carrying the sacred flame that shall rekindle the Light of a world fallen in darkness and decadence, they await their last battle, they await the Sign... with the faith that resurrects the dead, and the hope that defies the greatest tragedies, they await the first ray of the New Dawn, the first sign of the Coming God. They await *their god* and *their* prophet, for they have long been held under the yoke of strange gods and strange religions, and so they want to be themselves again, they want to be Masters again, they want to be divine again."

"*Those* are your real sons, Arya, *not* those who share your home and your bread, for the home is easily changed and exchanged, and ultimately one leaves one's home to seek and discover new worlds; and rarely does one see the light and depart this life under the same roof."

"*Not* those who speak your language, for language is easily learned and forgotten, while the blood never betrays, and the spirit never varies."

"*Not* those who read from the same book, for the eternal spirit needs not the faded letter to learn what it already knows and to become what it already is."

"*Not* those who share your past and its glories, for the past is dead and Glory needs evermore new warriors and new conquests and new victories to quench its longing for itself."

"*Not* those who pray with you and perform rites and burn candles to venerate a lifeless idol that they serve blindly, simply because that is what faith dictates and what tradition demands — for true faith need not dictate, and noble tradition need not demand, as the heart ultimately only truly serves its own faith and only follows its own commandments — . God needs neither burning altars nor muttered prayers, God needs neither empty rites nor solemn vows to weigh one's faith on a scale as a fisherman weighs his bounty — for God is no fisherman! Or at least, *our* God is no fisherman… He is the All That judges not and weighs not but hallows Life as a Whole and its innocence as the most sacred thing under the Sun."

"But *who* are my sons," said Arya to the stranger, "and *where* can I find them? *Where* are they?"

"Your sons, Arya, are those who share your blood and your spirit, *not* your bread and wine — for the blood *is* the spirit, and the spirit is divine —, those whose spirit runs in their veins and shapes their body, and whose blood transpires in their soul and dictates their will."

"Those who only find their home in their hearts — for the heart alone is true, and the mind secretly follows the dictates of the heart —, those who belong nowhere save in the values that they cherish and uphold, as ideas and ideals are a world unto their own."

"Those whose language is the ineffable and eternal voice of the gods that resonates in their souls, those whose culture is ingrained in their spirit, not on bookshelves where only dust and worms dwell."

"Those whose god dwells within, who need not kneel before a deity of sand or stone, or shudder upon hearing the name of an Almighty which terrorises and subdues, instead of inspiring and uplifting, but worship the Inner God and thus seek Him out in their own great deeds and lofty thoughts, and so truly serve the purpose of the universe, which is to perpetually overcome and to perpetually elevate."

"Those who choose their own god, and do not simply worship strange gods and strange prophets, for true religion is *chosen*, not inherited, and real gods are created, not imposed."

"Seek your sons in the spirit of your own blood, Arya, for that is where they dwell. Blood and Spirit are one's only true essence, for they never betray and never vary. And though Blood is vital, Spirit is thicker than Blood. Therefore, search for the noble spirit, and *there* you will find noble blood."

"But what of my home?" Arya, interrupting the man, asked, "where do I find my home? For I am seeking it as a child seeks his lost mother, I am seeking my last refuge, the safe harbour where my weary soul can set its sails, after its aimless journey on the sea of despair."

"You say you are seeking your home," the man answered. "Seek not your home, Arya, seek your sons, for *they* are your home."

"You say you are looking for your sons… but how can you find them if you do not *recognise* them first? You may have passed them by and looked away! For to recognise is not only to see, but to find… not only to behold the surface, but to find the depth, for the depth is the essence, and the ocean's soul lies at its profoundest."

"Arya, your heart is true but your mind is deluded; your blood is pure but your spirit, though sublime, is tainted… it is tainted by wrong beliefs cloaked in noble intentions, beliefs which blight its sight — and one only *truly* sees with one's spirit —; thus you create false hopes to quench your soul's deep longing for a long-lost dream of a forgotten past which you try to revive by projecting into the future… but the future has its own dreams, and a promise never was a regret."

"The future holds its own promises and fulfils its own purpose, and so it can never be a slave to the past, however great the past may be, for *Was* and *Will* never shall meet on the path of Time, which always leads *ahead*. Hence, only those who look ahead are the pioneers of Life, the Creators and the Light of the world; they are the shining rays that herald the Sun, they take from the fallen fruit of Yesterday the seeds that shall bestow the harvest of Tomorrow."

"You are deluded, Arya, though your aim is lofty. You invent false hopes to survive in a world which does not understand you and which you do not accept — for you need to *belong*, and to belong is to be understood —; and when these deceptive hopes betray you and fade back into the illusion whence they came, failing to deliver the fruit that you hoped to reap, you shall be left with a broken will and a dejected soul darkened by the agony of despair. And woe to him who harbours broken hopes and shattered dreams!"

"I know you, Arya, I know who you are, but do *you* know who you are? Knowledge of Self is knowledge of the world, for the universe is reflected in your dreams, and God speaks silently to your soul… and so your outer quest remains illusive and fraught with deception, tears, and regret, if it does not serve your inner quest, which ultimately leads to the god you so earnestly seek, for He dwells in you."

"As for your sons, you need not worry about them, for they shall find you so long as you seek them sincerely — for intention is everything, it alone determines the final outcome, and the seeds, once planted, shall grow, even in the harshest weather and the driest land. Worry not about the harvest, Arya; plant the seeds, and the fruit shall come... Build the divine temple, and your sons will come, for they are the sons of the gods, and in the end, one always finds one's way."

"But you should look forward, not backward, if you want to find *your* way. Thus you should redeem the past to conquer the future. And redeeming the past entails shedding all illusions, and having the courage to behold the mirror of Time and to say: 'it was so, now *I* will it so.' True freedom rests in Will, and your will should dictate your way."

"Stop clinging to the past, Arya, for the past should inspire, not enslave, and the present alone aspires and achieves and creates the future; thus the past should only inspire the future, and not hold it in bondage."

"Relinquish your illusions, Arya, lest you lose yourself and your way. You have grown attached to hollow beliefs, falling prey to distorted values, for you still cling to that which does not endure, while you disregard that which you should seek. It is time for you to open your eyes to the truth that shall free you from your worst enemy: your ego, that delusion which calls itself reality, that sweetest of poisons which clings to forms and appearances and everything shallow, that which flees all depth, while your Self cries out to you to look deeper, feel lighter, and think higher."

"You have been taught to think: my fatherland is my race. Fatherland, Race and God are one. Well *I* tell thee: Race is *above* Fatherland, *Race* and God are one, as Man and God are one; yet Race has yet to be defined, even as God and Man have yet to be defined... your *race* is your fatherland, your race is your god. But what *is* your race? *Who* are your legitimate sons?"

"Your race is divine, Arya, it is noble spirit cloaked in superior garb, but it is Spirit first and foremost, for, as I already said, Spirit is thicker than Blood... and do you not shudder with disgust and disbelief, each time a divine beauty mates with a human beast? Does not your whole belief crumble at such a revolting sight? Does it not make you want to become blind and curse all the gods and tear this awry world asunder?"

"But *that* is not what Race is about, though some have been taught to believe so… *that* is only the surface of a lake whose waters run deep; for how many beautiful flowers contain the deadliest poison! How many worms dwell in the loveliest apples! Do not cling much to form, Arya, for it deceives… and though spirit moulds the form, yet the form is *not* the spirit! Thus a higher soul always transpires in a superior body, but beauty on its own remains an empty shell and a bittersweet illusion to the senses."

"Spirit alone is supreme, all else is illusion, deception, and ignorance. *That* was *my* first lesson in life! And one only learns from one's own suffering and experience."

"Thus, seek the *spirit* of your race, for it alone will lead you to your *legitimate* sons, not those petty souls who belittle and debase your name by making it shallow — and shallowness is the worst sin against the sacred —, thinking they are praising you… for such praise does more harm than good, and some of your unworthy sons have harmed you more than your worst enemies, for, by clinging to your form, they took away your soul."

"Seek your sons, Arya, for *they* are your home… for what good is a home without its sons? And *that* is what your Fatherland is today… A desert of the spirit, a land filled with people, but empty of soul and meaning. Henceforth, wherever your sons stand, *there* shall be your fatherland."

"If you love your Home, you must forget it, for it belongs to the past, and even the most glorious past is dead. And to worship the dead is a curse to the living. But *Aryana* (6) will always be in your soul. If you love your homeland, let it rest in the peace of immortality; let it be, do not go there! For the past is best glorified when left to rest in its own memory. That is true love, which wants to behold itself in the brightest mirror, and gaze at itself from the highest peaks. And there is only mist and clouds in our beloved North today… ultimately your home is within, your kingdom is within, your god is within. In your soul and your memory, your Fatherland will remain the same, but out there, the sad reality is too hard to behold and to bear."

"Arya, you are higher than you think, I know you… but your genes betray your soul when you cling to your transient identities and mortal shells — however great these may be — and thus forsake your eternal Self, which is beyond time and space. For the Self is part of God, and God is the Whole, and the whole has no identity beyond itself. Your heart betrays your soul when you long for the glorious past, whereas you represent the future of man and his highest aspirations. Shed your outer garb, Arya, and reveal your naked soul to the world, for only when we are naked do we truly exist and do we truly create, as only then are we truly free; and only a free soul can create."

"Shed your mortal shell, and reveal the eternal within; set the inner goddess free, so that your true Self and your true purpose might reveal themselves to you. Do not care for the moment, for the moment will take care of itself, it will be gone in the blink of an eye, whereas the infinity within you will shine forever. Live for, and serve Eternity, and you will vanquish all earthly attachments and aims. You are not lost, Arya, for your spirit is boundless, it finds its source in God."

"My dear Arya, here is a little pearl of wisdom to help you find inner peace and serenity: never expect and never regret. The past exists no more, the future has yet to be; so dwell in the eternal present, which alone endures."

Arya was moved by such words that touched her very heart, and she spoke thus to the familiar stranger: "you are a prophet, stranger — for only prophets speak as you do, only prophets *inspire* as you do — and though you are still young, Wisdom has no age, thus you carry the wisdom of millennia."

"You speak words of wisdom to those who thirst for them as plants thirst for the source of Life. You are a prophet, for you speak directly to the heart, source of all wonders and creation. And the head cannot but follow the commandments of the heart, if one truly wants to create."

"You say the right words to the right person and reveal the true nature of men hidden beneath the cloak of mortality. You unveil the hidden wisdom and beauty, so that they may shine and thrive always upwards and above. You shall lead men, *that* is a certainty."

"Prophet, you have touched my soul with your truth, awaking the divine that was slumbering in me. You are no stranger to my immortal Self. Life has joined our kindred souls anew, and only death can separate us, now that Life has blessed our reunion."

On the meaning of Life

The prophet and Arya sat down for a while, enjoying the Silence about them, that breath of God which speaks more eloquently and more profoundly than the sweetest words of wisdom. As they looked with wonder at the countless stars that were illuminating the eternal night sky, they both fell into a contemplative state, each delving into his own world, communing with the divine, all-pervading presence of Nature. But Arya's spirit remained restless, thus she broke the silence, saying:

"Prophet, your wisdom flattered mine when you bestowed some of its divine pearls, but still, my soul remains thirsty, it needs to drink not just from the cup, but from the *source* of Truth and Wisdom, it needs to become one with the soul of God; only then will it fulfil its destiny and finally rest in the peace of Eternity. There are so many questions left unanswered, my mind is overwhelmed by Life's great questions, and my conscience dictates: 'you shall seek Truth in every atom and in every star, in every valley and on every mountaintop, in every tear and in every smile, in every laughter and in every cry, in the heart of life and in the abyss of death, in the lightning and the Sun'. Thus I strive and I seek, but I need guidance, and who better than you, my prophet and companion, to guide me?"

"I need your counsel, prophet, for how can I lead men, if I myself am lost? I want you to reorient me when I stray from the Path. And the first question that I put to you is this: what did I come here to teach?"

The prophet replied: "you should rather ask: what did you come here to *learn*? For how can one teach if one does not learn first? And many a teacher has yet to learn his own lessons! You should learn your own lessons in life, before you can teach men their way and their goal. Before one becomes a teacher, one must first be a pupil; and are we not all eternal students of that great school, Life?"

"You should learn before you can teach; do you have enough humility to accept that? For the first lesson in wisdom is humility. I shall be your guide, Arya, for I know you better than you know yourself, as *I* see your path, while all *you* see is your goal; and what good is a dream if it is never fulfilled? What good is a tree severed from its roots? Death awaits all hope that is not rooted in possibility; therefore, the path is more important than the end."

"Learn *your* lessons, Arya, walk *your* path, follow your destiny; only thus will you lead men to the Way, the way to divinity. Do not seek out your followers, they will come when *you* find your way, for yours is also theirs; and has a leader ever followed his disciples? You were born to lead, Arya, so lead the way, and others will follow. Live your dreams, serve your ideals, and they will become mankind's ideals, as *you* embody man's highest purpose: the divine."

"Learn from Life, Arya, learn to *live* your ideas — not just to seek them and dream them —, learn to turn your ideas into ideals to preach and to follow; only thus will they become real. For the best sermon sounds hollow if it does not translate into action and will, and the deepest wisdom remains chimera if does not become a practice and a way of life… and every idea that does not become an ideal is a wasted fruit in the garden of Life."

"Therefore, listen to the voice of Wisdom in your soul and the world — for your soul is the mirror of the world —, and you shall carry Her sacred flame and speak Her holy word to men."

"Know thyself, Arya, and you shall bestow your truth upon the world, which is: man is a God in the making, and though he has long shunned the path chosen for him, still he remains a hope and a promise of divinity. But only complete men can tread the path to divinity, the rest are sketchy trials and hopeless failures."

"You are a goddess and a woman, your heart is human, but your soul is divine; hence you embody man's highest ideal — God — but also his deepest pain — Love —, for up there on the cold heights of Supremacy, where only eagles dare, the heart weakens and longs for the warmth of the abyss... thus *your* heart grows weak and longs for the earth, when you gaze too long at the Boundless above you and within you."

"Arya, you should cross your own bridge, for *you* are the bridge that men — those still *worthy* of being called men — should cross in order to become gods. The way is steep, but the goal is sublime, and divine glory is attained at the highest price, for everything great comes at the highest price. Therefore, forsake your human side and pursue higher ideals, for the ego is but an illusion that brings pain, tears and regrets, though it sometimes likes to deceive you in its brief moments of glory and bliss."

"Shed your human side, Arya, and unveil the goddess within, for *there* is where you will find eternal glory and eternal bliss. Unveil the inner goddess, and you shall truly fulfil your destiny. You should teach men their highest goal, which is to become gods. But that lesson is the hardest to teach, and the longest to learn, and many before you have tried and failed; many saints and prophets and godmen and Sons of God have failed before you, and many will fail after you, but that is our destiny on this earth: ever to strive, ever to fall, ever to rise and uplift — and by rising one uplifts —, for redemption entails sacrifice;

thus we sacrifice our lives for the Life Divine, and our love for the Love Supreme: the God-man."

"And though most men remain more beasts than men, and more men than gods, still, do not despair, Arya, for Time is but a human invention, and Eternity belongs to those who serve it. Have faith in your mission, for history is timeless; thus it does not count the years and the aeons, but serves the cause of Truth and hallows Her warriors."

"But what of my suffering?" replied Arya with a hint of frustration, "how do I end it? How do I cross the bridge? Can one become divine in the land of humans? Can one make divine what is merely human? Oh the misery of gods on earth!" The prophet remained silent for a while, pondering the significance of Arya's lament, then he told her: "all suffering stems from lack and guilt, lack of unity with the purpose of the universe, and guilt for not treading the right path, not achieving what one was born to achieve. Therefore, pay heed to your suffering, for it is a sign that shows you the goal, it is a milestone to your destination... thus your suffering will end when you fulfil your mission. But to redeem men, Arya, you must first redeem yourself; therefore, know thyself, and *your* truth shall set you free. Redeem yourself, and you shall redeem the world."

Her frustration growing stronger, Arya hastily replied: "but how can I redeem myself, when I strive to reconcile the irreconcilable, the human and the divine, the real and the ideal? When I cling both to my present and my future, my pain and my cure, my predicament and my aspiration?"

"How can I become a goddess, when I still *feel* like a woman? — and one ultimately becomes what one *feels*, not what one thinks; for it is the heart which truly dictates its will to the mind, though the mind thinks itself supreme. Thus I still suffer most from those twin curses of mankind, desire and fear. Desire and fear: those are two sides of the same coin, though desire wears the mask of joy, while no mask can hide fear's ugly face. But beneath all veils, desire and fear are one and the same, for both produce pain, that worst nightmare of man."

"My highest desire is to embrace and bestow Love… but human love is denied me, and divine love is still beyond my reach; human love is forbidden to him who aspires after the divine, and divine love has yet to kindle man's eternal flame. Hence the Higher Man, that god in the making, remains trapped between heaven and earth — while men are trapped between earth and hell —, torn between his will to live and his will to Truth, clinging to Love but dreaming of Truth, attached to that great and most powerful deception, Passion — which is love at its most intense levels —, while desperately seeking his elusive and ever fleeting divine dream."

"Thus the human and the divine in me are constantly at war, and there is no real winner, when the loser secretly rules his victor through guilt, pain, and regret. There is no winner when victory tastes sour and defeat is desirable; for the heart and the mind can never truly part, and to separate them is to deny them both. And so my highest desire turns into the worst pain, for I am whole; which do I choose? Can one ever *really* choose between his heart and his spirit? Can one choose between his desire and his will, his essence and his goal? — for one's essence is ultimately one's goal, thus the God-Man is both a man and a god, *and* neither a man nor a god."

"Should I follow my heart, and forsake my goal, or pursue my spirit, and slay my soul? How do I choose? Ultimately, I lose… for Unity is the only victory, and to divide is to defeat. Can a mother ever choose a child over another? Has God ever chosen among his Sons? No, no, no! There are *no* chosen people, save those who have chosen out themselves, as *our* Great Prophet once said; all the others are lost in illusion and delusion. To separate is to deny, and to deny is to condemn; thus man remains doomed so long as he remains a fragment."

"Desire is therefore nothing but pain and loss… but I am in love with Love, and so I submit to drinking its sweet poison which bestows a few drops of joy, followed by the excruciating pain of loss; for nothing endures under the sun save that which has no form and bears no name. Hence, attachment begets loss, sublime love becomes bitter sorrow, passion turns into agony."

"As for my worst fear, it is the fear of loss, the fear of loneliness, the unbearable suffering of the solitary soul in that desert of men called earth. For loss of a loved one kills something in man, and loneliness is but death looking at itself in the mirror of life. Solitude reveals one's inner war, the war between the thinker and the witness, the Ego and the Self, the god and the man… thus its company is unbearable, save for those twice-born who have overcome the illusion of death and sit as equals with the gods."

When Arya fell silent, despondent and weary from her human drama, the prophet pushed a compassionate sigh of melancholy, as he knew the agony of separation that tortured the soul of every seeker of the Absolute; he knew the pain of attachment and the death of detachment — for to cling is to suffer, but to relinquish is to die, as death of the senses gives birth to the spirit — . A few minutes elapsed before he came closer to Arya, held both her hands, gazed deep into her tearful eyes, and spoke thus to her:

"My dear Arya, you speak highly of Love, but when you do so, the woman in you has silenced the goddess… you speak highly of Love, but know that human love is an addiction, and addiction is a curse disguised as a blessing, agony disguised as ecstasy. Learn from life, Arya, She is the greatest teacher, but man is Her worst student, and there is still much of the human in you. There is a higher kind of love, that which clings not and asks not and desires not, a love that bestows and overflows; *that* is divine love, love of God; for God is Love and Life."

"You confuse love with desire, and though you think highly of love *and* desire — unlike men, who confuse love with lust, and desire with depravity —, still the love you speak of is much too human; it comes from lack, for, as you said, it arises out of fear and ends in pain. Arya, you should look forward and seek upwards, lest you remain trapped in the abyss of the temporal and the transient. And there is nothing worse, for a god or a goddess, than the prison of matter which stifles the spirit and debases the soul... there is nothing worse for the spirit than this earth where nothing endures and all fades back into nothingness; where the dream of love turns into the nightmare of loss, where Life itself becomes a death wish, a curse unto itself."

"Life, Higher Life, has a higher meaning and serves a nobler purpose than man's narrow soul and flawed mind have hitherto given it. They say with pride, these petty humans of today, who naïvely think that they have discovered Life's meaning, when they do not even know that they know nothing — and nothing feeds ignorance better than the arrogance of certainty — they say with pride, these petty people: 'live life abundantly'. But to live life abundantly gives not Life its due; to give life a *meaning* is to serve it well, a higher meaning that grows wings to reach the heights of Being, and a deeper purpose that delves into the bowels of the mysteries of the universe. For only thus does life become worth living, only thus does the word 'absurd' become itself absurd, and fade back into the void that created it. And though Love hallows Life and fills the soul of the world with divine ecstasy, still it does not ennoble Life and serve it, and only by ennobling does one truly serve."

"Love serves the heart and the soul, but Spirit needs something more... Spirit needs Perfection and Elevation; it speaks not the language of love, it only hears the ineffable voice of God, which urges it to transcend, and to ascend, whereas love is nothing but attachment and fall. Therefore, to bless life by ennobling it is to truly live abundantly, for how can one drink to the fullest from a cup that remains empty, how can one quench one's thirst from a source that has dried out?"

"Life without Love is a wretched wreck in the sea of existence; for Joy, — that divine elixir — and Hope, that mother of all creation and all victories, need to taste the holy wine of Love and the intoxicating ecstasy of Passion to thrive and blossom; and where Love lacks, there the blissful garden of Life turns into a desert of sorrow and desperation, as existence becomes empty and unworthy, a bitter poison which perpetually tortures the soul until death itself becomes a sweet hope of liberation."

"Without love, life is empty; but without *meaning*, life is even emptier, it is but decay, apathy, and despair, for, as I said, Love hallows Life, but it does not give it meaning; and meaning is the breath of Life, the Soul of the World."

"Therefore, the worst verdict levelled against Life is to ask: 'what for?' For when a meaning lacks, Life loses its soul and becomes death. And if the whole earth is a desert today, is it not because man has ceased to find meaning in, and give meaning to, Life? Have not his foolish arrogance and his insatiable greed emptied existence from all meaning? That arrogance which banishes all questions and derides all answers, and that greed which ever wants to grab and accumulate and relish, always taking and never giving — and thus ever growing richer in possessions, but poorer in spirit?"

"Life on earth is a punishment for men and a trial for gods. Material life is a curse wrought upon man for his fall from the grace of God. For man became mortal when he ceased to think and believe that he is a god. Yet gods' journey on this earth and among men is neither a curse nor a punishment, though treading the human purgatory of suffering and regrets may seem like the closest thing to hell for a god. But things are never what they seem; thus, although gods share man's condition, they do not share man's fate and mission. And though gods on earth feel and desire as men do, yet their feelings and desires are of a higher nature, for they serve beyond themselves, they serve the Spirit."

"And *that* is the essential difference between men and gods: men, in their infinite conceit that knows no shame — the conceit of the ignorant — think of themselves as ends; their petty and arrogant egos — and pettiness is always arrogant — need to erect fences and to draw boundaries within and outside themselves in order to survive, for that is what the ego does: it separates and divides, for its essence is separation and division… whereas gods and human gods, those Higher Men with divine souls, those giants who have the humility of the wise, those who have experienced the indescribable bliss of Unity, know that even the highest among them is but a means to a higher end; thus they know that they are but different facets of the One, conscious parts of the Whole, they are mere drops in that river of Becoming which eternally flows into the boundless ocean of Being."

"Gods' sublime feelings and lofty desires are of a higher and nobler kind than men's lustful needs and petty cravings, for gods are but Warriors of the Light in its endless journey towards self-consciousness and self-overcoming, a journey that passes through the human plight of individuation, but rises above it, in that eternal transcendence of Spirit which only becomes conscious through the immanence of form."

"For there can be no self-overcoming without self-consciousness, hence separation is a necessary evil in the service of a higher good. Therefore, the agony of attachment and its twin sister, separation, is necessary for self-consciousness of the Spirit, as Unity — or God — cannot discover itself if it does not look into its own mirror — and that mirror is Life."

"Gods, as men, feel and fear, they desire and suffer, but their aching hearts and their aspiring souls feel deeper and aspire higher than themselves, serving the Pure Spirit which pervades all forms and all existence. And though gods, too, fall into the darkness of matter, theirs is but the fall *of* matter and the rise of awareness, the bright road that leads to elevation. For one has to fall deepest before one can rise highest; and when the abyss of Form gazes at the peaks of Spirit, is it not the river of Becoming which eternally flows into the infinite which gazes at its Higher Self?"

"Incarnation entails self-consciousness, and transcendence entails self-overcoming, and both are daughters of Unity, source and end of all things. Hence, by incarnating, gods acquire awareness, and by transcending, they rise back towards Unity, after Unity has gazed at itself in the mirror of consciousness, the mirror of matter. And so, having fulfilled their mission on earth, completing the sacred circle of fall and elevation, gods return whence they came, save those fallen gods who have chosen to become men. That is the meaning of Life as gods see it; as for men, they assign life motley meanings and manifold aims, but none seems quite worthy of Life, save those lofty deeds and sublime thoughts of noble men who, serving the divine purpose, become gods themselves."

"Only by serving the divine and ending the cycle of incarnation and transcendence does one know and experience Unity in its soul, the earth, and in its spirit, the universe. The human drama therefore becomes a divine mission, for it gives Spirit the gift of self-consciousness, and thus uplifts it on its eternal journey towards perfection."

"Therefore, gods need not choose between heart and mind, between soul and spirit; only humans make that choice and face that dilemma. Gods do not choose, they *fulfil*; their fate is sealed, and that is Unity. Their hearts serve their spirit, their souls serve God."

"You need not choose, Arya, for, as you said, to choose is to lose… thus you will be left with emptiness and despair, as emptiness is the worst kind of despair for him who strives ever higher and delves ever deeper, and the agony of separation awaits him who strives not after, and serves not, Totality."

"If you follow your heart, Arya, let it guide you upwards, towards your spirit, its source and its end; and if you follow your spirit, know that your heart will sing along in that joyous symphony of Love and Life, of Unity and Supremacy. But if your heart clings to men and all things human, it will kill the goddess in you, for your spirit is divine, and the divine cannot endure a life devoid of meaning, a life devoid of spirit. And will gods still matter, if they begin to think and act like men? Are they not the arrows that lead men to their divine destiny?"

"Beware passion, Arya, for passion is blind and makes blind; and it shall blind your spirit, if, entranced by the irresistible warmth of infatuation and the burning flame of temptation, your spirit chooses not to reign supreme and dances frantically to the heartbeats of your lower self, bowing before the passing whims of your human desires. For though passion uplifts, though it always has a sublime beginning, yet, like any addiction, it ends in agony, and, like any illusion, it ends in regret."

"But Higher Love is of a different nature and has a different end — or rather, it has no end, for Pure Love is Life, and Life is eternal —; Higher Love is divine, thus it never changes and never deceives. And so, serving the Spirit, the seeker of Truth becomes one with the object of his veneration, and basks in the shining glory and the ineffable bliss of Eternity."

"Therefore, Arya, let your spirit listen to the divine symphony of Higher Love, and remain deaf to the pounding beats of your heart which torture your soul and cloud your mind, for they shall lead you nowhere save to agony and misery. Aspire to the highest, and you shall attain it. Cling to the human, and you shall remain trapped in the dark cave of matter and mortality. That is the golden rule of Life."

"Beware the Ego, Arya; the ego is a devil in man; the ego is *the* devil *made* man, for it lives by the senses and serves them blindly, not paying heed to man's higher aspirations; and he who lives by the senses, dies to the spirit. The ego only sees matter in motion, it is blind to the divine stillness of the Spirit, and knows not its sublime peace. Its lord and master is immediate gain, its lord and master is the material world. The Ego is but an instrument of the Higher Self to discover and overcome itself, otherwise it becomes its slayer."

"Love is a noble feeling, it is lofty and sublime, but still, it is a human feeling, for it breeds attachment; and attachment is mankind's curse and blessing. It is a blessing, for it completes and makes a whole out of fragments, but it is also a curse, as it steals away and tears asunder that which it had conquered and united, and throws back the fragments it had sealed into the black hole of the void of existence. Attachment is a curse, for though it enraptures us with divine promises of Bliss and Eternity, ultimately it ends in loss, for nothing lasts forever save the Whole, not its parts. And we are all, the greatest and the lowest of us, fragmented parts of the Indivisible, changing forms of the Unmovable, perishable faces of the Eternal. Thus Higher Love alone is eternal, that love which ever reaches out beyond itself, that overflowing fountain of Joy and Light, a joy unto itself, a light unto itself, that love which need not give or take, but desires only itself, and lives contented as the sublime soul of God."

"Higher love is divine, undying, and perfect, whereas human love remains wretched, finite, and incomplete, although those blessed by its burning, purifying rays tend to think of themselves as immortals, as Love seems like the last remnant of divinity here on earth, for it deceitfully promises absolute and eternal Unity, while all it ultimately bestows is loss, tears, and regrets, shattering the very dreams that it had inspired and nourished. And though lovers meet again evermore on their endless journey through Time, bound by that sacred bond which links twin souls above, in the ocean of Infinity, and blesses their union below, in that garden of Love that is our earth, still, human love remains incomplete and unfulfilled, so long as it does not become divine and thus hallows itself with the seal of Eternity, rising above itself and serving the highest and noblest goal of the universe: perpetual Creation and Elevation."

"And so, true lovers, those blessed with that sacred flame which kindles the highest and greatest feelings in man, should bless their union by uplifting it and sublimating it, putting their love in the service of a higher love — love of Eternity —, and putting their union in the service of a higher union, the union of the human with the divine, its source and its end."

"Desire arises out of lack, and fear of loss. So forsake both, for they are illusions, and serve the eternal, which is the only reality. The key to peace and fulfilment is detachment, or *Amor Fati*, as that great prophet, that *only* prophet from the West once called Higher Life."

"To find yourself, you need not choose between your parts, Arya, for you are whole; so choose yourself, choose Unity, the Spirit Divine — which is the highest kind of love —, choose the Life divine — which is the highest kind of life —, and you shall attain peace and fulfil your destiny."

"Nothing is real save that which endures, and nothing endures save that which is real. Therefore, cling to spirit, Arya, not to form, for the Spirit alone remains and ever takes on and creates different forms; the Spirit alone is true, and Truth alone prevails and endures." Thus spoke the prophet, and he then fell into a deep silence that spoke louder than words, that sacred stillness which creates and inspires."

However, Arya's soul was still restless, and her mind was still tormented, and so she broke the silence of the prophet and said: "yet, still I suffer, for though I aspire after the divine, and yearn for the inner goddess to unfold, still I am enraptured by that most divine of human feelings, Love, which fills my mind with sweet words of bliss, and floods my heart with the sacred wine of ecstasy. Love is irresistible, even for a goddess… and choice seems like a cruel word, though it is necessary. I must choose between rising above, or sinking below. So I must know, which is worse, the agony of the heart, or the agony of the spirit? For to avoid the worst pain seems like a wise choice."

The prophet, somewhat bemused by that question which betrayed the innocence of a pure soul still unscathed by the dark fumes of the human realm, looked at Arya with a hint of a smile on his lips, gazed with deep compassion into her eyes, and said in a tender, loving tone: "you ask the wrong question, my dear, for to avoid pain is but to postpone it, not to heal it. Your question betrays a dark outlook on Life; you should look for the light in all things, only thus will you *see* the light in all things. Hence, your question should rather be: which is greater, the delight of the heart, or the bliss of the spirit? Which of these gifts bestowed upon men endures? Which of them does not fade and turn from the sweetest honey to the sourest poison? Life itself provides the answer to that question; and though it is better to have loved and lost, than never to have loved at all, as those eternal romantics say, still it is the delight of the Spirit which is eternal, whereas the intoxicating joy of Love is a self-consuming fire which burns the very joy that it once radiated."

"Forsake all human illusions, Arya—and Love is the greatest illusion—and surrender to your divine fate, for *you* have willed it and fashioned it on your journey to Eternity, though your ego denies Eternity and clings to the moment, for it only lives through the moment, as it alone serves its narrow aims and its petty desires."

"Overcome your weaknesses—for they are only human, and you are divine—and pay no heed to the human in you, for the human is your past, while the divine is your future; surrender to your fate while fulfilling your duty, for sowing you can, but reaping is an act of God. Surrender to the destiny you have chosen for yourself, for everything is as it should be, the greatest and the worst of occurrences has a meaning, and there are lessons to be learned in everything that happens on this earth. But you should learn to see beyond the surface of things, events, and people, to grasp that deep truth, for things and events and people are but instruments of a greater Will that wants to teach man his goal, and that is: to overcome himself, and create beyond himself. You have to see beyond the surface to grasp the meaning of Life. All that happens has a meaning and serves Life's higher meaning and aim. All that happens to you serves to awaken the real you, your Higher Self."

Arya, having listened with attention to the prophet's words, replied: "but though I am whole, still I remain torn between my parts... and though I serve the highest with my staunchest will and my deepest love, still I falter on the path to Immortality, as my aching heart makes my will waver, and my yearning soul makes my mind weak; for heart and mind serve different gods, and Eros and Logos remain ever strangers to each other."

"My story is an epic of Truth, Love, and Power. But these are constantly at war in me. All want to conquer, none wants to submit. Love wants to conquer all, Truth wants to prevail, Power wants to overflow. Which do I choose? Which of these shall win the internal war, so that finally I could rest in peace and wage my own war, in the coming battle for Supremacy, for the meaning of the universe?"

"Earthly love is a heaven to the senses, a hell to the spirit, for it brings pain, because it comes from lack and remains incomplete and unfulfilled, ever unsatisfied, ever thirsty of itself. So long as man remains man, love will never be complete or joyful; nonetheless, love will always haunt and torture men, so long as men have hearts that beat, and souls that dream."

"And what of Truth? It is lofty and noble, but ever unreachable to our fallible mind, that imperfect instrument which serves a perfect aim — and how could imperfection truly serve perfection? —. Hence, truth remains an empty word and a dead letter if it does not transpire in life and serve its purpose."

"And, as regards power, I long for it, I yearn for it, it needs to overflow and rule… but it remains an inexhaustible source of pure potential that squanders itself in the river of Impermanence and illusion. For power never really rules and never really lasts."

"Thus, I am torn between Truth, Love, and Power; I am Truth and will to Truth, I am Power and will to Power, I am Love and will to Love. I am a Trinity that cries out for Unity. I am a knight of knowledge, a lover of Wisdom, a saint who wants to conquer, a conqueror who dreams of Love. I am a warrior in love, a seeker of Truth, and a saint of Love; that is my pain and my blessing."

The prophet, sensible to Arya's lament and torment, but determined to guide her on the steep path to Wisdom, answered her with an austere determination: "Arya, know that Trinity is Unity expressed, and man's short sight sees diversity where there is only unity. Truth is the highest kind of love, it is a love which never varies, never betrays, and is never distorted. It is a love unto its own, and needs naught but itself to feel complete; for true Love and true Power are one, and Truth is Absolute Unity."

"Truth is Being seeking its own depths in the heart of God. Truth is the highest kind of power, it is the only kind of power that lasts, it is the Force that creates, regenerates, and uplifts. All else is evil, petty, and base. That is why men of power are seldom men of wisdom, and men of wisdom are seldom *in* power. That is not a coincidence or an injustice; that is a law. Power corrupts, it is possessive, and so it deludes and distorts all truth and all beauty. Therefore, saints can never be rulers."

"You are part of the Whole, so you *are* whole; thus all divisions and contrasts are illusions. Truth is Love and Power, it is the only lasting love and the only real power."

"Your greatest fears and your deepest pain are your best opportunities, for they urge you to overcome the illusion called separation and finiteness. Henceforth, when you feel fear or pain, think of yourself as an alchemist of the Spirit, and turn this fear into determination, and this pain into expectation; for these are your greatest lessons in life, as they show you the way to your inner legend. Men prefer the good and the joyful to the bad and the painful, but the former could not have meaning without the latter, as Truth is beyond good and evil, Love is beyond joy and pain, and Power is beyond victory and defeat."

"Your first lesson in life was: Race is above Nation; the river of Blood flows over the bridges of nations. Your second lesson is: Race is Spirit, and Spirit is beyond form. Your third lesson should be: Spirit is supreme, and Unity is absolute; all contrasts are illusions, more is less, all possession is loss, and all wealth of matter is poverty of spirit.

All power that does not serve Truth is weakness, baseness, and evil; and the love that does not gracefully pour itself into the sacred cup of Wisdom is a wasted wine that has lost its divine taste."

"Do not lament your loneliness, Arya, for all separation is illusion. Cherish your solitude, as solitude is wholeness. It is only when you are alone that you are with God; it is only when all is still that God manifests Himself in the world. Silence is divine, noise drives Spirit away. So dance joyfully in the stillness of heaven to the rhythm of your own divine melody."

On the plight of gods on earth

Having spoken his word, the prophet had an air of contentment upon his countenance; he felt that his words were sinking deep into Arya's soul, guiding her back on her way to her Higher Self. But in Arya's mind, there were still many questions unanswered, many mysteries unsolved. Thus she ever felt the need to inquire, and so she again asked her guide:

"You speak the truth when you talk about the unity of existence, the One behind the many, the Truth behind all mysteries. But why does the Whole need its parts to just *be*? Why does Being need Becoming? Why can't Perfection remain perfect, and Unity remain complete? Why does the higher need the lower? Why can't below be as above? Why can't men be perfect, as their Father in heaven is perfect?"

After a brief pause, during which she seemed to go into the very heart of Being, her soul reaching out to touch the soul of God, Arya went on questioning Life's mysteries: "why does the gloomy, human veil of *Maya* cover this beautiful, divine earth? Why does the shadow always follow the Light? Why does doubt always torture certainty, why does deceit always haunt Truth, casting a dark cloud on its shining path that leads to the stars? Why does the transient plague Life, which is Eternity? Why does the finite stifle the soul of Infinity?"

"Men remain wretched, and gods remain unfulfilled down under, in the density of matter, where the curse of gravity makes everything heavy and awry. So why do gods incarnate on earth? Why do gods still live among men? The Higher Man is a memory of the god that was, and a promise of the god to come; but men remain men, and gods remain gods, forever separated by a wall of silence and ignorance, forever misunderstood, forever strangers to one another."

"What have we gods to offer this hopeless humanity that shall forever remain alien to divinity? No act of man is divine, no thought of man is divine, save those very few — saints and prophets and hermits — who are more gods than men."

"All that is great on earth has been accomplished by lofty souls and godlike beings; men, however, remain mediocre and ignorant. So what is this obsession among gods which makes them think the unthinkable, and dare the impossible, and that is: to want to redeem humanity? Can one redeem that which is unredeemable? Can the seeds of Life grow in the fields of death? Gaïa is sinking to its doom, and today it is nothing but the graveyard of gods and the slaughterhouse of men. Man is but the shadow of himself and the wretched relic of a forlorn glory, and all that is left from his divine dream is the fading memory of a Golden Age kept in the infinite mind of Eternity." Thus spoke Arya, bemoaning her torment and her doubts to her prophet and companion.

"This earth," he answered, "has ever been a battlefield where the higher and the lower, the divine and the human, Light and darkness, mix and clash... a never-ending cycle of rise and fall, bliss and despair, glory and misery; but *who* has won the battle for Supremacy, gods or men? The Truth is that, never has the fate of the earth been sealed, and even as it drowns today, a war to the death still rages on between those who want to overcome man, and those who want to preserve him; those who fight for a divine destiny for the earth, those who want to uplift and sublimate Life, and those who want to keep the earth human, denying Life its own purpose, its own progress toward an ever higher and an ever greater destiny. An eternal war rages on between those reaching for the stars above and yearning to become gods again, and those clinging to material life and contented with their mediocrity and their mortality."

"And so the millenarian battle between Light and darkness still goes on; but the greatest battle of all, the battle of the Spirit, is about to begin, even as the earth sinks to its death. For the deepest yearns for the highest, death yearns for rebirth, and every fall must again ascend. The final battle, the battle for Supremacy, has yet to be fought on earth. All former battles have been mere preludes to this final one; all the gods, prophets, and saints who have come to this earth were but preludes to the Coming God, mere glimpses of the future of man, mere fragments of the meaning of the earth. What will be the outcome of that greatest of battles? Destiny alone bears the answer to that crucial question; will men become gods, and gods men, as the divine law of perfection dictates? Or will man regress, going back to the apes, and gods depart, going back to their own spheres, where no human has yet trodden?"

Arya pondered for a while what the prophet had said, then, all of a sudden, a feeling of despondency took hold of her soul and choked her spirit, and she burst out saying: "O the unbearable suffering incurred by gods on earth! For the spirits from higher spheres, who dwell in human flesh, suffer the limitations of mortality, which stifle the soul's infinity. Nonetheless, can there be creation without incarnation? Can there be perfection without manifestation? Can there be elevation without fall? Is divinity conceivable without humanity? But still, I suffer from the duality of this earth, and I long for that lost Unity that only gods know and live. I came to this earth to give, to bestow Light, but how can I bestow that which remains hidden? How can I preach the unity of all things, when I have yet to transcend the illusion of separation?"

"God Himself needs company," the prophet replied, "God Himself needs His gods, for what would divinity be, were it not to bestow itself and its grace upon the world? Would gods be gods if they did not reflect their own divinity in existence itself? Gods tread the earth and impregnate its soul with their divine seeds, so that they beget beings that are human in feeling and divine in longing, men that are gods, and gods that are men; men with godlike souls, and gods in human garb. Such is the wisdom of Life and Creation: the higher bends and bows before the lower to elevate him, and the lower longs for the higher to shed his base shell and nature, and overcome himself. Thus, as God needs gods, so do gods need men, and they almost forgive them for their imperfections and vileness; for how else would gods discover their own immortality, how else would they become conscious of their own divinity and perfection, if they did not experience the human tragedy of the Spirit?"

"Men should ask themselves: 'are our bodies the shining temples of our spirit? Do they incarnate and justify divinity, or are they a graveyard of the Spirit?' I say to the contemplative who seek nirvana through self-annihilation: we need our bodies to discover our souls, and we need our souls to discover the Spirit, God. We need the vehicle to discover the energy, we need the form to discover the essence which gives it life and keeps it alive; and so we must endure humanity in order to achieve divinity. That is our plight, but also our fate and our mission on this earth. Arya, know that gods on earth are but higher spirits trapped in human flesh, stifled by the limitations of matter, and crushed by the weight of gravity. Even the most perfect body remains a prison of the soul, ever longing for absolute freedom, for detachment from the heavy and tight chains of human existence. Gods too suffer on this earth, for this Eden is their hell, but, as hell crucifies the body, it immortalises the spirit."

Arya was moved by the prophet's response, and she felt that, beyond their words, there was a silent dialogue between their souls, which belonged to the invisible realm of the Spirit. He seemed to know her better than she knew herself, for he knew her Higher Self, and thus whispered to her his sublime words of wisdom. Looking at him with admiration mixed with affection, she said: "prophet, I have only known you in your present form for a short while, but our souls have known each other for aeons, and have danced with each other to the eternal music of the spheres; and they shall continue to meet each other evermore on the path to Immortality."

"I have a secret that I carry like a shackle to my soul and a thorn in my spirit; would you share my innermost suffering with me? For you seem to know me better than I know myself, as you *see* my path to Glory, whereas I only *feel* it." "Speak your word, my dear Arya," the prophet replied, "tell me your painful secret, unveil your hidden pain to me."

Finding solace and comfort in the prophet's encouragement, Arya spoke thus: "my prophet and eternal companion, I shall relate to you what has always been my secret, my eternal secret that will go down with me when I bid my time on this earth; for we higher beings all have a secret and a depth that no one can reach or penetrate, it is our refuge and our temple of peace, away from the noisy chaos of the world of men, and closer to the divine stillness of higher, subtler realms."

As she was about to say something that she had long held back, Arya took a long breath, then pushed a deep sigh, as though she was trying to find relief through her confession. "I have waited a long time to divulge my secret," she told him, "as I had yet to find a kindred soul to share it with, a soul worthy of the secret of the gods. I had yet to find the right person for whom that secret was destined, and for whom my soul was aching in anticipation; for all secrets are ultimately destined to be told, when the right time and the right persons cross paths. But now, finally, I can speak, and to the lonely heart, speech is a reward, though silence is divine."

"Speak your word, Arya," the prophet said, "for I am that kindred soul that you have been waiting for, ever since the breath of Life blessed your soul and awoke your spirit. Speak to me, daughter of Light, and in doing so, you shall be speaking to your Higher Self, revealing the goddess within; for every truth wants to be told, every mystery needs to be solved, and the time of reaping the harvest of Truth has dawned upon a world in dire need of redemption. The time has come for Truth to reclaim Her rights, and all higher souls are children of Light and warriors of Truth. So tell me your secret, Arya, relate to me your secret legend."

Emboldened by her guide's trust and belief in her, Arya finally opened her heart: "at last, I am speaking my word, which is the true word of divinity, and so I shall live forever, for he who utters the unutterable, he who speaks the ineffable Word of God, lives eternally like the gods."

"Finally I am speaking my word… for too long have I kept my heart shut and my lips sealed. My soul wants to burst out shouting and crying, it needs to express the anger and grief, the hopes and regrets, the frustrations and expectations that have tortured it during all these long years spent on this doomed earth."

"Finally I am telling my tale, unveiling my legend, uttering my truth, forged by the wisdom of millennia; for what is Truth but the inner legend which lies deep in each higher being's recesses of the soul? What is Truth but Life itself unfolding before God? Divine wisdom thus has it: one either serves the eternal or the temporal, one either serves God or man, one cannot serve both, for their paths and their purposes are of a different nature and essence. He who serves the eternal and forsakes all earthly desire and glory, enters the temple of immortality. And he who pursues his own glory and his lower destiny, remains trapped in the chains of Time, plagued by the curse of mortality. For all that is left in the soul of the universe, following our brief passage on this earth, long after our bodies return to dust, are our sublime thoughts and our noble deeds."

"Prophet, I shall now share my secret suffering with you. So let your ears listen with the awe and reverence that is reserved to the gods, for though I suffer and though I falter, my path — as yours — is divine. I am the warrior-goddess of Wisdom in this fallen world of men, where defeat is called peace, and deceit is called truth. Do you know what it feels like to be a god on earth? A Warrior of Light in the realm of darkness? A saint of knowledge in the abyss of ignorance? A seeker of Truth in a world of illusions? A human god torn between divinity and humanity, between the delights that Life has to offer our senses and to fill our souls, and the indescribable bliss of Eternity? Do you know what it feels like to be bound by the human fetters of time and space, while your inner infinity longs for the ether where it belongs?"

"Do you know the writhing pain of cosmic solitude amid the human crowds who remain impervious to your secret longing and your hidden suffering? For men live in the shadow of Truth and on the margin of Life, and idleness is their fate. Prophet, I shall now tell you *my* truth: real suffering is found not in an imaginary hell, but here on earth, in the human purgatory which has neither the bliss of heaven, nor the fatalism of hell. The earth bears hope, and in all hope lies the promise of a new dawn, but also the excruciating night of longing, for to long is to give birth to new suns, and all longing that does not turn into creation is a child yet unborn. The earth is lost in infinite space, and it escapes black holes of nothingness by revolving around the Sun; so too does man struggle to escape the black void of existence by revolving around *his* sun, *his* god, creating him if he cannot discover him."

"You say the universe is my home, but what worlds would I not squander, if only I could belong *somewhere*, if only I could find *my* peace and *my* home... for where one finds his peace, one finds his home; and where one finds his home, one finds his peace. The human in me shuns the vertigo of Infinity and clings to the safe haven of identity; and even the boundless in me has at times a longing for a little piece of reality... and even the truth that speaks through me has at times shivered to that little folly, earthly power and glory, away from the divine sphere of Eternity. But *where* will I find my home? When will *my* time come? Will I ever find my home, will my time ever come?"

"Such is the plight of gods on earth: to be like rays of the dawning Sun, rainbows of the bright future, while being consumed by the flame of their own sacred fire which kindles the Light of Truth upon the altar of divinity; for only that which goes down shall rise higher, and only that which goes the deepest rises the highest. It is the deepest valley which gives birth to the highest mountain, and the tree whose roots run deepest grows the highest and mightiest branches."

"Great is the suffering of gods, for the higher the being, the deeper the suffering, and the nobler the goal, the greater the burden; and he suffers the most who, as Atlas, carries the weight of the world upon his shoulders, he who has engraved on his forehead the divine seal of the future of humanity. The glory and tragedy of human gods is that, while their feet tread the earth below, their eyes behold the glory of the heavens above."

"We gods on earth look human, but act divine; and though, as men, we feel and suffer, still we always aspire and we always overcome. We are but humans with divine longing, men with higher souls, sons of Pure Spirit endowed with that most divine of human feelings: the gift of Love. We are the flesh of Nature, the Breath of God, and the Soul of the universe; in our memory and our future lies divinity. We are reflections on earth of the One cosmic principle, for God reveals Himself through gods, as man reveals his soul through his thoughts and deeds."

"Yet, as we tread the earth, we too suffer from the limitations of mortal life, its attachments, its weaknesses and finiteness; thus our inner infinity can find no abode on earth, and our inner eternity can find no peace in heaven; for the earth is too small for great souls, the earth is too round for those who look beyond appearance, those whose sharp eyes pierce the hollow shell of form. And heaven remains the realm of an unbearable, empty Silence which deafens our ears longing to hear the drumbeats of struggle, the cries of victory, and the rumblings of glory echoing in the valley of Eternity. Thus we remain trapped between heaven and earth, ever longing for Spirit, ever clinging to form."

"Do you know, prophet, what it feels like to belong neither to time nor to space? To be at home nowhere? But the universal longs for the particular as the particular longs for the universal, in the sacred Ring of Life; and Life is the battleground of that eternal struggle between finitude and perpetuity, between the glory of the One and the wealth of the many, though in truth all opposites are but different facets, various shades and degrees of the same essence, as Unity is absolute."

"Hence, we gods are the deepest roots of the Tree of Life, as well as its longest branches; we belong to the remote past and to the distant future. And so we remain torn between what was and what shall be, clinging to the former while longing for the latter. It oppresses me, this present, this ever-fleeting, evanescent present, vacuum of boundlessness, the glimpse of an eternity that forever disappears, is reborn ever again, and vanishes evermore."

"My prophet and friend, do you know what it feels like to belong nowhere and to no one, to feel no ties with kin, clan, or nation? To find both comfort and bitterness in solitude? — and the worst kind of solitude is that which one endures among men —. To wear one's various masks each day, and for each person a mask — for each person *deserves* a mask? —. To bury one's secret deep within one's soul, until death, and beyond death, for fear of defiling it by revealing it to unworthy eyes and ears? To remain eternally a stranger to the world, to the farthest and closest people, a stranger in a sea of strangers? O the bitter freedom of solitude! O wounded joy of freedom! O the misery of gods among men! For though their mission is great, their suffering is greater still. And if the price of divinity is incarnation, life on earth remains unworthy, for it defiles gods instead of raising men."

"Such is the plight of gods among men: to lift one's cross along Life's steep path to Immortality, enduring the agony of humanity in flesh, while living divinity in spirit; to feel nausea at mankind and flee into the safe haven of solitude, choosing the cold dangers of the pure and innocent wilderness over the warm comfort of the filthy and decadent human wastelands of civilisation; for where herds live, there you find the wastelands and the deserts of the spirit; and where no man has set foot, there the air remains pure and undefiled, and a ray of hope shines on the horizon of a better tomorrow."

"Gods are at home nowhere and with no one save themselves, in their abode of Light that draws no boundaries and knows no limits; for they are a world unto their own, a law unto themselves, a race apart."

"Such is the plight of gods on earth: to be eternally homeless, at once lost and at home everywhere and nowhere; to be timeless, eternal witnesses of millennia unfolding before their inner eyes, at once belonging to no age and to every age, to the Spirit of All Ages which blends the soul of past and future in the hallowed cup of Eternity."

"To search — hopelessly and aimlessly — for companions, brothers and soul-mates worthy of sharing one's cosmic solitude and inner silence, companions who are peers, not mere company; for to the Higher Man, bad company is worse than solitude, though he sometimes welcomes it, when his heart weakens in the presence of the Boundless, and his foot falters into unknown lands. Only the herd says: 'misery loves company', for misery *does* love company, and gods prefers solitude."

"Such is the plight of gods among men: to scoff at men's dire needs and greatest ambitions, their deepest desires and their highest dreams, for they are mere drops in the sea of Illusion that men call 'life', mere shadows in the realm of the transitory that men call 'the world', passing clouds in the sky of Impermanence, doomed to fade away and die, as death is the rule and the fate of all things down under. Such is the plight of gods on earth: to live in one's own world of ideals, which is as boundless as the universe, and as timeless as Eternity itself."

"Gods and men remain strangers to each other, for men will always look down and beneath themselves, and gods will always gaze up and beyond themselves, and even in their fall, they remain high and mighty, whereas men remain small, even in their glory. Men look down and fall, and gods look up and transcend; thus the eyes of gods and men never meet and never agree. And only those men who look beyond themselves and see across the veil of *Maya* become gods, for they alone have discovered Truth, and he who discovers Truth overcomes himself and joins the Absolute."

"Throughout history, gods were sent to men to impregnate the earth with the seeds of divine wisdom, and to create perfect beings from the soil of the earth and the spirit of the ether; yet evolution has always been selective, never collective. Hence, gods and human gods alone have evolved and ascended, whereas man is perpetually decaying and falling ever deeper into bestiality, ever a stranger to perfection, ever unworthy of divinity, instead of rising higher towards his destiny and end, the God-Man."

"Alas! Gods and men shall remain strangers, as men remain wretched, and gods sublime; that is man's curse and God's failure. And still, there is no light at the end of our dark tunnel, on that earth which is divine in essence and longing, but human in deed and fact. And how many men look above and beyond today, how many men still dream and still aspire? Who today still gazes at the deep blue sky of Day, and at the starlit ocean of Night? Man is becoming more human and less divine, thus gods remain remote and unreachable stars in the sky of a fallen humanity."

"But why is it so? Why does God remain unknown? Why do gods remain gods, and men remain men, instead of merging together in a holy union, thereby sealing the sacred circle of Perfection, which is immanence of Spirit, and transcendence of Form? What is the wisdom behind the mystery of Life, what is the wisdom behind all mysteries? Why were men born with a limited consciousness that could conceive a god, but not *witness* a god? A mind that could think of a god, yet not *live* the Life Divine? A soul that could long for the beyond, yet is unable to pierce the great cosmic mystery? This failed god who failed at his craft of creation, what kind of a god is he, to create such an imperfect creature, man? And if there is no God, what then is the blind force that created this world? Could chaos create Order? Could Order create chaos?"

"Only a conscious Force could be called God… but then what kind of a god creates imperfect creatures and asks them to be perfect as he is? What kind of a god creates dark and fallen creatures, and asks them to behold and become the Light, and rise to its peaks? No, no, no, men and God, men and gods remain eternal strangers, ever separated by the inviolable laws of Nature and Life; the higher and the lower remain distinct, for Nature is aristocratic, and the universe is an endless Hierarchy."

Having carefully listened to Arya's lament, the prophet replied: "you utter words of wisdom, you speak like a goddess; yet, dear Arya, even the wisdom of the gods is a wine that needs to mature in the dark caves of the earth, before it can deliver the sweet taste of Truth. Thus, you should suffer until you awake and hear the inner voice of God whisper in your ear the sublime words of a higher truth, and the entrancing symphony of a deeper reality. Until then, your suffering is the cross that you must carry on the way to your own crucifixion, for only those twice born in body and spirit know and live the divine life."

"I know your pain, Arya, it is the suffering of all seekers of Truth, and it carries in its bosom the future of man; and man's future is bright, though he knows it not and cannot lift the dark veil of gloom that engulfs this poor earth. The fate of God and Man is one, as Wholeness is the essence and aim of Life. I see your future, Arya, and it is bright; so do not despair, for things will unfold just the way they should, as

Life has its own reasons and serves a hidden purpose that we only grasp as we leave it, on the threshold of a new beginning."

"You suffer from man; do we not all suffer from man today? Man: that highest hope and biggest failure of the gods. But do not despair, for you must evermore invent a meaning for your life; how else would you bear its emptiness? You suffer on this earth, as a goddess, but you still have much of the woman in you; thus you should learn to control, to transcend, to overcome your humanity, so that you can free yourself from pain, for pain is a human curse that afflicts gods who tread the earth."

"Your suffering is your greatest lesson in life; you should accept it and learn from it. You should learn to transcend the human in you by overcoming the pain that pulls your soul ever closer to the abyss of despair. You search for a way out, but the whole universe is your home! You seek the Light, but the Light dwells in you. All else is a mere reflection of it, for Pure Light cannot be seen; it is felt and lived."

"Weep not because you suffer, for suffering is the beginning of birth, it is the key to change, the sign of creation. You are on the right path, the path of Wisdom, which is fraught with the thorns of Truth and the spears of Awakening that slay the flesh to awaken the spirit; but the Tree of Wisdom delivers the sweetest fruit, the fruit of the gods. You are pregnant with new ideas, you carry within a new dawn, that is why you suffer. All birth is painful, all creation involves a certain death. But all mothers welcome the pangs of birth and bless the pain of delivery, for a new life waits at the end of all suffering."

"You say you are a goddess, Arya, but you still have much of the human in you; you need to free yourself from your humanity, that humanity which needs and clings to identity. And the human in you resists your second birth, for it involves its own death. The Higher Self kills the ego, and the ego kills the Higher Self; both want to rule, and both either rule or die."

"Hence, only when you shed the human in you shall you live the Higher Life, which is above all forms and identities, a realm unto its own, the realm of Pure Spirit. You cannot remain torn between the human and the divine, you cannot remain torn between what you are and what you can be. You cannot remain a bridge, you have to cross the bridge, for bridges were made to be crossed. We are all bridges, and most of us decide to remain so; only gods cross the bridge that leads to their higher selves and thus fulfil their destiny, on this earth as in heaven."

"You condemn God as a failed creator; but there is *no* creator, God is Pan, He is the All, He has no beginning and no end, He has no past and no future, but is the Eternal Now which perpetually reinvents itself. Arya, before you declare war on the world and on God himself, you should wage your own war, the war against yourself; for it is the ultimate war, the hardest one you will ever have to wage. It is the war that will determine whether you remain a woman or become a goddess. For in every man a god and a demon are at war; and only when you have silenced the woman in you will the goddess in you awaken; only when you have silenced the voice of Man in you shall the voice of God speak *to* you and *through* you."

"You say you are lost, and you condemn Life for *your* misfortunes. Yet the truth is that life is innocent of all misfortunes; Life is innocence itself, a blank page upon which you write your own legend, with its joys and miseries. You think you are lost, but the truth is that your mind *thinks* you are lost, whereas your soul *knows* whence it came and whither it is going, for the soul has its own purpose beyond the mind's limited understanding and the senses' fallible touch."

"You should suffer in silence, for silence hallows all suffering; you should bless your pain, your pain should be your joy, for there is wisdom and meaning in all *true* suffering. You should suffer, so that you might bestow. Your suffering itself is divine, it unveils your hidden divinity which wants to transcend, and by transcending, create. Men do not understand your suffering, for yours stems from a divine longing, theirs is all-too-human. Yet your questions should be your answers, and your longing should be your goal. You should behold life with divine eyes, only thus shall you see beyond suffering and start looking at Life's hidden meaning and secret aim, beyond all limitations, and above all shadows."

"Arya, you should delve into your suffering, you should extract from it the divine, and learn the lessons to be learned; stop clinging to the ghosts of the past and the illusions of the future, and start creating your eternal present, your eternal glory that knows not the limits of time or space. Those who cling to the past are the unproductive and idle dreamers, for to ruminate the glory of the past is to slay its memory."

"You are treading the path to divinity, beyond nations, cultures, and all human identities, the greatest and lowest of them; you are walking towards Unity, where all contrasts and all shades fade into a divine harmony; where all questions find their Answer, where all wars lead to one victory: Supremacy; where the particular becomes universal, and the human becomes divine. You are shedding all your transitory and illusory—and the transitory *is* illusory—shells and identities on your glorious path to divinity."

"If your goal is noble, Arya, you shall attain it; for nobility is a divine virtue, and is there a nobler goal than the divine? I believe in you, Arya. I have always believed in you, for underneath your different forms shines the same eternal flame of divinity. You are walking the path to greatness, and greatness shall meet you halfway. Believe in yourself, live your dream, and it shall come true, and *you* shall come true, a goddess who inspires and lifts men. Serve your cause with all your faith and all your devotion, and worry not about the results; for to man belongs the will, and to God belongs the way."

The mission

Arya was moved by the prophet's words of wisdom, but though her mind was convinced, her heart had yet to submit to the dictates of reason; for the burning sun that beats in man knows not the coldness of the mind, as it only radiates the warmth of love, and ever kindles the flames of passion. And so, her soul still yearned for the land which bore her, and she sought to join again that broken link with the divine, which she believed still slumbered in the land of the gods. "My ears have heard the voice of Wisdom," Arya told the prophet, "but my heart only hears its own beats and dances to its own melody of Life and Love; thus it bids me to go back to my Hyperborea, my Ultima Thule, for only there will I find the Light that shall awaken the goddess within, only there will I seal my divine destiny. It is *there* that my sons await me, those shining stars that have survived unscathed in this darkest age, away from the filth and dust of human wastelands and deserts. And though Race is above Nation, still there are promised lands for those *truly* chosen to lead and to elevate."

Somewhat irritated by Arya's stubborn loyalty to the ghosts of a long-dead past, the prophet answered her in a stern voice: "you confuse soul with soil, and though some lands are chosen, and some places remain sacred, still, God draws no boundaries and knows no limits, as the Spirit is eternal and infinite. Thus, superiority is nameless and formless, and it only speaks the universal language of God."

"The noble spirit dwells within man and above nations. Therefore, forsake the illusion of time and space, and learn the lessons of the Spirit."

"Discover the geography of the Spirit, which is boundless, and unlearn the earthly geography of states, nations, cultures, and languages;

for the geography of the soul dances above the frontiers of nations and beyond the finite world of men, as it reflects the soul of the Absolute."

"Discover the history of the Spirit, which is timeless, and forget the history of men with its evanescent glories and its fading victories; for the Spirit, on its endless journey, unveils the sacred mysteries of the universe and the secret history of the Religion of Nature, that mother of all religions and daughter of Divine Wisdom."

"How can *you*, a goddess with a sacred mission and a holy message, cling to *any* land? For no land is holier than the religion it embraces, and no people are greater than the cause they fight for. The Spirit is above all identities, and gods are but Its messengers; therefore, you should serve the Spirit before and above all else. And though the land of the Goths used to be the land of the gods, today nation has little to do with race, and man has little to do with God."

"God dwells neither in the North nor in the South, neither in the East nor in the West. God dwells in the soul of each heart beating with the breath of Life, and He lives in the heart of each soul longing for the gift of Love. The Universal knows no boundaries, thus your mission is above men's shadows and dust — and know that the greatest of human feats remains shadows and dust in the eyes of God."

"Arya, you are above all identities, you are above all names and beyond all forms. You are the voice of Eternity singing in the winds of Infinity. You are the All that perpetually seeks and overcomes itself through its varying faces and its various shades. You are not a limited ego, but an infinite Self that merges its soul with the soul of God. If you cannot learn that first lesson in Life, how could you teach men their divine destiny?"

"But how can I forget the past," Arya replied, "how can I let go of that which made me who I am today? And though Race is above Fatherland, still *my* race and *my* Fatherland remain bound by that sacred, unbreakable link which joins the human with the divine. Thus, I cannot sever the golden chains which bind my soul to that last home of the last Great Race, for that would be betraying my soul and my race — and to the noble, honour is loyalty —; and Race is Spirit, and Spirit is God. I cannot, I *will* not fail my people. Nation is still the body of Race, and God is its soul, and one need not choose between body and soul."

"That is why I must go back to the future of my race, I must enter the dark tunnel of the past which leads to the golden dawn of the future, and thus redeems the present. I must find the lost land of the gods, for it is only there that I will become a goddess again, there where the glory of a higher race once shone on the whole world, illuminating the dark sea of mankind with shimmering rays of light, and hallowing the desert of man with the gift of life; there where the splendour of nobility elevated men into gods, lighting the night sky of a fallen humanity with the sacred flame of divinity. O how I long for my Eternal Fatherland, that abode of gods on earth!"

"I must go back, so that I may go ahead. I must remember, so that I may achieve; that is how I feel, and the heart betrays what the soul keeps secret and what the mind denies. *Gott* and Goth are one in the eyes of *my* truth. That is why I left the world of men to search for the land of the gods, up there in the North, where the divine odyssey on earth began."

The prophet, growing impatient with Arya's obstinacy, pushed a deep sigh of exasperation, saying in an austere tone: "matter enslaves, Spirit liberates. The material is a fall, a curse, a punishment; the spiritual is a promise of harmony and perfection. You are above all identities, the highest and the lowest of them. You are the Spirit Eternal, the Life Divine, the Love Supreme, Absolute Force. Arya, you are Eternity itself, so why do you cling to that which is illusory and transitory? You are a goddess, so why do you cling to earthly attachments? Honour is loyalty, indeed, but remain true to *yourself!* Remain true to your mission and your goal; to the essence, not the form, to the spirit, not the letter."

"I bring my people a gift," Arya answered with confidence, "I am going back to *my* promised land, the land of my forefathers and grandchildren, to fulfil my destiny and to seal my fate — and one only fulfils one's destiny in one's destined land. I am the standard-bearer of a new message, a new religion for the most godlike of men, those most pious among the godless, those most godless among the pious,"

"those whose faith betrays not the spirit of their race, and clings not to the mirage of superstition in the desert of human existence,"

"those whose reason denies not the unseen, and bows down in reverence to that which is beyond its realm,"

"those who refuse to worship strange gods and false prophets and prefer to remain godless, strangers to God rather than strangers to themselves,"

"those who believe in the eternal Spirit and shun the dead letter which fades and vanishes into the dust of transience — for Truth is eternal and immaculate and impervious to the distorting curse of Time,"

"those free men who kneel before no idol, but worship the god within."

"Those are my sons, those are my people; it is for them that I go back whence I came, it is for them that I carry my highest hopes and preach my greatest destiny: the God-Man, that god in the making, the man who has overcome himself and has reached the horizons of a brighter tomorrow."

"I am the messenger of the Coming God, I am the daughter of Pan, and the Mother of the future of Man. I am the harbinger of Light in a world drowning in darkness. I bring my people a gift, so that they may believe in themselves again and trust in *their* god again, for He has long been buried in the grave of Unbelief and Superstition — and is not unbelief the unwelcome child of superstition? My people need a new faith, for they lost theirs when they embraced strange gods, and to lose faith is to lose face in the eyes and the grace of God."

"The divine and the human clash on this earth, and though many wars have been fought, and much blood has been spilled between men, the *only* holy war, the only *real* struggle remains the struggle between the race of Light and the race of darkness, the struggle between gods and men. That war has yet to be won, that victory has yet to be achieved here on earth, so that the fate of Gaïa could be sealed; will it be human, or divine?"

"The holiest of wars has yet to be won, the noblest of goals has yet to be attained. The war of the Spirit, the war for the millenarian cause of Truth remains the only holy war; and is there anything holier than a war fought for a noble cause? And what nobler cause than Truth? *That* is my mission and my destiny. That is why I should seek the land of the gods, even if it only lives on in my memory and my imagination — for to remember is to revive, and to imagine is to create."

"My mission is to redeem my people, to make them great again, to find the Light that would again kindle their inner flame and guide them back on the shining path to glory and Immortality. For my sons have ever kindled the flame of divinity in men's hearts, and filled their minds with noble thoughts and higher ideals. My sons have ever imbued this wretched humanity with the breath of God, and sanctified Life below with the promise of elevation and perfection. My sons alone are the Sons of God, the Noble Warriors of Light and Life; they alone carry the seal of divinity on their foreheads and in their hearts, they alone deserve to be called god-men."

"But to redeem my sons and lead them on the right path, my soul should again be baptised in the blood of honour, up there in the cold North where Honour was first forged and Blood was first honoured, on the battlefields and in the hearts of men. My soul should again be blessed with the sacred rays of the boreal light, the light of that Sun of God which never sets. For that is what I am searching for: a holy land to rule, a higher race to guide, a coming god to revere. Ah, that I may sing again the divine hymn to my Eternal Fatherland, my Hyperborea!"

As Arya fell silent, contented with that divine feeling which swept her soul while she was reminiscing her divine origins, the prophet woke her up from her brief slumber, saying: "what has befallen the gods today? Have you gods become mad and blind? Mad about men's petty identities and idle definitions, and blind to the Spirit which bore you? Is it this earth which makes you cling to the illusory, and lose the essence? I speak to you of Divinity and Eternity, and you speak to me of Blood and Soil! What is this human curse that you carry like a chain to your divine soul? If gods start to think and act as men, *who* shall redeem humanity? For are not men but fallen gods and failed hopes? The human god fell when he was crucified, yet he rose again when he transcended the bounds of time and space; so do not crucify yourself on the cross of attachment, unless you are ready to rise again beyond all of Life's contingencies and limitations."

"Attachment is human, detachment is divine; so be attached to no land and to no man. Seek your sons with your heart, and your god with your soul, for the whole universe is in you, and what men call 'the world' is but a pale reflection of the realm of God. Know that your *real* sons are to be found all over this earth, for they are the beloved sons of Nature. But to find them, you need not seek them, you only need to find yourself, and *they* shall come to you; for they live not in nations and states, they live below the earth — whose depth they alone fathom — and above men — whose heights they alone perceive —; they thrive in their own divine realm, away from the stench of those lowest of men who rule this doomed earth today, and they await their next battle and their final victory. So stop seeking outside and start living inside, for only when you look into your own Self shall you find your sons and your home. Home is a state of mind, and men are but mirrors of one's soul."

"But if I was born to lead," asked Arya, "then where are my followers? Are *they* born yet?" "You seek your followers," the prophet answered, "but *they* should seek you; you await your sons, but *they* shall find you. So worry not about your followers, and focus on your path, for yours is the path of the future."

"A true leader does not seek his followers, he just leads the way, and others follow, for only *he* knows the way, only he *is* the Way. A true leader forges warriors and moulds heroes."

"And a true master does not have followers, he has disciples. Tyrants have followers, masters make disciples, leaders breed leaders. And you are both a master and a leader, though you still lack the maturity of the former, and the perseverance of the latter."

"Seek not your followers, Arya, for you should make disciples and breed leaders; and disciples do not follow, they *become,* they find themselves, whereas followers only follow and thereby lose themselves *and* their leader. For though there is One Goal, there are many ways. But yours is the Way of Creation, the Way of Transcendence and Elevation; so, control, Arya, control your senses and transcend your mind, for they are but instruments on your way to your Higher Self and your higher destiny."

"You yearn to preach the holy word to your sons, but, until you do so, you should write your thoughts with your blood, for the letter is the spirit of the word, and its silence speaks louder than the noise of language. The written word is holier than the spoken word, for it bears the stillness of divinity and the seal of Eternity. So write your legend on the pages of your own soul, and you shall inspire generations upon generations."

Arya was moved by the prophet's words of wisdom, yet, although they touched her soul, they did not convince her heart, and so, as in a trance, mesmerised by her long-hidden and forgotten fantasy that seemed closer than ever to be realised, she cried out: "O prophet! How I long to behold again the land that bore my soul, the land that bore all souls! What would I not give for a piece of my home! For I am seeking my home, and while I do so, my memory takes me back ages ago, beyond the dawn of Time, at that time when reality and legend were twins, when gods made the earth their home, and men, in their waking state, lived the divine dream,"

"at that time when my glorious Race of Light sowed the earth with its seeds of wisdom, when the only true nobility — the nobility that bore my name and spoke my truth — ruled the earth and spread the sacred words of gods to men, elevating them to the rank of titans,"

"at that time when the Master Race forged a nobility of blood and spirit, when one was a nobleman not by virtue of what he *had*, but by virtue of what he *was* and what he *did*, as spirit is inborn, not inherited, and *true* nobility cannot be bought or sold,"

"not a nobility of pompous titles and undeserved possessions, but a nobility based on superiority of the soul — and superiority is always innate, never acquired –, a superiority which transpired in noble deeds and lofty thoughts, and a title that was acquired by blood spilled on the battlefield of Honour — in the wars of men and ideas — and by honour upheld by loyalty, courage, and righteousness in both peace and war, and love and hate,"

"at that time when the highest ruled and the lowest followed, and the pyramid of Life was revered and preserved; for when the best rule, all are elevated and liberated, whereas when the worst rule, all are degraded and enslaved — and nothing is worse and more despicable than a tyranny which deceitfully calls itself Liberty."

"I lost my faith in mankind when it lost its faith in itself, and ceased to long for the divine. And men still wonder why the gods have abandoned them! Thus I search for my land, for my people, for only they are worthy of redemption." Thus spoke Arya, and a heavy silence fell upon the two soul-mates, a silence that seemed to last an eternity.

Arya's journey

A brief moment elapsed during which the prophet and Arya were absorbed in the unfathomable meaning of Life. But the prophet suddenly broke the peace, saying: "weep not for the fallen men and the fallen nations, for they have bid their time and served their meaning. And though everything recurs, nothing recurs in the same way and for the same reason. Thus, let bygones be bygones, let the past rest in peace, and its glory shine for all eternity in the timeless realm of the gods. But here on earth, things unfold in a different way, so learn to live and to love as men do, whilst fulfilling your divine dreams and achieving your highest ideals and reaching your farthest horizons."

"Learn to accept the law of Life which says: nations rise and fall, as men and stars and galaxies. For nothing endures under *our* sun — the sun of men, not the Sun of God —, as ultimately, the blessing of love surrenders to the curse of hate, and the bliss of attachment turns into the agony of loss, and the glory of power becomes the shame of defeat, and the splendour of the rise gives way to the misery of the fall… for life down under is ever thrown into the throes of death, as the Circle turns against itself when hopelessly it cannot transcend itself."

"Sand and dust can never turn to Life and Light, so abandon your illusions regarding the dead, even the greatest among them. Let the forgone heroes and their glories rest in the peace of Eternity and in the pantheon of Immortality, and fulfil your own mission on this earth — for one honours greatness best by perpetuating it, not by ruminating it. So seek not to revive the past, and worry not about the future, but live the present and thrive in its eternity, for the present alone is real. Your human genes cling to identity, as they long to belong, but your spirit is divine, and it recognises not the borders drawn by men and the flags raised by nations."

"You are lost in the details of men and the infinity of gods, torn between the illusion of belonging and the vertigo of transcendence; thus you find your home neither in the world of men, nor in the realm of gods, and you suffer eternally as a bridge between two shores, longing for both, belonging to neither… yet know that you are great, and your mission is greater still, *because* you are a bridge; for through the bridge, men cross into the world of higher forms and deeper meanings, and gods enter the realm of the possible and the real; and so, untold creation and unlimited fulfilment are joined together in a holy union and a divine symphony."

"You are both human and divine — human at heart and divine in spirit —, you are human in your divinity, and divine in your humanity ; that is why you are the messenger of the gods yearning for manifestation, and the hope of men in their divine aspiration. You are the bridge and the goal, so rejoice in your mission, and stop cursing your blessing."

"Know thyself, Arya, and you shall find meaning and purpose in life; discover your soul, and you shall find your path and your goal; for you are divine, and your mission is divine. Have you ever *truly* fathomed the depth and the height of your name? Have you ever shuddered with awe upon hearing your sublime name uttered by sages and saints as one of God's names? For your name bears the soul of divinity and the meaning of nobility — and nobility is the quality of the gods —, and in its sacred letters your eternal legend is unveiled, and your millenarian epic unfolds."

"Your name bears a divine essence and goal; therefore, know thyself, and you shall fulfil your destiny, which is the destiny of the highest and the deepest of men. Know thyself, and you shall redeem those still worthy of redemption in this unworthy age, in this dark world that has descended on us."

"But *who* am I, prophet?" asked Arya, "am I one, or many? Am I a fragment, or the Whole? Am I *me*, or the other? The object, or the subject? The witness, or the doer? The goddess, or the woman? When I am alone, basking in the hallowed presence of the Spirit, and bathing in the silence of the gods, I know my origin, my way and my end, and everything is clear and pure and bright. When I am alone, I am boundless and eternal, I am divine."

"But when I am among men, in this world where everything is in flux and nothing seems real, I feel like a stranger to my Self… and though my mind *knows* and my heart *feels*, still I have yet to remember my source, so that it may flow back into my sea. When I am among men, I am finite and mortal, I am a human wreck floating in the void of shattered illusions and unfulfilled hopes. So which am I, the goddess or the woman? For I am both, and neither!"

"Your soul knows whence it came and whither it is going," replied the prophet, "but your mind, numbed by the illusions of what men call the 'real world', has yet to fathom the secrets that lie buried within your inmost being. You know yourself, but you have yet to understand the language that your soul speaks, and *truly* listen to the voice of your heart. For heart and soul bear the essence, and the mind always lags behind in discovering what the soul is, and what the heart wants. So listen with your soul, listen *to* your soul, learn to speak its language, and you shall hear your own divine melody echoing in the infinite memory of the universe, which dwells in the boundless Being that *is* you. Learn to listen, Arya, and Truth shall bestow Her golden pearls upon you."

"Listen carefully, Arya, for I shall relate to you your millenarian tale, your eternal journey through Time. You are Arya, the human goddess, the Warrior Goddess of Light, Divine Spirit cloaked in human form. You are eternal, you are immortal, though you take on different forms to deliver the same divine message to different peoples — and the message remains the same, though men interpret it differently, for they only look at the form and ignore the essence."

"You saw the light in the North, where the Light first shone on the world, and you made your home in the heartland of this earth, in that cradle of divinity once called the kingdom of Gobi. Carrying the sacred flame of the gods to men, you travelled all over the earth, from North to South, from West to East, illuminating the world with the shining light of Truth and Beauty, sanctifying men with the divine dream of Justice and Harmony, and imbuing them with the holy cause of Elevation and Perfection. Your light has ever sanctified the hearts of men and transfigured their souls, bestowing upon them the gift of Consciousness and Awakening, and raising them into the higher spheres of the gods."

"With the divine inspiration of your radiant soul, and the heavenly power of your shining spirit, you erected monuments glorifying the memory of the gods who once trod this earth. With your iron will and your higher force, you laid the pillars of Civilisation, forging the Golden Chain of the Seven Sacred Nations which sanctified the world with the Word of God. And though these nations bore different names — men have called them India, Iran, Sumer, Surya, Egypt, Hellas, Germania —, though your homes have changed across Time, still their *real* name and *your* eternal nation remains the sacred abode that bears your name: Aryana, the home of the Aryas, the land of the gods, whose soul is Shambhala, and whose spirit is timeless."

"Your message is the eternal Word of God uttered in the silent prayers of the Masters, and hallowed in the Sacred Mysteries of the Initiates. Your names have changed through time — you have been called Saraswati, Shakti, Ishtar, Isis, Athena, Minerva, Ariadne, Freyja, Germania, and many other names — but your essence always remained the same. You remain forever Arya, Mother of All, the Noble Warrior of Light, the sacred labourer of Life sowing the seeds of a higher breed in the divine fields of Being. From you shall spring the future of man. Your dawn shall give birth to new suns, your Great Noontide shall beget the God-Man, the highest type of man. *That* is who you were, that is who you are and ever shall be."

"You are the virgin goddess of Wisdom, guardian of the sacred flame of Truth, for whose sake and in whose name you fought the hardest wars and achieved the greatest feats. With your blood, you wrote the word Glory on the wall of Immortality, and your soul sanctified the word Noble with the spirit of Divinity… yet your Kingdom has yet to come, and your warriors have yet to fight their final battle on this earth, a battle for the meaning of the universe, when the New Cycle shall dawn upon humanity."

"Throughout the ages, you spread the Light that redeems all darkness, and you preached the Word that erases all ignorance; and though most men shunned the Light, your *true* sons did not forsake you — and only those who kept your message immaculate and your spirit undefiled, deserve to be called your sons. Against all odds and beyond all tragedies, your sons remained true to you, they kept your spirit untainted by Time and unreachable to men, those distorted and distorting minds who smear all truth and curse all that is sacred and twist everything noble. Your real sons remained true to your spirit, honouring your name and immortalising your soul in word and deed; and everything great and beautiful that you see before you today is their work and your legacy."

"Your legend relates the sublime epic of Nobility, your cause carries the silent voice of millennia, your spirit speaks the ineffable word of Truth, and your mission reflects the Holy Spirit of divinity. You were sent on this earth to spread the divine word among men. You are born and reborn in the eternal odyssey of the Spirit and its endless journey in the universe."

"You are eternal and immortal: you were, you are, you shall become. You return eternally, across Time and beyond Space, and your boundless Self belongs to the inexhaustible ocean of stars above, and to the unfathomable depths of the earth."

"You dwell in the soul of God, and the soul of God lives through you. Thus, as you discover your Self, you discover the god that you serve and feel, for the way to God is within, and all quest ultimately ends where it started: in one's soul, which is the mirror of the Whole. And though you dwell in mortal bodies and suffer as men do, though your reason cannot reach higher truths, still your spirit is a luminous path that leads to God. To know and feel God, you need only to sink into your inner depth and unite with the source of all existence."

"You are That which was and which shall ever be, you are Pure Being and Eternal Becoming, That which is unborn and endless. You are the witness of Eternity, for you are part of it, and it is in you. You are history forever in the making, and divinity ever unfolding. You transcend Time, the Great Deceiver, you are Aïon, Time Eternal."

"Your Ego is but a garb worn by your Self to fulfil its divine destiny on earth. And though they often look and seem the same to you, know that the apparent is not the real, and your self is not your ego, for the essence is not the form. Your Self belongs everywhere at once, for the Whole is your home, your beginning and your end."

"You are boundless, you are Unity striving to fulfil itself in a world of varying shades and changing forms. Your god reveals himself to you in your inner infinity, and when you talk to your Self, you talk to God."

"Your soul connects you to the endless spirit of Time immemorial and the immeasurable soul of the Cosmos. And only when you rise above reason will you overcome your limitation and finiteness. For reason, on its own, stifles the spirit, even as passion, unbridled, clouds the mind. Intuition, not cold reason, is the gate to Eternity."

"You are the Ultimate Moment of the Spirit, you transcend nations and peoples, and the message that you carry to men is: seek God with your heart, do not seek him with your mind, for faith alone opens the gates of divinity; but true faith is pure and deep, it follows no rites and submits to no dogmas, but trusts in itself and listens to the voice of Intuition, which is the voice of gods whispered in the ears of men."

Arya was moved by the words of the prophet who knew her better than she knew herself, but a sudden feeling of sadness overcame her, and she said: "but, alas, prophet, what am I today? I am the goddess of Light in the age of darkness, the goddess of Wisdom in the age of ignorance, the spirit of Nobility in the era of the mob, in the era of decadence. I alone carry the flame of Freedom in a world of slaves who deem themselves free simply because they hold nothing sacred — save for lust and greed, which they revere as gods —, and trample on noble tradition and higher values… but those who hold nothing sacred are not the brave and the free, they are the worthless, the superfluous and the fruitless! For bondage to the senses and to the passions is not freedom, as those alone are free who have rid themselves of the tyranny of their own lower instincts, and the oppression of their own dark side."

"I am the goddess of Elevation in a fallen world, a lofty, enlightened soul in a base world of dark matter which knows neither the justice of Hierarchy nor the glory of Perfection. I am a higher spirit choking in a world of mist and sand and dust. I am the goddess of Perfection in the age of decay and mediocrity."

"Alas, prophet! Woe is me! I am a goddess in the age of men. I was born to lead and to rule, for the best *want* to lead, the best *need* to rule, and the best *should* rule! — thus commands justice —, but they seldom do — thus speaks reality — and justice and reality seldom meet in the world of men… for God has abandoned his Sons, and we are drowning in an age of darkness, perpetually falling, perpetually sinking into the abyss of the Void, into the void of the Abyss."

"Today the people rule, and the people never *could* rule, could they? Their values revolve around the immediate and the practical and the petty: immediate gain and practical living and petty delights… thus civilisation, to them, becomes accumulation, culture becomes leisure, ugliness is revered as beauty, money is worshipped as God, and justice is debased into equality — but true justice always was Hierarchy! — And so the world sinks ever deeper into its doom, ever a stranger to itself, ever farther from its divine essence and goal, a blissful illusion to men, a real misery to gods!"

"Alas, prophet! Of what account are my glorious past and my radiant future? What am I *today*? What has become of me today? For the present is all that matters in the end… and when the present is dark and awry, all glory and all hope fade away into the dust of illusions and delusions."

"Today I am but the shadow of my former glory, and my bright future is yet unseen to my eyes numbed by the clouds of my present misery. Today I am alone and weary and gloomy, I am a corpse waiting to be buried, and a soul waiting to be liberated. I am dead before dying, and with my demise my race will pass. My race has vanished, and it awaits its resurrection. My children are gone, and I await my grandchildren. The end of this world is near, and my god is coming: this alone is my redemption, my only hope and consolation. Thus today I search in vain for my lost golden race, for my lost god, for the lost Sacred Light, yet still I search and still I strive, for in all search there is hope, and hope gives life, as life carries hope."

"Yes, dear Arya, have hope," the prophet replied, "for your destiny flows into the destiny of the World. Your time shall come, you shall call on to the spirit of your race, your message shall go to the heirs of the Eternal Religion, the religion of Nature, the religion of Pan... and they shall be your race, your long-lost children and grandchildren."

"To those who belong to the deepest past and the distant future, you shall be their everlasting present."

"To those who belong everywhere and nowhere, finding their home neither among men nor among the stars, you shall be a refuge."

"To those who find no peace save in eternal self-overcoming, those who find no happiness save in the eternal quest for perfection, and find no purpose save in a creative and overflowing will to truth, you shall be their goal and their fulfilment."

"To those whose spirit is at home only on the heights, you shall be their peak."

"To those who are timeless, whose spirit is one with the Spirit of Infinity, you shall be the ocean into which their eternal Self flows back."

"To those who still dare to dream in a disillusioned world of broken wills and shattered ideals, you shall be their courage and their hope."

"To those who still believe in greatness and perfection in an age where greatness lacks and perfection is forbidden, you shall be their crowning and their glory."

"To those who are unmoved by defeat and impervious to tragedy, you shall be their greatest victory — the victory over themselves — and their deepest joy."

"To those who still believe in natural hierarchy, in an age where Nature is shunned and Hierarchy is banned, to those who still believe in Elevation in an era of mediocrity and degeneration, those who still trust in Nature's eternal law in a world that has turned against Nature, against itself, you shall be the throne upon which sits the redeeming soul of divinity, and through which speaks the uplifting voice of Pan."

"To those who know no god save the god they feel inside, you shall tell them: you shall be gods yourselves."

"As you discover yourself, Arya, you shall fulfil your destiny. As the inner goddess unfolds, the new religion will be revealed to you and to the world."

Having listened with the awe reserved for great words, Arya seemed at once moved and perplexed, and she asked the prophet: "but where are my peaks? Where shall I find my peaks? On which mountaintop? Are there any mountains left in this flat world we live in? Are there any peaks left in this round world we endure? Where shall I find my peaks, my refuge, my home? Will it be on the heights of God, or in the depths of Man? Can this earth again be called home, can Gaïa be redeemed? Or should we Sons of God look elsewhere for our peace and our goal?"

"Why am I here? Still this question haunts me, and no answer quenches my thirst! Why was I born here and now? Is it to find a light that has long faded, or a life that has long died?" Thus spoke Arya, and she sat gloomily, staring with empty eyes at the sky above her, steeped in the darkness of Night.

The divine odyssey

As the prophet did not respond, Arya seemed confused and somewhat dismayed at her companion's apparent indifference to her plight and lament. She looked at him with inquisitive eyes, desperately searching for a silent answer from the mirror of his soul, but, as she found none, she burst out saying: "why do you torture me so with your silence, my prophet and friend? For silence is the cruellest torture to those seeking answers and longing to hear the healing voice of the sacred Word."

"Do you not see the depth of my suffering, do you not feel the agony that grips my weary soul, that wretched wreck of divinity sinking in the sea of human misery, crushed by the weight of Life's heavy burdens and numerous riddles that find no answer save in the realm of ideals, there where Time's tyranny ends, and the reign of Truth begins?"

The prophet gazed deep into Arya's eyes and said: "Wisdom begins when questions become not ends in themselves, but milestones on the path to Truth, and pillars of the temple of Awakening; when the Quest leads to its destination and does not become a dead end of gloom and despair; when mystery does not overwhelm but turns into inspiration, and when inspiration turns into creation. Thus you should stop doubting and start affirming your truth, that immortal flame of divinity which dwells in you and need not be sought, but lived."

"Fear not, Arya, and have hope in Life and faith in yourself, for what you think is the end is only the beginning… what you think is eternal darkness is but the deepest night conceiving the Golden Dawn and delivering the brightest day, a new Sun for a new Earth and a new Man. Thus the curse of darkness shall turn into a promise of Light, and the end shall turn into accomplishment, and men shall again become gods."

"I have revealed to you your sacred path and your eternal journey through Time; I have unveiled before your inner eyes your divine origin and end. Now I shall speak to you of the journey of the gods, your fathers and forefathers… now I shall speak to you of the divine odyssey on earth, of the origin of the gods, their rise and fall, their demise and their promised rebirth."

"I shall now take you back to the dawn of Time to discover that Golden Age when the earth was the home of the gods, not their graveyard, and gods were the inspiration of men, not their rivals. I shall speak to you of a different world, a different god, and a different man. I shall speak to you of the real world and the real God."

"For the world we live in today is a dream, it is but the shadow of the real World; the god we worship today is but the ghost of the real God; and the men we see today are but fragments of the Higher Man. Today we live in an age of deceitful appearances and illusory certainties, an age of fleeting joys and constant suffering, where hope is a broken promise of liberation, and dreams are a hopeless longing for salvation."

"The world today is but a mirage in the desert of our thirsty souls and desolate minds… a strange mixture of pain and delight, of ecstasy and misery, an odd blend of heaven and hell, where life and death mix and clash, and men and gods meet and fight; where scepticism and superstition, those twin enemies, speak the same language of ignorance and decadence that deafens the voice of Truth. Ours is a world of fallen men and slain gods, ours is the Kali Yuga, the darkest of ages, the night of man and the death of God." Thus spoke the prophet as he gazed deep into the boundless sea of stars above, communing with the mysteries that slumber in the hidden memory of Eternal Night. He held his peace for a short moment, delving into his innermost Self, then he told Arya:

"We are thrown into the whirlwind of existence, helpless pawns caught in the clutches of unseen and blind Force, wretched creatures in a fallen world of darkness. We think we exist because we think, but existence and reality are two different things: existence is the outer shell of reality, it is the form taken by a deeper spiritual and eternal essence whose purpose ever evades the mind centred on the material and the finite. Hence we exist only as passing waves in the ocean of Eternity, insignificant grains of sand in the boundless shore of Infinity."

"But in man's inner recesses of the soul lies the unforgettable memory, but fading magic, of a better world and a Higher Life which he pursues as an ideal in an illusive future, unaware that it is but the reminiscence of a real past. Thus today man naïvely dreams of a better future, caught between the deceptive life of the apparent world, and the idle pursuit of the real world, lost in the void of irrelevance and absurdity. Still, that fallen and failed god remains a hope and a promise, for, though limited in his understanding and human in his limitations, he is infinite in his longing and divine in his aspiration."

"The world today is a dream and an illusion; the god we revere today is a mirage and a solace; and man remains a failure, the wasted fruit of the gods, a shattered dream and a lost hope. But there was a time, in a forgotten past unrecorded by human history — a time that men refer to as myth and legend, but that gods refer to as Satya Yuga — when the world was divine, when God and Nature were one, and men were the worthy sons and heirs of the gods. That was the Golden Age of gods and men, a divine spark of Light hallowing the eternal night of a Cosmos without beginning or end. For there is neither creation nor end to the universe, as Life is creative and perpetual evolution."

"That was the Golden Age of the dawn of mankind. But still, there is, and there ever remains, a different world and a different god and a different man for those Awakened Ones who look beyond and see through the dark veil of Night, their inner eyes piercing with arrows of fire the wall of ignorance that stifles this earth, uncovering the divine Light that lies beneath this fallen world of darkness. A better world, a higher world was and remains possible for us sons of the gods; that is our hope and our consolation, our ray of light in the darkness of man's night."

"Thus it all began at the dawn of time immemorial, in the realm of a timeless and boundless Whole, abode of Infinity and Spirit of Eternity, where the Alpha and the Omega perpetually joined each other in the sacred dance of the Cosmos."

"In the beginning was the Light, the Light of Pure Being, Absolute Silence, the sacred One who bore the Holy Trinity of Unity, Force, and Supremacy. The Light in His pure essence is unseen and shapeless, yet in the physical realm He takes form in the life-giving power of the Sun, whose rays radiate the invisible energy that rules the universe."

"The Light is One and remains One, though He has manifold names among men: His Sons, the sons of Nature, the pagans, worship Him as *Surya*, Savitri, Ar, Agni, Mithra, Shams, Shamash, Estan, Istanu, Suri, Sowelu, Sul, Aton, Helios, Aditi, Sunna, Sol. His Chosen Ones, the Initiates, call Him the I Am That, the Great Breath, the Great Principle, the Supreme Spirit, AUM, OM, the Tao. The philosophers, His seekers, call Him Sophia, *Geist*, Reason, Logos, the Good, the True, and the Beautiful. His lovers, the poets, call Him the Eternal and the Sublime, and sometimes Eros. The sceptics, His slayers, call Him Doubt — for even though doubt slays faith, still, is not doubt a veil worn by a wavering faith? — ; and even His ungrateful sons, those who call themselves godless and deny Him, still secretly acknowledge Him and openly revere Him as *Nihil*. The pious, His servants, know Him as the Unique and the Almighty. And among all His faithful, He is Known as Brahma, Ahura Mazda, Pan, Ammon, Baal, Ra, Apollo, An, Zeus, Jupiter, Odin, Wotan, God, Allah, and as many names as there are nations, religions, and cultures. But He remains One, indivisible and Supreme."

"With you, Arya, I shall refer to Him as God, Brahma, Pan, or *Surya*, the god of All who shines on all — for these names are the closest to your heart —, though throughout His manifestations, He has taken countless names, even if His qualities remain the same, and He remains the Unmanifest and nameless, That which is without form and beyond names."

"In the beginning was the Light of *Surya*. But the Perfect and the Absolute had His own divine longing for self-realisation and creation. And though His realm of Pure Ideas, of Unity and Supremacy was immaculate and ideal, still, even Perfection needs to look at Herself in the mirror of reality; even God needs to see Himself in the mirror of His sons and His creation. Thus, Pure Being became Eternal Becoming, the Unmanifest pervaded the World with His divine Energy, Unity manifested Herself in diversity, the One became the many, and God sent His gods and embraced Nature as his abode on earth."

"And so, in order to behold Himself in the mirror of reality, the Absolute and the Eternal, the One God with many names, *Surya* the Unmanifest and Brahma the Supreme, paid the ultimate price of divinity: He entered the realm of the finite and the limited. Thus began the divine odyssey on earth, the sacred journey of God in the realm of men. And the divine alchemy, which merged the immaculate Light of *Surya* and the Infinite Wisdom of Brahma with the world of phenomena, transformed the blind universe of Chaos into a harmonious Kosmos of Awakening, hallowing and uplifting Life below as a faithful reflection of Life above by imbuing Her with the divine essence of Pure Spirit, while bestowing upon That which is without form and above Time the blessing of self-awareness, and the gift of creation."

"*Surya* thus pervaded the universe with His Light, the life-force that imbues the world of forms with divine Energy, and bequeaths to the world of ideas the blessing of Life. Hence began God's descent into the spheres of men and the realm of creation, and His divine sacrifice, His fall into matter, gave birth to man's rise towards the peaks of the Spirit."

"I have revealed to you Brahma's nature, essence, and goal; now I shall reveal to you His different manifestations on earth and among men, although, Eternal and Infinite, He only takes form through the Divine Hierarchy of the cosmic spheres, first through His Sons, the gods, and then through *their* sons, the saints and prophets, those gods with a human face, those men with a divine soul. Brahma's eternal message to men ever remains the same: 'become gods yourselves', but His Word echoes differently in the ears of men, and His message touches in diverse ways the hearts and minds of the faithful."

"Thus, the Higher Men, those sons of the gods endowed with divine Sight and blessed with inner Light, see the eternal Spirit behind the fading Letter, and grasp with the depth of their sublime souls the timeless essence and the sacred mystery of His Truth, their inner eyes beholding with awe the glorious yet oft hidden meaning of His message; for Wisdom commands that Her Divine Daughter, Isis, wear a veil before men, as a shield against the wicked baseness of the ignorant — that ignorance of conceit which distorts and violates and mocks everything great —, and as an invisible entrance to the sacred Temple of the gods, a temple where no mortal can tread — and are not the wisest among men immortals, heirs and forerunners to the gods?"

"But to lower men, those flat souls and narrow minds unable and unwilling to look across the mirage of transience and see beyond the world of forms, the illusion of names, and the futility of rites, to those trapped in the blind darkness of matter, God remains a mystery eternally unsolved, and a Spirit ever unreachable, for they only see His fleeting shadow vanishing into the blond waves of sand in the desert of their existence, and they only hear the waning echo of His Word in their sombre valleys of death and desolation. Hence they cling to form and forego the spirit, they worship the name and ignore the essence, and they perform the rites, impervious to their meaning."

"Hence, Brahma the Unborn and the Undying remains eternally the same, His message remains ageless and His Spirit timeless, but it is men, those eternal prisoners of the Circle and its ruthless law, who differ and change, it is men who evolve and decline, who live and die, it is men who rise and fall, and with them, the image of the god that they created and venerated… and so men see *Surya* in a varying light and through motley shades and hues, according to their own level of evolution on the endless scale of the spiritual hierarchies, and He takes on different names and forms according to the age and culture into which He bestows His hallowed presence."

"Pan is changeless, but it is men who confer upon Him both their highest hopes and their deepest frustrations, and *they* create Him in *their* image and behold Him in *their* twisted mirror which reflects only the fleeting forms and the waning letters of the physical realm, ever blind to the invisible reality and the divine Energy that pervade and govern all Life."

"And so, That which is nameless and formless, both Pure Being and Non- Being, has been called manifold names, and has embodied various qualities among mortals, acquiring the attributes of men and races — for to each man and to each race their own god — , and His relationship with men is governed not by what He is — for He is the All That is beyond names and attributes and forms — , but by how *they* view Him: personal, tribal God, or impersonal, universal God; ruthless Tyrant, or loving Father; Creator or Destroyer; distant Lord, or Inner Christ; almighty Judge, or merciful Redeemer; god of Wrath, or god of Love."

"But beyond these attributes, different facets of the same God that men and races bestow upon Him as mirrors of their own soul, Brahma, *Surya*, Pan, remains the One God of Nature and Life, the Father of all gods, the God of Unity and opposites, the God of All and Everything: He is Ankh, the Life Eternal, and Anibus, guardian of the dead; He is Ahura Mazda, God of Light, and Ahriman, God of Darkness; He is Ares, God of War, and Eros, God of Love; He is Wotan, God of Wisdom and War; He is Thot, God of Wisdom, and Thor, God of Thunder; He is Apollo, God of Order, of Reason, and Elevation, and Dionysus the twice-born, Deva Nahusha (7), God of Frenzy, Passion,

Chaos and Creation; He is Adonis, God of enchanting Beauty, and Tammuz, God of eternal rebirth; He is the Creator, the Preserver and the Destroyer, Shiva, Vishnu, and Kalki, the divine Trinity, the Father, the Son, and the Holy Spirit, Osiris, Isis, and Horus."

"He is Krishna the Highest, Lord of Lords, and Buddha the humblest and the Selfless; He is Hermes Trismegistus, Messenger and guardian of the Occult; He is Allah the Just and the Merciful; He is Christ the Saviour and the Healer; He is the Judge and the Redeemer, the Avenger and the Liberator; He is the God of Good and Evil, the inner voice of the Archangel Gabriel, and the divine longing of Lucifer the Rebel Light bearer. These are all manifestations of the same God, for God is Whole, and the Whole cannot be separated from His parts, nor can He be reduced to His parts, or *confused* with His parts, even though the Whole takes shape *through* His parts and fragments, His perfect and His imperfect Sons: gods and men."

"The Light of *Surya* shines on All, and His redeeming rays radiate His Energy which blesses and permeates all existence, for He is endless and immeasurable, and so He remains innocent of men's ignorance and folly — that ignorance which wears the mask of sublime yet impenetrable Truth to hide its ugly, dark face, and claims to know everything and wants to label everything; and that folly which proclaims itself Wisdom, though it has never lifted the unfathomable veil of Isis —; but despite men's idle labels and hollow names, *Surya* cannot be confused with *Maya*; thus the god of men remains ever a stranger to the real God."

"*Surya* the Highest, Brahma the Absolute, Pan the Infinite, remains the One, the Light which reflects Himself in the World of motley forms and shades, the transcendent and the potential which lives through the immanent and the actual. The Light touches the world with His sacred rays and bestows upon it the gift of Life and the blessing of Love, yet He remains above the world and beyond all forms. Thus He reflects Himself in the life-giving Sun, in *Fohat*, the life-force, in the infinite power of the Vril, in the hidden force of *Kundalini*, in the divine beauty and harmonious hierarchy of Nature, in the electric Force of the Thunder and the divine spark of the Lightning, in the purifying flame of Fire, and in the all-pervading Energy which fills this universe. He is the faith that moves mountains and awakens the dead, He is the resurrection which triumphs over death; but His essence remains elusive, His Word remains ineffable, and, though His Spirit transforms the world, He remains ever indefinable."

"Thus began the Seven manifestations of Brahma in the world: Unity, to know Herself, descended into the visible realm of Duality, where the cosmic drama of opposites ever unfolds, begetting Life and Her twin daughters that deny each other, Good and Evil; and ever since, Light and Darkness have been at war within man and between men, and within Life itself. The One That became Two — both transcendent and immanent, potential and actual — then manifested Himself in the Trinity and Her Law of perfection which governs life and men below. Delving into the world of forms and phenomena, the Spirit then took shape and actualised Himself through the Seven realms of Nature and the microcosm man. Finally, Brahma manifested Himself in the Nine, then the Ten spheres that faithfully reflect the macrocosm on earth, thus closing the Sacred Circle of Life, above and below."

"Unity remains absolute, the Whole remains complete, but His manifestation is multiple and wears many shades and forms; and so the antinomy between God and gods is false, it is a mirage of the human mind, an illusive war that only rages within man's divisive spirit and narrow soul, as Pan rules All, and He alone is real, whatever names and forms He borrows to manifest Himself before men. There is a unity of God and gods, of God and His Sons. God is Life, God is Nature, and gods are the divine expression of Her forces on earth."

"Hence, in His longing to explore and pervade the lower spheres of forms, Brahma sent His Sons to earth, in the world of manifestation, to behold Himself, through them, in the mirror of awareness. In every deed they achieved, and in every word they uttered, the incarnated gods reflected God's Intention and Perfection, teaching men the Life Divine and leading them on Her shining Path. That is when civilisations, the only civilisations worthy of that name — not today's fake civilisation of accumulation, but the ancient civilisations of the Spirit, which served the divine will and goal on earth —, arose and blossomed, and men resembled the gods in body and soul, and upheld the divine harmony and hierarchy below, reflecting the divine harmony and hierarchy above. That is when Science and Religion greeted each other as sisters, not as enemies, and together formed the twin pillars of the Temple of Truth, through the knowledge that uplifts and the faith that transforms."

"Thus arose the kingdom of God on earth, whose lofty and noble rule transpired in the splendour of Gobi, in the glory of Atlantis, in the divine Thule, in the sublime Arcadia, in Babylon the city of God, in Ur the city of Light, in *Airyana Vaeïa* the land of the gods, in Ver the cradle of the Spirit, in Delphi the divine sanctuary, in the valley of the kings, land of the eternal pyramids, and in other great cities of the gods, living legends that testify to man's divine origin and nature, their ruins awaking in man glorious glimpses of his divine memory buried under the ashes of lost civilisations."

"But the Sons of Brahma grew attached to the spirit of gravity, that arch-rival of Elevation, and, enraptured by the immense power of attraction that emanates from human attachment, they gradually forgot the true bliss and divine stillness of the higher spheres whence they came. Thus they betrayed His Spirit by clinging to matter, entranced by its earthly delights, and addicted to the irresistible appeal of these two pillars of human existence: the intoxicating power of love, and the illusive dream of power. Therefore, instead of rising and transcending the material, gods fell into the black hole of matter and lost the consciousness and memory of their divinity, becoming more and more entangled in the human web of instincts and feelings and the corrupting pleasures of the flesh, ever more bound by the shackles of a world of shadows and dust."

"The earth-gods became victims of the human law of duality — which, though blessed with Love and Life, is also plagued by lust, fear, doubt, and death —, prisoners of a world where the illusion of separation distorts the nature and aim of existence, and thus curses it and impedes all progress upwards — for all *true* progress is a progress of the Spirit —, a world where quantity rules quality and the horizontal grows at the expense of the vertical."

"And so, instead of being a means for divine manifestation and creation, and a mirror of awareness, the human realm became the road to perdition and degeneracy, and the mirror of deceit which distorts all truth… and Gaïa the divine lost Her soul and became a world of ignorance and falsehood."

"Thus the play of opposites ceased to be the mirror in which Truth beholds and realises Herself, but became reality itself, that is, the human illusion called 'the world'. That is when Lucifer, the fallen angel, defied God, and the pride of the Ego crushed the divine Spirit that dwells in the Self; that is when hate became the sworn enemy of Love, and death plagued Life; that is when sickness and old age disfigured eternal youth and beauty, and the Fall dragged with it the winged spirit of Elevation."

"Gods became human, and they turned deaf and blind — deaf to the voice of God, and blind to His shining Light —, victims of that greatest of human follies, the delusion of good and evil, as they saw not that Lucifer was not absolute evil — for there is no such thing as pure evil, as Evil is the shadow of Good —, but a rebel waging war on the unreachable God,"

"and hate was not a sick feeling, but a Love unfulfilled, unexpressed, and unrequited,"

"and lust was but a love gone sick and awry, and expressed in its most contemptible form," "and ugliness was but Beauty disfigured by vice and impurity, and stripped of Spirit,"

"and death was but Life cursing itself for becoming devoid of meaning and purpose,"

"and sickness was Nature violated in Her essence and goal, punishing Her tormentors,"

"and old age was death knocking at the door of a life weary of itself,"

"and the fall was but divine hierarchy shunned and slain, and the expression of divine justice,"

"and deceit and ignorance were but Truth slandered, distorted, and defiled,"

"and weakness was but Force unmanifested and turning against itself."

"In this chaos of the senses and that desert of the spirit, divine innocence was lost, and divine memory faded into the fog of human chimera; and gods forgot whence they came and what they came to achieve on earth. And they became men."

"That is how the divine Atlanteans, those titans of the Spirit, became mindless giants. That is how Gobi became a lifeless desert, and Thule turned into a legend, and Arcadia was lost; that is how Babylon sank in the swamp of the chaos of races and cultures; and the light of Ur was buried in the shifting sands of idol worship; and the Spirit of Aryana was stifled by the smoke of a decaying humanity; and the valleys of the gods became the sacrificial altars and cemeteries of the divine; and the sublime monuments of the earth, erected to glorify the beauty of the heavens and echo the eternal voice of the Absolute, became ghastly and silent tombs of the unknown god; that is how gods sank ever deeper in the mud of earthly existence, and divine reality became human illusion."

"And so began the descent of the Light into the dark abyss of matter, and the odyssey of Brahma and His gods on earth became an endless cycle of rise and fall, of creation and decay, of death and rebirth;

for the divine, when manifested, is subjected to the law of karma that governs men."

"Thus began the fall of the gods and the cyclical law of evolution, the dance of the cosmos which unfolds in spirals of ascent and fall, whereby the ascent occurs as the higher bows down before the lower to elevate him, — thus perishing on the altar of a higher love, and in the service of a higher life —, and the lower in his turn is consumed by his own purifying flame of perfection, thus shedding his base shell and begetting a nobler soul. But, irrevocably, comes the time of the fall, which takes its revenge and drags in its dark chasm all life and all glory."

"And so the law of duality — which is the price paid by Unity in order to achieve self-consciousness and to perform the divine act of creation — put an end to the ascent, and a limit to the peak, and the apotheosis of the Spirit became the apocalypse of eternal recurrence wrought on gods and men by the devastating fall into the dark valley of the material and the finite; sent on earth to redeem and elevate men, gods themselves became victims of the scourge of the chain of incarnations."

"The glory of manifestation and the miracle of creation became the source of misery and suffering, for every living thing became caught in the inextricable net of separation, and the ruthless law of opposites, which put a limit to the realm of the Absolute, and an end to the reign of the Eternal. And so, manifestation slew the supremacy of the Spirit and brought on the decline and death of what once was ascending and creative life. And in our dark age, gods have been perpetually falling, drowning ever deeper in the dark and murky waters of sin and mortality."

"Unity was forever lost, and the Golden age of gods ended with the rise of man; the higher gods departed the earth, going back to the higher spheres of the eternal realm whence they came, and only the fallen gods remained below, mortals in a world of mortals, fallen gods in a fallen world; and hitherto, men have been desperately — but vainly — seeking to catch a glimpse of the fading light of divinity, to rekindle the sacred flame of man's divine origin and destiny, and to join anew the broken bond with that lost Unity: the lowest among men, the sensual, instinctive types, the Sudras and Vaishyas, through the base and fleeting pleasures of the senses, which gratify the body but slay the soul; the emotional, impulsive warrior types, or Kshatriyas, seek to recapture that lost unity through the heightened and sublime feeling of love, through the intoxicating feeling of power, the violent, destructive urge of war, the entrancing effect of music and dance, the uplifting power of faith and prayer, the ecstatic power of art and poetry, or through the gratifying feeling of right action."

"And the highest among men, the reflective and meditative types, the Brahmins, or Arhats, join anew the bond with the divine through pure reason and its selfless search for Truth, serving Her cause with unflinching devotion, through the earnest practice of meditation, an undying love of wisdom, and through the power of the word and its transforming magic that hallows the hearts of men and purifies their minds."

"Ever since the Fall, each man with a divine longing has followed and served Truth in his own way and according to his own nature and abilities, but Truth Herself remains One and indivisible, though She wears different forms, and Her same eternal message speaks different languages. And so, every human act, every human deed that brings man closer to divine Unity and revives Her spirit, brings joy and beauty, and elevates Life; and the further man departs from that original state of perfection, the more one suffers from the sorrow and agony of separation, and falls eternally into the dark, bottomless pit of death."

"But the divine odyssey on earth did not end with the fall of the gods, for their twilight heralded the dawn and the rise of men, as the highest among men retained the divine spark and memory of their forefathers, and strove along the ages to lead mankind towards the Light, that primal, abundant source of Higher Energy whence all life sprang. Hence, although the age of men dawned upon the earth, still those men with a divine longing, those gods with a human face, remained a hope and an inspiration for a humanity in search of meaning and purpose, shining solitary stars of a forlorn divinity, a beacon of hope from above lighting man's dark sky and deep night. Those were the Sons of God, the Great Initiates, the Masters and Seers, or Rishis, direct descendents and messengers of the gods, prophets and forerunners of the God-man."

"The Initiates kept the divine flame hidden and pure in the sacred temples of the Occult, away from the scorn of the ignorant and the filth of the unworthy, and they sought to teach the willing and the worthy the Great Mysteries of the divine origin and destiny of man, striving to awaken the spirit of divinity in the dormant consciousness of humanity. But their divine words fell into deaf human ears, and only among the Sons of the Sun, the sons of the divine Race of Light, did their celestial melody resonate in all its glory, echoing the heavenly music of the spheres in the depths of their noble souls. Those believers among the blind, those Awakened Ones among the sleepers, those Chosen Ones among the countless and the superfluous, became the adepts of the Natural Religion, which joined once more man's severed bond with Pan, and carried in its sacred teachings the original Word of Brahma, and the primeval fire of *Surya*."

"Thus began your epic, Arya, for it is with the Race of Light that the divine spark of creative genius lit the earth, heralding the rebirth of a new, divine Sun from the human ashes of fallen gods. Originally, in the Golden Age, before the hotchpotch of mob rule melted races and classes into a maelstrom from hell, there was one divine race on earth, God's glorious gift to mankind, the magnificent mirror of heaven below; and the sublime form faithfully reflected the divine spirit — unlike today, where everything is mixed and mixed up, and spirit and form seldom match; where gods, men and beasts mingle, and in their mingling lose their essence and their goal —. But after the gods fell, the Race of Light suffered the curse of division, as some of its unfaithful sons went astray, drifting away from the divine path, and sinking in the human swamps of earthly attachment, greed, idolatry, and lust for flesh and power."

"And so, the Race of Light soon split into two distinct groups that soon became two distinct species — for from the spirit evolves the body and the race —: those who remained true to Brahma and followed the Ram, symbol of Wisdom, Truth, and harmony, and those who forsook their divine vocation and worshipped the Bull, symbol of materialism, ignorance — with its twin offspring: unbelief and idolatry —, and blind fury."

"Those sons of *Surya* who revered the Light and lived in His splendour on the heights and served His Truth and His goal, hallowing the form and elevating matter in the divine act of creation and the human glory of manifestation, were known as the Aryas, or Noble Warriors of Light, the legitimate heirs to the divine throne, builders of the kingdom of God on earth, the divine ray of Light that shone on humanity and illuminated the night of man with the shining flame of Agni. Those were the disciples of the Rishis, sons of Manu and Rama, warriors of the Spirit fighting to spread His divine word among men, and to express the divine in human form and lofty deeds, thus joining anew man's severed link with God."

"The Aryas kept their spirit pure and their blood undefiled, thus they became immortals in spirit and perfect in body, gods in the making, and they upheld the divine cause in deed and word, communicating to the sons of men the message of the gods, in hope of redeeming them and rekindling the sacred flame of *Surya* in their frozen hearts and darkened souls. That was the divine origin of the Race of Light, the only divine race that has ever trodden this earth. Those were the warriors of Light, your only true sons, Arya. They were divine, and they remained divine until the end, proud in their defeat, honourable in their demise, dignified in their last breath and their last sigh of agony in this heaven of men, this hell of God called earth."

"But after the Fall, the bull worshippers, those bad seeds among the Sons of the Light, who preferred the shadow to the Light, attached to the material world, indulging in the ephemeral pleasures and bittersweet illusions of the senses, fell from the grace of Brahma and lost their divine sight; and they became mortals, caught up in the shackles of the curse of fear wearing the deceptive veil of power, and resentment disguised as justice and equality. Those were the fallen gods, who became men."

"And some of the men fell even lower, forever forgetting their divine origin, and stooped to the level of the animals, becoming mere human beasts, closer to the apes than to man. Those were the fallen men. That is the mystery behind the polygenetic origin of man, the origin of the secret and meaning of the variety of human races. For race is essentially a matter of spirit which moulds the form and perpetuates the genes of a higher or lower type."

"That is how divine memory faded into the fog of human illusion, and turned into a vague dream of a forlorn past, and an evanescent vision of an illusive future. And soon the Chosen Ones, misunderstood and spurned — for everything misunderstood is spurned by the masses — were persecuted by men, and driven into the underworld of the Occult as a refuge from a world fallen into the throes of blind ignorance and unbridled instincts, an oasis of Truth and Light in the dark sea of Night."

"Hence, the second fall occurred, the fall of man, as he failed to become what he was, a past and a future god. And out of the mixture between the remnants of the fallen gods, the various types of men, and fallen men, man as we know him today was born, neither a god nor a beast, but a rope and a bridge between two worlds, both a hope and a disappointment for the gods, a human failure that nonetheless remains a promise of divinity."

"Man as we know him today is radically different from the god-like creature—sublime in form and divine in spirit—of the forlorn Golden Age, whose beauty was immortalised in the statues of Greek gods, and whose spirit remains eternal in the ideals of a higher antiquity, in the divine wisdom of the Initiates, and in the occult meaning of the scriptures of saints and prophets; for at that time gods were men, and men were gods."

"In the beginning, Race and Nation were one, and both were divine; and the Seven Sacred Nations, the golden chain of *Surya* from India to Germania, drew the divine map of the world as the perfect reflection of the Macrocosm, and Brahma's faithful mirror on earth. That was the divine dawn of mankind."

"But today, Night has fallen on humanity, and a New Dawn awaits those men who have remained pure in blood and soul, gods in spirit, and supermen in body. Today the Circle rules men and nature below. And ever since gods became men, and men remained men, and fell even lower, ever since gods fell and men failed, the world of men has been revolving in circles and cycles, spirals of elevation and decay; and gods descend on earth as carriers of the divine Light, spiritual guides of humanity, and they experience the life of men, elevating them in their thrust upwards, while sacrificing their own immortality on the altar of self-consciousness and self-overcoming, pillars of all creation and all creativity."

"When the cosmic cycle reaches its climax, when the Great Noontide is upon the world, following aeons of noble words and deeds, and an earnest and honourable struggle in the service of Truth and Justice by the Sons of God and the sons of Man, gods manifest themselves on earth, and they are at the peak of their glory, and men are at the height of their splendour. In that Golden Age of gods and men, the Spirit rules supreme, reflecting His holy gift of Life, Love, and Beauty in the thoughts and acts of all creatures under the Sun; and everything turns into a living tribute to the divine, and a grateful praise to the Lord of the Worlds. And Life is hallowed in Her glory, Nature is revered in Her excellence, Hierarchy is upheld in Her justice, Truth is embraced in Her supremacy, Force is admired in Her energy, and Beauty is venerated in Her divinity."

"But when the Cycle is at an end, and another cycle is dawning, death and darkness loom on the horizon of man, bringing with their promise of a higher life untold misery and decay; for the law of Life commands that all that is born is destined to die, and all that dies is destined to be reborn, and so death is a condition of life. When the cycle is in its night, Nature is desecrated in Her laws and Her beauty, and the world becomes awry and crooked and base... and everything is turned upside down, death is revered and Life is reviled, darkness is preferred to Light, Truth is slandered and Justice is defiled, Hierarchy is crushed and Excellence is mocked, Love becomes lust, and loyalty turns into treachery... Honour becomes servility, and Supremacy gives way to blind force, the absolute is shunned and the relative is admired, Beauty is tarnished and bears the scar of impudence, shame, and impurity... and everything pure and natural dies out in the reeking wastelands of greed and decadence, those graveyards of the Spirit."

"That is when Brahma sends His gods to earth, to redeem a fallen humanity and purify Gaïa from Her bad seeds, and rid the Tree of Life from its rotten fruits; that is when Vishnu the preserver is reborn as Kalki the avenger and the destroyer, to cleanse the world of baseness and darkness that wear the mask of evil... and divine justice is carried out through floods, wars, and pestilence."

"Today, the Circle rules the world below as the nemesis of the gods, and the cross upon which man crucifies his lower nature and awakens his Higher Self. Indeed, the age of men soon fell into decadence, for, instead of striving on the divine path to perfection and immortality bequeathed by the gods, men fell even deeper into the prison of matter, strife, division, and limitations, as they ceased to think as gods and thus lost the memory of divinity and the spirit of Eternity."

"Men fell, giving rise to prophets and their religions — some of them real, godlike saints and faithful messengers of God, and others liars and hypocrites, traders of the spirit, prophets of doom or merchants of illusion —, whose aim was to revive God in man and redeem a humanity fallen into the throes of base and unbridled instincts. Hence, there was a fall in matter instead of an accomplishment of Spirit."

"The fall of men preceded their evolution, for though evolution is the law of life, Life began with a fall, Life began after death, as the rise of men followed the fall of gods, and men's rebirth followed their demise. That is the iron law of the Circle that rules this earth. That is where Science and Religion meet, as the law of evolution applies to fallen creatures. The ape is a fallen man — not his ancestor, as those superstitious among the scientists contend —, as man himself is a fallen god. That is what our world is made of: fallen gods, fallen men; men and beasts, beasts and men. That is where Divine Wisdom becomes the science of the Spirit, where Science and Religion merge and end their perennial useless and senseless war. And whenever Reason and Faith meet and agree, great feats are achieved, and God and man are reconciled in the glory of Unity, whereas only superstition and chaos arise out of their disunion, for Truth is one and indivisible."

"And so the second fall, the twilight of men, was the dawn of Religion. For when men fell and lost their divine memory, and became blind in a world of shadows, Religion became the standard-bearer of Truth, and the written word bore the eternal voice of God, to join once again the lost bond and the broken link with the divine; for the *real* missing link is not that between man and ape, but that between man and God."

"That, originally, was the aim of the Eternal Religion, the Natural Religion. But due to men's ignorance and rampant materialism which clouds the spirit of Truth, the Religion of Pan, which reconciled Nature with man, and Faith with Reason, soon gave way to men's countless religions, unfaithful imitations of the one divine message, each religion and creed seeking to appropriate Truth and to encapsulate Her infinite and indivisible essence in the narrow confines of rites and dogma and culture, drowning Her timeless soul in the quagmire of history, which sacrifices eternal Truth for the sake of immediate power. And, with the demise of their founders, these religions in their turn were further distorted, as the last spark of the divine faded, stifled by the smokes of the incense of idolatry and superstition."

"Thus, the one divine perfect message, heard, read, and understood differently by men, was torn asunder, splitting into several imperfect human creeds and sects. In the blind eyes of a deluded humanity, the messenger became more important than the message, the Son was confused with the Father, the Inner God became the outer idol, the Way became the end; and so the Sons of God were worshipped instead of emulated, and their worship turned into the instrument of superstition and the weapon of the wicked and the unconscious to serve their lust for power. The Messiah was no longer a symbol of inner liberation from the shackles of earthly limitations, but instead became a broken promise of a future that never comes; and the hidden meaning and essence of Religion was shunned for the sake of crude rites, shallow names, soulless beliefs, and meaningless ceremonies. That is how religions slew the very message they came to preach, and Truth went into the safe haven of the Occult, away from the rising tide of ignorance that swept a world sinking ever deeper into chaos and darkness."

"And so, religions followed one another in an endless but useless chain, after the Golden Chain of Divine Wisdom was severed by human delusion, as each religion sought in vain to correct the misinterpretations that distorted the previous one, and itself fell into falsehood and fragmentation. Hence, God's Word was read upside down, and His Truth was mutilated beyond recognition, prompting *our* prophet from Sils Maria, that most pious among the godless, to proclaim the death of the god of men, that curse to the real God. But it was the god of men who died, it was the tyrant-god of religions who died, not *our* God, *Surya*, whose all-pervading Light eternally shines on His Chosen Ones, even in the darkest night, as that light dwells in the soul of every true believer and can never be extinguished. Pan remains supreme and eternal, and, as Dionysus, He shall emerge again victorious and whole, when His Sun shall again dawn upon men, in the coming age of the God-man."

"As each religion came to correct the last distorted one, the divine message was lost in the details of men, and so religions too fell, their message disfigured, historical facts crushing the timeless reality, empty rites crushing the eternal spirit, idolatry replacing emulation, superstition replacing faith. When Truth was deformed and slandered, fragmentation ensued, thus the one divine Religion became several human religions, and religions in their turn split into countless factions and sects, waging war on each other for the sake of an illusive god, each claiming to preach the true message, but none bearing the divine and eternal seal of Truth."

"Blinded by ignorance and deafened by the drumbeats of hate, war, and division, men did not realise — ignorant and blind and deaf as they had become — that the message, the content, the soul and aim of each religion was essentially the same, though cloaked in different forms and bearing different names; and so, men mistook the hollow shell for the essence, and Truth was forever buried in the mud of ignorance."

"Religions became decadent and distorted, and, instead of raising and liberating men, awaking the god within, they themselves became instruments for the enslavement of man. And there is no greater tyranny on earth than the tyranny established in the name of God — for God is no tyrant! He is the all-loving and Life-bestowing Father. Truth, slandered, disfigured, defiled, was crushed to earth, Her divine voice deafened by the crossing of human swords fighting in Her name."

"Thus came the twilight of men and religions. But as the world revolves in cycles, and the Circle reigns supreme, the fall of men shall again herald a new sunrise, and a new day shall replace the long night of God and man."

"That is the story of God in the world, the divine odyssey—and tragedy—on earth, the rise and fall of gods, men, prophets, and religions. That is how the divine word was praised and hallowed, then shunned and slandered. But the divine race, the only genuine Master Race, the Master Race of the Spirit, remains the only ray of Light in that sea of human darkness, the only hope of redemption and rebirth for men and gods, for it has inherited the legacy of the gods, forever impregnating this earth with its golden seal of Perfection, and its own, eternally inspiring epic—which is yours, Arya."

"Therefore, I shall now take you further in the past, before the Fall, at a time when hierarchy on earth reflected Hierarchy in Heaven; I shall now relate to you the rise and fall of the Master Race, your forefathers and your children, that last remnant of the divine Sun on earth."

The rise and fall of the Master Race

1

"Before the Fall, there was one divine Race and one divine Religion on earth. Men lived in harmony with the gods, and divine hierarchy was faithfully reflected in Life, as Nature's law applied to all living beings. At that time, the sacred was revered, not reviled, and the pyramid of Life was praised in its perfection, and upheld by each man according to his rank on the scale of the Spirit. Thus, harmony ruled, justice prevailed, and perfection reigned supreme, and men knew not the misery of suffering and the curse of death. They were immortals living the

Life Divine and blessing and praising Her with their lofty thoughts and feats."

"That was the dawn of the Golden Age, the dawn of the Race of Light. That was when the epic of your race, the Master Race, began. The Golden Chain of Light, the golden thread which weaved the divine geography of the Spirit across the ages and above the frontiers, started with Manu, the Great Legislator, the first of your sons, Arya. Manu was a Rishi, a Son of God, founder of the first divine religion, at that time when Religion brought man closer to God, — not farther from Him —, when the sacred bond linking man with God still performed the perpetual miracle of creation, and bestowed upon gods and men the priceless gift of Awareness."

"But after the fall, as gods failed in their earthly mission, and men failed in their divine mission, the wrath of Pan was great, and Mother Nature, wounded and dishonoured, Her harmony broken and Her hierarchy defiled, reclaimed Her stolen rights and avenged Her beloved sons, those who had remained faithful to Her divine order. Thus there was a great deluge that wreaked havoc and engulfed the earth, and Gaïa sank to Her doom, paying for crimes of which She remains innocent, crimes committed by Her ungrateful and unworthy sons… and only a few higher beings, those chosen for the salvation and redemption of humanity, were saved from the cataclysm that befell the earth, among them Lord Manu, who was saved from the flood, as he, like all Chosen Ones, was blessed and protected by the gods. Heeding the warning of his divine inner voice, which echoes the divine voice of Shambhala, that Island of Wisdom, that eternal Oasis of Light, Manu built a ship upon which he embarked when the flood came. The Noah story speaks of this deluge, though *that* was but a myth copied from the scriptures of the Babylonians."

"After the flood, and from the same Dynasty of Light, came the divine Ram, or Rama, Noble Warrior and Son of God, an Arya and an Arhat, a Kshatriya at heart and a Brahmin in spirit. He chose the Ram, symbol of Wisdom, as a rallying banner for his disciples and followers, whom he showed the Way to the Light, as he strove to guide them back on the lost path of divinity. Born and raised in the awe-inspiring forests of Europa, his was a great destiny that would transcend all human boundaries and transform all established identities; that is how, as a young man, he had a divine vision in which Deva Nahusha appeared to him, urging him to go East and spread the Light of *Surya* to all men; for merely living in the bliss and splendour of the Light is not enough, one has to serve Him and fight for Him."

"Consequently, Rama gathered his best to embark on his divine mission to preach Brahma's eternal message, through the word and the sword—for the word sometimes needs the sword to conquer ignorance and pierce its dark veil which blinds and enslaves men—. But even a spotless sky is eventually scarred by a passing dark cloud that defiles its immaculate beauty; and even among the best apples, one ultimately finds a hidden worm. And so, among Rama's followers, there were those in whom lay the seeds of betrayal, namely the two evil extremes which met at the crossroads of ignorance: the sceptical materialists, and the superstitious idolaters; it is those unworthy of being called Aryas who turned their backs on the Light and worshipped the Bull, symbol of lower instincts, vice, lust, idolatry, and decadence, abandoning the path of virtue, honour, and perfection."

"Thus the curse of division struck at the heart of the Golden Race, and the sons of the Ram and those of the Bull parted, each following a different path and a different goal: Rama's faithful, the great Aryas, a race of bold conquerors, warriors, saints, and creators, headed East to fulfil their divine mission in deed and word; as for the fallen Aryas, those unworthy of their glorious name and unfaithful to their divine lineage, they remained in their towns and villages, forever abandoning the glorious destiny reserved to them by the gods."

"Shunning their duty, the Bull worshippers lost their privilege, that of belonging to a Higher Race, thus joining the countless lives unworthy of Life that pollute this earth. Their descendants are the corrupt rulers and amorphous masses of the present age, the darkest of ages, the age of slaves ruling slaves. And though to this day, some of them keep referring to themselves as the sons of the Aryas, still, with such unworthy offspring, that once glorious name soon became hollow and lost its divine essence and meaning, even if its fading spirit still faintly transpires in the waning beauty of those unconscious of their own divine past and glory. For divine karma commands that the beauty of form is doomed to fade when in it the spirit no longer radiates."

"But today only those very few pure and true followers of Rama can claim such a noble title and privilege, though theirs is a life of solitude and secrecy among a decadent majority, in the East as in the West."

"As for the Sons of the Ram, the only real Aryas, they remained true to their soul and their goal; thus they travelled the earth, carrying the sacred torch of *Surya*, that blessed gift from above which hallows life below and kindles in every living soul the light of Eternity. From Sagarmatha to Bam, from Gobi to Bamyan, Aryana the chosen land of Brahma became the cradle of divinity on earth, and the mother of all civilisations. Its radiant spirit soon beamed its holy rays of divine inspiration and celestial elevation to the Seven Sacred Nations, the civilisations of the Spirit, among which it was the first and the most glorious. That is how, having travelled from West to East, preaching the divine word, Rama and his faithful triumphantly went back, from East to West, as a rising sun of divine awareness and sublime creation, spreading the seeds of godly creation on the path to Truth."

"Nevertheless, as the tide of ignorance swept the world of men and drowned the flame of wisdom in the sea of darkness, the sons of Ram were soon persecuted by a humanity already fallen in the abyss of idolatry and superstition; and so, Truth went underground, away from the stench of incense and human sacrifices. And the world fell into its darkest night. And *Surya*'s glorious Noontide became the twilight of the gods, and the eternal night of the idols descended on this earth. And Aryana, Gobi, Atlantis, Arcadia, Thule disappeared into the human fog of illusion and chimera."

"But throughout history, long after Aryana disappeared in the sand and dust of the human desert, crushed under the dead weight of unbelief and scepticism, long after that divine reality turned into human legend, it still remained an inexhaustible source of inspiration to the Sons of the Sun — whether they sat on thrones or slept in caves —, for those are the immortal Aryas, Noble Warriors of the Light who bear the sacred light of *Surya* and exude its divine warmth through their radiant souls, in their lofty thoughts and their noble deeds."

"That is how the enlightened ones among the rulers, from Akhnaton to Hadrian, from the Sun-King to the Great Frederick, and many other immortals, known and less known, served the Light and spread His glory. That is how the Great Alexander, that Initiate among the conquerors, wore the thorns of Ram in his conquest of East and West, on his pilgrimage from Greece to India in search of a lost divine Unity. That is how the great Cities of God remained living legends that testify to man's once glorious link with the gods."

"That is how the Great Guides of humanity, the Brahmins, Bodhisattvas, and Arhats, kept alive the sacred flame of Agni in the hearts of their faithful; for a people's soul resides in their faith, and most men lost their soul when they lost their faith. Hence, the divine, eternal message of Brahma was kept by His sons, who continued the divine odyssey on earth, ever loyal to their mission and end."

"Across the ages and throughout the incarnations, the Sons of God completed the golden chain of Light from India to Germania. And though the Chosen Ones bore different names and spoke different languages, still they delivered the same divine message — for God's eternal Word is above men's fading letters — and they embodied the same ideal of the God-Man. And so, the pantheon of the Immortals was filled with those most sacred of names: the divine Krishna, highest Lord on earth, also made flesh as Dionysus and Christ; the great Zarathustra; Buddha the Enlightened; Hermes, messenger of the gods; the sublime Orpheus; Pythagoras the Initiate… and many others, known and unknown Superiors, who served Truth and were crucified — in flesh or in spirit — on Her divine altar and her glorious battlefields."

"But as men forgot the message and worshipped the messenger, the divine Word became hollow, its radiance faded, as religion parted with Truth and thus betrayed God, falling into the stagnant waters of dogma. And the lethargy of the Spirit ensued. And the dead human Letter ruled the divine spirit of Life. And ignorance crushed Wisdom. And the Chosen Ones disappeared into the realm of the Unknown, there where no filthy human foot can defile the sacred ground of the divine, there where no bloody human sword can wound the immaculate spirit of Eternity."

"Nonetheless, until this day, the Light remains hidden in the safe refuge of the Occult, waiting for the New Dawn to shine again on a new humanity and a higher type of man. For ours is the era of darkness and decadence. Ours is the rule of the lowest of men, the realm of the *Chandala*, mob rule above and below. Today, in the West as in the East, men have lost their divine memory — save for a few enlightened ones who see beyond the mist of illusion — and they live unconscious, praising what they should chastise, and chastising what they should praise."

"Among those who call themselves 'civilised', godlessness — that illegitimate child of superstition — reigns supreme, under the deceiving garb of Reason; and what little is left of piety sounds much like heresy… for holy words fall deaf in the ears of those who never listen, but claim to hear; and the Spirit remains invisible to the eyes of those who never look, but claim to see; and Wisdom remains uncharted territory to those who are unconscious, but who claim to *know*, just because they *think* — for true knowledge is not thought but consciousness —; thus they live subservient to a strange god and a strange religion, new slaves to old ones. How pitiful they look, these unconscious servants of an undying hatred — the hatred of eternal slaves — which, behind the deceptive mask of Love, enslaves the souls of the free and weakens the hearts of the brave. For when you stoop to the level of those whom you are supposed to despise, nothing distinguishes you from them, save an illusive and waning feeling of superiority. Thus, those who deem themselves 'civilised', those pompous men of the West, so ignorant in their conceit, and so conceited in their ignorance, accumulate wealth with unrelenting frenzy, in a desperate and futile bid to fill the unbearable emptiness and the infinite void that they feel inside, the void of a spirit unfulfilled, and the spleen of a soul imprisoned; but ultimately they discover that no material riches, no accumulated possessions can replace the only priceless wealth: the wealth of the Spirit."

"And among those who call themselves 'the faithful', those dark men of the East, who live in the shadow and worship the shadow, superstition prevails under the banner of Faith, as the willing slaves of deceit have turned the divine message of Love bestowed upon them by the grace of God, a message which liberates and elevates, into human commandments of wrath which enslave and subdue. Therefore, religion in their empty heads and clumsy hands has not hallowed God but given Him a bad name, as their narrow minds and blind faith have obscured the light of Wisdom and the soul of Truth — for Wisdom needs the union of faith and reason to bestow the divine gift of creation, and Truth needs to convert both heart and mind before She can rule. Those who deem themselves 'pious' in an age of unbelief, and proudly flaunt their faith as a prize — instead of *living* it! — , do they not know that it is their 'piety' itself which has murdered belief? Do they not know that Faith needs to breathe the fresh air of freedom to remain genuine and bathe joyfully in the overflowing fountain of Life? Therefore, they only see the shell of Truth and live on the margin of Life."

"Hence, in East as in West, ignorance reigns supreme — whether it wears the deceitful garb of 'reason' and 'progress', or bears the illusive banner of 'faith' and 'virtue' —, and a human veil of darkness covers the radiant face of the divine Gaïa. And the sons of Ram live as strangers among strangers, and the world is both the curse they flee and the refuge they seek, for solitude is both a curse and a refuge."

"The Aryas are those very few among the multitude, those noble among the vulgar, those lofty among the base, who have kept the Light of *Surya* in their hearts and minds, wherever they dwell, and whatever befalls them, to guide their way across the darkness of man's day, towards the source and end of All, serving Truth with the word and the sword, until death, and beyond death, as the river of Time flows endlessly into the sea of Eternity, and the warrior of Light returns evermore to serve and honour the righteous and the true."

"But those are your worthy, faithful sons, Arya; they are the rare gems that have survived unscathed by that plague of human existence: earthly attachment, which sows the seeds of greed, lust, and envy, and only breeds bondage to possession and accumulation, an unquenchable thirst for illusive power, waning glory, and evanescent joy. Those are the few and the *real* Chosen Ones, the creators, in a world of countless failures and worthless parasites. For your unworthy sons (and every mother has worthy and unworthy sons), who have given you a bad name — whether by wilfully denying you, by distorting your message, or by wrongly serving it — have betrayed your cause and your goal, willingly or unwillingly, consciously or unconsciously; and though the intention may be different, the crime remains the same."

"Thus, after the deluge of human ignorance that swept the world, and the ensuing apocalypse that befell mankind, came the fall of the Master Race, and your true sons, those who remain few and hidden among the countless and the common, those who still — secretly or openly — serve your cause, against all odds and beyond all tragedies, are shunned today and cast away as traitors, madmen, or heretics by their own people who know not what they are doing, who never knew what they were doing. For your unworthy sons have betrayed the Light, Arya. That is why they fought the Light when it reached them, and each time it reached them, preferring to live in the shadow, where nothing is defined and everything is debased or despised, where all values are scorned and reversed. Those are the wretched remnants, worthless outcasts of the once glorious race — for each race has its outcasts, as God has his fallen angels. And today there are no Aryas save those in Shambhala, that kingdom of God on earth, and those who *belong* to Shambhala in spirit, wherever their bodies are."

"The Fall was dreadful, and the decay that ensued was even more terrible, for a slow death is more painful than a sudden one. The schism, then the miscegenation and intermixture between human races, which greatly degraded and corrupted the higher, and did little to elevate the lower, came as the final blow to the purity and innocence of the primordial divine perfection bestowed by the gods upon this earth; and so the Master Race, that once glorious race, became glorious only in memory, a hollow name on an empty and waning beauty, where no spirit transpires, and no soul aspires."

"However, the fall through intermixture was not a cause, but a *consequence* of the decline of the spirit of the Great Race, for the body only decays when the spirit departs. Hence, all men became the same, equal in their mediocrity, equal in their insignificance; and Karma killed *Varna*, as all colours, black and white, red and yellow, became different shades of the same colour, the dullest colour, the most impure among colours: grey, which is not even a real colour... And ever since man fell, he has been continuously falling, for there is no end to the abyss of human existence."

"Yet in the end, Truth always prevails, as She chooses Her warriors and Her battlefields throughout the ages and across the boundaries of states and nations and religions. Thus, the Sons of God and Warriors of Light refuse defeat — for they are the eternal victors and conquerors — and shun the darkness as the ignorant shun the Light; and so, persecuted until this day, their divine message remains hidden behind the hidden meaning and metaphor of every true religion and every noble philosophy, and inside the heart and soul of every seeker of Truth, every knight of Knowledge, and every warrior of Wisdom. The Secret Doctrine remains the real, Eternal Religion of the real, Eternal God."

2

"That was the rise and fall of the Great Race of Light, the Master Race, the only divine race to have trodden this earth. That was the rise and fall of your children, Arya; but as death begets a new life, now you should beget new sons and new suns, so that a new dawn would break our long night, and a new horizon would lift that gloomy veil of doom that covers the bright face of Gaïa. Man is at an end, a mere rotten cog in the eternal wheel of Time, an insignificant dot in the sacred circle of Life. Man has bided his time on this earth, as gods have bided theirs down under. You are among the very few remaining Aryas on this earth; thus, as the chosen among the chosen, you should breed a new race for a new world. Your sons await you, but you should *create* them first! So stop chasing the phantoms of the past, and look ahead, for yours is a bright future, as the end always resembles the beginning in the sea of eternal recurrence."

"The world you seek is lost, Arya, your North is lost, it has long disappeared in the mist of an illusive reality which engulfs the world today, though its magic still lingers in our memories and guides our way. Seek the Light within, enter your inner sanctuary, build your divine temple in the depth of your soul, and a new world will emerge before your bewildered eyes and your delighted heart; for everything you need to know, everything you need to discover, already dwells in you."

"Your day is coming, Arya, even though you have yet to see the first ray of light on the horizon of a brighter future. So say your word… and *fight*! Fight with your heart and your soul, fight with your word and your sword. But fight for *your* word, fight for *your* cause, and do not wage an illusory war for an illusory goal; wage *your* war, fight *your* battle, the battle for the present, for the victories and defeats of yesterday are gone, and those of tomorrow have yet to come. And though the divine cause is eternal, Truth chooses Her own warriors and Her own battlefields throughout the ages."

"The greatest battle in the eternal war of the spirits has yet to be fought, so fight your own battle, not the battles of your forefathers or those of your children. Thus you serve your cause best. And though the battlefield has changed, the warriors are the same. And though battles were lost, *our* war still remains, and goes on, in the wheel of Eternity, until it serves its cause and rejoices in victory. The names and banners may differ, yet the cause is ever the same. So let the glorious battles and the slain heroes of the past rest in the peace of Immortality, and fight your own battle, for only thus you serve your cause and hallow its meaning, and only thus you venerate your heroes' memory and glorify their names."

"There is history, and there are facts. Facts are facts, but — alas! — History is written by men, and men always lie and cheat and distort everything they touch. There is real History, and there is the history of men. Real history is Truth unveiled, revealing Her divine beauty and Her human scars, naked before the purifying Sun of Life; but the history of men is lies upon lies. Therefore, have no faith in men's history, Arya; fight your own battles, wage your own wars, and achieve your own victories: only thus you write your own history with your blood and your honour on the eternal pages of the Book of Life, which alone speaks the innocent and noble language of Truth. Write your history with your word and your sword, engrave your glorious epic on the pages of your everlasting life, carve your victories in your noble soul and your shining spirit; thus you radiate the sacred light of Truth, piercing the dark sky of man with the golden spear of your divine destiny."

"Heed not the words of men, their perverted morality and their distorted facts. History is written by the victors of the moment, and those who doubt it and seek to revise it are slain as heretics on the modern altar of an inverted truth, by the new inquisition of a reason gone mad; for Reason too has Her deluded and unworthy sons. And so, today, history and Truth seldom meet and match, as Reason and Wisdom remain strangers to one another. That is why justice will only be upheld when the righteous win and Truth prevails, and harmony will only be achieved when the divine hierarchy of Nature is restored. And the gods will only return when men resemble them again. That is the holy mission and the millenarian cause of the Master Race."

"Today, a new battle has to be fought, a new war is looming on the horizon of a new world, and this war serves the same eternal cause of divinity, for in it resides the divine future of man. A new battle looms on our horizon, for the same dark enemies of Truth, Beauty, and Perfection have overthrown the order of Nature and Her divine laws through the revolt of the slaves, those masters of the present who have turned the world upside down."

"Today, *Surya* is shunned and the moon is mistaken for the Sun, today the shadow is mistaken for the Light, thus men worship the ghost of a dead god and the dust of a buried truth. These days, darkness reigns, and the Sons of the Light are persecuted and executed, in the name of a fake freedom which only enslaves, a perverted justice which only oppresses, and a twisted knowledge which, devoid of wisdom, only blinds."

"Today, the worst kind of tyranny, the tyranny of ignorance, rules supreme, under the most manifold names and forms; thus it often hides its ugly face under the deceitful mask of 'Liberty' and the hopeless slogan of equality; and its sick soul often allays its darkest fears by submitting to the despotic laws of Dogma and the oppressive commandments of Virtue."

"Modern man has a useless choice: he is either 'free' or 'virtuous' — but since when does one *have* to choose between one's essence and one's conscience? —, free to be a slave in a world of slaves, free to be a fallen man in a fallen world; but true freedom commands: 'you shall overcome yourself!' And of what account is virtue, when, instead of blessing and inspiring, it oppresses Life and denies Love, cursing the former and slaying the latter?"

"Today there is no Master Race, for in this dark world there are neither masters nor races, only slaves ruling slaves, of all colours and all creeds — for all faded colours and all fallen creeds look the same in the eyes of Truth. The spark of genius has drowned in the dark seas of modernity, and 'master' and 'slave' echo the same in the valleys of deceit and decay."

"Today the Golden Chain is broken, no nation is great, no people carry the sacred torch of *Surya* and serve His noble and divine mission. And Truth is only to be found in the shining minds of those who still listen to the original voice of Wisdom and hear Her heavenly whispers that fill their souls with the sublime bliss of Eternity. The world today is lost and waiting for salvation. But you must have faith in the Circle, for there is no redemption without fall, and there is no rebirth without death."

"Alas! The Master Race has fallen — save for a few specimens of the gods on earth, milestones of the human spirit on the divine path —, and all that is left from its glorious past are sublime monuments and the fading and hollow beauty of its unworthy and soulless children, who bear the form but no longer the race. For, as I always say, Race is Spirit first and foremost; and of what account is the form, when the spirit lacks? Of what account is the sacred cup, when the sacred wine that hallows it has dried out? Of what account is man, when the divine breath has left him?"

"The present cycle is at an end, yet, as dusk begets a new dawn, the Arhats — those accomplished Aryas — will inherit the earth, at the end of days and after the apocalypse, in a new cycle and a higher destiny. And *that* is your mission, Arya: to redeem those very few today who are still worthy of redemption,

"those solitaries of the heights, lofty souls fleeing the lowlands of mob rule,"

"those saints of higher spheres, martyrs of the divine crucified on the altar of a fallen world,"

"those creative men of genius who suffer the unbearable void of mediocrity,"

"those most pious in times of unbelief, and most godless in times of idolatry,"

"those Free Spirits, free from desire and lust for power and money, detached from a world of bondage to lower instincts and greed,"

"those enlightened ones in a world of darkness, those awakened ones in a sea of delusion,"

"those noble and virtuous in an age of sin and immorality, those proud and loyal in the era of servility and treachery,"

"those honest ones in a world that perpetually lies,"

"those heroic types who constantly affirm, in a world that perpetually debases and denies,"

"those brave men of honour, in these times of cowardice, shame and disgrace,"

"those valiant warriors in an epoch of submission, those bold conquerors in the age of defeat,"

"those gods in the age of men, they are the rays of the coming Sun bearing the divine Light that shall again illuminate this earth."

"Arya, I have related to you the epic of your forefathers, the gods, and your sons, the Aryas; remember whence you came and who you are… for only when you find yourself will you guide your race, as you are the divine spirit of that race, and the immortal conscience of its sons. You are the last ray of hope on the horizon of a world engulfed in darkness, so believe in your glorious destiny, as the streams of the past ever flow into the ocean of the future."

3

Arya, who had kept silent during the prophet's long discourse, falling under the spell of those magical words that filled her with the awe she had long sought, and the hope she had much awaited, awoke from her trance, her mind slowly regaining control, and, at first hesitant, she finally said: "you speak the truth, prophet, your words are drops of wisdom that sow the seeds of Life and awaken the soul of God in every son of this earth; but rest assured, for I do not seek ghosts in the darkness of a dead past, nor do I seek the rays of a distant sun in an undefined future; I too have hope in the present… but to me, the present is enshrined in the past, and so the world I seek, my beloved Hyperborea, cannot, *should* not die!"

"I do not seek consolation in the past or expectation in the future, I seek my present, my everlasting, glorious present! I believe in greatness in the present, I believe in victory in the present! For I am a Warrior of Light, and the Light never dies, and, behind these dark clouds, it shines just as much to those who see beyond the darkness and across the fog of illusion. Yes, I see beyond this darkness, though it oppresses me and fills my heart with gloom and despair… I see beyond this sombre present, for *my* present is different, *my* world is brighter, *my* skies are blue: I see other horizons of an age that can never die, though it has faded from the material world, but its spirit lives on forever in its sons. Therefore, I seek the Light neither in the divine past nor in the bright future, but in this dark, human present, for I know that somewhere, the divine flame still flickers, and its healing rays still bless the souls of those for whom they are destined."

"Somewhere on this earth, the breath of *Surya* still maintains the life of Gaïa... for there can be no life without the divine rays of the Sun, and there can be no hope when hope itself has given up! Thus I seek to fulfil my destiny, defying this overwhelming obscurity around me, ever hoping to find life in the midst of death, and light in the midst of darkness. And that which gives me hope and strength is memory... for in my memory lie the seeds of my destiny, and in reminiscing, I build the bridge that will take me across, towards my new lives and my eternal destiny. So do not ask me to deny that which affirms my essence and my goal, do not ask me to forget that which reminds me who I am, why I am here, and where I should be going."

"Somewhere in the depths of this dark earth, there is a sun waiting to emerge, for though the sea of darkness has engulfed the sky and drowned its peaks and doused the Light, yet it is in the depths that the spirit of the heights still lives on; thus the Sun went down under this sombre earth, into the inner realm and the unseen light of Gaïa the divine, to preserve its healing and life-giving rays from the curse of decadence and degeneration which today holds sway. For in the age of darkness, the Light dwells within and below, waiting for its new dawn and its new day to bless life anew in the new cycle of a higher humanity. That is the Black Sun which shall rise again on a higher kind of man, when the New Age comes."

"It is my memory which gives me hope, and it is my hope which gives me strength and faith; so do not ask me to forsake that divine spark of light that redeems the sombre sky of men with a sacred promise of renewal and rebirth. The past and the future are inextricably intertwined in my eternal present. Therefore, whenever my will flounders and my soul grows weary, my imagination takes me back to the Golden Age, when my forefathers, these last remnants of gods on earth, upheld cosmic justice by preserving the natural Pyramid of Life, in the divine hierarchy of Nature, whereby the highest men, the purest in blood and soul, the strongest in will and resolve, the healthiest in body and spirit, the boldest in war and struggle, the wisest in peace and government, the brightest in mind and soul, the noblest in deed and thought, the most creative and the most divine, ruled the lowest men, the impure, the weak and sickly of body and mind, the ignoble, the ignorant and the cowardly, the dumb and the base, the darkest men… thus maintaining cosmic harmony and perfection on earth; for the caste system embodied the divine order and the beauty, justice, and excellence of Brahma the Supreme."

"Yes," said the prophet, "thus began the odyssey of the human spirit towards perfection and elevation, impregnated by divine wisdom, and the flame of that wisdom gave birth to the greatest civilisations the world has ever known. But that magical, divine time, when the human pyramid was a reflection of cosmic perfection, is gone today, as the harmony is broken, and the hierarchy is shattered; for when nobility of titles ceased to reflect nobility of character, when titles no longer reflected — and justified — superiority, when nobility became a privilege based on an injustice, and no longer a duty toward oneself and others, when nobility became a title instead of a conduct, it lost its meaning and betrayed its purpose."

"When kings were no longer also warriors and philosophers, when warriors and philosophers where no longer kings, the monarchs turned into despots, and their throne became the seat of oppression. When the sons of kings became unworthy of their fathers and forefathers — who earned their titles with their sweat and blood, their honour and virtue —, heredity killed justice, and so nobility lost its legitimacy, as true superiority is seldom inherited, and true nobility is always righteous."

"But why, why the fall?" asked Arya, and her eyes sparkled with anger and despair. "Can the heights of Life and Light ever become the valleys of death and darkness? Supremacy, or death! Thus speaks the pride and honour of a true nobleman and a brave warrior — and every true nobleman is a brave warrior —; so why the fall? How could this be? Is not the twilight of the gods on earth the twilight of Life itself down under?"

"Your race was divine, Arya," the prophet replied, "your sons were noble, but that was a very long time ago, when myth and reality mixed, when the spirit of divinity pervaded the soul of humanity and transpired in the glory of creation and perfection. But today, all are human and all are mediocre, save those elect few, those solitaries in the age of the mob, eagles of the peaks who breathe the pure air of higher spheres and remain above men's polluted rivers and dark seas."

"Few men today can claim to be superior, as superiority died with the last nobleman, that aristocrat without a title, that natural aristocrat who needs no titles but bestows them! — for true nobility needs no titles, as it justifies itself and is sufficient unto itself—; and of what account are titles! They do not make noble! Real nobility is inborn, it cannot be granted; thus titles should not be inherited, but deserved!"

"Nobility is dead, for all kinds of people have sullied the word 'noble', both those who deny it, and those who defile it. Nobility died when wisdom and justice no longer sat on thrones, and only greed and conceit sat on the royal seat; nobility was doomed when natural aristocrats were no longer actual aristocrats, when the rulers were no longer noble, and the noble no longer ruled; when noble blood no longer reflected a noble spirit, when blood and honour parted, never to meet again. And what worse fate than the fate that befell nobility? What worse disgrace than the disgrace wrought on aristocrats? From rulers to paupers, from monarchs to buffoons: that is the fate and disgrace of the unworthy sons of the Master Race."

"Nobility was doomed when the order of rank, the divine order of Nature, collapsed; when the highest were no longer on top, when the lowest instincts and the worst sins became the highest values and the best virtues of a society gone mad and blind; when rulers and ruled resembled each other and became alike. Aristocracy fell when the best no longer ruled, when the best were no longer the first, and the first were no longer the best."

"Nobility lost its meaning when wealth — or lack thereof — determined one's rank and one's worth, when titles were bought and sold as commodities, and inherited as property — but superiority is something we *are*, not something we *have*! It is individual and selective, never hereditary and collective. And so, noble blood has little to do with heredity."

"Nobility died when honour and loyalty, blood and soul, all had their price... when birth, not virtue, and power, not talent, and possession, not superiority, determined status, and became the sole meaning and purpose of life."

"Nobility was doomed when a man's title became his worth, when men were judged according to the name they wore and the money they carried, for one only *wears* a name and *carries* money, as one is *not* his name, nor is he his possessions."

"Nobility was doomed when men were judged according to their titles, not their abilities, and where they come from, not what they do, and what they are, instead of who they are, and how much they have, not how much they give, and how rich they become, not how noble they are; when titles ceased to be the crowning of a man's worth, but became themselves the norm and the end. For titles never ennoble, they only crown a superior soul. One is *born* noble, one does not *become* noble. True superiority is innate, never inherited or granted, and noble blood runs in the veins of rich and poor and speaks several languages, as it knows not the divisions of classes and the boundaries of states."

"Nobility fell when it became hereditary. Yes, heredity killed nobility... the unjust law of heredity killed the universal soul of nobility; for though true nobility is innate, not acquired, it is selective, not determined, as karma has its own reasons and its own ends, and man's destiny unfolds in ways that are strange and mysterious to the limited mind, but following a divine order and harmony to the infinite soul."

"One is born noble of blood and spirit, regardless of *where* he is born, or *what* he is born into; one does not become noble by virtue of bestowed or inherited titles. Superiority is inborn, never imposed. A nobleman is never made, he is discovered. But alas! Do we not always speak of Higher Men in the *past* tense? Are not all Higher Men acknowledged and discovered *too late?*"

"Nobility failed because it was based on an injustice — heredity — and therefore it bred injustice; and injustice lies in granting titles and privileges to the unworthy, and withholding them from the worthy. Nobility failed because it became fake and hollow, based on birth, not virtue, and titles, not achievements, and privileges, not merit; thus it betrayed its original meaning and purpose, which is to reflect and uphold divine hierarchy and harmony, to ennoble and to elevate."

"As a result, kingdoms were shattered because they rested on shaky moral foundations, for the rulers were no longer virtuous — as are true noblemen, for virtue is inborn in every true nobleman —, and so they became corrupted by those two human evils, money and power, and in turn they corrupted their people with their fallen values. And when the first are no longer the best, aristocracy is doomed to destruction, and turns into tyranny... and even democracy, which is the will of the unwilling, unproductive masses, and the rule of the unruly, the mediocre, is better than tyranny, though both are mob rule; for democracy is the consensual rule of the herd, whereas tyranny is the absolute rule of one herdman; and equality of all is a lesser injustice to the Higher Man than the rule of the inferior over the superior."

"When the caste system no longer reflected natural hierarchy — as birth replaced merit, and heredity replaced achievement —, it became obsolete and hence collapsed. Noblemen, in their fallen thoughts and deeds, became a disgrace to the title they held. Accordingly, as the divine, spiritual hierarchy on earth turned into a material, human hierarchy of classes divided on the basis of possessions, traditional hereditary aristocracy was replaced by a money aristocracy, thrice worse. For that fakest of elites, the financial elite, is only distinguished from the lower classes by virtue of its wealth and possessions, not by virtue of its inherent spiritual or moral worth."

"That is why monarchy fell, and aristocracy failed; that is why democracy rules today. For when the gods departed, and their sons no longer ruled, the pyramid gradually became inverted, the many ruling the few, the base ruling the lofty, the vulgar ruling the noble. Thus, in the end, the common ruled the godlike, and the lowest ruled the highest."

"And so came the twilight of the Master Race, that last remnant of the gods on earth, through the intermixture of classes and races that ultimately became alike in essence, though different in form. The warrior caste of Kshatriyas dominated the human pyramid of power during the reign of war, as titles were earned on the battlefields and with one's blood. War created a new kind of elite, an elite of warriors and conquerors, aristocrats of the sword — who soon replaced the aristocrats of the court —, some of them righteous and enlightened, most of them corrupt tyrants."

"But war also created a mercantile class that amassed riches, and traded in war and peace, exploiting both to the fullest. That was the Vaishya caste, forefathers of today's bourgeoisie, for whom everything is bought and sold, including honour and loyalty and faith and power and God and man… for there are no moral limits to him for whom nothing is sacred and for whom everything has a price. And it was this class which promoted the unnatural idea and the perverted ideal of equality so that it could rule in times of peace, when the cowards and the brave become equal, and talent is drowned in the stagnant waters of mediocrity."

"In time, the bourgeoisie took over the reigns of power through revolutions, exploiting the people's sense of injustice and directing their anger and resentment at the rulers as the sole responsible for all their woes, whereas it was in fact these merchants of war and peace who benefited both from the absolute rule of kings, and later from the rule of the mob; for business goes on as usual, and anything goes to those devoid of conscience and principles, come war or peace, come prosperity or misery... and most of the revolutions that ensued in history were the work of these exploiters and traders, always lying to the people, while serving the rulers of the moment."

"And though wars continued to be fought, they were no longer for the sake of ideals, but for the sake of plundering; and during times of peace, the warriors and heroes are forgotten, their heroic deeds buried in the eternal memory of history, mere myths that feed the imagination of the people."

"Hence, decadence ensued, as the people's base values — the values of the Sudras, the lowest caste — reigned supreme, and rulers were no longer models of perfection, but servants of the people, a mere reflection of the common man's imperfections. The descent into darkness became inevitable, for the loss of harmony led to a disruption of the natural order, which is the divine order. And so, humanity plunged into the Kali Yuga, the darkest hour of man, and the human pyramid was completely inverted, as were all its values: the highest were treated as the lowest, and the lowest were lifted to the peak."

"Thus the Unknown Supermen took their sacred message underground and continued to serve their noble cause of Light in the sanctified shadow of Occult Truth, waiting for the day to come when their flame could light up the dormant fire of the world, purifying humanity from its sins, so that a new order could rise from the ashes of the old, corrupted order. That was the rise and fall of the Master Race, whose demise drowned mankind into its darkest night."

"But if the original meaning of nobility was corrupted," asked Arya, "then *what* is true nobility? *Who* is noble?" "True nobility," replied the prophet, "is nobility of blood and soul; but make no mistake about that, 'blood' is spirit, blood lies in spirit, as spirit is in the blood. True nobility is nobility not of birth, but of merit; not of ascription, but of achievement; not of titles, but of deeds; not of privileges, but of duty; not of rewards, but of sacrifice."

"True nobility is nobility of talent and genius, of virtue and courage, of honour and loyalty, of *higher* freedom and of *real* justice. *That* is nobility in its truest essence and its purest form."

"Not to take and to steal, but to give, to bestow from oneself and from one's possessions; not to be honoured and praised, but to honour one's rank by upholding justice and performing one's duty, thus praising the work of the Lord; not to be served and waited upon, but to serve Truth and to achieve Perfection and elevate all men to the level of kings by imbuing the world with the noble values of the higher order of Life: *that* is the sign of a noble soul."

"There is genuine, natural aristocracy, and there is fake, social aristocracy; the former is based on superiority of spirit, the latter on power and wealth."

"There are real aristocrats, aristocrats by selection, and there are fake aristocrats, aristocrats by heredity."

"There are born aristocrats, whatever their social status or wealth or power or influence, and there are aristocrats by heredity; only the former are real aristocrats, worthy of the name and the title."

"There are aristocrats by ascription, and aristocrats by achievement; the real aristocrat is he who *earns* his title, whether he inherited it or acquired it."

"There are natural aristocrats, and there are actual aristocrats; a natural aristocrat is not necessarily an actual aristocrat, and an actual aristocrat is seldom a natural aristocrat; for, as I already said, heredity does not determine superiority, superiority alone determines itself and justifies itself. And a born aristocrat is not necessarily born into a noble family."

"The real aristocrat is a complete human being, a synthetic man, an accomplished person. He combines a healthy body with a brilliant mind and a noble soul, a radiant spirit and beauty within and without. But the soul is primary, and a pure soul is more beautiful than the most perfect body."

"True nobility is based on wealth and power of spirit, not material wealth and political power — for the former are inborn, and the latter acquired; and real, natural superiority is always inborn, never acquired. Man is only what he achieves, what he becomes, not what he inherits or receives; for becoming is the essence of being, and justice lies in merit alone. Thus, a true aristocracy is a meritocracy, an aristocracy of merit, talent, honour, duty, and honesty; all else is injustice begetting injustice."

"True nobility is not based on wealth or titles or possessions or power, but on lofty values and noble virtues. Hence, nobility should be *deserved*, not granted upon birth; and titles should not be inherited, but earned by merit and courage, and bestowed not as a birthright, but as the accomplishment of a lifetime of virtue and honour. The crowning of a man should be an end, not a beginning."

"Therefore, nobility should be born again and taught anew; a new nobility is needed, one that is constantly recruited from all walks of life, for a nobility that perpetually renews itself never dies. The new nobility should be inspired by the nobility of antiquity, the only real nobility, when social hierarchy was based on genuine superiority, at that blessed time when the divine spirit still governed and inspired."

"The New Age, which will be an aristocratic age, the age of the Overman, the godlike man, shall witness the birth of a higher kind of nobility, a nobility hitherto undreamt of, a synthetic nobility of spirit and body, a genuine aristocracy of complete men, saints of Wisdom, knights of Virtue, warriors of the Spirit; for when wisdom, virtue, and power meet, great things are achieved."

"There is another kind of heredity, a higher kind of heredity, and that is: the heredity of the soul. There is another, deeper dimension to Race, and that is the spirit of blood. Hitherto, *varna* determined *karma*; but that was an injustice and an aberration. For it is karma which truly decides one's varna and one's *dharma*, as karma bears the Spirit in its endless journey through the incarnations."

"Immortals, those great guides of humanity, belong to the Dynasty of Light, the only true dynasty and the only genuine light in the world, not today's fake aristocrats with hollow names, shadows masquerading as light. The legacy, the heredity of the Spirit, *that* is the eternal soul of the Master Race... for those are the heirs to the divine spirit of the Aryas, wherever they are and whatever men call them."

The Inner Fatherland

"But *where* does the divine spirit, the noble spirit, dwell today?" Arya entreated the prophet, "where do I find *my* spirit today? Where do I find the sacred flame first carried by Lord Rama, which baptised the golden chain of Light and justified and blessed Life? And what is the race, what is the nation chosen to carry this flame?"

"Speak no more in terms of race and nation," the prophet answered, "for today there are neither races nor nations, neither colours nor creeds nor religions, but — and as in the beginning of Time, and always — only two species: the Masters and the slaves, the godmen and the undermen; those who emulate the gods, and those who stoop to the level of beasts. Those who want to elevate man to the heights of divinity, and those who want to drag him into the bowels of bestiality. Masters and slaves: that is how the world is divided today. All else is naught but idle labels and empty names, faded hues and shades of the same colour of decay: black, black, black, and its brightest shade, grey!"

"The spirit of blood: *that* is the higher and deeper dimension of Race. 'Blood' is spirit, it is an endless river that runs across men's arbitrary frontiers and silly creeds. For all frontiers are arbitrary, and all creeds look silly in the infinite realm of the immeasurable universe, and in the divine eyes of all-encompassing Truth. Superiority is innate, it is never a product of the environment or culture or education, and has little to do with language or nationality. Thus noble blood transcends the boundaries of nations and cultures, and speaks the universal language of God through the hallowed word of His sons."

"Masters and slaves: that is how the world is divided today, that is how the world has always been divided; all other divisions are arbitrary. What matters is one's varna, which is one's race, class, and faith. A higher class is also a higher race — or so it should be in the natural hierarchy —; and a higher race is always a higher class, a Master Race. Hence, race and class are inextricably intertwined, they are one. That is the deep meaning of the word 'caste', or varna, spiritually, morally, racially."

"The Master Race is not a 'race' in the ordinary sense; it is an invisible Knighthood of Unknown Supermen, unknown brothers bound by a divine mission and a millenarian cause. As such, the Master Race is *within* races and beyond nations, for there are elite races, and elites *within* races; and only the latter are the Master Race, the best class of the best race. Consequently, your cause is above men's nations, religions, and cultures. Yours is the universal aristocratic cause of the universal aristocratic race."

"The coming age will be a spiritual age; the coming war will be a spiritual war, not a war between nations and races and religions, but a battle of the spirits between the Warriors of Light and the servants of darkness; between those who want to elevate man to the rank of the gods, and those who want to debase him and deny him his divine destiny. The sons of the gods versus men and undermen: that will be the battle of the future; so forget about colours and forms and shades and hues, and focus on spirit, for it is the spirit which moulds all forms and paints all colours, and draws the divine rainbow of the *Geist*, the

Universal Spirit, upon the sky of men. Gods and beasts: that will be the future of this earth, and all those in the middle will perish or vanish, for in a war there is only black versus white, and nothing in between."

"The new war will be a universal war, a clash of the spirits, not a clash of civilisations; for all civilisations look the same nowadays, and though they may look different to the uninitiated — who focus on outward form — they are essentially the same human ignorance and illusion and delusion cloaked in different garb, hiding behind different masks, speaking different languages, bearing different banners, and worshipping different gods. The real clash will be between the hidden, invisible world of godmen, and the actual, visible world of similar and equal slaves, whatever their human colour or their human creed. The real war is a war of spirits, the real war is within man — not between men —, a war between man's higher Self and his lower self, a self-conquest and a self-overcoming."

"Therefore, seek no more to sail the lost seas of vanished races and fallen gods, Arya, for these seas will lead you nowhere save to perdition and despair... live the innocence of the present, live the freedom of the moment, walk *your* path, and your dreams will come true; for your outer journey is also — and mostly — an inner journey of self-discovery, as ultimately we experience only ourselves."

"The journey is within, and all the people we meet on our path, all the places we discover, all the things we do during our brief passage on this earth, are but lessons and pathways to our sacred journey and secret destiny, our inner path to the Spirit. And though few of us do complete that journey and reach that goal, most falter and stumble, and they either return to the human shore, or perish on the way. How could a human goddess seek a nation, *any* nation, even a sacred nation? Arya, the human in you still clings to your genes, whereas your divine spirit longs to transcend; therefore, you have to become divine, you have to burn in your own flame before you can find your *Nirvana* and your *Valhalla*, your redemption, your salvation; for the divine, hidden kingdom of Shambhala remains invisible to him who seeks it outside his Self."

"You have a gift, Arya, you should bestow it…You came to this earth, to this land, to fulfil a mission that will reveal itself to you as you progress along your path. It will unfold before your naked eyes as you travel along your inner spiritual journey, of which your journeys and travels on earth are but the outer manifestation and the human path to your ultimate divine goal. Ultimately we experience only our Inner Self and destiny, though we may conquer distant lands and sit upon mighty thrones and dictate our will to the world; but at the end of our journey on earth, before our soul departs to a new birth or a new world, we face our mirror and ask ourselves the final existential question: 'was it worth it? Was it meant to be? Was *that* … the *real* me?"

"What is important is the inner journey, Arya; therefore, have faith in your strength, and find strength in your faith, and worry not about the darkness, for the Light awaits you in your inner depths. And worry not about your warriors, for they will come when *you* wage your war, as true leaders are always the first on the battlefront. And worry not about your suffering, for you should know that with knowledge comes suffering, and with suffering comes awareness, and with awareness comes Wisdom, our meaning and our end. The path to Truth is steep, but the divine goal is worth all human sacrifices."

"All our battles and struggles are but imperfect manifestations of our greater inner battle and inner struggle: to find and conquer our Self, our higher being; to re-conquer our lost divinity, to recapture our faded divine memory, and fulfil our eternal divine destiny. Yet in order to do so, we Sons of *Surya* must first experience the earth and all its blessings and curses, for it is the battlefield where Life unveils Her secret meaning and Her sacred mysteries, and where our spirit undergoes the trial by fire, through the redeeming flame of *Agni*. In order to conquer our Self, we must first realise the sacred communion with Nature, divine Mother of All. Only then begins the journey within."

Visibly moved by the prophet's words of wisdom which deeply touched her soul, Arya said: "you bring out the pure goddess in me... you show me the way towards my Self, you light my path and you open up new horizons for my future. I need your guidance, prophet, for you are the light that shows me the way to the end, *my* end and *my* purpose."

"I shall be your guide along your inner journey," replied the prophet, "for we all need a guide, be he real or imaginary, inner or outer, man or spirit. Your mind may be lost, Arya, but your heart knows the way, and your spirit *is* the way. And do you know what is the Way, Arya? The Way is not something you *seek*, but something you *are*; not something you discover, but something you create; not something out there, but something within. Therefore, do not seek your purpose outside yourself, for you would be seeking the ever fleeting ghost of the void, and all you will ever behold is the dark, bottomless pit of nothingness. You have a purpose, divine daughter of Light, and that purpose is engraved in your inner depth. Hence, explore your own inner depths, Arya, and you shall find your true essence and purpose, the goal that the universe has fashioned for your soul throughout the ages; thus you will see your eternal destiny unravelled before you."

"And worry not about life's tribulations, woes, and tragedies; for nothing that happens on this earth occurs without a meaning, — though chaos seems to prevail —; all things, great and small, serve a purpose, serve *their* purpose... and even the little things serve a purpose in the Grand Design of Life. Even the little things have a meaning, even the little things matter, though you might think they are the product of chance and accident. But there is neither chance nor accident in this divine cosmos of order and harmony, and even chaos and mayhem ultimately serve creation and perfection; for only when the whole picture is complete does everything make sense to him who views the work of an artist — and the Spirit is the cosmic artist of Life."

"Yes, Arya, even the little things, even the tiniest pebbles are signs, milestones that lead to the Way; and even the greatest suffering is a blessing in disguise, for it serves your higher Self and moulds your higher destiny. And when you look behind, when you see the signs and unravel the mystery behind all suffering, you understand what's forward; you finally understand *why*... why it all happened, why it all *should* have happened. When you delve into the past, you understand the future. For all is written, and everything serves the scheme of divinity, though it is man himself who, through his thoughts and deeds, writes his own story on the pages of history. Man is an instrument of the gods; he is an integral part of Nature, as the soul of the universe pervades all aspects of Life. Man becomes great when he merges his Self and his destiny with the spirit and the destiny of the universe, which is the spirit and destiny of God. All else is folly, delusion, and wasted dreams."

"Therefore, do not go North, Arya, as there you will only find bitter disappointment, that is, if you find anything at all; for the land of the gods is emptier than a desert today." However, Arya did not heed the prophet's warning, as she resolved to seek the Light up yonder, for there is where she felt she belonged, and where salvation awaits. "My children, my beloved children await me... I cannot fail them, for they have never failed me," she said, and her eyes were glowing with pride mixed with a certain nostalgia.

"What children?" the prophet burst out saying, "my poor, lost child, today the divine race has vanished, today nobility is dead. It died with the demise of God and the fall of the gods. Today is the reign of the mob, above and below, in the North and the South, in the East and the West; for all are equal in their folly and their mediocrity. Yet Nature shall prevail over man, for man is fake from head to toe — though he thinks he is supreme —, and his reign is shaky and ephemeral... as only the natural is supreme and remains actual, and all else is doomed to fade with the wind of perpetual change, and decay like a dead leaf come the winter of existence."

"The divine order shall rise again with the golden dawn of the coming god. But in the iron age of men, materialism, which is both the cause and the consequence of the myth of equality, reigns supreme, for equality is always material, horizontal, and crushes all and everything under its ruthless yoke of mediocrity and its dead weight; whereas hierarchy is an endless scale upon which climb those who strive, and those who aspire, and under which submit those who never create and never seek, but only lust and vegetate, those who never dare but only dream, and never accomplish but only desire."

"They confuse freedom with equality, these foolish men of modernity, just as they confuse nation with race, and race with form; for everything is mixed up in the age of ignorance and decay. They confuse freedom with equality, and to them freedom is itself a chain of bondage that they carry, proud but unconscious, not the pure liberating wind of the heights; and equality is a powerful weapon and an oppressive tool that they use against the genius and the exception... and while freedom elevates and liberates the slave and exalts the master, equality debases and crushes the higher and empowers the lower."

"And is not freedom naught but the freedom to rise ever higher in the hierarchy of Life, and to tear asunder the human chains of attachment, lust, and desire? Is not higher freedom, *real* freedom? But the men of modernity talk of freedom, lust for freedom, like freed slaves, not like born freemen; they talk of freedom not as a given, but as a gift — yet has a given ever been a gift, save for slaves? —. For freedom is the greatest gift bestowed on a slave, but it is a given to the free soul, whether he walks free or lies in chains."

"Nowadays, they talk of equality as the new religion, or even as God. Yes, equality *is* the new religion and the new god in these decadent times... and the exception is a crime under the ruthless law of mediocrity and the despotic rule of equality; for the rule of the people is always the rule of mediocrity, as the mob is ruled by its instincts, while the nobleman rules with his spirit. For when a man's spirit masters his instincts, his rule is lofty and just. But when a man's spirit is ruled by his instincts, only injustice, greed, and chaos ensue; indeed, when a man cannot rule himself, he can never rule other men, and his rule becomes a despotic yoke and a ruthless oppression. Thus today chaos rules the world, whether the chaos of superstition or the chaos of unbelief; for both cause the loss of higher purpose and the debasement of man. Both are folly and delusion."

The prophet paused for a while, as he realised that Arya's spirit was elsewhere, hearing other voices and seeing other visions; she was in another world. And so he realised that she could not redeem the fall of her race — she whose divine pride refuses defeat —, she only remembered the heights, and was filled with the hope that comes from the sublime, magical, hidden energy of idealism. He nonetheless went on: "your race no longer dwells in the North. Today race is above nation, but race is also beyond form… Race is essentially a matter of spirit, and spirit transcends all human divisions and frontiers. So seek your race with your spirit and *in* your spirit, for there is where it lives and thrives."

"Geography is no longer sacred today, but if you must find inspiration outside your Self, and if you must seek a nation you could call home, you will find it nowhere in the West nor in the East, nowhere in the North nor in the South, but in the far North and the deep East… the far North and the deep East, *that* is where your spirit still dwells and lingers today. Hyperborea and Aryana… *those* are your nations, Arya, but they are no longer of this world, they no longer exist save in your inner Self and your infinite soul. Yet rest assured, for you need not go there, as the whole universe lies within your very soul, and its silent melody echoes in your very depths. So seek them with your heart, not your mind, and experience them within, for that is their essence and their meaning. That is your inner journey into your Inner Fatherland, that is the sacred path to the divine kingdom of Shambhala."

"Today there is only decadence, men have become blind and deaf, blind to Beauty and deaf to the Sacred Silence that bears the divine. The earth has turned ugly, and the unbearable noise of men has drowned the last sighs of the divine echo of the forlorn Golden Age. In this gloomy world that we endure, men have lost their manhood, and women have lost their virtue... these days, beauties mate with beasts, men and beasts look and act alike, and everything is distorted and sullied beyond recognition. Yet out of this folly which grips the world today, and which will bring but doom upon men, will spring a new race."

"Through men's folly, a new catastrophe will ensue, a new deluge of fire and ice and blood, which will cleanse the world of its human sins, and build a new man and a new world on the ashes of the old, fallen world; and only those chosen to redeem humanity will survive, and will sow the seeds of the divine garden of a better tomorrow."

"A New Dawn shall rise upon this earth, heralding the end of the old cycle, and the beginning of another cosmic age. Thus, Arya, you shall rise again, taking on a new form, as you always do across the ages. Your followers await their reign, they await *your* reign. Prepare yourself to lead, but in order to lead men, you must first conquer your own humanity, for only a goddess could rule men; and only a woman who has overcome herself could call herself a goddess."

"There is no beginning and no end, for creation is an ever turning wheel and a sacred circle. Evolution is the law, elevation is the path, and perfection is the end. So fear not, everything will fall back into place, it always does in the Ring of Eternity. Nature always prevails in the end, Truth always prevails in the end, for they are Life's eternal daughters and beloved creation."

"Despair not, Arya, for the fruit will fall when it is ripe, and so you will only attain wisdom and enlightenment when you become worthy of them; when you behold yourself in the mirror of Being and do *not* see yourself, but the Whole, *that* is when you will have become wise, and then you can bestow that fruit of the gods to men. What is important is the inner Light that shines on your infinite Self."

"I do not remember my ebb," Arya replied, "for I live on the highest mountain of the Spirit, there on the peaks of Supremacy, where only gods dwell and eagles dare... I, Arya, goddess of Light, the soul of nobility, the spirit of divinity, have given this world its most precious gift from above; I gave the world the Master Race, the most beautiful and most divine race, the best that has ever been conceived of and created on earth; the race of gods that bestowed the divine flame of Agni upon men. Thus I refuse my ebb, and I await my flow."

The prophet, looking at Arya with compassion mixed with affection, told her in a gentle but firm tone: "you lost your way because you were not heading the *right* way, the way towards Truth. And destiny has its own signposts—events, illuminations, even tragedies and defeats—to guide you back to your own Self. You lost your war because you were not being true to yourself, to your deepest essence, meaning, and goal; you chose to stay on the surface, and the surface of the lake is often distorted by the waves carried by strange winds, impure waves that defile the immaculate beauty and purity of its depths; for the depth always bears the genuine and the pure."

"You served Truth faithfully, you wanted Truth to prevail, and you fought for Truth to prevail; but when power was in your reach, you clung to it and forgot its purpose... you forgot that for power to last, it should serve a higher purpose, a purpose beyond itself. Thus you became intoxicated by the entrancing grip of power; your power became an end in itself and a path unto its own, away from Truth... thus it waned and died; for all power that serves no higher purpose loses its legitimacy and is doomed to fade."

"Arya, I beseech you, do not go North... do not waste your destiny by following forsaken paths and lost causes. Woe to a mother who outlives her children; and that is you, Arya, you have outlived your own children... for they are dead, and they await their resurrection; so do not lament their death, but get ready to give birth again, O divine mother of *Agni*, favourite daughter of *Surya*."

But Arya remained stubborn in her resolve to find her lost homeland. She was certain that it is there that she would find the light that bore her soul aeons ago. Faced with such obstinate obsession, the prophet pushed a sign of exasperation, saying: "do not cling to the past, do not look behind, look ahead, to the future, for the divine race is dead and has yet to be reborn. What you think is the end is only the beginning, for the divine Spirit has yet to be accomplished here on earth."

"Only in the North will there be redemption of humanity," Arya replied, "for that is where it all began... and if humanity now lives in darkness, it is because it has shunned the northern light of Life. The Light came from the North, the North gave the world its brightest light, but the world has shunned it, and now it lives in darkness. So if there is a light, a hope, a promise somewhere on this earth, it must be in the North, it must come from the North." That is what Arya thought and believed, and nothing could shake her resolve and her belief in her race and her mission.

"You lack maturity," said the prophet, visibly exasperated by Arya's stubborn loyalty to illusions, "you should be humble before you can be great. All greatness is humble and magnanimous, all baseness is wicked and conceited. A student of wisdom cannot preach wisdom, he should learn and master it first, for Wisdom is a school, the school of Life, and we are all Her students... and most of us remain failed students."

Deeply offended by the prophet's harsh words which wounded her pride, Arya — who still lacked the humility that comes with spiritual maturity — swiftly walked away and left her guide, albeit with a bitter feeling in her heart, for she had grown attached to that stranger whom she knew so well, and whom she needed so much; but her wounded pride forbade her to stay, and her will and hope urged her to leave this man who was telling her a truth she was not yet ready to hear or to face. Thus she continued on her northbound journey in search of her roots, of her Spiritual Fatherland."

On her way home, Arya started to daydream and said to herself: "*Heimat* (8), beloved *Heimat*! Ah! To behold again the land that witnessed the birth of the divine race, the land that bore my soul at the dawn of its existence!" As she thus spoke, her face lit up in expectation of the land of wonder and magic which bore her and which she was about to rediscover.

Time

Thus Arya headed North, seeking the Light that would redeem all darkness and cast aside the clouds of gloom and despair that have covered the earth, there where the Sun never sets, there in the land of white nights, where the wonder of *Aurora Borealis* glistens with the divine radiance of cosmic mystery, sending shivers of ecstasy across the realm of Infinity. As she walked for days on end finding neither light nor men, and as this no man's land seemed to escape the ruthless reign of Time, Arya's enraptured spirit spoke thus to the Spirit of Time:

"O eternal spirit of Time,
Time the destroyer, the avenger, the robber…
Cruel, unyielding, it runs, it passes, it fades…
It wanes and dies forever,
and evermore disappears in the gloomy mist
of wasted dreams, shattered hopes, and broken promises,
to be born ever again and again,
a promise of Life and Light,
a new dawn unto the dead night."

"Time flows, it goes by, unperturbed, irreversible,
impervious to our joy or pain,
oblivious to our hopes or regrets,
both changing in its perpetual movement,
and eternal in its divine circle of recurrence,
where there is neither loss nor gain,
only the creative thrust of boundless energy."

"Time moves, vanishes, only to reappear
in a new garment, with a new sunrise, on a new horizon,
caught up in the endless cycle of Life,
enthralled by the frantic dance of the cosmic night
where darkness eternally flirts with light."

"Time passes, it comes back and goes away
like a lonely cloud passing through a spotless sky,
like a stream that runs into the river of Eternity,
like a river that embraces the ocean of Infinity."

"Time robs us of our youth,
its relentless thrust ever caressing the spectre of death,
like a wind that stifles all breaths,
and a breath that pushes its last sigh."

"Time robs us of our love
through its inescapable journey
in the dark kingdom of death,
only to re-unite us lovers again
in the warm arms of Eternity."

"As Time passes, all things fade away and decay,
and in its realm only sorrow, pain, and regret hold sway…
but also, and always, the eternal promise of a new day."

"Time robs us of our labour and our harvest,
only to give it back to Life, its rightful owner,
that overflowing source of All,
whence we all came and whither we return,
again and again."

"For Life alone is eternal and everlasting.
So, lovers and saints, wise men and fools!
Let your hearts and souls only celebrate and venerate Life
and worry not about Time's running river,
for Time is Life's witness,
it is both the river and the sea,
it is both the moment and eternity."

"My unknown brothers, I entreat you:
Cling not to that which does not endure,
and worry not about that which is not timeless.
For all things on this earth are like evanescent waves and ripples,
shifting and shapeless,
perpetually pushed and thrown hither and thither
by the capricious winds of ruthless change
and they too shall pass in the river of Time
flowing into the boundless sea
of tears and heartache,
torturing Life's aching heart with the curse of misery and melancholy.
And all that's left of our earthly possessions, attachments and desires
are but vague memories of an innocent smile, a divine shiver,
a bygone thrill, and a fading magic,
lost in the cosmic wilderness

amid the dust of countless stars and galaxies,
blessed daughters of Infinity."

"Time passes and vanishes
yet again forever renews itself,
bathing in the divine fountain of Life,
and evermore flows back into itself
in an endless cycle of life and death,
different facets of one reality."

"Weep not, wretched humans of this divine earth,
the loss of youth, beauty, or love.
For youth is an inner state of mind,
it is an eternal renewal and rebirth.
And beauty remains unscathed and ageless in one's soul,
ever shining within, and glowing without
like a priceless blessing from above.
And love forever lives in one's heart,
as lovers are always young at heart
and beautiful in spirit."

"Weep not, men, the loss of youth, beauty, or love,
for each age has its own glory, its own wisdom,
and its special gifts,
bestowed with grace on the righteous and the worthy,
and withheld from the wicked and the greedy.
And we shall return evermore
to this same earth and this same life
which is forever changing
and forever remains the same."

Still under the spell of the eternal moment of bliss that mesmerised her ever longing soul, and her ever striving spirit, Arya said to herself: "I am walking through the dark maze of a life yet unexplored and unfulfilled, stumbling on its many painful obstacles and unsolved riddles, enduring its many miseries and relishing its little joys. But Life is Life, She goes on, unperturbed, endlessly flowing in the river of Eternity, and so me must accept and bless Her unseen goal and Her hidden meaning, for we are powerless human pawns of Her divine will, and we are blind and finite before Her infinite, eternal Light."

"I should find *my* way, I should tread *my* path, paying no heed to the deceitful ghosts and elusive dreams that I encounter on the path to my Higher Self. The past is dead; let it rest in the peace of perpetuity. The future is yet unborn; let it thrive through the soul of possibility. It is the present alone which bears the soul of Eternity."

"The breath of Pan has touched my soul… I feel reborn, I feel divine… I am immortal."

Thus spoke Arya, as she headed North, in search of the lost Sacred Light.

PART THREE

KALI YUGA

In the land of gloom

After a long journey spent walking across deserts, mountains, and forests, always in the darkness of the eternal night that has descended on Gaïa, but ever under the comforting guidance of the Northern Star, Arya realised that she was getting closer to her beloved land, the land of the North, and beyond the North, her sacred Hyperborea… for the forests were becoming thicker and darker, the air was becoming colder and harsher, and she felt that unique, divine shiver of the heights which first welcomed her into this world at her dawn, in that same abode of her soul, that abode of the gods.

"*Heimat*, beloved *Heimat*!" cried Arya, "my blessed Fatherland, my eternal Fatherland, finally within my reach! I have waited so long to behold again thy divine beauty, to embrace once more thy sublime soul, to feel ever more thine unique magic, to tread yet again thy sacred soil." As she spoke thus to the spirit of the land she called home, her eyes were full of tears, but those were tears of joy, the joy of a long-awaited reunion, and the rebirth of a long lost hope.

As she felt that she was getting nearer to her destination, to her destiny, Arya was gripped by the thrill of expectation, and a magical chill pervaded her soul and shook her body. At long last, she would behold once again the green pastures and dark forests of her eternal fatherland! The cold, refreshing wind would once more caress her face and lift her soul, instilling it with an ineffable feeling of bliss! Her ears would yet again hear their familiar song, the comforting voice of her native tongue… Her eyes, weary of looking at desolate lands and dark skies, would once again behold the light of the land where the Sun never sets, the land which bore her soul before time began, the land where all creation is made and all hopes are possible and all dreams are achieved…

Finally, a sign of life became visible to Arya's incredulous eyes, as she noticed in the far distance a city bustling with life and immersed in light. She hurried towards that welcome sight — for all sign of life is a welcome sight to a lonely heart —, gathering her remaining strength to get there. And, even though she expected to discover a totally different land, her mythical land of the gods, that cradle of the Light bearing the stillness of divinity, not a city filled with human noise and glowing with fake lights, still, Arya was contented to temporarily halt her solitary journey and rest for a while, trying to figure out where she was and how far she still was from her final destination.

When she got to the gate of the city, and as she was about to enter it, she noticed a strange phenomenon that bewildered her: the dark sky that accompanied her, ever since she opened her eyes to *this* world, had gradually given way, above this strange city-state, to a somewhat lighter shade of black, a faded black, a kind of greyish hue. Indeed, the sky was covered with heavy, grey clouds that stifled the air with a gloomy veil of despair; it was as though the countless clouds had permanently merged into an impenetrable dark barrier that blocked the sun's rays. The city was choking in a sea of grey. That was not a welcome sight to behold, even to a weary soul dejected by the unbearable silence of solitude.

In this strange new world, Arya's soul was gripped by a ghastly feeling of impending doom, as she was not used to beholding such a dismal sight… for even in the darkness that was plaguing her and following her wherever she went, she could nonetheless envision the birth of a new dawn by gazing at the stars that sparkled with the hope of Light and Life, breaking the overwhelming obscurity that engulfed the earth, and guiding her on her path towards her lost soul and eternal goal. But now, even the redeeming drops of light and the blessed seeds of hope were denied her in that new dreary reality, as the sky above that new land was shrouded by an ocean of grey, and the fumes of the city rendered everything grey below. This was a grey land of gloom, the end of life and the antechamber of death.

"So close to the North," Arya thought, "and yet the Light is still nowhere to be found… My boreal light, heaven's gift to the earth, wherefore art thou? Where is thine eternal flame that shall redeem all darkness and deliver man from the excruciating misery and the unbearable void of his earthly existence?" Thus bemoaned Arya her uncanny and cruel fate which kept pushing her ever deeper into the bottomless pit of despondency and melancholy.

"Grey? What is this strange murky ocean which drowns this strangest of worlds? Is grey even a colour? It is not black, it is not white, but both, and neither… grey is indefinable, it has no character, it is dull, lifeless, soulless … and if white is the colour of purity, of Life, and black is the colour of death, then surely grey is the colour of agony and despair… it is no longer life, and not yet death, but a declining life which bears the sinister soul and the cursed seeds of death."

"If darkness is death of mind and oppression of soul, if darkness is the end, then grey is the beginning of the end, and the end of all beginnings… grey is the twilight of all dawns, the fog of doom and gloom that casts away all life and quells all longing and slays all joy. Grey is the end of all hope, the loss of all faith, the lack of all purpose; grey is naught but decadence and decay."

"If God has died, then *this* surely is where he is buried… if God's soul has departed this earth, then this surely is where his body — Nature — lies, decomposed, rotting away, eaten by that worm that calls itself man, that strangest of creatures, that unworthy son of Nature who renders everything fake and awry and crooked. This is God's graveyard, the graveyard of the light of faith which alone bestows meaning upon the world."

"But perhaps I err when I thus condemn this land, and its soul, which I know so little about?" Arya asked herself, "perhaps one truly should not judge a book by its cover? Could it be that I am only looking at the *darker* side of grey? What if I looked at its brighter side? Could it be that grey is not the path to darkness, to death, but the path to Light and Life? Could it be that I am getting *closer to* — not farther from — the Light? The colour of the sky is in fact getting lighter here; and at least I know that, behind these oppressive and depressing clouds, there is... the Sun!"

"After all, there, in the East, it is even too dark to *think*, and too hot to *will*! There the sleepless dreamers have divorced reality and live unconscious in the shadow of life, calling their dream the 'real world'. Perhaps the light of reason lies hidden here in the cold, above these thick grey clouds, waiting to be discovered by those destined to bear the sacred flame of Truth? Perhaps the mist carries the spirit of freedom, and beyond it shines... *Surya*?"

Among the dreamless sleepers of the city

1

After her initial hesitation, Arya decided to discover this new world. "What strange reasons and shadowy ends has Destiny still in store for me?" she asked herself, weary and wary of Life's hidden designs and unknown motives which defy all human logic and shatter most divine aspirations.

Thus Arya submitted to her fate, while clinging to her dream; perhaps in this strange land she would find the clues and the signs that would lead her *back* to her beloved homeland. Upon entering the city, Arya was struck by the unsightly scene that lay before her eyes: it was a gloomy, overcrowded, noisy city teeming with people scurrying here and there in a chaotic manner, countless lonely atoms going their separate ways, impervious to the grey hell in which they were living. The air in that grey monster of concrete was stifling, as breathing freely was nearly impossible, given the smokes and fumes that surrounded the city and polluted its atmosphere.

Arya looked around her, desperate to find a sign of *real* life, that is, natural life… a tree, a plant, a bird, anything that *looked* alive… but all that lay before her dejected eyes were hollow mountains of grey concrete, and asphalt roads where no weed could breed. And all that she could hear was the deafening sound of the chaos of the senses and the unbearable noise of greed, in that wretched haven to forlorn souls and lost hopes.

Arya ventured deep into the city, trying to catch a glance of the magical, mythical world which haunted her cosmic dreams of divinity, hoping to find a familiar face in that sea of strangers, perhaps another lost soul from her beloved race… but all there was before her were small industrious creatures, a motley race and a melting chaos of all shapes and all colours, each walking briskly towards their separate lives and separate goals, paying no heed to one another or to the grey fog of monotony in which their atrophied souls were drowning.

She looked around her, again and again, but nowhere could she find the land that haunted her dreams, and her beloved godlike race. Such a lesser world she had hitherto never seen, for her soul dwelt in higher realms, there where Truth and Beauty sanctify Life, that divine daughter of Creation. Arya was visibly distraught at this disturbing scene taking place right before her eyes, although, still sceptical, she had a hard time believing what her eyes were beholding.

Arya's soul became dark and her spirit grew gloomy, as she realised that the land she used to call home, the land that was once her soul's birthplace, might forever remain beyond her reach; she shuddered at the awful thought that all she would ever behold was the hideous mask of darkness and despair covering godforsaken lands of gloom, where magic has vanished, and imagination is banished.

"Could it be? How could it be? That is impossible! The land of the gods... *where* has it vanished? Is it above this land? Below it? Beyond it? Where? It is nowhere to be found, save in the depth of my yearning heart and aspiring soul..."

Suddenly, a horrible thought tortured Arya's wary mind: could *this* be... the North? Could this have *become*... the North? Arya quivered from head to toe at the very possibility that this might actually be her land... "What horrible crime did I commit to deserve such fate, this hell that the mindless alone could call home? Is this the land that I have long searched for, the land of my dreams, the land of the gods, the land of the divine race whose name I carry? No God dwells in this land. The desert might well be in the East, but here it is the desert of the Spirit, the void of the heart, the gloom of the soul."

"No, no, no, that is impossible," she said, shunning such a mad thought from her mind, "this cannot be, it defies the very laws of Nature! And the laws of Nature are divine! A heaven turned into hell? Why would this happen? *How* could this happen? Would the gods allow such a crime to befall their sacred land?" Determined to convince herself of her brief folly, Arya shrugged off her unjustified fears, thus consoling herself: "I have travelled far and wide on my way to the North, but I have yet to reach my final destination. This is just a mirage in the desert of men, and soon I shall reach the realm of the gods."

Despite having cast away her initial fear, Arya was still deeply perturbed by this new reality which offended her mind and wounded her soul; despondent and bitter, she asked herself: "but where, in heaven's name, is my sacred land? Where is the land where gods dwelt and where men became gods? What is this strange city that is so full of living creatures, so full of motion, but so lacking in ... Life? For *that* is surely not Life! A living hell: that is what this is... and if hell has a colour, it is surely grey."

Notwithstanding her disgust and disbelief, Arya decided to continue wandering through the streets of this city, in order to find out where she was and how far she still was from her final destination.

Amid the clamour of the marketplace of this soulless city without a face, Arya pondered her cruel fate, cursing the gods who had abandoned her in a hostile world where the redeeming rays of Light held no sway. "Darkness here, darkness there, darkness everywhere!" she lamented. "Here, God lies in the grave, there he still lives on as a ghost... and a ghost is but the shadow of death haunting the living, and the fading memory of a vanished past torturing the present. Thus, everywhere God's demise has darkened our skies and drowned our sun and buried our hopes... This earth is my hell, this hell is my purgatory... but what crime am I expiating? What sin am I doing penance for? If there is a crime, then why is there no guilt? If there is a sin, then why is there no shame? I am guilty of a crime I did not perpetrate, and a sin I did not commit!"

"Is my suffering a curse? Is my curse, eternal suffering? Or is my pain also... my salvation? Does not resurrection entail... a crucifixion? Does not spring owe its glorious beauty and its abundant life to winter's agony and sacrifice, its dead trees and fallen leaves? Does not the sublime mix with the gruesome on this strange earth of contrasts, abode of gods, men, and beasts? Does not Life's green tree thrive and blossom on the grey ashes of death? For what is Life and Beauty but death conquered and overcome, and ugliness cleansed of its sins? And what is death and ugliness but Life slandered and denied, and Beauty stripped of virtue? Thus the darkness of man's night carries in its womb the divine seeds of Light..."

2

Despite her despondency, Arya remained steadfast in her will, and resolved to talk to some of the people of this strange city; perhaps they would help her find what she was looking for. She approached a middle-aged man of average height, who seemed to be less busy, friendlier, and more receptive than the other soulless beings scurrying back and forth to their various tasks like little conscientious ants at work. He was calm and serene, and this is what caught Arya's attention amid this hectic urban nightmare. "This man looks like an intellectual, a thinking being among all these conditioned slaves. I shall speak to him," Arya thought, as she greeted the stranger, who responded with a friendly smile.

"Pray tell, dear sir," Arya asked the man, "what is this city called?" The man, surprised to hear such an unusual question, looked at her attentively, as though he was trying to guess where she came from; then he said, solemnly and proudly: "this is the City of Light, the city that never sleeps, the pride of the West, the jewel of the Civilised World! Do you not recognise it? *Everyone* knows this city, if only by name, if only by imagination! Every living being on this planet dreams of visiting this great city, at least once in his lifetime... But where do *you* come from? You seem to be lost and confused. You obviously do not belong here; your eyes see different worlds, and your ears hear different voices."

"Where I come from is of no importance, it is where I am going which matters; for one ultimately *is* what one *becomes*, only thus one becomes who one truly is. I am heading North, but I seem to have lost my way. Could you tell me if I am on the right track? Does this land, which you call 'the West' and 'the Civilised World', does it lie on my path northwards?"

"But *why* are you heading North?" the man, stunned and perplexed, swiftly replied, "why would anyone go North, when all you could ever dream of is right here before your eyes? For *this* is the final destination for all those seeking peace, happiness, and prosperity; *this* is the pride and envy of the whole world today! Why would *anyone* seek the cold and harsh life, and forsake *this* life of warmth and comfort? What is it that you seek in the North, which you cannot find here in the West?"

"I am searching for the Light…" said Arya, imperturbable. "But I am telling you, *this* is the city of Light, the city of *all* lights!" replied the man, exasperated, "do you not hear what I am saying? In fact, *all* our cities are cities of Light! The whole civilised world glows with light! We are the beacon of the world… Today there is no North, there is only East and West, and all want to go West, all dream of going West… No one goes North these days, for there is nothing there but a lifeless desert of snow and ice."

Impervious to the man's conceited enthusiasm, Arya remained serene, and repeated calmly: "I am searching for the Light… not the light made by man, but the Light that made man… the Pure Light that comes from the divine heights, not the wretched light of human lowlands… what you call 'light' is only human light, it is fake and dim and petty, just like man. I am searching for the divine Light, the source of all creation, the sacred flame of divinity which blessed this earth with Life, at the dawn of Time, long before man sullied Gaïa's divine soil with his filthy foot, and polluted Her pure air with his foul breath, and broke Her divine silence with his noisy chatter, and scarred Her sublime beauty with his ugly greed."

"I do not understand your words," said the man, "they are strange and deep and unfathomable, they are not of this world, and in our age of speed, progress, and skill, there is no time for strange and deep and unfathomable matters, even for us intellectuals… we leave these questions to philosophers, poets, and dreamers, and I dare you to find *those* in our midst today. For *we* live in the real world… but *this* I can tell you: the light you seek is all around you! Look around, the city is flooded with light! Who in his right mind would want to leave such a great sight?"

"Who in his right mind would want to *stay* here?" Arya replied, "but *you* do not understand me... you do not see what *I* see, and I do not see what you see; we live in different worlds, though we tread the same earth... but still, I am perplexed: do you not *see* the grey sky above? Do you even still *care* to look above? Or are you so entranced by the illusive and elusive pleasures of the senses, that you only see that which gratifies your appetites and quenches your thirst for earthly delights? Is *this* what you call light? Have your eyes gone blind? Have they become so numb that they can no longer distinguish the real from the illusory, the eternal from the ephemeral? Grey skies above, grey souls below! Do you not see the gloomy ocean covering your highest horizons? Do you not see the grey shroud of gloom stifling your hearts? For do they not say 'home is where the heart is?' You poor souls are drowning in darkness, but you do not realise it... and woe to those who sleep with their eyes open, and neither dream nor *live*, neither hope nor create, but walk unconscious and devoid of sight and imagination, dreamless sleepers of a disenchanted world where God is dead and man, lost in a moral void, wretched and meaningless, lives in despair."

"When below looks so nice, who cares about above? Who still looks above nowadays?" said the man, "only dreamers and poets and fools and madmen still bother to look above these days, and seek to flee the real world by naïvely dreaming of a better world that exists not save in their delusive minds and deluded souls. *We* in the West live in the *real* world, we are realists and free spirits who follow the liberating dictates of Reason and Logic, refusing to submit to the tyrannical commandments of Faith and Virtue. You seek the light, but the light is right here before your eyes! Why do you raise your eyes to behold that which is right before you? Look at the beautiful buildings of our beautiful new world! Look at the awesome monuments of our glorious civilisation!

Look at our great culture, the culture of the Enlightenment! *That* is true light, that is the light you idly seek in the North..."

"Man is the source of all light, man *is* the light. Therefore, all light, all life, all truth is human, all else is sweet deception and comforting lies. There is no God, there is no worthy life and lasting truth beyond man; man is the centre of the universe! When you reach this truth, when you accept this truth and espouse it, you will have become an enlightened one like us. We are the city of Enlightenment, we are the light of the world. Do not seek the light above, in the North, the light is right down below!"

"My poor, deluded friend," Arya told the man, "you utter words of wisdom that you yourself do not understand... for it is true that one need not raise one's eyes to behold that which is below and within... but do you *know* what is below and within? Do you *see* what is before you and within you? Have you ever delved into your own inner universe? Have you ever gauged the depth of your own soul? Does your soul even *have* a depth?"

"You shun what's above as madness and fantasy, but do you not see that it is the darkness within your souls that has covered your skies with the colour of doom and gloom? The skies above you reflect the depths of your own ocean, your own soul. Your soul contains the whole universe, your soul *creates* its own universe... as you think and as you feel, so is your life and so is your destiny; and it is the greyness *within* you that tells me that *your* 'reality' is but death of soul disguised as will to live, and poverty of spirit wearing the mask of knowledge, and decay of mind calling itself progress, and the misery of an empty existence masquerading as joy and abundance."

"You wretched, lost souls, you speak of 'above' and 'below' as two different things... but how can you separate the human from the divine, man from the universe? How can you separate that which cannot be separated, save in your narrow minds?"

"How can you sever the river from its source? How can you deny Becoming its essence and its soul, which is Being? How can you ignore the thought that gives life to the deed, and the word that gives form to the dream, and the dream behind every act of creation? Know thou not that the heart of creation beats through your own heart, and that its soul echoes the melody sung by your own breath and written with your own spirit? For the whole universe is contained in your innermost being!"

"How can you despise the stars, when you glorify their son, man? How can you deny God, when you embrace His soul, Life? For Life, as Truth, is one, and earth and sky are bound by a sacred union and blessed with the sacred breath of creation. Life is neither above, nor below, but All and Everything, Being and Becoming… it is the seed contained in the fruit, and the fruit concealed in the seed; it is the soul giving life to the body, and the body giving form to the soul; it is the atom and the cosmos, the ideal and the real, bound forever in a divine totality and an indivisible whole, a closed Circle of eternal becoming."

"And if man is alone in this universe, how poor and wretched life is doomed to be! How many worlds squandered, how many dreams denied! But is our earth not the daughter of the universe? Is man not the son of Creation? Is your 'realism' not a sin against… reality itself? For what is reality but Life, in Her motley forms and Her divine unity? By denying the higher meaning of Life, do you not also deny… Life? Do you not also deny your higher self and your higher destiny?"

"You spurn what's above and praise what's below, but do you not know, you blind men who foolishly and arrogantly — and foolishness is often arrogant — speak of the Light, that in the boundless realm of Being there is neither above nor below, only Wholeness ever unfolding, ever evolving, ever expressing and revealing itself through Life's myriad forms and aspects? For though the Spirit wears countless faces and borrows different shapes and creates infinite worlds, still there is a sacred invisible bond that lies at the source of all living things and pervades everything, everywhere."

"Hence 'below' and 'above', as all earthly divisions, are words and worlds invented by man, whose short-sighted, narrow soul, unable to behold the Whole, perceives glimpses of the Light and deems itself enlightened, and whose fallible, limited mind, unable to conceive the Whole, needs to reduce and divide and label and weigh and measure all things according to human logic and human understanding, deeming itself wise, unaware, in its blind ignorance, that in doing so, it debases and distorts Truth, whilst thinking it is discovering and embracing it... But the *truly* enlightened ones see through the deceiving shroud of relativity and diversity, and with their sharp eyes pierce the veil of *Maya* and behold the One behind the many, and the Absolute behind the relative, and the Eternal beyond the transient. Those are the Great Masters who see the eye of God in the soul of Life, and touch the heart of Truth beating with the breath of Creation."

"There is a wise saying among the Initiates, those bearing the last spark of divinity on earth: 'as above, so below'; although that axiom remains timeless as the universe, yet it was especially true when the earth was still divine, and in its various manifestations reflected divine will and divine harmony. But today the earth is a distorted mirror which only reflects the dark and base soul of the lower order of those rejects of Nature, soulless and faceless creatures that are more beasts than men, wretched refuse of a declining life unworthy of itself... nonetheless, men still cling to the comforting illusion and lost ideal that man *as we know him* is in the image of God, as that is what their fading divine memory, which is engraved in their very souls, still faintly captures from its original source."

"But now that Gaïa rots in human filth and decay — though you men call this filth and decay 'civilisation' —, now that man lives in the shadow of his divine past, *we* the gods say: 'neither above, nor below!' Speak no more in these human terms! Everything is one, everything is whole, 'above' and 'below' are but different facets of the same reality. For even as man longs for the divine and the Unmanifest, gods long for human manifestation, the miracle of creation. That is how the Sacred Circle is completed, that is why men and gods share a common destiny. There is neither above nor below! That, my benighted friend, is the kernel of what you common mortals call 'reality', and what we gods and Initiates simply call 'Life'. For Life is the ideal and the real, the seen and the unseen, it is the 'aught' that transforms the 'is', and the idea that shapes all forms. And it is the unseen *within* you that moves your body and moves your heart. It is the unseen within you that reflects itself in your world, below and above."

"That is how we, the gods, view the world and understand Life, for we are Her beloved sons. But in your 'relative' or 'real' world of lost and lonely atoms, in your wretched human world, each man beholds and creates his own world, his own god, his own heaven and his own hell. Each man beholds the universe through his own soul, and sees his own soul in the universe; but he himself has created *his own* universe! And so, down under, *every man* is an island, every man is a world unto himself, a miserable worm that thinks itself a god."

"Hence, I say unto you: 'as below, so above' is *your* sad reality today; for by darkening your souls, you have darkened your skies... by slaying the god within, you have slain all gods and shattered all beliefs and buried all longing and emptied this earth from all meaning... by denying your Higher Self, you have denied your higher destiny... by stifling the voice of the divine in you, you have cursed Life and turned the world into a desert. That is why I seek *my* world and *my* light beyond your world of shadows and dust, for *my* reality lies elsewhere, as in the Dark Age of man, where all meaning lacks, to each belongs his own god and his own world that his own soul has created."

"Therefore, I tell you: it is the darkness within your souls that has covered your skies with the colour of doom and gloom... it is the worm in you that has eaten away the heart of Life... it is the devil in you who has killed the god in you… it is the dwarf in you who has cursed all higher longing… it is the disease in you that has defiled Nature's divine innocence and distorted all reality and scarred all beauty and turned the world upside down… you have dried all the oceans and sullied all the rivers and polluted the skies with your unquenchable greed… you have buried all faith and drowned all hope, you have denied all purpose and taken away from Life its purity and its innocence, its joy and its magic… you have turned this heaven into a hell, you have made this divine earth human."

"And the 'light' you speak of, the light you see, is but the faint shadow of the original Light of Life, the Light of Creation, the gift of the gods to men. Your so-called light is but human illusion… your so-called 'enlightenment' is but a deceiving garb worn by your deceived minds to cover the dark void left by a reason unsatisfied and unfulfilled, a reason which has conquered superstition but has failed to conquer itself, by giving itself a higher meaning and serving beyond itself and exceeding its own limits, as only thus it serves Life best and embraces Her hallowed spirit. For reason is but a tool in the service of the Spirit, and when it becomes an end in itself, it loses its meaning. And reason devoid of meaning is but one of the various masks worn by ignorance. And reason devoid of spirit is but a blind tool at the mercy of unbridled base instincts."

"Therefore, my vain, shallow friend, steer clear of the conceit of the ignorant, for conceit is often ignorant, and Wisdom is always humble; and by learning, one teaches best. Do you not *see*, O blind men who preach enlightenment, that the 'reason' you unreasonably worship today, is yet another idol that you kneel before, though you claim to be wise, and yet another shackle that you carry, though you claim to be free? Is not reason the new idol of modernity, or what you falsely call 'the age of the Enlightenment'? Is not reason the new god of those who proclaim themselves godless? But true enlightenment has no idols, and true piety needs no gods."

"Do you not know, you fools pretending to be wise, you self-proclaimed 'free thinkers' who are neither thinkers nor free, that reason devoid of purpose is just another superstition draped in the mirage of realism, a human sigh lost in the vastness of space, as faith alone gives meaning to Life, and gives life to all meanings? And without purpose, there can be no faith!"

"And, pray tell, *why* do you speak of reason and faith as though they were enemies, separating them instead of uniting them? For reason without faith is cold and empty, and faith without reason is blind and dark; but together, they are supreme, together they are the twin souls of Higher Life, and through their holy union speaks the eternal voice of Truth."

"Why do you oppose freedom with virtue, as though they were irreconcilable? Does freedom *have* to be immoral, does virtue *have* to be a yoke? Is not *true* freedom, higher freedom? The freedom of the heights, which ever wants to overcome and transcend and climb the endless scale of Perfection, above all desire, want, and need? Does freedom have to debase man and drag him down beneath himself, should it rather not lift him up above and beyond himself? Seen in this light, is not true freedom the essence of virtue? Is not true virtue the highest kind of freedom, the freedom from earthly shackles and human attachment, pain, and fear?"

"You call yourselves 'free spirits', you little men of modernity, but you are as far removed from the spirit of freedom as you are from the freedom of the Spirit; for yours is not the freedom of the peaks, the overflowing spirit of Supremacy that dwells among the stars and breaks all the human chains which enslave the soul and debase the mind, and soars supreme in the divine spheres of Infinity... no, you shallow and petty souls *think* you are free (do you even *know* what that word *truly* means?), yet in truth you shun your higher longing as idle illusion and remain slaves to your basest instincts which rule you and blind you... your 'freedom' is naught but the lust of freed slaves who surrender to their lowest desires and confuse free will with sickness of mind and darkness of soul."

"Freedom in your perverted eyes is not a beginning, but an end, a dead end for the aspiring soul and a wanton license for unbridled perversion, a license for licentiousness, the unquenchable thirst of the vile and the lustful. Your freedom is not the pure freedom of open skies and infinite possibilities, but mere freedom from morality, freedom from *responsibility*. But true freedom entails responsibility, otherwise it would merely be the infinite foolishness of immature minds and incomplete souls. And responsibility is impossible without consciousness and virtue, for only a conscious mind and a pure soul can truly be free, that is, lofty and supreme."

"There is higher freedom and lower freedom. There is the freedom of the master and the freedom of the slave. Yours is the freedom of slaves… for freedom in your perverted ears deafened by the sounds of primal instincts, is naught but a hollow word that echoes only in the dark valleys of a fallen humanity."

"There is higher freedom and lower freedom. There is the freedom that shines from within, a boundless overflowing Will that pours its blessed drops of creation in the sacred cup of Life, a divine inner sun which eternally dawns unto itself and the world and dances joyfully with the liberating wind of Infinity, radiating its hallowed rays of Light into the depths of Being. And there is the freedom that is buried within, the freedom that comes from lack, the insatiable lust which cries out for unfettered indulgence of the senses and ever longs for itself, but ever remains unfulfilled, an endless twilight and a constant fall… Thus the born master, even in capture or defeat, remains proud and free, for he is free *inside* — and freedom, as bondage, is in the mind —, while the born slave, even when he runs in the open air, remains ever a stranger to freedom, as his soul remains dark and lowly, ever trapped in the bondage of his own blind instincts."

"True freedom is never sought or conquered, but ever lived and felt; it is never a yearning or a promise, but a path that leads beyond and above itself, even as the arrow longs for its highest target. Thus, your unquenchable thirst for freedom betrays the hidden shame of an enslaved soul; that is why you should free yourselves from your own lust for freedom before you can truly be free… you should sever the chains of your soul before you can walk unbounded and unfettered in the garden of Life. That is true freedom, that is the higher freedom that only the gods and godmen know and live."

"Ours is the freedom that liberates, yours is the freedom that enslaves. For bondage to the senses is the worst kind of bondage, and when the tyrant in you cries 'Liberty!', it is naught but the desperate sigh of an inner slave unable to free himself from his own yoke and sever the chains that bind him to his darkest, lowest desires. Hence, few people are truly free, as freedom is a gift bestowed solely upon the pure and the lofty, otherwise it is naught but slavery in disguise."

"You proud peacocks of freedom, you remain motley-coloured failures… for though you beg to differ, is there *really* a difference between different kinds of failures? And tell me, you shallow men of the modern age, what have you done with your freedom? Have you served it well, as it has served you? Have you used it wisely? Has it lifted you upwards towards your highest longings? Has it built bridges to higher realms and deeper meanings? Has it been a stairway to creativity and perfection? Has it allowed you to overcome yourselves, thus fulfilling its true purpose? Or has it dragged you into the bottomless pit of bestiality, lust, and decadence? Has your freedom made gods or beasts out of you?"

"Tell me, men of the Free World, have you *earned* your freedom? Has your freedom justified itself before the eyes of Eternity? Or has it been your downfall and your shame? Has your freedom grown wings to carry your noblest longings to their ultimate destination, up yonder on the peaks of Higher Life, or has it burned these very longings, by satisfying the cravings of your lower self? I tell you, your freedom is itself a cross that your deluded souls carry to their own crucifixion on the path of death, though you call your crucifixion a blessing."

"You self-proclaimed free spirits, the truth is that you have not honoured freedom but slandered it; you have emptied that noble word from all meaning, for in your foul mouths it has acquired a foul taste… and all I see before me today is a freedom that is ill-understood, ill-used, and ill-deserved. All I see, above and below, in the East as in the West, are slaves who walk unbounded, carrying their chains within their souls — and the chains that are within are the hardest to break. All I see is a new bondage of the spirit calling itself freedom, and a new tyranny calling itself reason."

"You call yourselves 'realists', but you remain strangers to reality and blind to its totality, dreamless sleepers wandering aimlessly in search of life's true meaning and purpose which lie buried among the ruins of your own greatest longings."

"You call yourselves 'civilised', but yours is the civilisation of accumulation and mediocrity bearing the banner of justice and equality, a sham civilisation which buries all higher aspirations in the stagnant mud of materialism, and drowns all will to elevation in the murky waters of degeneracy."

"You call yourselves 'cultured', but yours is the dark culture of greed and ignorance wearing pompous names, the contemptible culture of perverted minds and empty souls."

"You poor souls of the rich world, I tell you: you can *have* your 'dream city', your dark culture and hollow civilisation, you can *have* your glowing fake lights — for all that glows is not gold! —, your petty pleasures — are not *all* pleasures petty? — and fountains of delights, for they mean nothing to me… *I* yearn for something else, something much higher, much deeper; *my* dream is different, *my* land is divine. I seek *my* light elsewhere, I seek *my* god in higher realms and in better worlds. I search for the divine spirit of a distant future that shall inherit the deepest past and redeem the human present; and what are your great monuments but wretched remnants and posthumous tributes to that divine past which is innocent of you? Yes, your own past is innocent of you, for you are unworthy of your great forefathers... *they lived a healthy, pure, noble life in accordance with Nature, Mother of All and daughter of Creation.* You are strangers to your own past, for the divine past is innocent of the human present, and the future alone shall redeem the glorious memory of the vanished Civilisations of the Spirit."

Offended by Arya's violent diatribe which hurt his firm beliefs, the stranger looked at her with bewilderment, baffled by that scathing attack against a world that he considered supreme and perfect. "How can you criticise that which is beyond criticism?" he said with apparent irritation, "for ours is the ideal city on earth, the City of Man, the earthly Eden made reality. We have reached the highest stage of human evolution, the end of history and the accomplishment of man's millennial dream of the Good Life."

"*This* is the centre of the modern world, the essence of civilisation, the capital of culture, the beacon of freedom, the land of solidarity and fraternity. Here, we are all free and equal brothers and sisters, people of all faiths, classes, races and cultures, living side by side in peace and harmony. We have found eternal happiness, we are the envy of the whole world! How can you not *see* this glory, how can you not *recognise* such glory?"

"I fail to see what is so special about this city which you depict as an earthly paradise," Arya replied, indifferent to the man's excessive enthusiasm, "all *I* see is a human hell packed with empty souls and desolate hearts, a gloomy hell filled with noise and reeking of lust and greed... all *I* see are grey skies above, grey souls below... and where you see a land of wonders and delights, I see an ocean of gloom drowning your highest horizons and crushing your deepest longing. For I have no interest in your human pleasures, the greatest and smallest of them. I have no interest in your human values, the highest and lowest of them. For what is your heaven but *our* hell, we the gods? What is your dream but our nightmare? What is your civilisation, your 'liberty' and your 'equality', but bondage to the darkest instincts, and equal mediocrity? Your heaven reeks of lust, it is naught but poverty of spirit and misery of soul."

"And what of this 'diversity' that you so proudly speak of? Diversity is one thing, harmony is another; and one does not necessarily lead to the other. For inharmonious mixture produces a bastardised, mediocre uniformity, soulless orphans and failed heirs; and diversity best serves harmony when through it sings not the ugly noise of chaos and confusion, but the divine symphony of Order and Unity. And so, while man, in his blind arrogance, thinks that through intermixture, he is preserving diversity, yet in reality he is destroying it! Thus you speak much of freedom, justice, and harmony, but *we* are already free, and *our* justice speaks thus: 'equality is human, hierarchy is divine. And purity alone bears the immaculate beauty of the divine."

"Man, in his infinite conceit that knows no shame, and his blind ignorance that knows no boundaries, has shattered the divine harmony… man has severed the sacred bond with Nature, the bond with his higher Self… that is why his soul has become dark and hollow, and violence, treachery, decadence, ignorance, vice and greed rule this fallen earth. Everywhere I see culture, but nowhere Wisdom! Everywhere I see knowledge, but nowhere Truth! Everywhere there is civilisation, but nowhere elevation! Man is everywhere, and God nowhere! The earth has become dark, the earth has become human. Woe to the living, woe to the children!"

"Therefore, you can *have* your dark culture and hollow civilisation, for *I* am seeking higher goals and deeper meanings, I am striving to be one again with Mother Nature, I am seeking my Great God Pan, god of Nature, god of Life… I am seeking the spirit of Wotan, I am seeking the pure life, the divine life of the beginning and the end."

"Who needs Nature?" the man interrupted Arya, "we have culture! Who needs to seek out your so-called 'pure life' up yonder in the cold desert of departed gods, when the human pleasures of the flesh and the rapture of the senses are offered to you in this garden of delights? Your 'ideal' world is an illusion, you are a dreamer. Wake up to the real world! *Our* world is a world of relativity, there is no absolute truth or ideal, there is neither God nor heaven nor hell, there is only this imperfect world of imperfect lives and imperfect goals. Therefore, live this live abundantly, while it lasts! Nothing is absolute, everything is relative. We have found the ultimate truth, and that is: there is no truth! And as that great thinker, the prophet of all free spirits, once said, 'nothing is true, everything is permitted!', we follow this precept of abundant life. Why do you fail to grasp *this* truth? For the only truth is that which can be grasped and understood and lived."

Arya held a moment's silence, as she was gauging the deep chasm that separated her from men; she was saddened by the conviction that now firmly imposed itself upon her, namely that gods and men shall ever dwell in two different, mutually exclusive worlds constantly clashing in an eternal battle between eternal strangers. In this brief moment of heavy silence that filled the air with the extreme tension produced by the meeting of opposites, Arya spoke thus to herself: "this man remains a stranger to my soul, he remains deaf to my wisdom, and blind to my truth. Woe is me! Why do I insist on bridging the unbridgeable gap between men and gods, why do I seek to cross the impenetrable barrier separating gods and men? Why do I seek out the other shore, hoping to save a fallen mankind from itself, and elevate it above itself? Can one save the damned? Can one elevate the fallen? Can one raise the dead? Woe to the living! The divine flame which kindled the dawn of Life on this earth is dead and buried, and the millenarian dream of the God-Man has become a nightmare; for when dreams remain unfulfilled, they poison past and present…"

Thus Arya pursued her internal dialogue with her soul: "this man and I could go on forever in our dialogue of the deaf, but we remain worlds apart... so why do I still seek to join that which can no longer be joined? Can one explain to a man born blind the concept of colour? Can a deaf man ever savour the sound of music? Will a fallen man ever breathe the pure air of the heights, and behold the glory of Life from Her highest peaks?"

"This human mess of colours and faiths, this confused and failed mixture of every race and every faith, transpires in their values and beliefs; the inharmonious blend of forms and colours, and the unsuccessful mixture of spirits, has created this dark, ugly culture of confusion which cannot define itself nor be defined... that is why these so-called 'realists' shun the ideal and the absolute, and believe in compromise and relativity. For it is the confusion within their souls, and the noise within their minds, which make them submit to their fate, the dark fate of noise and confusion, within and without, which deafens their ears to the silence of the gods, and blinds their eyes to the Light of Eternal Truth. And, what's more, these petty souls cite *our* prophet and defile his liberating message to justify their petty beliefs and sanctify their petty pleasures, unaware that *our* truth opens new horizons to man, while theirs closes all doors and denies man his higher destiny."

Suddenly remembering the presence of the stranger, Arya again addressed him, saying dejectedly: "you petty souls of a fallen world, your world is what you make it, your life is what you make of it; and, as you say, there is no truth save the truth that can be grasped and understood and lived; but what *is* that truth which *you* grasp and understand and live? *Your* truth is but fall and decadence, death of soul and sickness of mind."

"You have made your world in your image, you have made your god in your image; your god is now called reason, your god is now cold reason... but a reason which strives not beyond itself remains trapped in the cage of matter, and becomes the slave of blind passion;

and reason in the service of the senses is but a tool to gratify the vilest instincts, not a way to reach self-fulfilment and self-overcoming. For reason only fulfils itself when it overcomes itself and thus leads to Awareness. But *your* reason has driven you to bestiality, instead of making men out of you — for is not man first and foremost a *thinking* being? — . But how *could* you think like men, when the cry of the beast has stifled the voice of the god in you? Thus your 'reality' is as far removed from Life as you are removed from the true spirit of man... for the human realm is governed by reason, while your reason is governed by your senses, though it proclaims itself supreme."

"Tell me, you proud sceptics, has reason on its own ever achieved anything great? Is not faith the gift of the gods which imbues reason with meaning, and blesses it with hope? Is not reason an instrument of Intuition, that divine breath of God bestowed upon men? Is it not faith which inspires your artists and poets, your saints and conquerors, in fulfilling their dreams of Beauty, Perfection, Truth, and Supremacy? Does not all greatness entail a drop of madness, but of that creative madness which only comes from above and tears asunder the word 'impossibility'? Are not all dreamers madmen? Have not all men of genius defied all human boundaries by serving their divine aspirations? For it is faith, not reason, which truly separates man from the animals, and the higher man from the ordinary mortal, and gods from men."

"I tell you, your world has been drowning in darkness, and it is heading — blind and unconscious — ever closer towards its doom, ever since the divine spark of genius that kindled man's soul ever again was forever buried under the sands of the desert of the Mind and the desert of the Spirit."

"I tell you, even the coldest reason needs a drop of madness to find meaning in Life... even the coldest of worlds needs the warmth of faith to light its dark and long nights... and he is truly blessed who has been struck by the lightning of the gods, he who has tasted the sacred wine of Eternity, he who has drunk from the overflowing fountain of Truth.

But your world remains poor and wretched, for true wealth comes from the Spirit, all else is dust in the wind of Infinity."

"Do you not realise, you lost souls of a lost world, that *you* are the ones who are removed from reality, for you live on the margin of Life, though you cannot even be called dreamers—for dreamers are endowed with the gift of faith—, only sleepers with no dream, no hope, and no purpose, unconscious and uncreative... 'when nothing is true, everything is permitted': *that* is a truth which I also embrace, but in your mouth it acquires a sour taste; for *what* is permitted? Is it to fall to the lowest level and become like beasts, or to rise to the highest peaks, and stand as equals among the gods? That is how we *true* Free Spirits—free in thought and in deed—understand the meaning of Freedom and embrace the soul of Life. For *our* freedom speaks thus: 'you shall rise ever higher on the infinite scale of your own destiny, you shall ever transcend and overcome yourself, and in transcending and overcoming, create yourself ever anew'. Thus *our* freedom is a creative will which elevates and transcends, while yours is a dark craving which debases and destroys."

"You claim to have broken all idols and shattered all illusions, yet in truth you worship the worst of idols and you cling to the greatest of illusions: you worship the flesh and you cling to this material world of evanescent and changing forms... hence, you only see the clouds, you only see the shadow of Light and the dust of Truth, while I see beyond... beyond the clouds, beyond your world of ghosts and shadows. And I know that beyond these dark clouds of gloom and decay, there is Infinity, boundless Light; and beyond your human world of ephemeral pleasures and elusive reality, there is Eternity, Supreme Truth."

"You self-proclaimed sons of the 'Enlightenment', the truth is that darkness pervades your soul and numbs your mind... thus you are dead men walking through the dark maze of an empty, meaningless existence. Yours is the land of illusion, a mirage in the desert of a disillusioned world without faith, without purpose."

"You have killed God, you proud realists spell-bound by the tyranny of reason... Yet have *you* yourselves justified this crime? What have you done to fill the abysmal void left by God's demise? Have your lives justified Life, so as to make amends for your deicide? For one redeems one's crime by overcoming it. But what have you done to overcome yourselves? You have killed God, you petty mortals, but have you yourselves become gods to redeem his death?"

"But how could *you* become gods, when the worm still dwells in your body and gnaws at your soul? How could you enter the realm of the unfathomable, and explore the infinite soul of Life, when your mind is still entangled in the entrails of bestiality, and lives in perpetual fall? How could *you* become gods, you pompous dwarfs of the Spirit, when you have yet to become men, *whole* men? Become whole men, before you act like gods! But you do not fool me, for beneath your inflated conceit lies a deep lament and a secret shame... the void in you speaks to me, and even as you flaunt your wealth, your starving soul cries out: 'you have killed God, but what have you done to replace him? You have cursed God and denied all gods, but have you given Life a new meaning? Have you given man a new meaning? Has a new dawn redeemed your darkest night?' "

"You have broken old idols and removed all altars, turning churches into sepulchres of the old god; yet have you not also sacrificed all your higher ideals upon the altar of Truth itself? Godless mortals, what will be your new belief, now that your god lies in the grave? Or would you rather go back to the animals, lacking all purpose and surrendering to your basic instincts? Your god is dead, and you lie hopeless and bitter before his grave, secretly grieving your loss of faith. For you have become realists, that is, deniers of all perfection and all elevation. Your 'realism' is but another word for impotence, the highest form of cowardice. You have become realists, empty shells of men, unworthy of belief, incapable of love, self-deluded 'free spirits'... but a free spirit is he who overcomes himself again and again, and always aims higher and goes deeper into the mysteries of Life."

"You killed your dream when you killed your god, and now you are left soulless, godless, and purposeless; but you *had* to kill him, for he was your own invention, an imperfect god for an imperfect humanity. Hence you could no longer bear to look above and see your own imperfections in the mirror of your highest hopes. But do you not know that verily you killed your *real* god, your inner god, the eternal and boundless in you, when you killed your deepest dream, the divine dream which gives meaning to this earth? Do you not know that it is when you killed your highest longing that you truly killed your god? And is not the highest longing the dream of the God-man, the god in the making, the divine wearing a human face?"

"But it did not have to be so! For when you awoke from your divine dream and realised that you were dreaming the world, dreaming God, dreaming yourselves, you decided to stay awake, for fear of falling again in the sweet but poisonous illusion of a life that denies Life; yet in doing so, you fell into another illusion, the illusion of the world of forms, and the deception of the mind which thinks itself supreme and thus strips reality from its own purpose and denies it its own dream of transcendence. For Unity knows no separation, and mind and soul belong to the same realm of Being. Therefore, by submitting to the yoke of the material world, you also deprived your thirsty and aspiring souls of the drop of madness that separates human reason from divine intuition, and human logic from divine magic, and human fate from divine destiny. By relinquishing your deepest dream and your highest longing, you also relinquished your deepest essence and your highest goal, you became but shadows of your higher selves."

"You poor mortals, you shall remain wretched and lonely in this vast universe of infinite possibilities, for you have chosen the dwarf over the Higher Man, the buffoon over the prophet, the petty comfort of mediocrity over the divine glory of Supremacy. Thus you pay the price of your own folly, and you bear the guilt of your own crime."

"Darkness in the East, darkness in the West! Over there, in the East, they are the sleepless dreamers, people who dream while they're awake, who dream *that* they're awake... but here, in the West, is the land of the dreamless sleepers, for here even dreams have faded, even hope has vanished under the ruthless tyranny of the 'reasonable' and the 'correct'; there, they lack reason and freedom and worship the void, but here you lack faith and purpose, here you *are* the void, and all of you are fragments of men and fragments of Truth."

"Over there, in the desert of the Mind, faith, misunderstood, twisted, and blind, has killed the soul of Truth. But here, in the desert of the Spirit, reason, misused, abused, and emptied of its purpose, has buried the light of faith. And though East and West, in their illusory war, both claim to have conquered Truth — through faith or reason —, yet in truth the whole world drowns in eternal darkness and illusion and worships the same idols of ignorance bearing different names; and is not ignorance the daughter of death? For faith without reason is death of mind, and reason without faith is death of soul."

"Equal in your folly, equal in your mediocrity! That is how *I* view East and West today... this whole earth has become mad, this whole earth has become blind, this whole earth has become sick; everything is twisted and scarred beyond recognition, freedom and justice and right and wrong and good and bad and higher and lower... God is dead, Eternal Night has descended upon humanity, and men have become blind, blind to beauty, blind to Truth; and where else than in Truth and Beauty does the Divine dwell and blossom?"

"And if one day, you open your eyes and you finally *see*, you shall see that darkness has engulfed you. And when you see that the world has become black and awry, you shall realise that you yourselves have made this world dark and ugly, you yourselves have brought this dismal fate unto yourselves. For the whole world is your own representation, your world is the reflection of your will, your reality is the fulfilment of your own thoughts and ideals. Thus the 'reality' you behold today is the dream you made yesterday, and the burgeoning promise of a new day."

"Equal in mediocrity! That is the norm today. Equal in misery and decay: that is *your* reality today. But *I* pay no heed to men's changing worlds and idle wars, for I bring the most sacred sign of Light and Life in man's darkest hour: I bring the Wheel of Fire to light man's night and kindle man's inner flame anew."

Arya suddenly fell silent, as she pondered her strange fate and Destiny's mysterious ways: "here too, they live in the dark and do not know it, do not see it," she thought, "here too, they call their night day, and their abyss the peak. All this time I *thought* I was heading North, while in fact I was heading West! Yet how could this be? How could I confuse what can never, what *should* never be confused? Have I lost the North, or has the North lost me? Have the gods betrayed their sons, or have the sons betrayed the gods? Must I cross this divine hell, this human purgatory, to find my Northern heaven?" Thus spoke Arya to herself, and, lost in her secret thoughts and her hidden world, she pursued her inner dialogue with her soul:

"But no one should make that gravest of mistakes: the West is not the North, and though their paths may meet on this earth where everything is confused, still they remain worlds apart... Alas! People today confuse West with North, but what do the people know? When have the people *ever* known? Is everything not mixed and mixed up nowadays, good and evil and higher and lower and East and South and North and West?"

"Nay, nay! The West is *not* the North! In fact, the West is the *opposite* of the North... even though there may have been a time when West and North were the same, when West and North *meant* the same thing, and their sons venerated the same gods and shared the same spirit... when the spirit of Wotan ran through the veins of all the sons of Ar, the Sons of the Sun, wherever they were, and blessed their thoughts and guided their deeds."

"Yes, there was a time when West and North were the same and meant the same, but that was at the Golden Dawn of gods on earth, when God and Man were one, when the god in man spoke through him and created beyond him, before the Dark Age of a faith gone mad and a reason gone blind stifled the voice of God in man, before the Divine was buried under the mud of superstition and materialism, in the name of the god of piety and the god of unbelief… for the twisted minds and narrow souls of men often confuse piety with unbelief, and unbelief with piety; thus piety leads to unbelief when it loses its soul, and unbelief loses its meaning when it turns into idolatry."

"The West betrayed the North when on its soil and in its soul the religions of the Book slaughtered the Religion of Nature, and the hollow words of men murdered the hallowed Word of God,"

"when the flesh was despised, then worshipped, and the Lord was idolised, then buried, and the Spirit was feared, then denied,"

"and reason and faith turned against each other, and the kingdoms of God and Man turned this earth into a hell for gods and men."

"The West betrayed the North when in the eyes of its sons God became a ghost, then a lie, an unreachable dream, then a fading sigh,"

"when faith became empty and reason became dry, and Life became a burden and a will to die,"

"when the tyrant became a god, and God became a tyrant, a curse unto himself and the world, an invisible despot whose dark reign sowed the seeds of death and smothered the soul of Life, and rendered man a helpless pawn in the hands of a ruthless fate."

"The sons of the West were doomed when they went astray from the path to perfection set forth by the divine Rama,"

"when the dawn of the gods became the twilight of men,"

"when the Son of God became not the Way but the end,"

"when the god on the cross was praised, and the god within was despised,"

"when the proud and noble warriors of Light, who lived and felt the divine within, became pious and humble servants of darkness,"

"And laid down their swords along with their honour, and thus betrayed their blood — for blood is honour — on the altar of death and shame."

"The sons of Agni betrayed the divine spirit of their great legacy,"

"when they abandoned the Wheel of Fire and its shining path to Immortality,"

"and bowed down before the cross of Death and its dark path of suffering and misery."

"Aye, when the sons betrayed their fathers and forefathers, they lost their divine memory, and West and North became strangers to one another and parted ways, never to meet again."

"The West lost its soul when it lost its memory and betrayed its goal,"

"when dishonour was preferred to death, and peace was preferred to victory,"

"and defeat was preferred to sacrifice, and pride turned to shame, and shame to pride,"

"when the blood was sullied and the spirit was lost,"

"and manliness turned to weakness, and love turned to lust,"

"and loyalty turned to greed, and honour was vilified,"

"when nobility became a slander, and virtue was reviled,"

"and the common became the norm, and the exception was cast aside."

"Verily, the West lost the North forever when its sons, humbled and misled,"

"turned from Knights of Truth into slaves of deceit,"

"when in their shrines an alien god was worshipped, and the god within their souls was shunned," "when in their hearts the cross of death was revered, and the Wheel of Life was despised."

"Thus the divine flame faded and died, and the Sun went down in the West, a dark veil of gloom descending on this godforsaken land of fallen men and lost pride."

"The West is not the North. The West will never be the North, and the North shall never become the West, so long as gods and men remain strangers; for the divine and human realms never could meet, save in the souls of those who have joined both shores and live the Life Divine in word and in deed."

"Here in the land of culture, they proudly proclaim the death of God and the end of history and the supremacy of reason over all superstitions. Here they claim to have reached truth by denying all earthly and heavenly creeds and slaying all illusions and breaking all idols — and is not God the greatest illusion and the greatest idol today? But they know not, these petty men of the civilised world, blinded as they are, that they have yet to slay the greatest illusion and the greatest lie of modernity: their absolute belief in relativity... for when nothing is true, everything is worthless; when nothing is true, everything is useless, and the world becomes empty and awry... and man becomes worthless and useless and empty and awry. Where meaning lacks, hope fades and death of soul and body ensues. And that is the wretched state of the world today."

"Modern man pretends to be above belief and free from idols, but he has yet to overcome his last belief: his belief in unbelief, and to break his last idol: reason. Man has yet to overcome his own greatest illusion and his own greatest lie: the illusion and the lie of his own supremacy, the illusion and the lie of reason's infallibility. Until then, his 'truth' will remain lies and deception, and his 'light' will remain shadows and illusions. For man's reason — as his senses — remains fallible and imperfect, and to worship reason is no lesser folly than to submit to passion; and to be blinded by science is no lesser folly than to be blinded by faith; and to worship the flesh is no lesser madness than to worship the ghost of an illusive god."

"Here in the West, they claim to have slain all gods and broken all chains and conquered all shame, yet in truth they have only replaced the old idols with new ones, and given new names to old superstitions. They built new idols with the same clay that moulded the old ones, and they serve these new idols blindly; and are not the cult of matter and the worship of the flesh the worst of superstitions and the greatest of follies? Does not ignorance remain the rule, in the East as in the West, in the past as in the present? Is man doomed to live in the shadow and abandon all higher paths?"

"Here in the land of gloom, they claim to live the abundant life, but never have I seen such poverty calling itself wealth! For the desert of the Spirit is emptier than all deserts... and in the midst of all that abundance in material things, man remains poor and wretched, hollow and meaningless, a lost lamb and a shadow of his divine Self."

"But there, in the North, in the land of the gods, Nature has remained undefiled, and in Her blessed womb She bears the eternal dawn of *Surya*. There the pure air carries with its refreshing breath the spirit of the heights, the Spirit of Supremacy, and the divine murmurs of the forests and sacred whispers of the wind together sing the sublime melody of Pan that echoes the hidden voice of Life's mysteries."

"Over there, the air has remained pure and Life has remained immaculate and man has remained divine. For to stray away from Nature is to stray away from God! Thus teaches *my* religion, thus speaks *my* wisdom... There, the silence of the gods relates the divine dawn of mankind which still lives on in the magical imagination of men."

"The West is not the North, the West will never be the North. North and West remain two different worlds and two different visions that shall never meet. This land is the end of all worlds, the graveyard of faith, the twilight of the Spirit, the death of all higher longing. Does not the Sun set in the West? Do not *all* suns set in the West? In the grey land of gloom, people confuse black with white, and West with North, and so mix them; but the North is not the West! And the East is not the South... and although people still confuse Light with darkness, still Truth is above men and beyond confusion."

Pushing a deep sigh of despondency, Arya thought: "I have seen enough! There is nothing for me here but disgust and contempt, I should go away, as far as I can, from the hell of modernity... Woe is me! I was fleeing the darkness in the East, I found it in the West, and with it, the unbearable noise of men. And if there is a hell on this earth, it is in the city." Thus spoke Arya to herself, inwardly and silently, and she bade the man farewell and decided to leave this strange land that she could never call home, and seek a more hospitable world where her soul could belong and her spirit could finally rest in the peace of divine Eternity.

3

As she briskly walked back toward the gate of the city, Arya's thoughts were already wandering beyond this world of dust and fumes, hoping again to find their peace in the stillness of their original abode, the realm of the gods. She walked through the narrow streets of the city, trying to remember whence she had entered it, but she was unable to tell one street from another, as all looked the same. She was caught in an infernal urban maze from which there seemed to be no way out. She panicked and shivered with horror at the terrible thought that she might actually remain trapped in this urban nightmare, doomed to wander forever in that concrete hell of the soulless and the godless, this grey world of dead souls and gloomy hearts.

The inverted pyramid

While bewailing the dark fate that befell her, Arya noticed a commotion nearby, in the city's main square, and she heard loud sounds of laughter mixed with jeers. She wondered what was causing all this noise, and approached the scene, curious to find out what this was all about. As she reached the main square, she saw a group of people gathered around a man who was standing on his head, his feet upwards.

The people were all jeering him, some laughing, others staring with disbelief or disdain. But the man was clearly not a street entertainer, as he was not performing any tricks or acrobatics. Nor did he seem deranged or unbalanced in any way, as he had a serious expression on his face. He was simply standing there, upside down, a serious man in a silly position. It was that paradox which caught Arya's attention. She approached the man and asked him: "why are you standing upside down? Do you not see how silly you look? What is the point that you are trying to make?"

"You all look surprised to see me standing upside down," the man answered with an expression of contentment upon his face, "but do you not see that the world itself is upside down? Should you not rather laugh at yourselves, and despise yourselves, instead of mocking me, for making you look in your own mirror? You look at me and see something unnatural, something absurd and awry… but have you looked at your world today? The world itself is standing on its head! The world has gone mad and dark and awry… everything has been turned upside down, good and evil and higher and lower and black and white and God and the devil! And if I stand this way, it is to behold the world as it once was, the world as it should be… the world as God intended it, for that is the natural order of things. But today man and Nature are strangers to one another, man and God are enemies, and this earthly heaven has become a human hell."

Upon hearing these solemn words coming out of what they saw as a mere buffoon, the people laughed even harder and heckled the man, shouting and booing, some even throwing things at him in order to make him fall. Then, visibly bored, the mob dispersed, and each went back to his or her usual tasks, quickly forgetting that brief encounter with that strange man. But soon, the same crowd assembled again in the same square, this time around a couple of dancers who were moving and jumping frantically, uncannily similar to apes. "Are these men pretending to be apes?" Arya, baffled, asked herself, "or apes pretending to be men? But why would *men* pretend to be apes?"

This time, the crowd was delighted, and it loudly cheered and applauded the dancers. Arya was stunned. She had witnessed both scenes and was amazed at the mob's strange behaviour: scornful of the tragic, respectful of the ridicule. Deeply touched by that human paradox, she spoke thus to herself:

"What a strange creature is man, so pitiful and foolish... such a shame, such a waste... man would rather go back to the beasts than overcome himself. He has chosen the ape over the Overman, the pigmy over the god. The world has become blind, the world has become mad... but man has yet to be aware that he is blind and mad; for without consciousness, there can be no redemption."

"I have travelled to different lands and I have seen different cultures, yet everywhere I saw the divine order of Nature defiled in the name of the hollow glory of an unknown god, or the illusive rights of fallen men... everywhere I went, I saw an inverted pyramid standing on the ashes of the Pyramid of Life."

"Verily, an inverted pyramid has been set up, an inversion of all natural values... everything has been turned upside down, everything has been mixed and has become mixed up: races and classes and man and woman and worm and god...the beast is praised and the god is derided, the fool is revered and the saint vilified, everything is inverted and fake, man lives against Nature and against God."

"All values have been perverted and turned into their opposites... thus evil reigns in the name of the good, the lowest are treated as the highest, and the highest are degraded and reviled."

"The outcasts now call themselves the chosen, justice is the will of the strongest, and Truth is tainted and despised."

"Vice is confused with virtue, beauty no longer transpires in art, and everywhere the sacred is defiled."

"The body is not the temple but the graveyard of the soul, men are ashamed of their honour, and to sin is now a woman's pride."

"Alas! The world is standing on its head... the illusory has become reality, the futile has become essential, and the material has crushed the ideal... and the Light has faded and died."

"Power is in the hands of incompetents and liars, wealth is in the hands of crooks and scoundrels, and humanity's fate is decided by fools and madmen; and today everything and everyone has a price..."

"Modern man is obsessed with possession and accumulation, and he calls his obsession 'civilisation'; but property is the source of all evil, it sows discord and feeds greed and drowns all meaning in the stagnant mud of matter... thus quantity has crushed quality, and matter has crushed Spirit, and man has buried God, and the world has become empty and meaningless."

"Man has scarred God's image, and the Pyramid of Life, drawn in the stars by the gods and conceived in the depths of the cosmic night, has been reversed, and all we behold today is the opposite of what originally was."

"Alas! Woe is me, for I am living in the Kali Yuga, the end of all times, the darkest of ages, the decline of man and the death of all gods. I am preaching Life's blessings and unveiling Her mysteries wherever I go, but all I ever see around me is a lifeless mass of the soulless and the hollow. I am preaching Love to those who can only hate, invoking the spirits in the land where gods no longer dwell, and evoking greatness to petty souls and weak hearts. Woe is me! I am preaching Life to the living dead, and enlightenment to eternal sleepers, and elevation to fallen souls, and purity to the stained and the damned."

The worm in man

With sadness in her heart, Arya left the city's main square and pursued her elusive quest of a lost world and a forlorn age. As she continued to search for a way out of the city, with stubborn determination but increasing despair, she stumbled on something on the sidewalk, and, as she looked down to see what it was, she swiftly looked away with disgust; it was a dead rat's decomposed remains, upon which countless worms were feasting. Sickened by that revolting view, Arya rushed away from the carcass, eager to forget that ugly image of death and decay.

But whilst she hurriedly walked towards her unknown destination, the image of death kept haunting her mind and tormenting her soul. "Death is truly an ugly thing," she said to herself, "even though it is in Her dark fields that the shining seeds of Life await their harvest at the rising dawn. Still, there is nothing worse, for a seeker of Light, than to behold the ugly face of death in the midst of Life's beating heart… and does not the worm dwell in man today? Is not man's soul rotting evermore, every day?"

"I have travelled to the confines of the earth… I have been East and West, where the Sun rises and sets, yet nowhere have I seen the Light. All I ever saw was darkness, gloom, and decay, begetting darkness, gloom, and decay… The Light has died, the light in man has died, the sun has set on this earth. The god in man has died, if ever there were one. And that which is left in him, that which thrives and grows and prospers in man, is the worm…"

"All that's left of man is the worm; the worm in man… the worm that *is* man… the worm that eats away man's soul and all that's divine in him, all higher thoughts and honourable feelings. No, there is no light in each man, as the idealists like to say… for man is neither divine, nor even human anymore… and man is no longer a beast, for to beasts belongs innocence, and man has lost his innocence and is driven by greed and envy, while beasts are driven by instinct and necessity. Thus beasts are innocent even in their cruelty, and man is guilty even in his innocence."

"I have travelled everywhere on this earth, I have seen the mightiest men sitting haughtily on their glorious thrones, I have seen the wealthiest men sitting contented on their mountains of gold, I have seen the holiest men standing as gods before their worshipping crowds… but nowhere have I found real power, the power that grows from inner peace and wisdom… nowhere have I found real wealth, the wealth that stems from a pure heart and a noble soul… nowhere have I found real faith, the faith that is imbued with a higher kind of love… nowhere have I found the Light… for how could the Light shine where there is no flame?"

"Nowhere have I found the Light… for the flame in the world has been extinguished, and fire has turned to ashes, and dust has returned to dust, as the soul alone is endowed with the breath of Life; and where Spirit lacks, darkness prevails and death ensues."

"The Son of God was right: there is none good… There is none good because they all live under the spell of *Maya*; and in the realm of illusion, the Ego is king… and the ego breeds on having, while the Self blossoms in Being and shines in Becoming… thus they all want to accumulate possessions, and they all want to attain power, and they all want to find happiness — as if happiness dwelt in power or wealth! — and the more they accumulate riches, the poorer they become in spirit… and the more they acquire power, the less they attain wisdom. But there are no limits to man's greed… and where it finds nothing to feed on and to gnaw at, it feeds on itself and destroys man. And man is left hollow and hopeless, a shadow in search of the Light."

"There are no limits to man's greed... ask anything of the highest or the lowest of men today, except to give, not of himself, but of the lowest in him, of that which is alien to him: what he *has*, not what he *is*. No, it is not of his highest but of his lowest that man is least willing to give... *ecce homo*!"

"Today, mankind is pushing its last sigh, mankind is doomed; for when the soul departs, the body decays... The soul of the world has left the earth, and all that's left is its decaying body. And all we see before us today: hate, war, pettiness, selfishness, resentment, perversion, vice, violence... are but symptoms of man's ultimate disease: greed... but man has yet to admit that he is sick, for ignorance feeds the disease, and consciousness cures it."

"Look at men today, running after power, running after money, running after women... those who run after ghosts and *away* from themselves, do they not know that happiness remains elusive to him who seeks it outside himself? Look at how they run after ghosts, these petty men of the present... I pity them and despise them. Do they not know that when we die, we are all naked, the highest and the lowest amongst us, the most powerful and the weakest, the wealthiest and the most deprived? And all we ever take with us to the grave, to the other life or the other world, are the higher thoughts that have enlightened our minds, the sublime feelings that have blessed our souls, and the righteous deeds that have purified our hearts, and this earth, and our fellow man? Do they not know that Life is a trial, and nothing else? But most of us are failures..."

"How little they rule, these men of power! How little they inspire, these men of faith! How little they own, these men of wealth! For true power and true faith and true wealth come from that which cannot be conquered, and that which cannot be granted, and that which cannot be weighed: the divine Self that dwells in man and serves naught but the Absolute and the Eternal. But nowhere on this earth have I seen a good man, nowhere in this world have I witnessed a selfless deed, never in this age have I heard a divine word."

"Man is a worm... the sentence has been delivered by Nature, daughter of Life: man should perish. Man *shall* perish. And only he who bears the sacred flame and serves not his kind, not his race or nation, but that which is beyond human identities and earthly divisions, only he serves the divine purpose and the march of history, and is worthy of inheriting this earth. For God is the Spirit, and Earth is the womb, and the God-man is the Son of Creation."

"And it is not death that man should fear most, but a life unworthy of Life... but where have all the higher men gone? Where have all the *men* gone? Truly man must have been greater, and nobler, than the shadow of man that we see before us today... This world has become dark, men have become dark, the end is near... but a new dawn is upon us, so let us redeem our passing night and await our coming day."

The darkest man

With unflinching will and unflagging faith, Arya continued walking towards her unknown destination. While wandering aimlessly through the streets, trying to find the gate of the city, she came across two men who were standing next to a woman outside a sleazy, dimly-lit bar. The woman, scantily and indecently dressed, caught Arya's attention and elicited her disgust; she was clearly a whore, and the two men were chatting with her, laughing loudly from time to time, both looking with lustful eyes at her worn-out body. But as Arya hastily passed them by, eager to get away from such an unsightly scene, she was struck by the fact that one of the men's face had undefined, blurred features... it was as though he had no face, and only his eyes were barely visible across the haze covering his countenance.

Arya was shocked by that uncanny sight, and she looked back, after she had passed the group. She stared again, from a distance, at the strange man, perplexed by that phenomenon. The man without a face was looking at the other man with admiration, as a disciple looks at one's mentor, emulating him in everything that he said or did. He was like his shadow, mimicking his every move and repeating his every word. Arya's curiosity grew, and she looked at the other man, trying to find what the faceless man saw in him.

As she beheld the second man, Arya was disturbed by his repulsive features, and she noticed that his appearance was different from the other people she had encountered in the city; was he an alien passing for a native? He clearly did not belong… but *where* does an alien *ever* belong? She scrutinised him attentively, trying to pierce, through the veil of form, the essence of his soul.

"Curly hair, round face, curved nose… bulging eyes, skewed look, crooked legs: nothing is straight with that man! Everything about him is crooked, everything about him lies… but how can a round head think straight? How can a twisted mind see Beauty and know Truth?" Thus spoke Arya to herself, and it suddenly occurred to her, like a flash of lightning: "I recognise that man," she thought, "he belongs to that wandering tribe which belongs nowhere and claims the earth as its own… they are known as the *Chandala*, the wretched refuse of all races and all faiths, but *they* refer to themselves as 'the Elect'…"

"I know him, he is the darkest man, he who has murdered God and defamed Life… it is he who has stifled the divine breath in man, and buried the sacred Light of Truth… it is he who renders everything dark and ugly wherever he sets his filthy foot and utters his unholy word and spews his lethal venom into the soul of existence."

"He is the ultimate decadent who defiles all that is sacred and debases all that is noble and crushes all that is lofty… it is he who smears purity and corrupts innocence and mars beauty, and spreads the scourge of nausea upon mankind, stripping man of his reasons and his ends. He is hell for others, he tempts and taunts and mocks everything and everyone, despoiling Life and preaching the cult of the flesh and the death of the spirit."

"He is the great falsifier, the sly deceiver whose whole life is a sham… it is he who perpetually lies and perpetually denies, turning all truths into lies and all lies into truths… he is the wry scoundrel who survives by stealing and grows by cheating; he is the merchant of illusions and the master of deception whose abject existence is a curse cast upon mankind, and whose demise is a liberation."

"He curses God and denies Life and is ruled by the spirit of revenge… he cannot create, so he thrives on destruction. He cannot inspire, so he instils despair in the hearts of men. He cannot believe, so he renders everyone godless. He cannot rise, so he wants to abase. He cannot uplift, so he wants to level. He is ugly, so he makes everything and everyone ugly. He is base, so he demeans and preaches equality for all, so none would be above him. He is the ugliest man, the darkest man, cursed by the gods and the prophets, and cursing God and Life itself."

"He was born dark of soul and sick of mind and weak of will, thus he sees and seeks darkness and sickness and weakness in the world. He sees the world through his dark eyes, he beholds the sun through his blind eyes; thus he remains alien to Life and blind to Light."

"He is the destroyer of values and virtues, the slayer of dreams, the denier of hope, enemy of heaven and earth. God to him is either a tyrant or a foe; therefore, he either lives on his knees or in despair, cursing a life devoid of freedom and a world devoid of meaning."

"He created a god so he would not sin, then he killed this witness to his sin. And now he worships the god of money and the god of vice and serves them from his very heart."

"He is the enemy of Nature and all things natural, for he is Nature's only sin, he is Nature's only imperfection. He is the anti-natural creature *par excellence*, that is why he has declared war on Nature and on

God for creating him sinful and base. He is outside Nature and against God."

"He is the damned and the cursed, the fallen and the outcast; he is the guilty who plays the innocent, the murderer who pretends to be the victim, and the oppressor who claims to be persecuted."

"Now he has revealed himself to the world, now he is naked before his victims and his tormentors — for victims often turn into tormentors —, this darkest of men, this ugliest of creatures. The ultimate decadent has now come out of his dark cave and aims to rule the world, for he rules best in this Dark Age, the iron age of decadence, and in this faceless West, a world which has lost its soul. Yes, the epitome of decadence rules best today. But his fall is near, his twilight has begun, as the first rays of the divine dawn emerge on the horizon of a new earth."

Thus spoke Arya's soul to herself, and, all of a sudden, she remembered that she had a mission to accomplish and a land to discover, so she hastily left the group and pursued her journey northwards.

Arya's lament

Walking aimlessly in the streets, Arya's desperation grew, and her patience waned. "Pain is the cancer of the soul," she thought, "and human pain is the hell of gods… but how can the Higher Man live today? When will I find my home? Where will I find my peace? Who shall heed my word?"

Distressed and gloomy, Arya continued her secret lament, and her tearful eyes stared hopelessly at the dark sky, imploring the gods to end her human plight. "Am I awaiting a dawn that never comes," she asked herself, "a sun which rises only on the horizon of my inner infinity? Woe is me! Am I doomed to wander the earth aimlessly, homeless and purposeless, an eternal stranger, an eternal seeker of a long lost light?"

"They say 'when there's a will, there's a way'; they say a strong will overcomes all obstacles. But there are times when even the most unbreakable will says to Life: 'your many blows have broken my spine, and now I lie powerless on the ground, too weak to fight, too bitter to hope, too crushed to rise.'"

"Oh the despair of a life without hope, the misery of a world without light… will my night ever end? Will my day ever come? This earth sickens me… My beloved Gaïa! I do not recognise you… what has befallen you? O Sacred Mother of Man, O divine daughter of Heaven, what has your ungrateful son done to you? Why did man become mad, why did he turn against you, and deface your sublime beauty? Who will restore your ancient splendour, who will revive your lifeless soul? Alas! Is it… too late? Too late to save you from man's greed and folly? Too late to save man from himself? Are your wounds beyond healing? Is man beyond salvation?"

"Disgust, disgust! I only feel disgust today… the nausea of man, the nausea at man grips my heart and smothers my soul. The time has come to rebel, the time has come to fight and turn all rules and all values and all virtues upside down, and restore the natural order, the divine order; only thus will the world become straight again, only thus will the world become sane again… and the beauty of innocence will shine yet again on a purified earth and a born-again man."

"The time has come for the Sons of Light to rebel against the servants of darkness and kindle anew the divine flame of *Surya* in the soul of Gaïa… the time has come for the New Age of the Divine Life to rise from the ruins of a doomed world bent on its own destruction through its blind veneration of death and ugliness."

"I have felt enough contempt at the false gods and their imaginary kingdoms of heaven which only bring hell on earth,"

"at the fake religions and their unholy wars waged in the name of God, against God," "at the crooked beliefs and their divisive versions of indivisible Truth,"

"at the narrow identities and their flawed visions of glory,"

"and all arbitrary labels which only sow hatred and instil fear and breed envy in the hearts and minds of men."

"I have felt enough contempt at the decay calling itself progress, the bondage disguised as liberation, the injustice inflicted in the name of justice, and the tyranny deeming itself virtue, to be able to speak my word… and *fight!* But when will I speak my word? Where shall I preach my truth? When will *my* god come?"

"The highest slander on earth — the myth of equality — called 'truth'! The greatest crime against Nature — man's alienation — called 'civilisation'! The worst immorality — the animalisation of man — called 'freedom'! O that I were blind, so that I would not behold man's ugly face and dark soul! O that I were deaf, so that I would not hear the noise of fallen souls indulging in unabashed bestiality… O that I could lose the sense of smell, so that the stench of the filth which has engulfed this earth would not reach me! O that I could lose all feeling, so as not to bear the unbearable: the loss of meaning and purpose."

"My heart aches, though my spirit is divine. In feeling, we are all human; but in longing, we are all gods. Thus I suffer like all humans, though I am a goddess… yes, even gods suffer on this earth; in fact, *only* gods suffer on this earth, for they alone never belong to a reality which they also cannot transcend, as they were born to change it — and how can one belong to something one was born to change? — And only those who suffer, only those who do not belong today, are those who shall be redeemed, those who shall survive the coming catastrophe. It is to them, those pure of heart and mind, that I address my highest hopes… It is to them that I speak my word and utter my truth."

"My suffering knows no boundaries… it is the affliction of forerunners, prophets, and visionaries. I was born at the wrong time, I was born in the wrong age… yet is there ever a 'right' time to be born for higher souls? Are not those chosen for redemption born above time, and against time, to redress the right, and redeem the fallen, and heal the offended, turning all defeats into victory, and all miseries into glory? In the eyes of Destiny, is not the wrong time, the best time? For Light proceeds from darkness, and Life from death, and dawn is conceived in the darkest night. And though this darkness overwhelms me, I should never lose hope, for I am the goddess of Light, and Light never fades and never dies."

"I should never lose hope, even when hope itself has given up; for though God's will works in mysterious ways, it never lacks purpose. And I was born for a purpose, I was born to *give* a purpose to this lost world and this doomed earth. This is my mission, this is my destiny; and one's mission *is* one's destiny."

"Today, humanity stands at a crossroads, hanging between heaven and hell; this is the threshold of a new beginning: who shall prevail in man, the god or the worm? Will man rise from his ashes, or will he remain ashes? Will he be the dust or the wind? Will he ever behold the Light, or live forever in the shadow? Is man doomed to stare eternally into the bottomless abyss of an unworthy existence, or will the time come when he will look above and within, and find himself, and by finding himself, redeem God?"

"And what of God? Man was born to feel one with God and Nature — the Father and the Mother —, but religions have taught him to think of God outside Nature and outside himself; but how can a creator stay away from his creation? How can a mother stay away from her son? Thus man lost God and became the enemy of Nature, alien to Life, alien to himself. And he lost heaven and earth."

"To conceive God outside Nature, outside Life… *that* is pure blasphemy, and the root cause of godlessness… and gods intervene each time humans commit this folly. The god of men has died, killed by reason; but the *real* god lives on, for he never was created, thus he can never be killed. Weep not, men, the death of the old god, for he was your own creation... you created him out of fear, and killed him out of despair; so do not mourn him, for he was your own worst fear and your own worst despair. And today he is the most pious who is the most godless."

"Philosophy has always asked questions, and religion has always answered them. But when philosophy ceased to ask questions, and religion ceased to give answers, the world was lost. For that which does not evolve is doomed for destruction, and so our present humanity is declining, for, instead of drawing its inspiration from the past, living the present, and building the future, it is denying a past of which it is unworthy, dreaming a present which ever eludes it, and remains blind to the future which defines it."

The vision

Lost in her thoughts, Arya did not realise that she had been walking for several hours without interruption. She was exhausted and needed to rest in order to be able to continue her quest. She sat on a bench and soon fell into a deep sleep. She had the strangest dream, in which the Great Alexander appeared to her on his magnificent white horse, wearing his shining armour and his splendid gold helmet. He was smiling and looked contented, his piercing eyes sparkling with divine inspiration, his handsome face glowing with higher energy. He got down from his horse, removed his helmet and offered it to Arya, saying:

"Arya, Great Mother of Agni, blessed child of *Surya*... you are the last breath of God on this earth, and the ultimate hope for man, ever. You are the last ray of the divine Sun that has hallowed this earth since the dawn of Time. You are the last ancestor and heir of the Dynasty of Light. That is why I have come to you, to bestow upon you this symbol of my holy quest and my sacred struggle. For I, too, was a Warrior of Light, I too was a seeker of Truth. And my great conquests were but a humble pilgrimage, from Greece to India, on the hallowed footsteps of my god, Dionysus, who joined East and West under One Supreme Truth which transcends all petty creeds, and under the Eternal Light which is above all fleeting shadows."

"Wear this helmet, Arya, and honour its meaning. It belongs to you now; it has always belonged to you, for I am but one of your many sons. All our hopes are invested in you, all our faith is devoted to you. If you fail, the Light will die with you, forever; but if you succeed, God will be reborn, and this earth will be healed, and man will be saved. Go, Arya, and speak your word, spread your message. Your mission has just begun. May the gods protect you on your sacred journey."

Having thus spoken, Alexander disappeared behind a blinding sea of Light. And then there was total silence, total obscurity. Was it a dream or a vision? It did not matter, for the message was delivered, and the mission was espoused. Her body still lying in a deep trance, Arya's soul thus asked herself: "is this the *Sign*? The sign of the Great Change, the Great Upheaval? Has the time come when the spirit of Alexander, the spirit of Hadrian, leave their sanctuaries of Light and their temples of Truth, and come back to inspire the righteous, and torment the wicked?"

"For when the unwise Pope of a faith inverted and usurped will sow his words of discord, and when the blind masses of a faith misguided and misused rise up, and religions wage wars against each other, and against themselves, the Wheel of Time shall again turn, and a new cycle shall begin. Aye, when the religions of the Book will go to war, *our* religion, the Religion of Life — *Natura Divina* —, which is beyond words and above strife, shall shine again on an awakened world."

"The Great Change will occur when Religion sheds Her empty, used shells, Her twisted goals and abused meanings, and Her Soul directly speaks to the souls of men, and Her Truth directly reaches their minds and captures their hearts. But every new birth is achieved through pain, and every new life grows from death; and, to be reborn, one must first perish. Thus the divine in man will only arise when the human in him dies."

"That is why Gaïa now pushes Her last sigh, that is why Life Herself humbly bows before death, and Light submits to darkness, and Truth yields to deceit, and Virtue is slaughtered on the altar of a perverted freedom, and Justice is trampled under the boots of brute force, and Wisdom is derided by the mindless, and Beauty is mutilated by the blind, and Nature, in the name of culture, is slain by the soulless."

"That is why, when the Great Upheaval shall come upon us, the Good shall wear the mask of evil, and Christ shall wield a sword, and Eros will become Ares, and Shiva will joyfully dance his dance of destruction; and God Himself will look away while men are submerged by the Wrath of Pan… Men, beware the wrath of Pan! It shall be ruthless… that is why the New Cycle will be born amid ruins, and the God-Man will walk over corpses. Alas! That is the tragedy of Life on earth, where consciousness is only achieved through suffering, and awakening is only possible in the midst of darkness, and elevation only occurs after the fall."

"For when purity has been eradicated from the hearts of men, it reincarnates in the form of destruction. And when innocence has been wiped off the face of the earth, it comes back with a vengeance. Thus Vishnu the Creator shall return, at the End of Days, as Kalki the Avenger."

Upon contemplating the terrible fate that awaited mankind, Arya's body quivered and her soul sought to tear down its human cage and join the higher spheres where it belongs, there in the realm of everlasting peace, beyond the cruel laws of the material world. But no one can escape Destiny, for She chooses her own heroes and her own martyrs — and all heroes are martyrs —. Unable to wake up, Arya remained in a deep trance, as though the Higher Powers had hypnotised her so that she could hear their voice and submit to their will. Plunged once more in a deep sleep where the border between reality and fiction disappears, Arya was dragged in an endless whirlwind beyond Time and Space, thrust into the black hole of an infinite void.

In another vision, Arya saw herself alone at night, on a mountaintop, holding a stone covered with dirt. She was staring at the stone attentively, for she was convinced that, despite the filth on the outside, it bore something magical. She broke the stone in half, eager to see what was inside it, and was amazed to behold, at its very core, a small, barely visible, but brightly shining diamond. Delighted to find this sliver of light in this utter darkness, Arya looked up at the sky above her, thanking the heavens for discovering this small piece of earthly heaven and divine earth, a promise of joy and prosperity for men, and a faint shadow of the original Light of the gods.

However, as she looked up at the night sky, Arya was absolutely stunned: millions upon millions of stars were shining above her, countless diamonds floating in an endless sea of cosmic mystery. After her initial astonishment, which sent shivers all over her body and filled her soul with an indescribable feeling of inner peace, Arya looked down again at her stone, and, as she was pondering the meaning of the magical link between heaven and earth, a voice that seemed to come from nowhere and everywhere said to her: "as Above, so Below… that is the timeless Wisdom which ever was, and which ever shall be; that is AUM, Supreme Truth, Absolute Unity."

The Voice continued, in a calm and steady tone: "Arya, you are seeking the Light, but how can the Light seek itself? The Light is all around you, for it is *in* you! Therefore, how can you seek That which already dwells in you? But you do not see It yet, you did not discover It yet, for you have yet to know yourself and to discover yourself. And you will never find the Light if you seek it outside yourself. Your search will be vain, and your life will be wasted, if you do not understand and accept this truth, which is the root of the Tree of Wisdom. Seek the Light where it began, Arya, not where it ended: seek it within, not outside!"

"As above, so below: if you, the goddess, cannot embrace this axiom, what distinguishes you from humans? Do they not all seek the Light? Do they ever find It? How can you lead men, if *you* have yet to find *your* path? And there is no path outside the soul, for the soul is the gate to the heavens. You are searching for That which can never be sought. Find yourself, and your search will be over."

"We are all the sons of the stars, the Light is in each one of us, but we have unlearned to see from within, we have lost our inner sight; and so we are left, hollow and blind, wasted rays of a lost sun. We are all hidden diamonds waiting to be uncovered through the light of consciousness, which breaks all shells and cleanses all ears and opens all eyes. For consciousness is the key to the temple of Awakening. The soul is the Gate, the Light is the Key."

"When the shell of Dogma breaks, and the Light of Truth is released, when the chains of identities are severed, and the essence of Unity is embraced, when men recognise the supremacy of the Spirit, and see the futility of division, then the Secret Doctrine, the eternal message of Wisdom which lies at the root of all religions — yet, as the diamond, remains hidden from the vulgar and the ignorant — shall be revealed to a higher humanity, a humanity awakened and reborn. And it is then that the divine will be redeemed, and the real god will appear, and man will be free."

The plea

When the Voice fell silent, Arya woke up. As she opened her eyes and looked around her, she had a sad look upon her face, for she realised that she was still in the city. She had not escaped, as she had hoped, from that dismal reality, save in her dreams. "Was it a dream, or a vision?" she again asked herself, and her answer was prompt: "does it really matter? What can I do, anyway? I have a vision, I have a mission, but I am *alone!* Where are my disciples? Where are my sons, my warriors? How do I find them, how do I find those for whom my message is destined? And how do I tell the good seeds from the bad ones?"

"And if the Light is to be found inside me, inside everything and everyone, *how* do I find my inner path? How can I attain Wisdom, when Her fruit has yet to ripen in my soul, and Her sun has yet to shine on my world? Who shall guide me? My prophet is gone, and I need him so! I have no guide and no followers… whom do I follow, and how shall I lead? Alas! I am a cause without warriors, a dream without foundations, a cry of hope drowning in a sea of despair…"

"Is my dream a vision, or is my vision a dream? If that was a vision, where is the path? And if that was just a dream, why does it haunt me so? Do not the seeds of creation blossom in the mystery of imagination? But what does it matter? I am alone, powerless, hopeless… I am a fading twilight and an unborn sun."

"Prophet, O my prophet… where art thou? Do you hear my plea, will you heed my call? And you, my unknown brothers and my unborn sons, where will I find you? Will you ever come back to me? Most of you have died on the battlefields of Truth, immortal martyrs of an immortal cause, slain, crucified, burnt, and sacrificed by the ignorant who did not understand you, and the wicked who did. Some of you are lost, some of you *want* to be lost… some of you have denied me, others have betrayed me, and most have abandoned me… but few, very few have remained true to me, very few have honoured my name and immortalised my spirit. Those are my worthy sons, those alone deserve to bear my name and carry my torch."

"Woe is me! Most of my children have abandoned me… and here I am, a solitary orphan, a childless mother, a broken shadow of a goddess, without roots, without horizons… O the shame of breeding unworthy seeds! My fallen sons, why did you dishonour your divine legacy? You are my shame and my sorrow… you are the traitors who have denied your souls, you are the cowards who have abandoned your swords, you are the defeated who never fought… you have twisted my words and emptied my meaning, you have belittled my name and shunned my glory."

"I was overflowing, you made me hollow. I was soaring, you made me fall. I was shining, you darkened my soul. The most divine word slandered by the most despicable mouths — and are not traitors the most despicable of men? — . A curse be upon you! You shall be damned for all eternity, you shall be overwhelmed by the darkness that you have brought upon yourselves and upon this pure earth. Thus alone shall you expiate your crime and pay the price of your betrayal; for the punishment should fit the crime. And when you wake up and see that darkness surrounds you, it will be too late, for you will be drowning in the dead sea of obscurity, finally reaping the rotten fruit of the unholy seeds that you have sown."

"O ungrateful heirs, the gods you have slain have cursed you; thus you are doomed to live in perpetual disgrace and untold pain, the disgrace of defeat and the pain of regret, having neither fought for your honour, nor repented for your crime; and your crime is unforgivable, my fallen sons, that is why you are beyond redemption, you who have scarred the immaculate face of purity, and flirted with the ugly soul of vice. For you can erase the traces of lust from your body, but can you ever erase the stain of betrayal from your soul? And guilt is the heavy price of sin."

"I have come to punish the guilty and redeem the innocent, for I am the Great Avenger of a stolen justice and a murdered truth. The time has come for Truth to rise from the Underground where human ignorance and folly have buried it, and shine again upon the world. Thus I cry out to you, my highest hopes, my deepest longings, my unborn suns, my faithful Aryas! It is to you that I speak my word, for you are the reason I still hope, you are the reason I still dream, you are the reason I still live in this disenchanted world of despair!"

"You who have remained pure when the whole world has gone dark, you who have remained true when the whole world has gone blind, you who held on to your beliefs when all others lost faith... it is to you that I raise all my hopes, it is to you that I deliver my ultimate message... and though you too have lost my way, I forgive you, O purest of breeds, for still you seek and still you strive... and all true seekers deserve salvation."

"But what shall I say to you, my Aryas, my beloved children, my noble Warriors of Light, when I finally find you? How do I preach my sacred Word, when I have yet to decipher its hidden meaning? And everything sacred has a hidden meaning, that is the wisdom of Life. What shall I say to you, my dear children, at our final reunion? For it is only when I find myself that you shall find me. But this I ask of you now, this I beseech you: become one! Forget your shallow differences, and cherish your deep bond; for your differences are shallow, and your bond is deep... and though you may speak different languages, though you may bear different flags and worship different gods, the blood that runs through your veins and transpires in your deeds and shines in your spirits carries the soul of Ur, your original sacred homeland, your first and eternal god. One is born into a race, but one chooses one's faith; thus one's true god lies in one's blood."

"O lost sons of a fragmented home, how I yearn to hear you sing again with one voice, and pray again with one heart, how I yearn to see you dance evermore to the rhythm of your primal song of creation... it is with sadness that I look at the complex maps of states and nations that you have woven out of that insidious spirit of division which has gripped you, ever since your gods were slain and your souls were sacrificed by the enemies of Life, and you were scattered into warring tribes oblivious to their common roots."

"I look at your maps, my beloved children, and all I see, from Aryana to Hyperborea, is One Holy Empire torn asunder, at war with itself and denying itself... all I see are shifting borders and sham cultures, brothers who have become strangers, separated by arbitrary fences, raised apart, pitted against each other, fighting amongst themselves, and dying for the sake of alien gods and strange creeds. All I see is discord where there should be harmony, and adversity where there should be comradeship, and enmity where there should be unity. All I see is division and hatred among the branches of *Yggdrasil* (9), the Holy Tree which bestowed this earth with the hallowed fruit of creation."

"Ah that I may see all my sons and daughters united under one flag and bound by one symbol — the Wheel of *Surya*, the Wheel of Life — and one destiny: Supremacy!" Arya abruptly changed her tone as she spoke in a solemn, almost holy manner, for the words were now coming out from within, as though dictated by a higher power and presence that dwelt in her: "I have come to teach the totality of all things," she said. "Life is a Whole, God is everywhere, and man is the son of Nature. Therefore, children of the stars, Sons of *Surya*, shed your petty identities and your human chains of time and space, and sing in unison the hymn to that inexhaustible fountain of Life whence you sprang!"

"Each sees in my divine eyes the mirror of his own soul, each looks through my eyes to behold his own soul. My sons, that is how you shall recognise me, that is how I shall recognise you. O noble warriors of Truth — and no one is nobler than the warrior of Truth —, you shall be the seeds of the new breed… that is why I still await you, you who remain as humble in victory as you are proud in defeat, you who are sincere in your longing and true to your destiny!"

"That is why I still believe in you, O nameless heroes whose will never falters and whose head never bows, save before the bolder and the wiser, you who alone have the courage to speak your word and utter your truth, when words are slaughtered and Truth is slain, while others shift with the wind and bow before the truth of the day and the victor of the moment."

"That is why I shall come to you, you who are rich in spirit and possess naught save that which has value — and nothing has value save that which is not possessed —, you the eternal victors and conquerors who never surrender and never submit, whose will grows stronger with each defeat, and bolder with each danger… you who never waver and hold on to your principles, in glory or defeat, and even more so in defeat; for that is the true test of a nobleman: to be able to withstand the capricious and ruthless winds of change, and the treacherous and deceitful scale of justice."

"But alas! The Master Race is dead… and the new seeds have yet to blossom at the dawn of the New Age. I am the last Arya, the last ray of the divine Sun on this earth… I am the last orphan and the last mother of the glorious Race of Light. I bear an unbearable burden: I am the seed, and I bear the seeds of salvation."

Kshatriya

Thus spoke Arya to her unborn stars, and she pursued her unfinished journey northwards. With an iron will and a brave heart, she walked for endless hours through the urban maze, in search of the liberating Gate that would lead her closer to her destination, closer to her destiny. But still, there was no gate in sight, and no light at the horizon — and when was there ever a horizon in the city?

Just as she was beginning to lose hope and abandon her path, Arya was astonished to see a man dressed as a knight marching, alone, in the middle of a deserted road. Her disbelief gradually turned to admiration, as she attentively stared at the man's stern countenance and his sharp eyes which seemed to behold other worlds and higher goals. He had the firmness and determination of a warrior, but there was also a hidden, gentler side to him which betrayed a deeply sensitive soul that only a woman could perceive. "Pray tell, kind sir, why are you dressed like that?" Arya, amused, asked the knight, and, giving in to her growing curiosity, further inquired: "why do you march alone in this strange city, and where is your army? Should you not be on the battlefield? But you belong to another age!"

The knight, surprised to see that he was not alone, turned around and looked at Arya. When their eyes met, something strange happened, a powerful feeling took hold of them; it was as though they were struck by a lightning bolt. It was pure magic, the kind that all men dream of, but few experience: it was love at first sight. There was a spark in their eyes which encapsulated their immortal story, through the ages and above the boundaries. It was an eternal, unbreakable bond which took form and renewed itself and blessed itself again and again, growing ever stronger, ever deeper and nobler with every birth and every dawn.

But the magical spell which briefly engulfed them was abruptly interrupted when the knight, suddenly remembering Arya's many questions, looked straight into her eyes and said: "fair maiden, you ask why I, a knight from another age and another world, march here on my own, away from the battlefield, away from my warriors, away from myself... here is my tragic story: I come from a long line of knights who served Truth, honoured Hierarchy, and upheld Justice. Our blood was our honour, and war was our baptism; and by fighting, we sanctified our faith and forged our characters. For in those times, blood still meant honour, and war still was holy. And the blood we spilled on the battlefields was our immortal glory, the ultimate tribute to a cause worth fighting and dying for."

"But now my king is dead, and my warriors have abandoned me. For today no one wants to serve, and no one wants to fight, as there are no kings, and no cause is worthy; and, in the age of equality and mediocrity, who wants to serve a servant, or die for nothing? Aye, today no cause is worthy, and no war is holy. And rulers and ruled alike serve one god: Mammon. Today peace tastes bitter, and strife is folly. Thus I march alone, the last knight of a forlorn glory and a vanished kingdom, the last warrior of a lost cause. I march alone in this city of gloom, away from the path of Light, away from all meaning, away from all purpose."

Whilst listening carefully to the knight's words, Arya was also secretly wondering: "this man… I know him well, though the fog of the ages has blurred my memory. But the heart never lies, and its arrows never miss their target. I know this man, I have always known him, and I will always love him. But is he a man, or a message? What should I learn from him? Is he Ares, or Eros? Or Eros incarnated as Ares? O Eros, irresistible in your power, unfathomable in your mystery! Could you have been sent for me, again? Did our paths meet by chance, or by a higher will? Are we destined to be together, or doomed to part, evermore?"

Arya had so many questions, but no answers. She was no yet ripe for her answers. All she knew, for now, is what she felt; and love had come back to haunt her mind and torment her soul. She was both ecstatic and terrified by that divine feeling which swept her. For though love brings joy, it ends in loss, as nothing and no one lasts forever, save That which is not born and which never dies. Thus she longed for love's intoxicating bliss, but dreaded its doomed end. She could not endure the suffering of men, for she was on a mission from the gods, and that divine mission was above all human happiness. Therefore, she was not free to share the joys of men and relish their wantonness, for the Chosen Ones are seldom free, as they serve a higher destiny.

"I must leave," Arya briskly told the knight, who was astounded by that unexpected and premature decision. "Duty calls, and duty is higher than love," she said, trying to convince herself that she was doing the right thing. But she was not convinced, and nor was he. "I must leave," she repeated aloud, "my path is elsewhere, I long for my peaks; and this earth is too flat for me."

"Nothing is higher than Love," the knight answered, "you need a reason to stay? Love justifies everything! Love is supreme; everything speaks of love, everyone dreams of love, the whole universe sings its celestial symphony; and even the gods are enraptured by its entrancing spell."

"Every soul that is blessed with love becomes a temple of God, for God is Love, and Life is His shrine."

"Every thought that is not imbued with love is fruitless, for love is the fount of creation and the river of inspiration."

"Every touch that is not sanctified by love is sin, for love is purity and innocence."

"Every act that is not dictated by love is unholy, for Love alone hallows Life and endows Her with meaning."

"Every prayer that is not filled with love is wasted, for Love itself is a prayer, and the answer to all prayers."

"The power of love is greater than any power in the universe, and many are the blessings bestowed upon our lives by the grace of love. Love is an infinite ocean of bliss which renews itself with every new life and every new purpose."

"Love is ageless, it is the overflowing spring of youth and the endless river of creation, it is a perpetual dawn and an eternal noontide."

"Through love, the earth turns into heaven; and where you do not find love, there you find your hell."

"Without love, the oceans would be dry, the skies would be empty, and the earth would be a desert; and God Himself would die. And is not our world today dry and empty, a desert without God? Where Love lacks, God fades and darkness reigns."

"Love is the greatest hymn to Life and the highest tribute to creation. Love is the eternal dance of joy, the highest gift bequeathed to us from above. Love is the highest of meanings, and the ultimate end."

"But why do you speak of love," Arya, perplexed, asked the knight, "how could *you* speak of love, you who have only known the scourge of war?"

"And who better to speak of love," the knight replied, "than him who has only known war? He who has tasted the sour grapes of war will long most for the sweet wine of the gods; for it is the divine elixir of Love which heals the wounds that scar the body and the hatred that wounds the soul. Only he who has known war can know the meaning of love; for even as war sows death and destruction, Love breeds Life and instils the world with joy. And are not all wars waged for the sake of love? Love of country, love of power, love of God? But Love for its own sake remains the highest kind of love."

"But Love does not give meaning to Life," Arya said, "something higher is needed to justify existence."

"Love justifies all," the knight answered, "Love need not give meaning to Life, Love *is* the meaning of Life and the end of all ends. Love is Life, Love is God, and God is Love. And though there are several gods and several paths, is not the god of Love the highest among gods, and the path of Love the most sacred of paths?" As the knight fell silent, Arya was speechless. "Why," she silently wondered, "why did *he* come to me, just as I was awaking from my human dream, and seeking to reach the other shore? Was it meant to be? Is there any wisdom in this encounter? Is he an obstacle that I must overcome, or the ship that shall take me to the other shore?"

"Why did you come *now*?" she cried out, "I was on the right path, my choice was made, my destiny was sealed. And now I am torn again, at war with myself." Tears were now flowing from Arya's eyes, as her heart was shattered and her mind was confused. "Do not cry, my princess, my queen, my goddess!" the knight implored her, wiping her tears and embracing her tenderly. "I came back to love you, again and again... I came back to teach you that you can never reach the heights that you so earnestly seek without the blessing of Love... for it is precisely at the peaks that Love resides and takes you, as Love is the Way and the End. And know thou not that the highest mountain stems from the deepest valley? And there are no limits to the depth of Love."

Arya was clearly upset by that conversation with the knight, for, although it soothed her wounded heart, she was hearing the answers that she did not want to hear, as she was seeking other shores and higher meanings, away from men's words and worlds. Thus she fled

Love, and the warmth of Love, and sought the cold solitude of her highest peaks, for it is there that she would find herself and her god. That was her ultimate destination, and nothing else mattered... even Love, *especially* Love, for it was a hindrance on her way to her higher destiny.

"I have but one love," she said, "and it is called Truth. I have but one companion, and he is called solitude. For we who live on the mountaintop have unlearned to love, at least as humans do. And though they say 'it's lonely at the top', still I prefer the solitude of the peaks, where the divine Spirit dwells, to the noise of the valleys, where men vegetate; and where there are men, there is noise, that hell of gods. And though men talk a lot, though they analyse and evaluate and weigh a lot, still they remain deaf to the silence of the gods, which is the gate of Wisdom and the realm of Truth. That is why I have relinquished my dream of love, for a dream unfulfilled is a wasted dream and becomes a nightmare that haunts one's nights."

"But dreams are our only reality," the knight answered, "for they dwell in our souls, which are a world unto themselves. And did anyone ever desire to wake up from the dream of love?"

"I am wasting my time talking to you," she said with a hint of exasperation. "Love is a beautiful flower with many thorns... love is a promise of bliss that is never fulfilled, a sweet taste of heaven — the *only* taste of heaven down under —, but it is a taste that turns bitter and poisons heart and soul; for when you fall into its throes, it delivers naught but misery. Love is a mirage in our desolate sea of heartache, love is the wreck of a fallen sun taken hither and thither by the cruel winds of change and the passing waves of evanescence. I shall not suffer such a dismal fate. I serve other gods and higher goals. That is why I must leave you now, my knight, for we have no future together."

Thus spoke Arya to her distraught love, and, as she embraced him and bade him farewell, she looked for the last time into his eyes and said: "with you, my love, I saw the world through human eyes, and for once the woman conquered the goddess in me. I will never forget you, for you will always be a part of me, until death, and beyond death."

"Do not go, my love!" the knight begged her, "do not leave me… I cannot live without your love, just as you cannot live without mine, for I was born to love you forever, and you were born to be loved." But Arya did not answer, as she turned around and walked briskly away from him, never turning back. The knight, seeing his love drift away from him, again, and evermore, was speechless. His heart was shattered as he gazed with disbelief at his lost happiness, walking further and further away from him.

"She will come back to me," he said to himself, sad but confident. "She belongs to me, and I belong to her. We are bound by the same flame and the same fate, our souls flow from the same source and into the same ocean, but she does not know it yet. She will come back when she realises it, and I will be waiting for her, in this life or the next…"

Her eyes in tears and her soul in tatters, Arya kept walking away from the knight, forcing herself not to look back. She was devastated. It was as though her heart was ripped from her and torn to shreds. Something in her died as she left her dream behind; something always dies in man when he abandons his dream. "Forgive me, my love, even if I never forgive myself," she whispered to her invisible love, "but I have a mission to fulfil, and I serve a higher end which transcends my joy and my misery. And though I yearn for Love, Love is not my destiny."

"But what is that strange feeling which conquers all and everyone, the scoundrel and the saint, the peasant and the prince, the fool and the prophet?" she wondered. "O Love, sin of mortals, envy of gods… or is it the envy of mortals, and the sin of the gods? This blessing and this curse, it brings so much misery and so little joy… so why do we cling so much to it? Why do we long so desperately for it? Love tortures our hearts, torments our minds, and slays our souls… so why do we still cling to it, ever yearning to taste its sweet but deadly poison,

Passion? Is it not because Love is the very breath of Life, and the brief joy that it bestows upon our souls and sows in our hearts is worth the untold misery that it reaps, and all the pains in the world? Could it be that Love alone gives meaning to our lives, and all else is lies upon lies? Where Love is, heaven finds its home."

The dream of love

Thus bewailed Arya the end of her brief encounter with Love. Pushing a deep sigh of despondency, she finally turned back to catch one last glance of her knight. She was weeping as she waved farewell to the love that would never be hers, the love that she sacrificed on the altar of her higher destiny. In an outburst of fury at the hidden powers which rule the lives and mould the destinies of gods and men, Arya cried out in despair:

> "Ecstasy of Love! Misery of Love!
> Ah, this fleeting dream of Eternity
> that haunts the minds of men
> and fills their thirsty souls
> with the divine shiver of the heights
> and the ineffable feeling of bliss,
> it is a blessing, but also a curse!
> For it takes back what it gives,
> and steals away the evanescent joy
> that it bestows on mortals,
> when Time's ruthless reign erases,
> with the stroke of a pen,
> the love story that it once wrote and blessed."

> "We remain ever longing for the bliss of Eternity,
> ever thirsty for the ecstasy of Infinity,

in a world where nothing is real,
and nothing endures…"

"Glory of love! Wretchedness of love!
It imbues us with the sacred breath of Life,
only to slay the very hearts
that it once sanctified,
whenever its capricious grace
turns into unbridled cruelty,
and destroys the divine temple
that it once built
in every man and in every woman,
to glorify its hallowed name
and immortalise its divine spirit."

"When Love spreads its wings,
the gods themselves fall silent
and bow down before its sacred presence;
but then it folds them back, and, as an eagle,
plunges into the abyss of existence,
taking with it in its free fall
its preys' broken hearts
and shattered dreams."

"There he is, the knight of Love and Light
who turned my dream into life
and my life into a dream.
There he stands before me, and far from me,
the warrior who taught me love,
and the glory of love,
the knight who serves love
as he serves his king,
whose heart is hard as a lion's

and tender as a dove."

"But, alas! Ours is a love that is blessed by the heavens
but forbidden on earth.
For he who kindled the flame of my aching soul,
he who warmed my cold heart,
he shall remain the hero of my dreams,
my secret and my hope,
the captor of my soul,
but not its conqueror on this earth
and in this life."

"Alas! Ours shall remain the union that never was,
a love unfulfilled, a bittersweet taste of heaven
that shall forever linger in our hearts and memory
until our souls meet again,
in a new day and a new beginning,
separated on earth, united in Eternity."

"He has not lived, who has not loved,
for to live is to love,
and to love is to *live*!
And to have truly lived
is to have truly loved…"

"We are doomed to remain human
so long as we have bodies…
We are doomed to have bodies
so long as we remain human…
We are destined to love
so long as we aspire to become gods,
For are we not blessed with eternal and immortal souls?"

Of higher love

Distressed but resolute, Arya tried to find solace in the path that lay ahead, but her heart ached and betrayed a deep grief and a hidden regret; and the heart alone is true, all else is lies and deception. She walked even faster, as though she was trying to flee her own inner voice which urged her to turn back and live the happiness that she had always sought. Drowning her gloomy mind with lofty thoughts of a higher order, Arya thus spoke to the wind that blew over and around her:

> "I should pay no heed to the pounding beats of my aching heart, for I long for a higher kind of love, love of the Absolute."

> "The fleeting senses are a sweet illusion,
> an evanescent delight and an elusive joy,
> but the Spirit, eternal, never lies.
> Blessed be a higher love, a union of souls
> made in heaven
> and sanctified on earth.
> Blessed be a divine love worthy of the gods,
> for the love of men is but a wretched misery
> that remains incomplete and unfulfilled."

> "The flame of desire gnaws at the souls of men:
> it blights their minds and stifles their spirits.
> Temptation and pleasure are a curse in disguise,
> a sweet poison that inflames and consumes the heart
> and drowns the mind.
> And are not mindless men beasts that walk on two legs?"

> "O the agony of a heart fallen into the throes of desire,
> for it shall know no peace and shall perish unfulfilled,

its thirst unquenchable
and its love incomplete."

"Blessed be a higher love,
a love that's pure and ethereal,
a union of souls and a meeting of minds,
for this love is made in heaven,
and it shall last an eternity,
while the merged writhing bodies
remain ever unsatisfied
and their flame shall wane
when death severs the human bond of the senses
and stifles life and love."

The great temptation

The knight was now far behind, but his memory was forever engraved in Arya's heart. Overwhelmed with grief, crushed by despair, she started to question her fateful decision: was she right to act as she did, relinquishing her dream of Love and pursuing her vision of Light, or would she regret her decision all her life? Her human torment came back to haunt her, and temptation again teased her soul and confused her mind. All the love she had searched for ever since she came to this world, came to her when she had given up her humanity… what would she do? What should she do? What *could* she do? There were two voices speaking to her, and two worlds at war within her; which voice would she listen to, which world should she embrace? Her heart was at war with her mind, and her soul, confused, was torn between the human and the divine.

Would she listen to her crying heart, and drown in the sea of humanity, with its glory and misery, breaking her divine promise, and forsaking her path of Light? Or would she heed the voice of duty urging her to fulfil her destiny, thus sacrificing her love of man for love of God, love of the deepest for love of the highest?

"Do we love because we are human," she wondered, "or because we are divine? Is Love human or divine? Could it be that, by denying love, I have spurned, not espoused, the divine? Could Love, even love of man, be divine? Is not Love's strange hold and entrancing spell a gift from heaven? Is not shunning it also shutting our eyes to the divine? If love would conquer the world, as men fantasise, would our earth not become a heaven?" A horrible doubt now took hold of Arya, as she realised that she might have ruined her only chance of happiness; she asked herself:

"Why should Love be the enemy of Truth? Why should duty clash with passion? Why does man oppose that which should be joined? Why can't I have both? Could it be that they only go together, and fulfil each other? Could it be that Love is impossible without Truth, and Truth is unreachable without Love? Could it be that duty is unfulfilled without passion, and passion is meaningless without duty?"

"Should I go back? What would *you* do, children of this earth, and seekers of the universe, if you were torn between two loves? Which would you choose, love of God, or love of man? The bliss of Eternity, or this life's ecstasy? Which do I choose, *how* do I choose? I cannot have both, thus reality teaches me… Is that not how Divine Wisdom intended it? But if I cannot have both, I am neither! For are we not all bridges, doomed to remain bridges? But why, why should I choose, when the choice is cruel, when the choice is impossible? Is not Life the greatest teacher? And Life teaches us this: 'everything is one'. Therefore, to transcend, one first has to fall. And one rises higher after a fall. I am not whole if I do not embrace both worlds that dwell in me."

"I, the goddess of Wisdom, the Warrior of Light, have fallen prey to the clutches of Love… Love, that most sublime of human feelings, that most divine of human longings… This is my secret, my pain and my joy, my pride and my shame. This is my secret, my hidden torment: I am torn between two loves, I am a broken bridge between two parallel universes…"

"Ecstasy of Love! Misery of Love! Which do I choose, Eros or Logos? Eros or Ares? Passion, or Duty? Who shall solve this eternal riddle? Who shall conquer, the goddess or the woman? Which is man's destiny, which is God's destiny?"

> "La flamme d'amour qui brûlait dans mon coeur,
> il n'en reste aujourd'hui que les cendres et les pleurs…
> Mais où sont mes cîmes?"[1]

"I have abandoned my love, but where are my peaks? I have sacrificed my happiness, but where is my truth? Thus I stand in a twilight zone, a lake between two shores… I was told to look within and find the inner Light, but all I found was Love. Could Love be… the Light? The light of this world, and the other? The light of men and gods? Does not Love give wings to men, and bestow a heart upon gods? But where are my peaks?"

"You never really lose your love, it always finds you… maybe I will come back to him, one day, when I have all the answers. Maybe when I am whole again, I will truly embrace my human side as I seek my divine path." Thus ended Arya's torment, and she continued her search, even though her heart was forever wounded, and would only heal when the soul for whom it was destined is again reunited with it.

Arya's rebirth

Walking for hours on end in all directions, desperately trying to flee the chaos of noise and smoke that engulfed the city, Arya's will remained unwavering, having as sole consolation the hope of finally finding

---

[1] "The flame of love which burned in my heart, naught is left of it today but ashes and tears… but where are my peaks?"

the liberating sight of the Gate of Salvation. Nonetheless, despite her strong determination and her relentless efforts, she could not find any way out of this city that was holding her soul captive and wearing down her body. It was in vain that she sought to escape: wherever she went, the streets all looked the same, the buildings all looked the same, the people all looked the same… everywhere she walked, she found the same sad faces and empty stares, and there was no end in sight to the hollow walls of concrete that overwhelmed the city.

While she was walking, Arya looked closely at the people and the buildings, trying again, desperately, to find a familiar face in this faceless crowd, or a familiar sight in this strange land; but there was simply no way out of this urban mess. Tired and depressed, she rested for a moment on a bench on the sidewalk, trying to regain her strength before she continued her northern quest.

Filled with anxiety and uncertainty, Arya spoke thus to herself: "this earthly heaven has become the mirror of hell, the whole world has become a desert… sand or stone, dust or smoke, it is the same desert, it is the same hell… the desert of the Spirit, and the hell of a world without God, a world without meaning."

"This divine earth has become a hell for gods and men… what befell man? What befell God? When the god in man died, the world was emptied of meaning; thus the skies were cloaked in the colour of death, and the heavens mourned the demise of the Father, and the stars lost their divine glow, as the Spirit that pervaded them was no more; and the Mother was torn asunder, and the Son became an orphan, and the Unity of eternal dawn was lost."

"Only a miracle could now save me from this hell… only a *sign*—from above or within—, only a ray of light could cast away this darkness which overwhelms me… but *where* do I find hope in the midst of despair? How do I find my dawn in the depth of this night? Is there no end to this darkness which haunts me, like a curse, wherever I go? And this city of hell… where does it end? Where does *my* world begin? Is there no escape from this fate? Am I doomed to suffer until I transcend? *Should* I suffer, so that I can transcend? I have a vision, I have a mission, but *where* is the path?"

Arya paused for a while, as she closed her eyes to contemplate the Soul of the World; and, all of a sudden, it struck her like a thunderbolt: "could this darkness be the sign? The sign that I was awaiting, the salvation that I was seeking? Could my curse be a blessing? Could the road to hell lead me to the gate of heaven? For without darkness, there would be no Light, and without man, there would be no God, as the Sun needs to shine, and God needs to be revered. And without the silence of solitude, the voice of Eternity would never speak to my inner infinity, and the goddess who slumbers in me would never awake and blossom."

Arya was elated, and she joyfully exclaimed: "finally I understand! I had eyes, but I did not see, I had ears, but I did not hear… but these wise words now make sense to my awakened mind: the Light dwells *in* me, so why do I seek it outside? The Sun never seeks its shadow. Thus the North — *my* North — lives *in* me and *through* me… and my sons shall be the divine seeds of creation that I spread in the fields of a Higher Life. I finally understand: the path is to be sought with the *heart*, the goal is to be reached through the soul, for the mind on its own is poor and wretched, and the senses are deaf to the inner voice, and blind to the inner sun. But my heart should remain pure, and my soul should remain true, if my mission is to be accomplished, and my destiny fulfilled. Only thus will the divine in me be reborn, and my message will heal and redeem."

Arya's eyes were now glowing with the spark of those who have been struck by the lightning of the gods, and her soul was filled with the thrill of those who have drunk from the fountain of Truth and tasted the sacred wine of Creation. "Losing my ego, I found my Self, and I became free," she thought… "I was dead, and now I am born again… I was lost, and now I found myself… for one only finds oneself when one has ceased to seek outside oneself."

"I redeemed myself of God and all worshipping, but now my spirit wants to be redeemed from its godlessness and break all idols — and godlessness is yet another idol — which oppress it. Only thus will it overcome itself and soar free and unbounded in the realm of everlasting stillness. My spirit yearns to break free and sever the chains of dogma which enslave it; but there are as many idols as there are men, and Dogma wears motley masks and speaks many languages, thus it desecrates the holiness of faith and stifles the light of reason. But most lethal to the Spirit is the dogma of godlessness, for it strips Life from all meaning and renders man hollow and worthless."

"I am a believer in a god who has yet to be born, and a religion that has yet to be preached. Therefore, I shall create my own god and spread my own word. And how many worlds still lie undiscovered in the depths of my Being!"

"I shall seek my lost land, I shall seek my new race, I shall seek the coming God, I shall seek them all within; for in the knowledge of the Self lies the Divine, the meaning of the universe."

Exalted by her new vision, beholding the world through different eyes, Arya murmured to the passing wind, addressing an invisible crowd: "you think you know me, men, yet none of you know what higher spheres my soul inhabits, when night comes and you are asleep… none of you know the magic which seizes my soul, in the tranquillity of dawn and the serenity of dusk. My body may well belong to this earth, but my spirit dwells in the heavens, there in the realm of Absolute Unity, beyond the fleeting waves and shifting sands of transience. My mind may carry human thoughts, but these find their purpose and their end in the vast ocean of the unbounded Spirit."

Arya was now shining from within, beaming rays of renewed hope and newfound faith. Her eyes were closed, so she could see what the eyes cannot see, and hear what the ears cannot hear: the hidden words and worlds of Infinity. Her search was over. She had found the Gate; she *was* the Gate. Words of inspiration were now flowing out of her infinite soul, and Verses of Light were uttered through her mouth by an unknown power which seized her whole enthused being:

"All is vain, save that which has no purpose beyond itself; and that is Pure Being, the source and end of all. Therefore, my brothers, shed your human chains of time and space, and dive into the boundless ocean of cosmic mystery, which bears the running rivers of the ages and the infinite worlds of possibility... only thus shall you sing the heavenly hymn to Eternity, and relish the sheer bliss of divine detachment."

"Sons of men, cling not to your possessions, and do not lust after power or women; for power and possessions are as easily lost as they are painfully acquired, and beauty is doomed to fade if, surrendering to lust, it ceases to shine from within. Know that everything you now own, and everyone you now know, you shall lose one day. And the one thing that you shall never lose is the one thing that you do not own, the one thing that you can never own; and that is the immortal Spirit that dwells in you, but is not you, your beginning and your end."

"Think with your heart, feel with your blood, will with your spirit; only thus shall you remain true to yourself and fulfil your destiny."

"Poor mortals, you stuff your mouths and starve your souls, and you complain of the despair that grips the world today?"

"Some people save lives, others feed mouths. Those are called the righteous. I save souls and feed the spirits of men. I am the Great Healer."

"They say 'money talks', but its ring sounds hollow in the soul of Life, and falls deaf in the ears of Eternity. But the wealth of the Spirit is priceless and inexhaustible."

"Passion blinds us, reason opens our eyes, but it is the Spirit which gives us wings to fly."

"Man likes to weigh and measure everything. That is how he has been trained, that is what he is: the evaluator. But I say unto you, the immortal and boundless Spirit cannot be weighed and measured on the scale of man, for It speaks for Itself and *It* weighs all else on the scale of Life."

"Do you not know, seekers of the Light, that when you talk to your Self, you are truly talking to God, and when you talk to God, you are talking to your Self? For God is in man, and man is in God. God and man are one, their soul is Nature, even as the blood of the Father runs in the veins of the Son."

"Ask not what you want from Life, but what Life wants from you, for, by serving Her, She serves you."

"Truth needs Her warriors; where are the warriors of Truth? All I see are mercenaries of greed and merchants of death."

"I have travelled far and wide and have seen all shades and shapes of people; yet all I ever saw were herds that looked too much alike; for all herds look alike, though they wear different faces and speak different languages. There are no higher people today; everywhere there are only herds, above and below, and the Higher Man remains lonely and homeless, a holy seed which awaits its harvest at the dawn of the New Age."

"Each failure that you undergo makes you grow... each suffering that you endure makes you pure. As you transcend and overcome all of Life's illusions, and cast away Her ghosts and shadows, you discover the meaning of Being: eternal, creative evolution, and you relish the pure freedom of the heights."

"Each person who hurts you makes you free, free from your ego and its illusions and delusions. For you are not your ego; you are the boundless Self made flesh, ever transcending and evolving towards Unity. By enduring, you transcend, and by transcending, you transform; and transformation is the wheel of creation, which is the soul of Life."

"Whatever *should* be, *shall* be; all is for the best. In the end, all falls into place… and when you put the last piece of your life's puzzle in its place, at the very end, as your soul prepares to depart on its journey of discovery, you see that everything is as it should be, everything is as it should have been; and finally it all makes sense to you, finally you understand: whatever is, was meant to be. Whatever is not, never was. Everything that should have happened, *did* happen. This is the Voice of Wisdom talking to the Soul of Life."

"Children of the earth, your identities are your fetters; and only when you will have broken your last fetter shall you be truly free, and bask in the Sun of Awakening."

"Become mad! But of that madness which creates, which wants to tear asunder all bounds and all barriers. For only thus do you *truly* live."

"Power is meaningless and becomes evil, if it does not serve Truth and elevate Life."

"L'ennui, c'est la mort qui frappe à la porte de la vie. Enfants de la vie, fuyez l'ennui ! Créez, découvrez, aimez ! Donnez un sens à la vie."[2]

"Life is a school, and we are all pupils. We undo ourselves and recreate ourselves… thus we learn from Life; we learn to live, and we live to learn."

"They condemn Life for being perfect, for today perfection is the worst sin, and equality is the antidote for it. They condemn Nature for being divine, for today God is the worst enemy, and man is his pitiful, ungrateful heir."

"Feed your soul as you feed your body, for the soul is the breath of Life and the source of all creation."

"Man is Nature's enemy; that is why he is Life's enemy, and God's fallen son."

---

2   "Boredom is death knocking at the door of Life. Children of Life, flee boredom! Create, discover, love! Give a meaning to Life."

"To the man of riches, I say: you do not own your possessions, they own you… they bind you to the earth, while your spirit belongs in the heavens. The only thing you truly own is the eternal in you, the god in you, your immortal Self."

"My brothers, I entreat you: relinquish your greed, for it shall only consume you; and the more you accumulate, the less you own. For one only truly owns that which can never be lost."

"Strive not after Love, for Love dwells in you and speaks through you, and need not be sought, but lived."

"We give value to things and to people. But values have no worth on their own, and they only acquire meaning when they serve the meaning of Life."

"All values that have hitherto governed humanity should be transcended for a cosmic consciousness to emerge and lift man above himself. For man is a promise, not a goal; he remains a broken promise, but an eternal hope of divinity."

"Sons and daughters of Gaïa, how could you become gods, if you do not first become men? And, as our prophet once said, there is still much of the worm in you… how many of you have silenced the beast within, so that the voice of God can speak to itself and resound in your inner depths, turning your human body into a divine temple? How many of you have forsaken desire, ambition, and fear, so that the Divine Light can kindle your purified souls and your pacified hearts?"

"In each man, a god and a demon are at war… who shall conquer, who shall inherit this earth, the god or the beast?"

"In every man, beauty mixes with ugliness, in every man, there is depth and shallowness, and Light flirts with darkness. In every man, a choice is made, and a war is won."

"Reason, stifled and idolised, and freedom, denied and abused, have slain the soul of Life."

"It is by delving into your deepest core that you ascend to your highest destiny."

"The mystery of God resides in your soul. Therefore, uncover your own mystery, and you shall find God."

"Man will cease to suffer, fall, and repent, and God will cease to punish, pity, and forgive, when man redeems himself in God, and God redeems Himself in man."

"Life is a healing process, and only when the healed become the healers shall man become one with God."

"The key to happiness and inner peace is detachment. Therefore, perform your duty, but cling not to the fruit of your labour; sow the seeds, but worry not about the harvest, for your acts write your own destiny."

"Son of Man, you have a higher power, a hidden god within you: it is *Atman*, the indwelling divine breath."

The message

Arya's northern quest was over, for she had found the hidden gate of a higher reality; but her inner journey, her Nordic dream, had just begun. She was now living her dream, living her destiny, and in her inner world past and future merged and unfolded their sacred mysteries in an everlasting present.

Arya's exhilarated and liberated soul was glowing. She had overcome her fears and desires, she had transformed her suffering into enlightenment, and her solitude of the heart into wealth of the spirit. She was now an Awakened One, a seeker who had just embarked on her inner quest of self-discovery, a holy quest which opened the gates to the depths of Being. Her eyes were still closed — for one only truly sees when the eyes are closed — when she heard a voice whisper in her ear: "Arya, you have found the Gate; you have yet to enter the Sanctuary of Light. No one treads that sacred realm save he who is worth, and he who is ready."

Startled, Arya thought: "that voice, I know it… it is the voice of a familiar soul…" And then it hit her: "the prophet! My prophet!" She could not see him, but she knew that it was him, she sensed his sacred presence. "Our paths meet again," she told the formless voice, "was it willed by fate? Did you come for me, or did I come to you? It matters not, for our path is the same, as we speak the same language of the Spirit, and drink from the same spring of Wisdom. And since you have grasped my essence and taught me to look within and to listen to the silence of the gods, my soul is yours forever. You shall be my guide, and I shall be your disciple, though I am the goddess and you are the prophet. For gods too need their prophets."

"I want to rekindle the light of faith in men, for faith, as reason, is the Light of Life. And man cannot live without meaning, without God, though some have deluded themselves into believing this folly. And are not the most godless the most desperate of men? Are not those who deny God those who need Him most?"

"You have learned your lessons the hard way," the prophet answered, "but one only truly learns the hard way. One has to live to learn, and you have lived and learned. We Higher Men bear the weight of the world on our shoulders, and the destiny of mankind on our conscience. And the greater the mission, the heavier the burden and the deeper the suffering. And are we gods and prophets not always crucified, one way or another, in flesh or in spirit?"

"You are treading the shining path of divinity. Have faith, Arya, for, as you become one with the Light, you shall be the sacred flame in man's darkness, and the divine spark in his heart and mind. Your life is the myth; you are the eternal myth that shall inspire the coming generations. This is your vocation and your divine message: to redeem God in men."

"You left the idolatrous South for the godless West, seeking a divine North which no longer exists, and a sacred Light long lost on this earth. But there is a Hidden North, a Secret North, a sacred geography from Hyperborea to Aryana, whose borders are drawn not by the arbitrary and capricious will of men, but by the conscious hand of Divine Wisdom. This holy land is known among Initiates as the Kingdom of Shambhala, and some of them also call it the Inner Earth or Inner Fatherland. It is also known as Agharta, Asgard (10), Thule, Arcadia, or Atlantis; however, these are but different names for the same land. There is where your god dwells and where your soul finds its abode, its origin and its end. There is where your spiritual journey shall lead you."

"Your mission, Arya, is to revive your god and to preach the new religion. For the god of men is dead, and his religions are dying too, pushing their last sigh among their disenchanted faithful; and is not everyone today an orphan waiting to be reborn, and a sceptic waiting to be converted?"

"You should revive the only eternal religion, the Religion of Nature, which is above time and space, above names and rites, the Religion which is above all religions, because it is Truth itself — and, as Divine Wisdom dictates, 'there is no religion above Truth'. For, unlike the fleeting religions of men, the Wisdom Religion needs no holy wars, no crucifixions or miracles, as Life itself is its greatest conquest and its highest manifestation."

"Again, I tell thee, Arya: your mission is to revive your god, for only by reviving your faith will you revive your race and bring back its former glory. It is only through an invocation of the spirits of the depths, and a return to your forgotten divine roots, following the footsteps of the gods whose sacred presence hallowed this earth, at the dawn of Time immemorial, that your long lost sons will be born again as Children of the Light; for the spirit alone ennobles the form, and faith alone preserves the spirit. Thus a spiritual consciousness is needed, for it alone preserves the purity of the race, which in turn preserves its spirit."

"Your message shall transform your sons, and, by transforming them, it shall bring upon them a spiritual awareness that bears in its depth the higher destiny of this divine race: God's resurrection from the ashes of the old idols. It is then that the Armies of the East — those sons of the North — shall rise, and the Spirit of Rama shall return, and the Sons of *Surya* shall rule, and Truth shall prevail."

"The war was lost when the message went unheeded… and the power of *Fohat* is only bestowed upon those who tread the right path. And that is your mission: to *be* that path. Again, I tell thee: your life is the myth… and myths are the only reality. What great truths lie in legends! Often legends are the only repositories of Truth. And your legend shall be the beacon of Truth and the voice of God echoing in Eternity."

"You are the message and the messenger. The god within will speak through you if you just surrender to him. You are the goddess of Light, Arya, always remember that. You should believe in your destiny, and greatness *is* your destiny. And worry not, revelation will come to you if you do not ask for it. Truth just comes to you, if you seek Her you lose Her. We are Her beloved sons and daughters, to whom else would She reveal Herself, if not to us? Revelation will come to you… but you should destroy your own idols to liberate the god who dwells in you, and by liberating him you will be freed, and the Sacred Word will flow from your depth as an invisible inexhaustible source."

"But how can I preach my word to men," Arya asked the prophet, "when I do not understand them, and they do not understand me? How can I redeem those for whom I only feel pity or contempt? I only care for my sons! The common man is not my concern… that is why I am fleeing men."

"Some people flee noise," she said, "for it disturbs their peace and offends their ears. But most people flee silence, as silence reveals one's self, and the naked truth is unbearable to most men, the mirror is unbearable to most men… and, as I said earlier, silence is the language of the gods, and music is their prayer. As for me, I seek my holy realm of eternal peace, I long to hear the silence of the gods… thus I am fleeing men, I am fleeing the noise of idle chatter and empty words that stifle the soul of God in the Higher Man, that homeless god; for there is nothing worse, for the solitary man, than the noise of the herd, the noise of the void that speaks of itself, to itself."

"Why do we gods have to live among men? Why do we have to suffer the company of men? That is life's strangest mystery and unsolved riddle: that gods should be crucified on mankind's cross, for being gods. For *that* is the ultimate crime for men: to behold gods on earth — masters in flesh and blood — who deny the god in heaven before whom all are equal; that is the ultimate crime that man can never forgive: to behold perfection, not as a distant dream, but as manifested and incarnated on earth, in the Higher Man, that god made flesh. That is a mirror man refuses to look into, that is a truth man would rather not hear… that is why the earth gods are crucified by men. So do not ask me to care for man!"

"But only gods care for men!" the prophet answered, "has man ever truly cared for his fellow man? Only gods do that! And if gods abandon man, how will he overcome himself, how will he become a god? Who would guide him, who would teach him the difference between the shadow and the Light, between the peak and the abyss? A god is either compassionate or indifferent; either you redeem man, or you redeem yourself from man. Which goddess will you be, Arya? Ultimately, all gods are both. But do you want to shout your word from the mountaintops, where no one will hear you? You will die mad and bitter, and men will only venerate your memory, when they finally understand you. For all visionaries are against their time. But if you carry your human cross, if you go down to men, you will fulfil your destiny, and you will live to see your own glory: the redemption of your sons. Thus your dream will be realised."

"What is your dream? What is your destiny? Your dream is ultimately your destiny, though very few people realise their destiny because they relinquish their dreams; they do not dare to dream, for they are driven by fear, and, as they say, fortune awaits the bold. So, what is your dream, dear Child of Light? Is it Love? Truth? God? Dare to dream, Arya, and you will live your dream. And that is the secret of happiness: to live your life as a dream, not taking it seriously, the best and worst of it. For Life itself is but a dream, the dream of God, and when we wake up, we shall be gods ourselves."

"You are on the right path, the shining path of self-discovery. Follow the signs along your way, they are the milestones to your destiny. Men, metaphors, events, all are ultimately signs. Farewell, divine being, our love is our heavenly dream. My soul shall be with you wherever you are. A new dawn of the divine race shall rise with you. Always remember, Arya, the Sun rises from the depth of darkness. May Pan bless you."

PART FOUR

SHAMBHALA, SANCTUARY OF LIGHT

Beyond the Gate

When the voice fell silent, Arya opened her eyes; instinctively, she looked up at the sky and, for the first time, it was not darkness that greeted her, but Light, the Sacred Light of *Surya*. It was noon, and the Sun was at its peak, glorious, triumphant, supreme. And the sky… the sky was finally blue, spotless, pure, heavenly. "*Sol Invictus!*" she shouted jubilantly, hardly believing her spellbound eyes. Her whole body was shuddering with ecstasy, and her liberated soul was filled with an indescribable awe. Then, solemnly, she raised her arm, saluting her god. Her human nightmare was over, her divine dream had begun.

"Hail *Surya*, holiest of stars, AUM, Supreme Truth! No religion is higher than thee, no god is greater than thee, no life is worthy without thee, no cause is loftier than thee! Thou art the Soul of the World and the Breath of God echoing in the valley of Infinity, and hallowing Life, above and below. Thou alone art my god, my faith, my path and my destiny, my source and my sea. Blessed be our sacred hour of reunion, my beloved circle of Light, O inextinguishable flame of my soul!"

Arya was so enthralled that tears were abundantly flowing from her eyes, tears of a hope long awaited and a joy long denied. And, as she looked down, what she beheld was even more breathtaking; it was a sight beyond words, beyond imagination: bathed in a sea of Light, a wonderful world of majestic mountains, enchanting forests, charming lakes, and magnificent waterfalls surrounded her. It was Nature in Her purest form, Nature in Her divine beauty, the earth as it once was: a heaven. Gone was the darkness, gone was the noise, gone were men and their fleeting glories, useless wars, and petty concerns. She had found the Gate. Now she had stepped beyond it, into its secret and forbidden realm, where neither those who worship nor those who deny can tread, only those who stand as equals before God.

The realm of the gods

Arya was immersed in Light, relishing this long awaited dream of divine bliss. She had found her Valhalla, her Shambhala, beyond the conflictive world of men, there in the realm of silence where all opposites fade in the glory of Supremacy. For matter is division, and Spirit is Unity. "Where there are men," she said to herself, "there is conflict and confusion. And only in solitude reigns the silence of the gods."

"O Shambhala, holiest of kingdoms! Asgard, my beloved Fatherland, finally I have found you, though you were always in me, and I always belonged to you! O Nature, Divine Mother of earth! Finally I found my home, finally I found my peace… for one finds one's home where one finds one's peace."

Intoxicated with celestial delight, drowning in sheer bliss, Arya thus chanted her hymn to Pan:

"Pan, O Pan, Father of earth, Son of Heaven, hallowed be thy name! My heart beats through thee, my soul lives in thee. God of Nature, god of Life, thou art my cradle, my shrine, my sanctuary, my sepulchre. Thy kingdom alone is holy, thou art my only god, the only truth."

"O beloved Nature, fountain of Mystery, what worlds lie hidden in thy sacred womb?"

"Beloved Nature, abode of harmony, the voice of Wisdom speaks through thee, and Her soul lives in thee."

"Beloved Nature, ocean of purity, Truth reveals her secrets in thy creation, and Life unfolds her wonders in thy glory."

"Beloved Nature, soul of Hierarchy, in thee Justice is upheld, and all are free."

"Beloved Nature, mirror of divinity, the Spirit of Creation unfolds in thy majesty."

"Beloved Nature, spring of Life, the soul of God dwells in thine ineffable beauty."

"Beloved Pan, hallowed be thy name! Beauty is thy soul looking at herself in the mirror of God… for Beauty is the soul of God, and the essence of Life."

Thus sang Arya her gratitude to Life, and said triumphantly: "I am that divine ray of Light that shall kindle anew man's darkest night. My dawn has risen, I am the New Sun!"

Moksha (11)

Still under the entrancing spell of the heavenly sight that lay before her bewildered eyes, Arya could hardly believe that her long lost dream was at last realised, and her destiny was fulfilled. She wandered, elated and serene, in this land that she could finally call home, her soul at peace with itself, her heart filled with love, her mind cleared of fear and worry, her spirit liberated and reborn. The hour of the Great Awakening had come.

Gazing with admiration at this landscape of unparalleled beauty, Arya wondered why and how she got here, pondering the meaning of her life's journey, with its joys and regrets, its glories and tragedies; her whole life started unfolding before her eyes, as she became the silent witness to the good and bad events that moulded her destiny, and the righteous and wicked people whom she encountered along her path.

"I have ceased to suffer," she told herself, "I seek no more, I yearn no more, I have become who I am: I am Arya, the soul of nobility, the breath of divinity, the warrior-goddess of Light, the virgin lover of Wisdom, a goddess who feels like a woman, a woman who thinks like a goddess. I am the seed of the gods and the future of man."

"Now I am whole, my mission is accomplished and my destiny is fulfilled. I have accepted my humanity and embraced my divinity; thus my path is the end, and my end is an eternal beginning. And though I remain a bridge, my worlds are no longer at war, and God and Man have finally merged in the depths of my being."

"The war that raged in me is over, I have achieved victory over myself, and my divine past and future are joined at the crossroads of my human present, to bless this earth with a divine destiny."

Relishing the blessing of Awakening, Arya's soul thus sang its praise to *Surya*: "I have finally seen the Light, a ray of sunshine has warmed my loneliness and has ended my night. O *Surya*, thy will is done, thy glory has come!"

"For thee, O womb of Creation, for thee, Supreme Truth before whom all shadows vanish and all lies perish, I have destroyed all my idols, those poisoned illusions which were buried in me and which buried me. But before I could rise, I had to suffer the agony of man, so that thy divine flame could be bestowed upon this lost heaven."

"My path was written in my blood, my destiny was engraved in my soul. I had to redeem the past so that I could conquer the future and sanctify the present."

"But now I suffer no more, my disgust has turned to pity, my pity to grace; and Grace is the quality of the gods and the salvation of men."

"Now I am whole, now I am free. My end was a new beginning, my decline heralded my rise, my crucifixion was my resurrection; and there is no resurrection without crucifixion. Thus the cross of death shall turn into the Wheel of Life, and the agony of Golgotha shall end in the glory of *Surya*."

Thus sang Arya her song of joy and her hymn to Life.

The King of the World

Lured by the captivating mystery and magical beauty of a thick, dark forest, Arya went inside it and wandered through its narrow paths, admiring its imposing, ageless trees and rich vegetation. Her soul became giddy, joyfully surrendering to the overwhelming wave of bliss that swept it; it was a feeling of total wantonness and profound happiness unknown to mortals, save during the brief glimpses of Eternity that pierce their dark worlds.

Listening with veneration to the natural symphony sung by the birds and other creatures of the forest, relishing the sound of the soft rustling of leaves and the shy murmurs of the wind breathing life into life, Arya thought: "it is in the forest that God speaks to Life, and Life sings of Love, and Beauty reveals Her glory, and Truth sheds Her veil of mystery and stands naked, eternal, supreme."

"It is in the forest that gods are born, and faith is awoken, and Life is imbued with awe. For the desert only breeds mirages, shadows of gods and dust of faith and semblance of Life. This is a truth that few people know: the gods of Nature are the soul of the world and the seeds of Light, but the god of the desert is a curse cast upon Life and a scourge wrought upon men. And when man left the forest, he lost his soul and abandoned God. But ultimately, Destiny always finds Her chosen ones and Her lost path."

Immersed in her reflections, Arya failed to notice that she had reached a glade in the midst of the forest. The clearing was bathed in light and radiated a heavenly glow, a kind of luminous mist which seemed to form an invisible circle around her. Suddenly, a ray of light came from above, and a man appeared out of nowhere before Arya's startled eyes. Stunned and breathless, her soul filled with reverence, her body quivering in fear, she looked with great wonder at that spirit made flesh that just descended on her from another dimension.

There stood before her a tall, slim, imposing man of fascinating beauty, a beauty unmatched on earth since time immemorial. She was enchanted by all that magnificence that lay before her eyes. But what astonished her most was what the man was wearing: a strange outfit that she had never seen before, which was nonetheless vaguely similar to the ones worn by the ancient Norsemen, those noble warriors and bold conquerors of yore known as the Vikings. Still, his were quite unusual and indefinable clothes, and one could not really tell whether they belonged to a priest or a warrior, to the remote past or the distant future.

At first hesitant and fearful, but gradually emboldened by curiosity and filled with wonder, Arya moved towards the man in order to take a closer look at him. It was with great admiration that she beheld his extremely handsome, angular face, which had clear-cut, ideal features reminiscent of the Greek gods of Antiquity; his body was also perfectly proportioned, a masterpiece drawn by the hand of God—and is not God the Great Artist?

"Is that man a god, is that god a man?" she asked herself, mystified. He was a god chiselled by a god, a man who was the envy of all gods. Arya was amazed by all that beauty, a beauty long lost on this earth. "Man today is such an ugly creature, a fading shadow and a waning spark of divinity," she thought; "our poor earth, that fallen heaven... how ugly, how sinful it is today! And do they not say 'ugly as sin'? True, ugliness *is* a sin, and beauty is divine... but true beauty stems from purity of soul; and there is no lasting beauty without virtue. And when inner and outer beauty meet, a god is born."

Still staring with admiration at the strange man, Arya discerned in his gentle but austere facial expression a serenity characteristic of the Blessed Sons of Light. A divine glow emanated from his entire being, his radiant aura emitting redeeming rays of an inner sun. He was shining with youth and vigour, yet there was also the unfathomable depth and mystery of millennia in his piercing, fearless blue eyes which reflected a timeless wisdom.

"Who... are... you?" Arya stuttered inaudibly, still paralysed by fear, "*what* are you, man, god, or spirit?" The man smiled affectionately and said: "man, god, spirit... what is there in the words? Words cannot describe that which is beyond words, just as thoughts can never capture that which is beyond form; and the voice of the Silence — the primal voice of Being — is beyond all words, unutterable, formless, divine. But if you must put a label on everything, as men do, know that I am naught but your own mirror reflecting itself eternally and infinitely, your endless dream of divinity and your eternal quest for perfection."

"I am That which was and which ever shall be, I am the breath of Brahma and the soul of Pan, I am the Formless taking form, and the Boundless giving life. I am the voice of God that whispers the unutterable in your ear, and the eye of God that guides your soul through the path of its destiny."

"I am the Creator and the Destroyer in the perpetual dance of the Cosmos, I am He who comes back eternally to redeem and to redress. I come down to men when they lose themselves, and each time they lose themselves, to rekindle the light that ends their night, and lift the veil that blights their sight."

"I witnessed the birth of gods on earth, and the glory of Rama, the first Arya; and I shall witness the death and rebirth of..."

"I know who you are!" Arya unintentionally and abruptly interrupted the man (albeit with regret, for she was curious to hear the end of his sentence), "legends of vanished civilisations refer to you as the 'King of the World', and Initiates call you 'the Great One', the first 'Unknown Superior' ". As she spoke, Arya realised with satisfaction and surprise that her fear had gradually given way to her curiosity; and it was with confidence that she added: "according to the myth, you are the ruler of the sacred land of Shambhala, a kingdom that is not of this world, an oasis of Light which survived the onslaught of darkness that swept humanity when gods fell and men ceased to be in their image."

"Your kingdom was an ideal made real, a mirror of the heavens reflecting the perfection and splendour of the order of Nature, the divine order manifested. It was an earthly heaven ruled by Truth and Justice, and blessed with peace, harmony, and beauty. In these hallowed times, power was in the service of Wisdom, and, in their union, Science and Religion honoured Truth and did not distort Her by fragmenting Her."

"But then came the Fall, and gods became like men, and men like beasts, and Gaïa lost Her divine soul and fell under the spell of *Maya*... and the world sank to its doom. That is when Shambhala disappeared from the surface of the earth, which was swept by the scourge of death and darkness, and became the sacred underworld where the ones chosen for the redemption of humanity took refuge, preserving the divine flame that would one day kindle anew the soul of the world with its sacred light, when the Wheel again turns, and a new cycle is upon us."

"My dear Arya, you seem to have all the answers, although one should first know all the questions," the king replied, visibly amused by her overflowing enthusiasm which reflected the innocence of the pure-hearted and noble-minded. "But why do you refer to my kingdom as a 'myth'? Your myth sounds much like reality to those of us who know the hidden and occult facets of Truth... and are not all myths allegories and metaphors of Truth, motley-coloured leaves of the same Tree of Knowledge? The leaves change and fall, but the tree remains the same, its roots reaching the heart of existence."

"People change, thoughts evolve, beliefs vary, but Truth remains eternally the same, behind Her manifold masks and countless symbols. So do not let your mind surrender to the curse of scepticism — that plague of modernity — which slays the heart of Truth and shatters all dreams and denies all hope, drying out the infinite seas of possibility, and turning the inexhaustible fountains of imagination into deserts of negation and swamps of decay and stagnation."

"Believe in your myths as you believe in your dreams, for what is a man without a dream but a wretched wreck thrown hither and thither onto the shores of despair by the capricious winds of chance, and the ruthless waves of change?"

"It is not the truth of the myth that one should question, but the truth *behind* the myth that one should ponder and learn from, the wisdom behind the symbol, the meaning behind the metaphor, the spirit behind the letter. For Wisdom alone gives meaning to our lives, and faith alone gives life to our dreams."

"That is why Shambhala is only real to those who live beyond what men call 'reality', this world of illusions, and it is only illusory to those who deny the real and worship the ideal, and those who deny the ideal and worship the real… for Life is indivisible, and when it is divided, it becomes its own worst enemy, a curse unto itself."

"Verily, I tell thee: Shambhala is only real to those who live the glorious Unity of Being, and it is only visible to those who see beyond what the blind human eyes see, those who still believe, in this unholy age where faith is derided and hope is forbidden… those whose hearts have remained pure, freed from the hatred, desire, and greed that plague life and demean its meaning… those whose noble blood has remained untainted and unblemished, and whose radiant spirit has remained unscathed in this crumbling world of confusion. Only those tread beyond the Golden Gate and enter into the Parallel Universe, that deeper reality unreachable to mortals."

"Arya, divine daughter of *Surya*, you, an Immortal on a human mission, a human with a divine plan, are the gem of those chosen among the chosen, those Unknown Superiors. You are the Great Mother who gave birth to the Golden Race that has blessed this earth with Ar, the Celestial Fire. You always have been, and always will be, an inseparable part of the boundless soul of Shambhala. Your destiny is linked to hers by a sacred, unbreakable, mystical bond. You belong to her, and she dwells in you."

"But how can I belong to something I have hitherto never been?" Arya asked the king. "Where your spirit dwells, there is where your home is," he answered. "Your spirit alone knows whence it came and whither it is going, and only an enlightened mind can fathom the mysteries of the soul, and break the human shackles of time and space which bind it to the material world of transience. But the truth is that the spirit has its own realm, and its realm has no boundaries. Thus, the whole earth, the whole universe is its home. And Shambhala is the spirit of the earth, and the soul of the universe."

"You have searched the four corners of the earth to find what was always in you, what was always you: your god, your home, your race, your faith… they all live in you, you need not seek them outside yourself, and thus deny them out of despair. The light is in you… seek it with your heart, and your spirit will unveil its secrets to your awakened mind. Love is the key, Truth is the Gate, God is the Sanctuary."

"You are here today because you heeded my silent call, by answering the prayer of your soul. It was your heart that led you to your sacred haven. But now your spirit needs to blossom in its own light, not the light of Love, but the Light of God. For, as you have been told earlier, love of God is the highest kind of love, and the only love that is enduring and selfless, free from attachment, fear, and suffering; and even as love of man is but a lost ray of the original divine Light, so the light of man is but a faint glimmer of the original divine Love."

"You utter the unutterable words of wisdom which heal the soul and awaken the spirit," Arya said. "I beseech you, O Great One," she pleaded, "enlighten me with your infinite wisdom, drown my thirsty soul in your boundless ocean of light. Show me your inner sanctuary, let me explore its depths and soar in its heights. Unveil yourself before me, if I am worthy, if I am ready."

"To you, beloved Child of Light, I shall divulge my deepest secrets and my highest truth," the king replied. "Behold, O Arya, my many faces… behold the wealth of creation, and the glory of manifestation!"

As soon as he ceased talking, his face rapidly changed, consecutively taking, at lightning speed, the form of the faces of all the Initiates who, throughout the ages, have blessed this earth with the light of heaven. Some of the faces were those of known gods, prophets, saints, philosophers, and artists, but there were also numerous unknown faces among them. "Those are the Blessed Ones, the Great Guides of humanity," he said, "the Immortals who have forged the Golden Chain of Light, across the ages and above the frontiers."

"And now, behold the glory of your own legend," the king told Arya, "these are your many faces throughout history." With inexpressible marvel, Arya beheld her various manifestations in an invisible mirror, sending shivers of ineffable joy all over her body. The many forms that her immortal spirit borrowed through time moved past her, and they finally merged in her actual form.

"These are your many incarnations, Arya," the king said, "though they are but different facets of the same immortal, infinite spirit that is in you, that is you. Your mission is sacred, your cause is eternal: you are the Light bearer, messenger of gods and redeemer of men. Nothing else matters, nothing and no one else *should* matter. And in your present incarnation, this was your path, these were the signs, the milestones that led you to me, to us, to yourself."

As the king spoke, there appeared on his face and before Arya's startled eyes the faces of all the people who had touched her life in so many different ways: the old wise man from the East, the old woman from the North, the prophet, and the knight. Wisdom, Faith, Truth, Love: the various facets of Life, which bless Her with meaning and purpose, were all mixed, then united, when the king's face finally took its original, divine form. "In the divine, all things are united," he said, "Truth, Wisdom, Faith, and Love lead to God. I take on different forms, but I am the One, the Supreme, the Eternal. All things find their origin and end in divine Unity. This is the meaning of Shambhala, the spirit of the earth, and the soul of the universe."

Spellbound and overwhelmed by the incredible visions she just saw, Arya exclaimed: "you are the king of *all* worlds! The real kings never had thrones, and the real gods never had religions, as the only sacred kingdom is the Kingdom of God, which is without boundaries, and the only lasting religion is the Religion of Nature, which is Truth at its highest. This is your kingdom, this is Shambhala."

The Spirit of Shambhala

Elated and moved, Arya urged the king: "I entreat you, Great Master, tell me more about your holy kingdom. So many different things have been said about it, that I am confused. I want to know, I need to know whence my soul came, and whither it is going… I need to know more about my Inner Self, by knowing more about my Inner Fatherland."

"But, as I said, I am confused. I have so many unanswered questions, so many shadows haunting my light… you say that Shambhala is real, and I believe it with all my heart, and see it with my own eyes; however, why do most men still consider it a myth? Why do they remain blind to its light? If it is real, why has it remained a mystery? Is there wisdom behind this mystery, or is this land simply lost and forgotten in this Dark Age that we live in?"

"And if Shambhala is only a legend, a collective dream of a longing humanity, why does it still linger in this age of reason? How has this beacon of faith survived the rising tide of unbelief which has swept this earth? What is this strange and powerful hold that it has on men, dreamers and deniers, mystics and sceptics alike?"

"But, as I always ask, what is real, what is unreal? Can one truly tell, will one truly know? Idealists say that Shambhala is real, that *only* Shambhala is real — as the ideal alone is real, and the Spirit alone lasts —; but sceptics contend that it is a mirage, that only the material is true, and all else is illusion. And in this clash of worlds, and war of words, something dies in man: the innocence of being, and the meaning of becoming..."

"What's more, if Shambhala is boundless, as you affirm, and as I feel, why does the legend say that it is located somewhere beneath the Himalayas, in the once fertile land that is now the Gobi desert? How can Infinity be confined to the narrow bounds of the physical realm? And the same legend adds to our confusion when it also situates the Sanctuary of Light in the extreme North, in what was once known as Hyperborea... how can the same land be in two distant locations at the same time? Is Shambhala in the East, or in the North? What are its boundaries? And, if it is infinite, how can it be manifested?"

"Forgive my many questions, O Great Master, but the legend nowhere provides answers, and it only elicits further questions... the mystery of Shambhala remains complete, and its veil remains impenetrable to humanity. Why this shroud of secrecy, why this conspiracy of silence? Should the Light remain hidden, should the Word remain unspoken? Should not the Sun shine on all men, and defeat the darkness that is in them and around them? Why does darkness always triumph, why does the noise of men, the noise of deceit, always stifle the silence of the gods, the silence of Truth?"

"The mystics speak of an Inner Sun, but how can the Light remain buried beneath the earth, or in man, when its healing rays should bless and redeem Life, everywhere, all the time? What good is a sun that hides from its own shadows, what good is an enlightened man who does not partake of his wisdom? Only death and destruction await a world devoid of Light... thus the dwarfs of the surface wreak havoc unto themselves and unto this earth, while the gods of the depths remain silent witnesses to the end of the world."

"Verily, the world above is sinking to its doom, while Shambhala remains buried below, out of reach, out of sight... and is Shambhala truly beneath this earth, or beyond it? Does it belong to this world, or to the other? Is it at the heart of Life, or in an unreachable Beyond that remains an unfulfilled promise of salvation? But then the Religion of Life, which is the soul of Nature and the essence of Shambhala, would be no better than the religions of men, which offer only promises, and no redemption!"

"And if there really is a beyond, how do I reach it? I went beyond the Gate, but I still do not know *how* and *where* I found Shambhala! And I see neither an Inner Earth, nor another world! All I see is an earthly heaven, very real, very human! What, then, is the nature of Shambhala?"

When Arya's endless questions were asked, she became silent and serene, as though she had relieved her conscience from the heavy weight of Life's countless questions that have hitherto not found their answers in her troubled heart and her longing soul. Her face again became composed, and it lit up with expectation, as she eagerly awaited the king's response. He looked at her with gentle, caring eyes, the kind of pure, paternal affection that a Master has for his favourite, most promising disciple. Then he spoke solemnly, as one does when one is about to divulge a long withheld secret:

"You are finally asking the right questions," he said, "and only when one asks the right questions does Truth lift Her veil and reveal Her face before Her beloved child. Everything you heard about Shambhala is true, even the most diverse and contradictory tales and suppositions. For the human mind cannot fathom the divine realms, and what sounds senseless and incoherent is harmonious to the Initiate, as he alone deciphers the secret language of the gods, and hears their silent melody."

"Every question you asked finds the same answer, Arya, as all rivers flow into the sea. And when I explain the unexplainable to you, everything will make sense to your transformed soul. I shall now relate to you the legend of Shambhala. This is the realm of the gods, the land of Sham-b-allah, the Sun of God, the Sun-God. No mortal soul has ever trodden this sacred land, no human mind has ever lifted its veil of mystery. Various cultures have given various names to this holiest of kingdoms, some referring to it as Agharta, Asgard, Ultima Thule, Atlantis, Hyperborea, or Arcadia, others as the Inner Earth, the Hollow Earth, or Inner Fatherland… but these are all different names for the same earthly paradise. This is where the odyssey of gods on earth started, where the first seeds of the divine Race of Light first blossomed."

"But when gods failed below, God failed above, and the Ring of Eternity was broken… and heaven and earth were torn asunder… and the Father was worshipped, then cursed, and the Son crucified, idolised, then denied,"

"and the flesh fell instead of rising, and men's darkened eyes, beholding the Sun, only saw its shadows."

"When Freedom parted with Virtue, and Reason parted with Faith, and Truth and reality parted ways in man's deluded mind,"

"that is when the Light no longer found refuge in the dark sea of men, and retreated away from them and beyond their noise and dust, into this safe haven where only the pure of heart and noble of soul can tread."

"But deep inside each man, there remains a spark of light waiting to be rekindled, and a glimmer of faith waiting to be revived… in each man's unknown depths, the flame of Shambhala flickers, waiting for its long-lost Sun."

"Man, torn away from his spiritual roots by a mind that perpetually denies, and a heart that perpetually desires, ever a stranger to the stillness of Being and the peace of contentment, lost in a world that has yet to make sense to him, vainly seeks his primal light amid the rubble of fallen idols, and searches for his god in the closed horizons of his dark skies. Separated from the Whole, alone, worthless, longing for a lost unity, yearning for a lost divinity, he exists on the margin of Life and at the doorstep of heaven, neither entering nor living, caught in an endless twilight that never becomes a dawn."

"That is how men lost the gift of inner sight — which alone conceives and perceives the Spirit in all its manifestations —, and the blessing of pure faith, which alone kindles His flame in man. For how can the shadow conceive the Light? And that is what man became: a shadow desperately seeking its lost light, a dry river seeking its lost source, a lonely drop thirsting for its ocean."

"That is why Shambhala is a living reality to all true believers, those who have eyes to see and ears to hear, but it remains a mystery to the soulless and the godless... that is why there is only darkness in the world of men, and the Light is hidden from mortals and withheld from this fallen earth, like a Black Sun waiting to burst out its rays of Life unto the heart of death, when the Wheel again turns, and man is reborn, and God returns. Thus the Inner Sun only beams its sacred rays unto the souls of its chosen sons, awaiting its Golden Dawn."

"Nothing endures save that which is real... all else is doomed to fade in the mist of Eternity. And Shambhala is the soul of Eternity and the heart of Life; thus it remains the beacon of a higher kind of man, and the abode of another kind of god. But hidden it shall remain from the wicked and the ignorant, the godless and the impure, thus Divine Wisdom will have it, for She was crucified too many times for casting Her pearls unto the swine, and bestowing Her Light upon the unworthy. And not until the Coming Race treads this earth, and the Coming God redeems its lost sons, will the ineffable voice of Shambhala's Silence be heard by all, and its sacred flame shall then burn in every beating heart."

"Shambhala is only real to those who themselves are real, those who have preserved the sacred bond with Nature, the secret link with the Soul of the World; those who still dance to the magical flute of Pan, and bless the One Spirit who has many names. For the Spirit alone is real, all else derives from His boundless Ocean, and manifests His abundant Life. That is why sceptics and idealists, in their illusory and futile war, commit the greatest blasphemy against Truth, which is indivisible and supreme. And, as the Spirit moulds matter in His own image, so is the whole world God's Idea taking form. But ever since man severed his link with God, he separates the Creator from His creation, and thus denies both."

"Have faith, dear Child of Light, for the destiny of this earth, as its past, is divine; in the end, Justice is always achieved, and Truth always prevails. But why has man wrongly learned and taught that the divine is unreachable? *That* is a myth invented by life-deniers. You are here, so how could Shambhala be unreachable? It is only unreachable to those who do not belong to it in spirit, those who kneel and those who doubt. And only those who touch the depths of Being, and the heart of Truth, there where the human and the divine meet, know the bliss of Wholeness and the peace of Harmony. Know that the earth is divine, only man is human… verily, *Gaïa* bears *Surya* in Her bowels, and the skies above are but the reflection of that divine Inner Sun."

"That is how Shambhala is both the centre of the earth, and the gate of the universe; it is in the here and now, and in the beyond, both in time and above time, in space and beyond space. For in the realm of the Spirit, the boundary between reality and fiction, the visible and the invisible, the material and the ethereal disappears, and a new dimension emerges, and everything is merged in a divine wholeness. Thus inner and outer worlds meet, and 'above' and 'below' fade in a beyond, an ideal that becomes real. And Eternity fuses past and future, as Time's ruthless reign ends, and space expands into infinity, and embraces the heart of Life. That is when the three dimensions of Being — physical, rational, divine — unite, and the two worlds become one, and the centre of the earth becomes the centre of the universe."

"That is the nature of Shambhala: it is both everywhere and nowhere, without boundaries, the mirror of the heavens reflected in the earth's inner depths; it is the Soul of the World that one enters through one's heart and lives with one's spirit, a cry of divinity in man's infinity… it is the realm where the inner and the beyond, the physical and spiritual realms meet and merge, a parallel universe, another dimension unknown to mortals, a deeper reality and a higher plane of existence. Its gate is everywhere, its frontiers nowhere, it is reached through a higher kind of faith. It is an Inner Earth illuminated by an invisible Inner Sun, the White Light of God."

Arya was listening intently to the king when, suddenly, he fell silent and looked straight at the noontide Sun above them. The strangest thing happened, when his eyes, beholding the scorching star, remained wide open, not in the least irritated by its burning rays... his eyes themselves seemed to be on fire, emitting an unusual glow which seemed to reflect the very depths of existence and its many mysteries. Arya observed him attentively, trying to detect his deepest thoughts behind that impenetrable look characteristic of the Great Masters.

A brief moment elapsed, after which the king broke his temporary silence and said solemnly to Arya: "you wonder how you reached this unreachable land, this hidden sanctuary of the gods known only to the initiates as the White Island, the Sacred Imperishable Land. Listen carefully, for I shall tell you about the secret passageway through which your soul travelled in order to get where you are now. But first, observe the sun above you; what you behold *above* is the Central Sun of the Inner Earth... yes, Arya, believe the unbelievable: this is the centre of the earth, which is the gateway to Infinity!"

"The earth is hollow, and in its midst a whole new dimension opens up, and countless worlds unfold... but this happens at the level of the spirit, that is why men have hitherto vainly searched for Shambahala with their picks and shovels and compasses, desperately seeking it inside caves and under mountains. But Shambhala only unveils itself before the Initiates — the seekers of Truth, those who seek within, the explorers of the Soul —, and it remains a mystery to adventurers — the seekers of glory, those who seek the void. The Gate is everywhere, but sadly, men like to touch that which cannot be touched, but felt, and they need to understand that which cannot be understood, but lived."

"Shambhala — as man — is terrestrial and celestial; its nature is triune and its realm endless. And it was your inner infinity which sought itself, and your Inner Fatherland which found itself, when you embarked on your inner journey, when you began your divine dream of Eternity. Everything you now behold, everything you now touch, you have dreamt before, you have wished for... your whole world is contained within your spirit, reality is naught but your ideas taking form. You were seeking the North, you found infinity. And in the vertigo of Infinity, all borders fade and all barriers break. Thus your search ended where it began: in your boundless Self, which is the Gate to Shambhala."

"You were seeking your fatherland, you found it within... for it is in your heart that the flame of Hyperborea and Aryana still flickers; and ultimately, it is where one finds his flame that one finds his home. You belong to Shambhala if it dwells in you; and whoever seeks Shambhala with a pure heart reaches it. The time has come for men to free themselves from the delusions of time and space, and live the Life Divine for which their souls were destined. But in order to do so, they must shed their petty goals and narrow identities, and embrace their higher goal and their higher destiny."

"The ego, or lower self, clings to origins, and identities are but inflated egos. But the Higher Self longs for self-overcoming, it longs for man's higher destiny: the Divine. The origins, perceived as identities, belong to the mind and the ego; the end belongs to the Spirit. Shambhala is not about the origins but the end, not where you come from, but where you are heading; it's a destination, a way upwards and beyond, an end that forever renews itself in a new beginning, an endless Circle of Light. Thus, in the Sacred Sanctuary of Light, the divine origin and end of the earth reconcile and merge in supreme wholeness."

"You ask if Shambhala is in the East or in the North... but East and North are one, moulded by the same sacred spirit, and imbued with the same divine breath... few people know that, save those who shun the artificial borders erected by men, those for whom only the borders of the Spirit last — and matter —, as only spiritual borders make spiritual nations, nations with a universal message and a divine vocation. And those are the only nations that have built great civilisations; others are but warring tribes with flags, or idle citizens of hollow states."

"Aryana and Hyperborea are one and the same, and North meets East in the heart of Infinity, which is the soul of Shambhala. These are the spiritual borders, the invisible frontiers of the Holy Kingdom of Light, whose map was woven by the divine thread of Wisdom through which Edda and Veda remain forever intertwined."

"Verily, I tell thee, when Initiates speak of North and East, they do not refer to borders, but to *this* Inner Fatherland, they refer to the sacred geography of the Spirit, where the lost North finds itself in the hidden East, where the heart of Gaïa longs for its divine destiny. This is the spirit of Shambhala, where North meets East, and Man meets God."

"When I speak of North and East, I speak of soul, not soil, and of blood, not language, I speak of the spirit of Shambhala... for the Soul of the World knows no boundaries, and noble blood speaks many languages; thus the Golden Chain spread from North to South, and from East to West, blessing the Sons of Light wherever they were born, and whatever tongue they spoke. And only those who, wherever they are, and whoever they are, still bear the sacred flame of Shambhala, only those are worthy to hold the title 'Arya'; for *that* is an honour bestowed only upon the worthy, thus it ever was and ever shall be."

The king, pondering the depth of his words, fell into a meditative silence, and, after a brief moment, he again looked at Arya with his deep and mysterious eyes, and, with the unshakable confidence of those blessed with a higher faith, he spoke thus:

"Shambhala will soon become a reality to all men, when the time of purification comes, and the Sons of the Sun emerge in all their glory from their abode of Light. The earth is now entering a new phase in its evolution, and a new consciousness is dawning on man. The long night of humanity is at an end, and the Black Sun, which bears in its depths the hidden light of divinity and the dormant force of the cosmos, awaits its coming resurrection and inexorable glory at the coming dawn of the new Cycle. For when the Great Upheaval is upon us, the Central Fire, that divine, invisible flame which burns in the soul of man and imbues the Soul of the World with life and creation, will release and radiate its redeeming rays unto the heart of darkness, heralding the New Age of the God-Man. That is when the divine odyssey of the Spirit will be accomplished, and the Circle will be completed, and men will be free, and they will walk as equals with the gods. Thus, Absolute Unity is Supremacy, which is God's essence and man's destiny."

The new religion

Entirely captivated by the king's prophecy, Arya was speechless; for when the voice of Wisdom speaks, one honours Her best with one's silence. "Life itself is a miracle," he told her, with a hint of a smile upon his lips, "Life is a daily miracle… miracles surround us, but men do not lend an ear to their silence, and they shut their eyes to their light. Therefore, they remain trapped in a world without magic, a world without greatness, a life denied and demeaned. Men, alas, remain fools… and fools do not believe, fools either kneel or deny, they never truly believe. A believer is one thing, a worshipper another; the former is liberated by his faith, the latter becomes its slave. That is how one should judge religions: whether they liberate or enslave. And, henceforth, that is how religions shall be judged: not by their tenets, but by their fruits… not by their promises, but by their achievements… not by the miracles they promise, but by the miracles they achieve. But religions have thus far only promised, never delivered, for they were made in the image of man, not in the image of God."

"Thus, a new religion is needed, a religion for free men, a religion that does not command and enslave, but liberates and elevates. For religions have hitherto only made slaves and killed God... aye, the 'religions of heaven' have only brought hell on this earth, and no man has ever heeded their commandments, as only a free man can truly be virtuous. That is why the coming religion will replace the old, rotten ones, and the coming god will redeem the divine and awaken man."

"The world was doomed when man ceased to believe. Never stop believing, Arya, for the dreams of yesterday are the glories of tomorrow and the inspiration of today. And, as I already said, faith alone gives life to our dreams... and a life without dreams is a life without meaning; for faith is the inextinguishable flame which awakens man to the meaning of life, his deeper dream and his greater destiny. That is why religions lost their meaning when men lost faith in them. That is why the new religion will imbue the sons of this earth with a higher faith and a higher meaning."

"Few people today are concerned about preserving the purity of the Race, which is the source of all values; but in order to preserve the body, one first has to preserve the spirit, as only a higher soul can create a higher body and claim superiority. The form dies when the spirit fades, and the spirit fades when the faith lacks. Therefore, you need to revive your faith, Arya, you need to believe again, in yourself and in your god, so that your sons can survive and thrive in this world of confusion and decay; for they are the seeds of the coming race that shall again kindle the divine flame in man."

"You need to preach your own religion, a religion that bears your name, so that your sons again unite under one banner and no longer go astray on the crooked paths of false gods and alien creeds, losing themselves in lost meanings and useless wars. For henceforth, the word 'Arya' shall be healed from its many scars and wounds, and the shame wrought upon it by its enemies who denied it, and its idolaters who made it hollow, shall forever be erased."

"Now you are whole, now you became whole, Arya; but being whole entails being a bridge, a bridge between two worlds, the human and the divine, the physical and the ethereal. And, like Shambhala, we are all bridges, even the most divine, even the most human among us. We are all bridges, microcosms of the universe, even men, even gods — and is not the God-Man our highest goal and our greatest bridge? That is why the new religion shall accept Life as it is, it shall neither worship nor deny any aspect of existence; it shall neither despise nor reject 'this world' or 'the other', and it shall bless Life in Her wholeness and Her perfection. And wholeness alone is perfection. For everything is one, all suffering proceeds from separation, and all bliss from unity. Separation breeds sorrow, alienation, and conflict. Unity breeds harmony, joy and perfection. Thus teaches the new faith that is dawning upon us."

"The purpose of Life is to attain unity, and the goal of man is to become God. And only when Unity and Hierarchy meet is there Supremacy, and the Cosmic Pyramid shines in all its glory unto the heart of Being. But man has yet to know his goal, man has yet to become whole. In truth, man was born in chains (though he *thinks* he is free), but freedom is his destiny. And Freedom is the essence of Unity."

"That is how Life views Herself in Her own mirror, not the distorted mirror of man, which renders everything small and insignificant. Man should no longer think in human terms, he should hereafter look at the sky, and, remembering whence he came, he should move with the stars, going beyond the human clouds of forbidden horizons and forsaken dreams."

"Everything has become small on earth, Life lost Her divine meaning and man lost his divine memory down under. Thus we need to behold new horizons and open new skies, that is what the new faith promises: neither heaven nor hell, neither salvation nor punishment, but the boundless horizon of Eternity ever unfolding in man's destiny."

"The new religion shall teach man not to kneel or fight or love or hate, but simply to *live*... for few men truly live, most spend their lives learning how to live, and ultimately they fail to live *and* to learn. Most men are failures... and how many wasted lives and shattered hopes have poisoned the meaning of Life! For millennia, man has striven to live better, to live longer, to live happier, but still he knows not how to *live*. That is why the new faith shall teach man not to make the world a better place, not to fight for a brighter tomorrow or regret a lost past, but to *look* at the world in a different way, to view Life as She *is*, not as *he* sees Her. That is the heroic vision of life whereby all contrasts are transcended in a higher reality."

"Therefore, Arya, in the message that you bring to men, you shall preach not submission or defiance or piety or godlessness, but reverence for Life, acceptance of change, freedom from desire, and renunciation of greed. For only thus is Life honoured in Her totality and lived in Her simplicity; only thus is Life reconciled with Nature, and man is reconciled with God." There was a brief moment of stillness, as both the king and Arya seemed absorbed in their vision of a brighter future for humanity, in the new era of the earth's destiny.

"You speak the truth, and your words are wise, O king," Arya said, "but if Life is whole, then one should accept evil as one accepts the good, and the fall as the rise, and misery as glory; even death, which is part of Life, should cease to be anathema in the eyes of men. So why should we still choose virtue over vice, and good over evil? For Life is as absurd as it is meaningful, and as cruel as it is beautiful. In fact, everything in life tends to remind us and force upon us the impression that the world is essentially cruel, unjust, full of suffering, sorrow, and plagued by death and illness, an aimless cycle of misery and decay. Hence, the question that imposes itself upon us is: is the world, is Life truly naught but misery and decay? Or is suffering a necessary aspect of the human stage of evolution, in a world made up of opposites? Does not this sombre aspect of existence force us to ponder the meaning of existence and extract the lonely, sublime rose from the many thorns that surround it? Is Life the thorns or the rose? Is life bound for death, or death for life? How should we look at Life, and learn from Her?"

"I say unto you," the king replied, "Life is one, the world is one, and death and life are inseparable like night and day, for the world of forms revolves around opposites, which cannot exist apart. Can you relish life without knowing death? King and servant stand equal before death, and lovers, separated by death, are united in eternity. Can you conceive joy without experiencing sorrow? Can you enjoy youth without dreading old age? Can you appreciate the blessing of good health, without having known the crippling scourge of sickness? Can you truly feel free without having known bondage? Can you be virtuous without experiencing injustice? Can you be merciful without shuddering before the ugly face of cruelty? The material world is ruled by contrasts, yet these are not a curse but a blessing which serves to awaken man's consciousness and push him to overcome them — and himself — for a higher reality. I tell you, the world revolves around opposites, yet these serve a purpose and find their unity and reconciliation in the bosom of the Life Divine, above the world of forms and limitations."

"Life unfolds in eternal creation, transformation is the wheel of life. The world revolves in cycles, hence the earth, which holds in its womb the memory of millennia, like man falls into forgetfulness when a new dawn comes, and the Wheel again turns, and a new Cycle begins. And that is the wisdom behind the Circle: the wheel of Karma moves the Mandala, which in turn creates or destroys worlds, stars, gods, and men, and transforms heaven into hell, and hell into heaven. That is how Life dies to be reborn ever anew. Amidst this cosmic drama, man is allowed glimpses of joy and glimmers of light in his human sea of darkness and despair, to remember what once was Eternity, with its blissful perfection and celestial unity, and strive to re-conquer his lost divinity."

"Thus, you shall reinvent yourself ever anew, you shall transform and recreate yourself eternally, for cyclical is the path of Life, an ever expanding spiral of creation, a whirlwind which nowhere begins and never ends. And though you have declined, still you perish to be reborn. And so, the twilight of the gods heralds their dawn, and the fall of man heralds his ascent. That is the wisdom of the symbol of Life, Ananta, the serpent that swallows its own tail, the Serpent of Eternity. That is the Sacred Circle which eternally moves — and is moved by — the world."

"The Higher Man's vocation is similar to the alchemist: transforming the base into the divine. And that is the true meaning of good and evil: elevating or debasing Life. Higher and lower: that is what good and evil *truly* mean. That is how *we*, the Sons of the Light, view the world."

"Ours is a tragic conception of Life whereby all opposites are reconciled in a holy union and an ultimate reality; this is called transcendence in immanence. For Light proceeds from darkness, harmony proceeds from conflict, and order from chaos. Hence, Unity is the only reality, and Supremacy is man's destiny."

"Yet how do we escape this endless cycle of death and birth?" asked Arya. "Are we doomed to live and die, again and again? Are we doomed to live to die, and die to live? What is the vital driving force of the universe, and in man, which makes Life worth living, and man worth saving?"

"There is no creation, no end," the king answered, "there is only infinite and eternal Being ever transforming and overcoming itself in Becoming. Evolution is perpetual, creation is endless. The cycle of incarnations ends when Divine Unity above is reflected and achieved below. For God and the universe are one, the seen is the manifestation of the unseen, as Spirit pervades the world and is manifested — and moves — in matter."

"Evolution is the law of Nature, elevation is the law of Life; both take place in cyclical rounds of birth, blossoming, decay, death, and rebirth. Those are the seasons of Life. Elevation leads to Wholeness, begetting love and harmony, whereas decay leads to separation and chaos — the curses of the world of gravity —, and breeds strife and hatred. Supremacy is the highest stage of elevation and the driving force of the universe; it is in Supremacy that divine harmony is attained, at the peak of the Pyramid, the climax of the Spirit, where all opposites fade and all things unite."

"Man is not the centre of the universe, he is its mirror. For the Absolute, the Eternal manifests itself in the particular and the transient, becoming conscious of itself, then transcending itself in higher spheres of creation. The cosmos is in endless expansion, Spirit shapes matter, involution turns the wheel of evolution, and this perpetual self-overcoming is done through the 'thrust to unity', which is the higher manifestation of the will to power, and the highest manifestation of the will to truth. Thus, the God-Man is the ultimate goal of man."

"Therefore, man should no longer seek God in an unreachable beyond, but behold the mirror of his own divine destiny; for man himself is the lyre and the melody, he himself is the dreamer and the dream..." Thus spoke the king, when he was abruptly interrupted by Arya, who eagerly asked him: "but *where* is this god whose advent you preach? Where is the coming god who shall redeem the divine and awaken man from his earthly slumber? Why does God still lie in his grave, vainly awaiting his own resurrection?"

The coming god

The king looked at Arya with his deep, impenetrable gaze that bore a world unto its own, and he told her in a solemn voice: "know that it was but one god who died on the cross, and many are waiting to be born. 'God is dead!' said a true believer, but that was the voice of God

Himself who spoke thus... for it is the god of religions, the god created by men, who died, and the divine still lies dormant in men's buried souls, waiting to be awakened and resurrected."

"The old god is dead, he died of men's unbelief—that cursed offspring of superstition—; for it is unbelief, not the cross, which kills gods. But man cannot survive without the divine; hence, to those who say 'there is no God,' those deluded, empty souls who deem themselves wise simply because they doubt and deny, I ask: where does our divine longing come from? Does not the source of our longing find its ocean in our inner depths? By aspiring, are we not... remembering? For God is man's past and his future."

"Religions killed God, but it is godlessness which killed the divine in man, by rendering him hopeless. That is why, hereafter, a new mode of divinity, a New Sun, shall bless every dawn and every day. For, if reason forbids us to believe in the old god, faith forbids us to remain godless. And Reason and Faith are the twin pillars of the temple of Truth."

"Your god dwells in you, your sun shines in you, but soon you will see His face upon the face of this earth. For no one yet has seen the real face of God—only his imperfect masks—, but soon men will behold it in all its glory. It is then that the divine rays of Ar—the primal fire—shall sanctify all men, and they shall bathe in the Light of Awareness. And they shall know and live the Joy of Being—Ananda—, when every word uttered becomes a prayer, and every prayer sung becomes a symphony and a hymn to Life."

Thus spoke the king, and his face lit up with a heavenly glow. "I have this vision, Arya," he said, "men will come to you for enlightenment and salvation, as they came to the Great Masters of humanity, the Rishis and Arhats. *We* firmly believe in you, so believe in yourself, for you are the chosen among the chosen, those who carry God's Eternal Message to men, those who are called *Zarathustras*, the Light bearers."

"You have travelled to the confines of the earth in search of your long lost sons, but you did not find them. For your sons, as you, do not belong to this earth, neither are they lost; they belong to Shambhala, they have always belonged to Shambhala."

The Armies of Shambhala

As he spoke, the king stretched his arm forward, unveiling before Arya's stunned eyes a sea of black-clad, steel-helmeted, heavily armed and ruthless-looking knights aligned in perfect order. There was no end in sight to the endless columns of these magnificent soldiers whose iron discipline, imposing helmets, and aristocratic capes reminded Arya of the great legions of Rome and the valiant warriors of Sparta. But, as with the king, there was an indefinable character to the garb worn by these strangely handsome warriors, as their uniforms, which were vaguely reminiscent of the past, also looked like something from the future, or even from outside this earth.

"Behold, Arya," the king said triumphantly, "behold your sons, your Holy Warriors of Light, those alone who are worthy of your name... behold the noble Aryas, the Great Armies of Shambhala!" Spellbound by this glorious scene of innumerable black knights in shining armour — how many were there? No human eye could tell — who stood before her, mesmerised by this amazing show of force and beauty, Arya remained speechless, relishing this unique, defining moment of her Life. Her eyes were filled with tears, and her heart was overwhelmed with joy. She was witnessing her greatest dream come true, her long-awaited reunion with her sons.

"These are the last Aryas," the king told her, "these are the armies of the hidden East, the sons of the lost North; for the Light always comes from the East — *ex Oriente lux* — but it shines in the North. These are the last rays of *Surya*, our hidden, divine Sun which shall rise again on a new earth. You were seeking your sons, and they were waiting for you… now the prophecy shall be fulfilled, now your destiny shall be accomplished, as the Armies of Shambhala come out of their sanctuary, and the Underground rises to the surface, and Truth ascends from the shadow and into the Light."

"Hitherto, we sent our divine emissaries, our *Bodhisattvas*, to the world of men, in order to enlighten them and raise them above the darkness… but all our messengers were crucified, in flesh or in spirit, as men shunned the Light over and again, out of ignorance or wickedness. Men have never learned, nor will they ever learn… nay, the deaf shall never hear, and the blind shall never see: that is a truth that we now accept."

"Hence, we shall now send the world not our saints but our armies, to accomplish with the sword what the Word, falling into deaf ears, and the Light, shining above blind eyes, failed to achieve. It is with their swords that men greeted the Word, and so, it is with the sword that the Word shall henceforth — and again — be preached. And there is no holier war than a war fought for the sake of Truth."

"These are your warriors, Arya. Lead them and go to men, and teach them their destiny. Bring them your word and your sword; the word to those who seek Truth — as the Word heals those who aspire —, and the sword to those who slay Truth, for those are the unredeemable — and the sword alone cleanses the sins of the wicked and the ignorant —. That is how you will know your own. *That* is natural selection at its best, which is above and before all else spiritual."

"Go to men, Arya, and fight! Wage your holy war with your sacred word and your mighty sword. And worry not about the outcome of that ultimate battle, nor fear your numerous enemies; for yours are the invincible warriors who know no fear — and those who know no fear know no defeat —. Have faith, warrior-goddess of Light, for yours are the mightiest warriors who fear nothing, neither God nor death, as God dwells in them, and they belong to Eternity. And those who fear nothing are those who should be feared the most… and they shall sow terror in the hearts of their enemies, and love in the hearts of the faithful."

"You are the last warrior of Truth, Arya. Serve Her with your blood and your soul, honour Her with your loyalty, until death, and beyond death. For Truth alone is eternal, and by serving Eternity, you become an Immortal. And nothing is nobler than to fight and to die for Her glory. May the gods be with you. Hail *Surya*!"

A call to arms

Upon hearing the king's war cry, those defiant words filled with wisdom which comforted Arya's long-wounded pride and filled her anxious heart with great hope and a higher faith, further strengthening her iron resolve and her unshakable will, she saluted her master with a humble bow of the head, in a sign of deference; then she raised her arm forward and gave him the salute to the Sun, thereby pledging her undying loyalty to that highest and noblest symbol of Life.

She then turned to face her warriors who stood perfectly still and silent, eagerly awaiting their leader's speech. "Hail *Surya*!" she cried, saluting them the same way she did the king, and, with a voice filled with pride and defiance, she spoke thus to them: "AUM. My sons, my warriors, noble Aryas! Finally I have found you, finally we are reunited! Now my mission has begun, now my destiny can unfold!" Tears were flowing from her eyes, but she remained steadfast, and her voice remained strong, as she continued her address: "too long have we waited for this holy reunion… our swords became dull and our hearts grew weary as we waited for our final and most glorious battle, to avenge the blood of our brothers fallen on the fields of Truth, Honour, and Justice, and to revive the spirit of *Surya* in the waning heart of Gaïa."

"Holy Knights! We are the last Sanctuary of Light in this world of shadows and this age of darkness; that is why, in our last battle, the future of humanity will be decided… who shall inherit this earth, gods or beasts? For man, as a species, is at an end; his way is either upwards or downwards. Gods and beasts: that is what the future will be. Thus we fight for a higher humanity, for the meaning of the earth. The future of man is in our hands, in our souls and in our swords! Therefore, my warriors, sing with me our Hymn to Supremacy!" With one voice, they all began to chant:

> "A new dawn is breaking,
> the dawn of a new order, AUM!
> A higher species is in the making,
> this is the age of Supremacy,
> of the God-man!"

> "This is our morning,
> our day is dawning,
> rise up now, rise up, Aryas!
> The greatest battle shall soon begin.
> The battle for Supremacy,
> for the meaning of the universe:
> a higher humanity,
> the Master Race that will rule the earth."

> "Life is power, overcoming,
> creation is forever unfolding,
> Unity, Force, Supremacy:
> this is the ultimate reality: AUM!
> This is our destiny,
> this is the march of history,
> the will of divinity,
> Aryas, fight until victory!"

> "Can you hear it, Aryas,
> the thunder of Absolute Force?

Can you see it, Aryas,
the lightning of Supreme Truth?
Can you feel it, Aryas,
the Spirit of Hadrian, again?"

"Ours is the Dynasty of Light,
the bridge to the Overman.
Let thine honour command:
Supremacy, or death!
For Supremacy is our only destiny,
therefore let thy justice be:
Spiritual hierarchy!"

"Occult force is unleashed,
lower forms will all perish,
Truth shall rise again,
AUM shall prevail.
We are the Sons of the Sun,
Surya, thy will shall be done!"

Right after the hymn was sung, a heavy silence fell, a silence of contentment, elation, and pride. As Arya saluted her warriors again, lifting her arm towards the Sun, they all raised their swords, and it is with great joy that she listened to their thunderous greeting — the greeting of the Warriors of Light: 'hail, *Surya*!' — repeated over and over again. But as she turned to the king, seeking to share her greatest moment of pride with her master, and awaiting his blessing before she left for battle, she did not find him; she looked around her, searching for his deep and comforting gaze, but he was nowhere to be found. He was gone... "He went back whence he came, to the realm of Pure Light," she said to herself, "there where Being and Non-Being fade in the bosom of Absolute Unity."

Overtaken at first by a deep feeling of sorrow and anxiety, Arya suddenly understood. "The time has come, *my* time has come," she thought, and a timid smile lit up her face. Her initiation had ended, she was now ready to carry her torch on her own. She was no longer a disciple and a seeker, but an Initiate and a leader. She turned again to face her warriors and, looking with immense pride at that ultimate hope for humanity, she addressed them thus:

"Aryas! Our time has come! Destiny chose us to achieve the holiest of goals, the noblest of causes: to serve, restore, and honour Truth. Let us heed her call, so that our lives are not lived in vain! We are the last Aryas, the *only* Aryas, the last rays of the divine Sun!"

"In our hearts beats the heart of Gaïa,
in our souls shines the flame of *Surya*,
in our dreams lives the dream of Brahma,
in our thoughts God speaks to us,
and in our deeds He breathes through us."

"In our glory, Life finds Her meaning,
and Her meaning finds its glory.
And Justice is no longer a forlorn dream,
and Truth is no longer the enemy of Life,
and God is no longer the enemy of man."

"That is who we are, that is why we fight. We are the last Aryas, and this is our last and greatest battle. Supremacy, or death! Thus it shall be. For Truth is indivisible, She either prevails or dies, only to be reborn, again and evermore."

"My beloved sons, my pride and my hope! Henceforth our wars shall no longer be fought in vain, won for little and lost for nothing… our wars shall no longer be lost in petty meanings and lower ends, but fought for Eternity! For all victories lack glory, and all defeats lack dignity, if they are not fought for the sake of Truth. And Truth alone serves and belongs to Eternity."

"Never has the world been richer in possessions but poorer in spirit. Never has wealth begotten so much misery. Never has Life been richer in deeds but poorer in meaning... we are the Light of the world, we shall bring the Light back to the dark desert of man, so that Life is reborn, and man is risen, and God is redeemed. For Truth is the only lasting wealth of Life. This is our mission, our honour, our glory; only thus will each one of us be able to face himself when, pushing his last sigh of life, before the great leap into the unknown, he can say with contentment: 'thus did *I* live!' "

After she uttered these solemn words which sent shivers of intense pride into the hearts of her faithful warriors, Arya held a moment's silence, and she looked at the sky which was getting darker. It was dusk, and the fading rays of the Sun cast a golden glow upon the trees of the surrounding forest. The richness of colours and their subtle variations endowed Nature with great beauty. Arya gazed at length at that scene of ravishing splendour; never before had she seen a dawn or a sunset, as only in the Oasis of Light does Life unfold in Her totality, and the cycles of the days and the seasons embrace the Circle of Eternity. She admired the beautiful landscape, absorbed in her own thoughts of immortal beauty.

Hymns to Life

With regret but determination, Arya quickly put an end to her reverie, as she remembered that she had a mission to fulfil and an army to lead. "Now is not the time to dream, but to act," she told herself, "for all dreams that remain unfulfilled are wasted drops of heaven in the sea of Infinity." But it is with a softer, gentler tone that she now addressed her knights, for she was about to utter not words of war, but words of peace, the peace of Wisdom that springs from the endless ocean of Being.

"Listen, Aryas," she said, "open your hearts, for now I shall not speak to your pride, but to your humility. And if fortune awaits the bold, wisdom awaits the humble. However, true humility never stems from weakness, but from strength — otherwise it is just servility —, thus pride is reconciled with humility when they both serve Truth."

"Aryas, noblest of knights! I exhorted you to fight, but every war cry should serve a higher end; hence, I shall now exhort you to conquer yourselves, before you conquer the world. And before you achieve your highest deeds, you should first discover the highest in you. My beloved sons, I shall tell you a secret. One day, at the dawn of my awakening, Life Herself spoke thus to me: 'Arya, daughter of *Surya*, I, Eternal Life, shall bestow upon you my most precious gift, the gift of Wisdom, which is naught but Life in Her purest form, and Truth in Her noblest manifestation.'

'Hitherto, humanity has fallen on its knees before the commandments of death and the verses of darkness; little souls have revered little virtues, dark souls have worshipped dark gods, lost souls have denied all gods. Let the rabble and the slaves follow the commandments of hate, wrath, and delusion; for those only who lack faith need to be commanded. You, mother of all free spirits and higher souls, shall teach your sons not the commandments that enslave, but the words that liberate; you shall teach them not how to submit to fear or surrender to illusion, but how to live the Life Divine in every thought and every deed. Therefore, you shall henceforth sing to them these hymns to Life, this Ode to Eternity:

'Thou shalt worship no idol, no god or man or power or money — these are all idols wearing the motley masks of deception —; for everything worshipped becomes an idol, and every idol is a veil that blinds and a chain that enslaves. Let Truth alone be your guide, and Wisdom your goal, and God shall dwell in your soul.'

'Thou shalt seek no god beyond the world, and no Truth outside Life, for the world is God's temple, and Life is the heart of Truth. Let Life Herself be your daily conquest and your eternal inspiration, and you shall see the divine in everything.'

'Your mind shall forever wander in the boundless ocean of your inner infinity, source of all Truth, Beauty and Perfection. Look within, and you shall discover that which no eye can see and no mind can fathom.'

'Fear no god above or devil below, for heaven and hell are but illusions of the mind, and God and Satan are but man's inner nature at war with itself. The divine lies in the depths of your undiscovered Self.'

'Thou shalt be an eternal seeker of Truth, an eternal lover of Wisdom, an eternal explorer of the Spirit, never resting in the idle comfort of a fixed idea or ideal, ever seeking deeper seas, broader horizons, and higher skies, ever overcoming yourself on Life's stairway to Eternity.'

'Thou shalt honour tradition, for it bears the wisdom of millennia, and its voice echoes the primal word that blessed this earth at the dawn of the gods. But beware not to bury your head in its deep sands, lest you stifle the breath of creation and dry the fount of inspiration that lie in you; for then you will drown in the sterile swamp of stagnation, which breeds mediocrity and decay. Rather look to the past for inspiration, and to the future for creation.'

'Thou shalt accept and revere Life as a whole, in Her human cycles and divine harmony, in Her joy and misery, Her splendour and despair, Her innocence and cruelty, accepting the good with gratitude, and enduring the bad with grace and fortitude. Thus you tread the path to peace and wisdom.'

'Thou shalt dance upon all of Life's tribulations, as a god dances upon the flames of his own hell, consuming himself only to be born anew, having shed his mortal shell. For to rise higher, one first has to fall deeper.'

'Thou shalt recognise no boundaries in life, neither those erected within man, nor those erected between men — for these are all man-made limitations, illusions of the ego and delusions of the mind. Cling to no nation, no tribe, and no creed, these are but chains of enslavement to the limited and the transient. How could you call a nation your own, you whose soul dwells with the gods? How could you embrace but one creed, when Truth is the source of all creeds, the fount of Life whence all rivers spring? Do not mistake the branch for the tree, and the drop for the ocean. Shed your lower identities so that you can embrace your Higher Self and your higher destiny. Your only home is your soul, your only nation is your goal, and Truth alone is your religion; upwards and forwards is your path.'

'Live for, and love nothing but Eternity, all else is illusion and deception. And know that it is only when you relinquish everything that you are truly free; and it is only when you give away everything that you are truly rich; for the wealth of the Spirit that dwells in you is an endless source of joy and love.'

'Know that you are born naked, and you die naked. Everything you are, everything you have, you shall one day give back to Life — its rightful owner —, when dust again turns to dust, and spirit to spirit; and all that remains from your human journey in the memory of Eternity are the higher thoughts, noble feelings, and righteous deeds that have enriched your life and endowed it with meaning. And the lessons of love and wisdom you will have learned and bestowed upon this earth shall remain forever engraved in your eternal destiny.'

'Beware the thieves of the spirit, those who do commerce with lofty things and buy and sell that which can never be bought or sold: Wisdom. Flee all those who murder the Word of God each time they utter an aberration, for they shall distort your message and invert your truth. And in their foul mouths and perverted minds, Truth Herself becomes an abomination, and God a devil, and Life a plague.'

'Live a heroic life, in word and in deed, and die with honour and dignity; that is the only life worth living, and the only death worth dying. For to live and to die with contentment is a blessing few men know.'

'Live among men, but not with them; for you will never belong to them, and they will never understand you. Different worlds and different gods never were meant to meet. And worry not: you will recognise your own with ease, as they will be those who do not belong. You shall remain islands, strangers in your own lands and among your own people.'

'Speak no more idle words, and pay no heed to the noise of the world. Let there be silence within you; only then shall Truth whisper Her eternal words to your awakened soul, and you shall know the meaning of Life and behold Her beauty.'

'Live to love, only then will you love to live.'

'The Tree of Wisdom is rooted in sorrow and suffering, but its branches reach out to the infinite sky of blissful peace. Therefore, laugh at all your tragedies, and carry your human cross with a smile upon your face, for the divine Light awaits you at the end of your path.'

'We are all passing waves, and what remains is Eternity. Therefore, cling not to the waves, but embrace the sea.'

'Arya, you shall forever sing these hymns to Life, this symphony of the gods, to give you strength when strength is needed, and faith when faith lacks, and hope when hope abandons you.' "

"That is how Life spoke to me," Arya told her warriors, "that is what I now teach you, and what you shall teach your sons and your grandsons, for Truth is eternal. Warriors of Light, Sons of *Surya*! By serving Truth, we serve Life and praise God. That is the Higher Life and the highest Love. That is the only way to live and to die for true believers and holy warriors — and every true believer is a holy warrior —. Under our banner, we shall fight our last battle, and the earth shall tremble each time our flags pass by!"

EPILOGUE

The departure

As she thus spoke, Arya turned around and lifted her arm, proudly showing her astonished warriors a huge flag that seemed to be hanging from the sky. Indeed, night had fallen, and no one could really tell where the flag was hanging from. Was it a vision? It was an amazing, even breathtaking, sight. Everybody stared with awe at that black and gold banner — black above, gold below —, which had in its centre a solar disc split into two colours — gold above, black below.

"This is our banner," Arya said, "the banner of Shambhala, which symbolises who we are and what we fight for. Behold the future of this earth! Behold our symbol: darkness above, Light below, and our Black Sun emerging from the Inner Light of Shambhala into the dark world of men, its healing rays heralding the Golden Dawn of a higher humanity."

"Our Sun cometh, our God cometh, therefore, Noble Aryas, sing a song of praise and joy to *Surya*! Our time cometh, we are now ripe for our fruits! Onwards, sons of Shambhala!" Thus spoke Arya and, raising her sword, she led her warriors out of Shambhala and into the world of men. She turned to behold one last time her sacred, eternal abode. "Farewell, O Sanctuary of Light," she said aloud, "you shall remain our guiding light and our endless inspiration, wherever we go, whatever we do."

However, as they were leaving Shambhala, Arya suddenly stopped, as a flash of lightning that came out of nowhere struck her eyes;

overwhelmed by that blinding light, she shut her eyes for a moment, not comprehending what had just happened. When she opened her eyes again, all she could see was an endless ocean of pure Light. In one last conscious glimpse, she thought: "only those who remain are those who die…" Then she faded into the luminous mist. Her dream was over. She woke up. She was dead; dead to the world, living in Eternity. But another dawn shall rise, another noontide shall greet her, ever again, when the Wheel again turns, and a new dream begins, and the odyssey of the Spirit continues.

NOTES

-1- *Surya* (Sanskrit): the Vedic Sun-God, the Sun.

-2- *Maya* (Sanskrit): illusion.

-3- Our Sea: *Mare Nostrum* (Latin). That is how the Romans referred to the Mediterranean.

-4- *Heimkehr* (German): homecoming.

-5- *Gott* (German): God.

-6- *Aryana:* "land of the Aryans", also known as *Airyana Vaeïa*; in former ages, the name used to describe a region stretching from Iran to India. The names Iran, India derive from the word Arya.

-7- Deva Nahusha: Hindu god identified with Dionysus.

-8- *Heimat* (German): homeland.

-9- *Yggdrasil:* in Norse mythology, the World Tree, the Tree of Life.

-10- Asgard: in Norse mythology, the realm of the gods and slain heroes of war.

-11- *Moksha* (Sanskrit): liberation.

ABOUT THE AUTHOR

Diplomat, thinker, writer, and poet, Abir Taha holds a postgraduate degree in Philosophy from the Sorbonne. A career diplomat for the Government of Lebanon, she has previously served as the Consul of Lebanon in Paris and as First Secretary at Lebanon's Permanent Mission to the United Nations in Geneva.

Versed in philosophy and Eastern and Western mysticism, the author espouses a spiritual worldview and believes that man's ultimate purpose and vocation in life is the fulfilment of his divine nature and destiny.

ALSO BY THE AUTHOR

- *Twelve Resolutions for a Happy Life – A Manual of Happiness* (Numen, Australia, 2015).
- *Verses of Light* (Arktos, London, 2014).
- *Defining Terrorism: the End of Double Standards* (Arktos, London, 2014). The book was translated into Portuguese and published in Brazil.
- *Le Dieu à Venir de Nietzsche, ou la Rédemption du Divin* (Editions Connaissances et Savoirs, Paris, 2005). The book was translated into English under the title *Nietzsche's Coming God, or the Redemption of the Divine,* and published by Arktos in London in 2013.
- *Nietzsche, Prophet of Nazism: the Cult of the Superman* (AuthorHouse, USA, 2005). The book was translated into Portuguese and published in Brazil.

OTHER BOOKS FROM ARKTOS

Sri Dharma Pravartaka Acharya — *The Dharma Manifesto*

Alain de Benoist — *Beyond Human Rights*
Carl Schmitt Today
Manifesto for a European Renaissance
On the Brink of the Abyss
The Problem of Democracy

Arthur Moeller van den Bruck — *Germany's Third Empire*

Kerry Bolton — *Revolution from Above*

Alexander Dugin — *Eurasian Mission: An Introduction to Neo-Eurasianism*
The Fourth Political Theory
Last War of the World-Island
Putin vs Putin

Koenraad Elst — *Return of the Swastika*

Julius Evola — *Fascism Viewed from the Right*
Metaphysics of War
Notes on the Third Reich
The Path of Cinnabar
A Traditionalist Confronts Fascism

Guillaume Faye — *Archeofuturism*
Convergence of Catastrophes
Sex and Deviance
Why We Fight

Daniel S. Forrest — *Suprahumanism*

Andrew Fraser — *The WASP Question*

Daniel Friberg — *The Real Right Returns*

OTHER BOOKS FROM ARKTOS

Génération Identitaire	*We are Generation Identity*
Paul Gottfried	*War and Democracy*
Porus Homi Havewala	*The Saga of the Aryan Race*
Rachel Haywire	*The New Reaction*
Lars Holger Holm	*Hiding in Broad Daylight* *Homo Maximus* *The Owls of Afrasiab*
Alexander Jacob	*De Naturae Natura*
Peter King	*Keeping Things Close: Essays on the Conservative Disposition*
Ludwig Klages	*The Biocentric Worldview* *Cosmogonic Reflections: Selected Aphorisms from Ludwig Klages*
Pierre Krebs	*Fighting for the Essence*
Pentti Linkola	*Can Life Prevail?*
H. P. Lovecraft	*The Conservative*
Brian Anse Patrick	*The NRA and the Media* *Rise of the Anti-Media* *The Ten Commandments of Propaganda* *Zombology*
Tito Perdue	*Morning Crafts*
Raido	*A Handbook of Traditional Living*

OTHER BOOKS FROM ARKTOS

Steven J. Rosen	*The Agni and the Ecstasy*
	The Jedi in the Lotus
Richard Rudgley	*Barbarians*
	Essential Substances
	Wildest Dreams
Ernst von Salomon	*It Cannot Be Stormed*
	The Outlaws
Troy Southgate	*Tradition & Revolution*
Oswald Spengler	*Man and Technics*
Tomislav Sunic	*Against Democracy and Equality*
Abir Taha	*Defining Terrorism: The End of Double Standards*
	Nietzsche's Coming God, or the Redemption of the Divine
	Verses of Light
Bal Gangadhar Tilak	*The Arctic Home in the Vedas*
Dominique Venner	*The Shock of History: Religion, Memory, Identity*
Markus Willinger	*A Europe of Nations*
	Generation Identity
David J. Wingfield (ed.)	*The Initiate: Journal of Traditional Studies*

CPSIA information can be obtained
at www.ICGtesting.com
Printed in the USA
BVHW050240011022
648443BV00001B/18